HE COULD BE THE ONE

"Why do you keep doing that?" Eve asked.

"Doing what?"

"Answering my statements with a question."

"Am I doing that?"

He smiled at her, and unable to help herself, Eve smiled back. "You always could get a rise out of me," she said softly, "doing nothing more than being within arm's reach."

"Yeah, well, I could say the same thing about you, you know."

He studied her with some intensity for a moment, and she wondered if he would try to revisit the past or stay here in the present. Part of her wanted very much to go backward in time, just to see if they both remembered it all the same way. Then again, if they did, what was the point in revisiting?

Other Avon Contemporary Romances by
Elizabeth Bevarly

HER MAN FRIDAY
HOW TO TRAP A TYCOON
MY MAN PENDLETON

ELIZABETH BEVARLY

He Could Be The One

AVON BOOKS
An Imprint of HarperCollins*Publishers*

This is a work of fiction. Names, characters, places, and incidents are products of the author's imagination or are used fictitiously and are not to be construed as real. Any resemblance to actual events, locales, organizations, or persons, living or dead, is entirely coincidental.

AVON BOOKS
An Imprint of HarperCollins*Publishers*
10 East 53rd Street
New York, New York 10022-5299

First Avon Books paperback printing: April 2001
First Avon Books special printing: November 2000

Avon Trademark Reg. U.S. Pat. Off. and in Other Countries, Marca Registrada, Hecho en U.S.A.
HarperCollins® is a trademark of HarperCollins Publishers Inc.

Printed in the U.S.A.

10 9 8 7 6 5 4 3 2 1

For the Seneca High School class of '79,
especially my colleagues
on the *Arrow* yearbook staff
and my colleagues on "The 82 Legs."
Oh, what fun we had.

And for the English teachers who inspired me
and encouraged me, and made a *big* difference
in my attitude, my ambition and my life:
Nancy Shepherd, David Gleaves,
Barbara Springer, Tom McPaul, and Mildred Abbott.

Many, *many* thanks to all of you.

Acknowledgments

As always, thanks to my editor, Lucia Macro, for being, as always, wonderful. Thanks to Christie Ridgway for answering questions about her native California, and thanks to Valerie Taylor and Lynn Miller for answering questions about their lovely city of residence, Cincinnati. (But for my own selfish reasons, I've taken the liberty of creating the fictional suburb of Woodhaven and the fictional historic hotel, the Stanhope. I'm invoking literary license. Sue me.) Thanks also to Teresa Hill, for assisting me in literary surgery.

Many, many thanks to Rhino Records, for putting together the phenomenal—and very inspirational—collection of music, "Just Can't Get Enough: New Wave Hits of the '80s," volumes one through fifteen. Not only did it charge me up for writing the book but all the songs have a good beat and are easy to dance to.

And finally, as always, thanks to David and Eli, who keep me grounded and reasonably sane, and who ensure that my phone is always charged, that there's always money in my wallet and gas in my car, and that I don't go to the grocery store in my pajamas or anything like that. I love you guys. You're the best.

 *One*

"**F**or this we flew two thousand miles?"

Wyatt Culver noted the wariness in his partner's voice, but he couldn't quite share Julian Varga's distaste for the view—even if it did lay on the opposite side of a security gate. Oh, sure, he could see right away why Luther Van Dormer's Santa Barbara estate was also known as "The Keep," but that didn't necessarily mean that he and Julian would actually be *prisoners* here during their stay. Probably not, anyway. Not unless Luther Van Dormer really had gone off the deep end this time—well, a deeper end than he'd been going off of the last time Wyatt had seen him. Of course, that had been nearly two decades ago, and a lot could happen in twenty years. Like, for example, deep ends could become really, *really* deep.

So Wyatt only replied, "Four thousand miles, if you count the trip back to Cincinnati."

The observation didn't seem to appease Julian. Go

figure. "And why is it, exactly, that we came?" the other man asked. "You promised you'd give me all the details once we got here."

Wyatt grinned. "Oh, we came to kidnap a woman. Did I forget to tell you that part?"

Julian turned to gape at him. "We came to *what*?"

"Oh, man, I did forget to tell you," Wyatt said, feigning contrition. "I could have sworn I at least *mentioned* to you how we'd be perpetrating a felony while we were visiting sunny California." He smacked his open palm against his forehead, dislodging a handful of light brown hair. "Gee, I really apologize, Julian. Imagine my chagrin."

Instead of replying, Julian only continued to gape. So, in turn, Wyatt only continued to grin. Then he turned his attention back to the view he had been surveying.

In spite of its oppressive moniker, the Van Dormer estate was breathtakingly beautiful, a sprawling, low-lying, Spanish-style villa that was invitingly lit, inside and out, now that twilight was falling. The elegantly manicured grounds, canopied by moss-dripping jacarandas and lush bougainvillea, evoked a sense of utter tranquility, and the very air Wyatt inhaled was heavy with the mixed and narcotic aromas of jasmine and gardenia and fast-falling night.

Yeah, all right, so there was the small matter of the double-steel, reinforced, Mediterranean-style fence that surrounded the place, and the double-steel, reinforced, Mediterranean-style bars striping each of the windows. There was the oh-so-casually strolling trio of Dobermans who gazed back at him with frank and identical expressions of challenge. And, of course, the one, two, three—my goodness, *four*—armed guards placed strategically about the roof and balconies did sorta contribute to that prisonlike quality.

Maybe Luther Van Dormer really *had* gone off the deepest of deep ends this time, Wyatt thought. He hadn't honestly considered that to be a real possibility when Luther had called him earlier in the week, not even when the old man had asked Wyatt to kidnap his daughter. Luther Van Dormer had always been considered eccentric by the residents of tiny, suburban Woodhaven, Ohio. Still, Wyatt thought, eccentricity did sometimes have a rather bothersome tendency to turn into other things. Other things like, oh . . . Wyatt didn't know . . . stark, raving lunacy, for instance. Criminal insanity, for another.

Okay, so Luther's place was a fortress, he conceded, regardless of its indolent beauty. *Lots* of people lived in fortresses. Granted, most of those people had either committed heinous crimes or were madder than hatters, but that was beside the point . . . probably. For now, Wyatt decided, it might just be best to reserve judgment on that deep end business.

"Um, I didn't think it would be necessary to remind you," Julian said, scattering Wyatt's thoughts, "but we work as private investigators. Which means we're the guys who would normally *investigate* a kidnapping. Not commit one."

"A minor technicality," Wyatt assured his partner. "We go where the jobs take us. And this job should be *verrrry* interesting."

"Oh, I don't like the sound of that at all," Julian said.

"Trust me," Wyatt told him.

"I like the sound of that even less." Instead of waiting for a reply to that comment—since none seemed necessary—Julian nodded toward the estate again. "So, this Van Dormer. Is he a total security freak, or what?" he asked, having evidently chosen not to pursue the kidnapping question for now.

"Nah," Wyatt answered. "Luther's just your garden variety paranoid, that's all. Except that he has a couple hundred million more dollars than most paranoids have."

"Mm," Julian remarked eloquently.

"He also has one of the most unbelievably delicious daughters on the planet," Wyatt added cheerfully before he could stop himself. Because in recalling Luther Van Dormer, he inevitably also recalled the lovely and talented Eve Van Dormer, with whom he'd attended Woodhaven High School back in suburban Cincinnati. And also with whom he'd shared one of the most . . .

Well, best not to go there. He had a long night ahead of him, after all. Not to mention that kidnapping business to consider, which he decided not to mention—or consider—for now. Mostly, because he still wasn't sure what to make of it, unless he wanted to bring up Luther Van Dormer and that deep end again. And he really didn't want to do that.

"Finally, you say something that makes you sound like your usual self," Julian said. "I was beginning to get concerned about you, Wyatt."

"Luther's daughter is the one we're supposed to kidnap." Okay, okay, so Wyatt couldn't quite help considering—or mentioning—the kidnapping thing again. So sue him.

Julian sighed. "Okay, I'm concerned about you again."

"Not to worry," Wyatt told him. "I have a plan."

"Now I'm *really* concerned," his partner replied.

Oh, that Julian, Wyatt thought. He took everything so seriously. "Then I guess I shouldn't tell you the other stuff about Eve Van Dormer," he said.

"What other stuff?"

"Oh, like how she was such a firebrand in high school."

"Firebrand, huh?" Julian didn't sound impressed.

"She could scratch a man's eyes out at twenty paces," Wyatt told him.

"Must have had some long arms."

"I was speaking figuratively."

"Whoa. You've been reading those How to Expand Your Vocabulary books again, haven't you?" Julian asked dryly. "I didn't realize you had a figurative bone in your body. Figuratively speaking, I mean."

Wyatt narrowed his eyes at the other man. "Why do I suddenly feel like I'm the Costello to your Abbott?"

"Better than being the Lewis to my Martin."

Well, Wyatt certainly couldn't disagree with that, even if the French did love Jerry. The French also thought naming a boy Maurice was a good idea. 'Nuff said.

"Are we early?" Julian asked, indicating the still-closed gate.

Wyatt shook his head. "Seven o'clock. Right on time."

As if hearing his remark, the gate slowly began to roll to the left, its soft hum accompanied by the whisper of the warm California breeze and the distant splash of the Pacific. Wyatt turned around to double-check that their rental car was parked safely off the street. As he did so he could see the ocean some distance beyond, rising and falling like bright sapphire satin. The sun hovered just above the watery ribbon of the horizon, fat and red and fiery, holding, holding, holding, as if reluctant to disappear.

Funny, he thought. In spite of his curiosity about Luther Van Dormer's cockamamie kidnapping scheme, Wyatt almost envied that sun. The thought of plunging into the ocean and staying there until dawn held a strange, but definite, appeal. Maybe by dawn Luther would have changed his mind about hiring Wyatt and Julian. Then Wyatt could go back to Ohio and live the life he'd mapped out for himself and try to forget all about the Van Dormers. His wasn't the most spectacular life, but it wasn't bad. Certainly it was free enough of potholes and pitfalls and other such annoyances. At least, it had been until now. Now, however . . .

He sighed heavily as he turned his attention back to The Keep, and he tried not to think about *now.* He tried even harder not to think about *then.* But somehow, the two kept getting tangled up with each other. And the joining factor between them was, inescapably, Eve.

The gate had completed its journey by now, leaving nothing but warm, fragrant air between Wyatt and his new destiny. Julian, he saw, had already passed through to the other side, but Wyatt found himself hesitating before taking the necessary steps. Funny, he thought. He'd never hesitated about anything before. Well, nothing except for Eve Van Dormer.

"So tell me more about this disagreeable, delicious daughter," Julian said, as if he'd read Wyatt's thoughts.

Wyatt forced his feet forward and contemplated the question before responding to it, wondering how to describe Eve Van Dormer without coming off sounding like a lovesick puppy—even if lovesick puppy was a nauseatingly accurate portrayal of what he'd always felt like around her. After all, he'd spent most of his high school years panting and drooling after her, howling at the moon because he knew he'd never have her.

What could he tell Julian, after all, about how her eyes and hair had been the color of rich espresso, both features touched with golden highlights when she stood in the sunlight just so? How could he tell his partner about her low, husky laughter, laughter that was as intoxicating as good Irish whiskey on a rowdy Saturday night? And how could he describe, without sounding like an idiot, Eve's pink, lacy bras and panties that matched exactly, underthings that smelled as sweet as ripe roses after a soft summer rain?

Lovesick, Wyatt thought again. Yeah, that pretty much covered how he'd felt about Eve Van Dormer back then. Good thing he'd changed a lot over the last twenty years. Good thing he couldn't possibly succumb to her now as easily and completely as he had as a teenager. Good thing he wasn't some oversexed, overwrought kid who had sappy, poetic thoughts about things like a woman's eyes and hair and underwear. Good thing he couldn't care less about what Eve might be like now. Good thing that didn't matter to him *at all*.

Damn straight.

"Eh, she was all right, I guess," he finally said with profound understatement in response to Julian's question.

And he tried to imagine what she might be like now.

Briefly, he pictured her in a black leather miniskirt and screaming red halter top, wearing mile-high heels with fishnet stockings. Not that Eve had ever dressed that way—no, she'd gone more for the cute, frumpy

Annie Hall look back in high school—but it was Wyatt's fantasy, and he'd dress her any way he damn well pleased. She wasn't seventeen anymore. There was nothing illegal—or icky—about his current train of thought.

"Did I mention she also has a sister?" he interjected quickly, before his thoughts *did* stray to the illegal or icky. Only after he voiced the question did Wyatt realize that, as had been the case twenty years ago, Simone Van Dormer was an afterthought.

"Um, no," Julian said. "That was another minor detail you neglected to bring up. Will we be kidnapping her, too?" His voice was touched with just the merest hint of sarcasm.

"Don't know yet," Wyatt said. "Luther wasn't real clear on what his plans for Simone are. But I'm all atwitter with curiosity just thinking about it." He couldn't quite keep his own voice from dripping with sarcasm. Wyatt had never been the understated type, the way Julian was.

"And what's *she* like?" the other man asked as they strode again toward the house.

Wyatt kept an eye on the Dobermans as he went, unwilling to turn his back on anything that had teeth that sharp and breath that hot. He shoved a hand restlessly through his pale brown hair, then nervously fingered his necktie.

His *necktie*, for God's sake, he marveled again. He couldn't remember the last time he'd put on a tie for anybody, yet here he was, approaching this latest job dressed like an undertaker. Okay, so a really cut-rate undertaker, seeing as how he hadn't had pants that were any dressier than dark Dockers, or a shirt more sophisticated than a white button-down Oxford, and his necktie sported an image of a hand-painted hula dancer swaying beneath a palm tree. He was still way overdressed from his usual blue jeans and button-down Oxford *without* necktie. Which just went to illustrate how very seriously he was taking this job.

"Simone was always kind of . . . I don't know," he told his friend, who was even more overdressed, because Julian had actually flung on a navy sport coat over charcoal trousers, dress shirt, and—very taste-ful—necktie. "I guess I just never thought much about her," Wyatt finally continued. "Nobody did."

"Why not?" Julian asked. "What was wrong with her? Was she that unattractive? Was she one of those girls who had a"—he shuddered for effect—"a *great personality?*"

Wyatt realized he couldn't answer Julian's question right away. Not because Simone Van Dormer wasn't easily described, but because he honestly *hadn't* given her much thought before, even though she was Eve's fraternal twin and one would think that twins would naturally constitute collective thinking—especially to a guy like Wyatt.

"I don't know," he said again. "Back in high school, she was just one of those easily overlooked kids. Quiet without being shy, smart without being brainy, plain without being unattractive, unremarkable without being invisible. She was nothing like her sister."

But then, nobody was like Eve Van Dormer, Wyatt couldn't help thinking further to himself.

"I can't tell you what kind of personality she has," he went on, "because I never really knew her. Nobody did. She didn't even seem to be that close to her sister."

Julian nodded, obviously giving the description much consideration. As they approached the lighted front entrance of the big house, Wyatt noted that his companion's jet black hair became flecked with silver-blue highlights that mirrored the unearthly color of his pale, gray-blue eyes. The impression unnerved Wyatt in a way, but then, that was hardly surprising. Julian himself unnerved Wyatt at times. Wyatt wasn't sure why, but there was something about the other man sometimes that was just, well . . . unnerving.

Topping Wyatt's own six feet, his partner out-weighed him, too, by a good twenty pounds. Hell, Julian probably checked in at two hundred, easy, every last ounce of it rock-solid muscle. Even though he was Wyatt's junior by ten years, there was something about him that made him seem even older than Wyatt. And Julian was one of those Eastern mystic, soul-at-peace kind of guys, one who fed his mind only the most nutritious contemplations, who considered his body to be a holy shrine. As a result, he took very good care of his . . . pagoda.

Wyatt, on the other hand . . . Reluctantly, he gazed down at his own pagoda and sighed. Earlier, they'd stopped for dinner between the airport in Goleta and the Van Dormer estate, at a little beachside café outside Montecito. Julian, not surprisingly, had taken advantage of the California setting and ordered a tofu-alfalfa pasta dish. The wuss. Wyatt, once he had stopped gagging over his partner's choice, had opted for the bacon-double-cheeseburger with grilled onions instead.

His pride swelled manfully now as he recalled his choice. Of course, his belly had swelled, too, he conceded unwillingly, and not quite so manfully. And Julian, wuss that he was, probably wasn't battling a wicked case of heartburn right now. Nevertheless,

Wyatt would bet his cholesterol level in gold that his friend wasn't enjoying that charbroil-generated, red meat–induced, testosterone high at the moment, either.

So there.

"I know the type you mean," Julian finally said. It took Wyatt a moment to backpedal to where they had been in the conversation and remember that they had been discussing the sisters Van Dormer. "I assume Simone was one of those girls who are invisible to the naked eye."

"Let me put it this way," Wyatt told him. "Whenever Simone Van Dormer was in the room, there was nothing naked going on anywhere."

Julian nodded. "I got it."

"No, that's my point—*nobody* got it," Wyatt countered. "Not from Simone Van Dormer."

Her sister, on the other hand . . .

Well, he admonished himself again, best not to go there, either. Especially not on a warm, balmy May evening that smelled heavily of flowers and promise. That was just too much like prom night, Cincinnati, Ohio, 1981. And that was the last year, the last place, the last night, Wyatt ever wanted to visit again.

By now he and Julian had survived the walk across the expansive front yard without being riddled by bullets or bloodied by fangs, and both stood at the entrance of Luther Van Dormer's abode. The double doors might seem like standard-issue, thousands-of-dollars'-worth-of-really-nice mahogany to the casual observer, but to someone like Wyatt, who made his living as a private investigator, they were the equivalent of a shark-infested moat—really mean sharks at that—when it came to keeping out the riffraff.

No sooner had he pressed the doorbell than a liveried housemaid opened the front door. In her early fifties, she wore the standard domestic's uniform of gray polyester dress and white apron, along with sensible, crepe-soled shoes. Her hair, a mix of gray and white, was bound discreetly at her nape, and her face was schooled into the standard servant's expression of total and unequivocal ennui.

Her arms, Wyatt couldn't help but note further, were the size of sanitation trucks, and he realized then that Luther had hired his domestics for more than their household skills and obsequiousness. Those crepe souls seemed perfectly capable of unmanning a guy with one swift, calculated maneuver, and the long sleeves of the gray polyester dress might very well hide a flamethrower or two. A guy like Luther would doubtless demand such overtime from his employees.

"Señor," the woman said with a slight nod to Wyatt. She then repeated the gesture with Julian. "Señor Van Dormer is expecting you, no?"

"Oh, yes, ma'am," he replied with the same carefully constructed courtesy the housemaid/hit woman had assumed herself. "He's expecting us."

"This way, *por favor.*"

Never one to disregard an order from someone who could unman him with one swift, calculated maneuver, Wyatt readily obeyed. Julian, he noted, did likewise. The moment they entered the house, the maid closed the door and discreetly bolted it—three times—then turned to make her way silently across the cavernous foyer and into the bowels of the estate. As he followed her through the massive house and up a flight of stairs, Wyatt formed a quick impression of terra-cotta tiles, earth-toned walls, Mediterranean furnishings, expensive, abstract art, and soft Spanish guitar music that seemed to accompany them from room to room to room to room to room . . .

So intent on forming impressions had he become, in fact, that he nearly barreled over Luther's housemaid/hired gun when she came to a halt in front of another one of those seemingly innocent—but actually menacing—security doors, this one standing sentinel over what Wyatt concluded must be Luther Van Dormer's office. Or den. Or padded cell. Whatever.

The maid rapped lightly on the door three times, paused, then rapped twice more. An answering trio of raps came from the other side, then the woman tapped two more times.

Somehow, Wyatt refrained from rolling his eyes and muttering "Oh, brother." A code? he wondered. With all the other security measures in place, Luther Van Dormer actually insisted on a secret knock at his office/den/padded cell/whatever door?

The sound of yet another bolt turning brought Wyatt's attention back around, and then the door was creaking open slowly, ominously, almost cinematically. His heart actually began to hammer harder in his chest, and heat flamed in his belly as he watched the seemingly endless movement, until—finally, finally— Luther Van Dormer appeared on the other side.

The last time Wyatt had seen the man, he had been eighteen years old and bleeding from the lip. That, of course, would have been because Luther Van Dormer had just popped him one, but good, in the mouth. And *that* would have been because Wyatt hadn't brought Eve home from the senior prom like he should have. No, Wyatt had just left her there, in the backseat of Stuart Turner's Chevy Nova, half-dressed and crying.

In hindsight, he supposed he couldn't really blame Luther at all for his reaction. Hell, Wyatt would have split a lot more than a lip on any guy who'd deserted *his* daughter—if he'd had a daughter for any guy to desert. Still, he wished the old man had bothered to get the whole story before he'd come gunning for Wyatt.

The years had been good to Luther, Wyatt had to admit. True, the old man's formerly dark hair was liberally threaded with silver now, but he was as fit and tall as ever. Biceps strained against a navy blue polo, and his belly was as flat as a steam iron beneath his khaki trousers. Although his face bore faint lines of age, his skin was burnished a deep tan, and the lines really did enhance his already rugged features. He held a cut-crystal tumbler of something dark amber, and undoubtedly expensive, in one hand and a smoldering, and undoubtedly expensive, cigar in the other.

California living agreed with the guy. Where Wyatt recalled Luther as being pretty much a joyless, suspicious, paranoid person back in Ohio, he seemed now like a . . . like a . . . hmmm. Well, like a . . . less joyless, less suspicious, still paranoid person.

Hey, every little bit helped.

"Wyatt," Luther greeted him with a surprisingly amiable smile. On the phone three days ago, he had been all gruff businessman and professional courtesy. "Good of you to come. Thank you, Carmen," he added in a brief aside to the housemaid/hardened criminal. She nodded once, then turned without a second glance at her employer or his guests.

Probably, Wyatt thought as he watched her go, when you had a flamethrower up your sleeve, you didn't mind so much turning your back on people.

"Come in, come in," Luther added, stepping aside so that Wyatt and Julian could enter. "What are you drinking?"

Wyatt glanced first at his own empty hands, then at Julian's. "Um, nothing at the moment, sir."

Luther chuckled. "Very funny, Wyatt. I remember you always were a joker."

"Mm," Wyatt replied noncommittally. Somehow he refrained from asking the old man if he himself had just been joshing twenty years ago when he'd fed Wyatt that knuckle sandwich. Instead, he said, "Whatever you're having is fine, Mr. Van Dormer."

"Call me Luther," the older man decreed. "How about you, Mr. . . . Varga, is it?"

"Julian is fine," Julian said. "I'll just have bottled water."

Wuss, Wyatt thought. He really was going to have to take Julian out some night and get him loaded. Drag him from one seedy dive to another. Until they'd pissed off a group of apelike men. Preferably bikers. Who outnumbered them three to one. And chased them down a dark, dead-end alley. And have the whole thing turn into a bloody free-for-all. Where the two of them just barely escaped by the skin of their teeth.

Julian really did have no idea how to enjoy himself.

As their host and potential employer went about seeing to their libations, Wyatt took in the rest of the office and immediately felt as if he had wandered onto the set of a daytime drama.

The room reeked of wealth and West Coast affability, and it was in keeping with the decor of the rest of the house—elegant without being formal, beautiful without being feminine, expensive without being intimidating. French doors—which Wyatt couldn't help but note were closed, and no doubt locked, on such a beautiful evening—offered a panoramic view of the setting sun, the lush front yard, and the ocean beyond.

Luther finished preparing and distributing their drinks, then returned to the bar to retrieve his own. Spinning back around to face his guests, he said, "I guess you're wondering why I've called you here tonight." He smiled again. "God, that was dramatic, wasn't it? I've always wanted to say that to someone."

"Is, um, is that why you called us here tonight?" Wyatt asked blandly.

Luther's smile fell. "No. I called you here because I want to hire you. Both of you," he qualified, including Julian in the conversation.

"Yes, you did mention that on the phone," Wyatt said. "And as much as I appreciate your footing the bill to bring us out here to sunny California for the weekend this way, I think, Mr. Van Dormer, that we need to discuss this little job you want us to complete."

Luther enjoyed another thoughtful swallow of his drink. "Oh?" he asked. "I thought I made myself clear when we spoke on the phone."

Wyatt thought carefully before continuing. "Uh, forgive me, sir—"

"Luther."

"—sir, but, I'm kind of confused about why, exactly, you'd like Julian and me to kidnap Eve."

Luther immediately looked troubled. "Oh, no," he said. "No, Wyatt, you misunderstood me on the phone. I don't want you and Julian to kidnap Evie."

Wyatt narrowed his eyes at him. "You don't? But—"

"No, of course I don't. What kind of father do you think I am, to ask such a thing?"

"Well . . ."

"I mean asking two men to kidnap one unsuspecting woman? That's crazy."

Boy, was Wyatt relieved to hear Luther admit that the plan was nuts. That would save Wyatt the trouble of having to point out that the plan was nuts. Because he feared that in suggesting to Luther that his plan was nuts, Luther might interpret that to mean that Wyatt thought Luther was nuts. And that could potentially open the door for Luther to go, well, nuts.

"It will only be necessary for *one* of you to kidnap Evie," Luther told him.

Uh-oh. He *was* nuts.

"You, Wyatt," Luther said further. "Evie knows you. It will work better if you're the kidnapper. Julian here can take Simone."

"What?" Julian exclaimed. Then, inanely, he added, "But I've never even met her."

"Oh, don't worry," Luther told him. "I don't think it will be necessary to kidnap Simone. She's infinitely more reasonable than Evie. Simone was always the good twin, you know. Always did what she was supposed to. But Evie has always been a handful, ever since their mother died, when the girls were nine. Evie never did what she was told, always behaved exactly opposite to how she knew she was supposed to behave. She was such a wild child." He turned then to Wyatt. "But then, I don't guess I need to tell you that, do I, Wyatt?"

Okay, here it comes . . .

Putting aside for now any observations he might

offer about the whole kidnapping scheme—and also hoping to intercept another right hook before he wound up with a broken jaw—Wyatt began, "Sir, about what happened on prom night—"

But his host waved him off before he had a chance to continue. "You don't have to explain," Luther said. "I know what actually happened that night. I found out the real story the following day."

Oh, great, Wyatt thought, his stomach knotting into a fist, even if Luther's hand wasn't. "So then Eve told you—"

"Everything."

Oh, man . . .

"That night, when she got home, she was too upset to make sense of anything. Much of what she did tell me was just bits and pieces, and I drew my own erroneous conclusions. The next day, she was in better shape, and she explained what really happened. And I apologize, Wyatt, for . . . you know . . ."

"The fat lip?"

"Yes, that." Luther had the decency to look sheepish as he glanced away, focusing on something over Wyatt's left shoulder. "Anyway, I shouldn't have gone off half-cocked the way I did," he added.

"Don't worry about it," Wyatt told him, wincing inwardly at the other man's phrasing even as his gut unclenched a bit. "It was a long time ago."

"It wasn't that long ago," Luther said cryptically. "Still, I suppose I should have apologized to you twenty years ago, but, well . . . it was a touchy situation."

"And, um, there was also that small matter of you and Eve and Simone leaving Woodhaven under cover of darkness a week after it happened," Wyatt threw in for good measure. "Without leaving a forwarding address."

Luther dropped his gaze back down to his drink. "Well, yes, that, too, did sort of hinder any apology, didn't it?"

Among other things, Wyatt thought.

"Time out," Julian interjected. "You guys just took off down another road completely and left me standing here eating your dust."

Which, Wyatt thought, was not an unusual thing to have happen whenever the Van Dormer family was involved.

Wyatt's next words were offered for Julian's benefit, but he was sure Luther would have something to contribute, too, once he heard them. "There was a lot of talk in the old neighborhood about Mr. Van Dormer here—"

"Luther," the other man corrected him again.

"Mr. Van Dormer here," Wyatt continued heedlessly, "making some shady business deals that went bad, and how some shifty characters were looking for him. But that could have all been small-town gossip."

"Cincinnati's not a small town," Julian observed.

"No, but Woodhaven might as well be," Wyatt said.

Nobody disagreed with the statement. In spite of its "downtown" district and spread-out geography, Woodhaven was very residential, and everybody knew everybody else's business. It had been that way twenty years ago, and, even if Wyatt called Cincinnati proper his home now, he was confident that nothing had changed in the old neighborhood.

But, surprisingly, nobody disagreed with the shady business deal part, either. Not even Luther.

"It was just a misunderstanding," was all he said.

Wyatt studied Luther thoughtfully, wondering, not for the first time, just what the hell had happened twenty years ago to make the man abandon a house and a community that had been a part of his family for generations, to uproot his college-bound daughters and move across more than half a continent, to continue his life in a fortress populated with armed guards and vicious dogs and flamethrowing domestics.

Must have been one hell of a misunderstanding.

Before Wyatt could ask him to clarify, though, Luther hastened on. "But getting back to kidnapping Evie."

Oh, yes, let's do, Wyatt thought. He eyed Luther thoughtfully for a moment. Then he began, "You know, Mr. Van Dormer—"

"Luther, please."

"Mr. Van Dormer," Wyatt continued, "I think I speak for both Julian and myself when, in regard to this kidnapping scheme of yours, I say, What the *hell* are you thinking?"

Julian nodded. "He is speaking for me, too, when he says that."

Luther inhaled a deep breath and released it slowly. "It's a long story," he said.

"And we flew two thousand miles to hear it," Wyatt reminded him.

Luther nodded, looking fatigued. "My daughters are intent on attending their twenty-year high school reunion in Cincinnati next week," he began. But he was eyeing Wyatt with some confusion as he concluded the announcement, probably detecting Wyatt's total and complete surprise at hearing it. "What?" Luther asked. "You didn't know about the reunion?

Didn't you receive an invitation? Evie and Simone got theirs months ago."

"Of course I received an invitation," Wyatt lied.

And he told himself that the reason he hadn't heard about any reunion until now was just because he hadn't had much personal contact with anyone from high school for a good four or five years, at least, and even then, it had just been in passing.

Plus, nobody had his new address. Plus, he'd moved around a lot over the last several years. Plus, he had an unlisted residential number—even if his business number *was* listed in three different places in the Cincinnati phone book. He was just hard to find these days, that was all.

That was the reason no one had mentioned anything to him about any reunion. It wasn't because they all still loathed and despised him because of that whole prom night fiasco.

Yeah, that was it. It was because he was a man of mystery. And clearly, he was really good at being a man of mystery if no one from his senior class could even find him to send him an invitation to the twenty-year reunion. Because he *had* attended the ten-year reunion, if only for a little while—long enough to see if Eve Van Dormer would show up—and hardly anyone then had commented on that whole prom night thing. Which was probably, he recalled now, because no one had spoken to him at all at the ten-year reunion. In fact, he recalled further, whenever he'd made eye contact with anyone, they'd all immediately glanced—and then walked—away.

In a word, *hmmm.*

Then again, he recalled further still, he hadn't actually received an invitation to the ten-year reunion, either, had he? No, he'd found out about it accidentally and had basically had to crash the function, in spite of the protests voiced by Mitzi Halloran, senior class secretary, who'd been guarding the door like a Bourbon Street bouncer and had insisted he absolutely could *not* get in without an invitation.

But he'd been a man of mystery then, too, Wyatt reminded himself. And men of mystery almost never got invited to their class reunions. Mainly because they were so . . . mysterious.

"But Eve and Simone didn't come to the ten-year reunion," Wyatt pointed out. "Why would they want to come to the twenty-year?"

"Simone didn't come ten years ago because she couldn't fit it into her work schedule—her work is very important to her. Eve didn't attend because her prick husband wouldn't let her."

Two parts of Luther's statement caught Wyatt's attention simultaneously. The part about her "prick husband" and the part about "wouldn't let." Strangely, the latter far outpaced the former in registering in his brain. Because he'd never heard the words "wouldn't let" used in conjunction with Eve Van Dormer. There was no *wouldn't let* with Eve. Ever. She went her own way, spoke her own mind, embraced her own views, spouted her own opinions. She never asked for—or wanted—anyone's permission to do anything. Yet this "prick husband," whom Luther so easily mentioned, had somehow managed to prevent her from doing something she'd evidently wanted to do.

Her husband, Wyatt marveled yet again. *Wouldn't let.* Both realizations made him equally sick to his stomach.

"Eve is married?" he asked, his voice sounding thin and hollow, even to his own ears.

"Divorced," Luther quickly corrected both Wyatt and himself.

And just like that, the world began to turn again on its axis. Slowly, Wyatt's heart began to beat again. Slowly, he was able to fill and empty his lungs with breath. Slowly, the room stopped spinning and reality stopped shifting, and he felt—almost—normal.

"The divorce was final just a few months ago," Luther added, "and only after a very long and very ugly separation. Eve's been living here at the estate for the last three months. Simone talked her into it, even if *I* couldn't. None of us trusts her prick ex-husband not to come looking for her."

The sick feeling roiled through Wyatt's belly again. "You think he'd hurt her?" he asked.

Luther hesitated before responding. "I don't know," he finally said, his voice gritty. "To be honest, I'm more worried that he'd try to talk her into going back to him."

"And would she?"

Luther's jaw clenched tight. "I hope not."

That sick feeling in Wyatt's belly intensified, and he wondered what any of this had to do with Luther's wanting him to kidnap Eve.

"Anyway," Luther rushed on, "because of that, you know, *misunderstanding* in Woodhaven twenty years ago, when Evie and Simone return to Cincinnati, they're going to be returning to a community where—"

Luther halted abruptly, just, Wyatt thought, as he was getting to the good part.

"A community where . . . ?" Wyatt spurred mildly, hoping to finally discover just why the Van Dormers had skipped town under such mysterious circumstances two decades ago.

Luther seemed to realize how close he had come to putting real detail to a vague rumor, because he studied Wyatt in thoughtful silence before continuing. "A community where . . . there's still the potential for mischief to occur where the Van Dormers are concerned," he finally concluded.

"What kind of mischief?" Wyatt asked.

Again Luther hedged. "Let's just say that, shortly before I left Cincinnati with Evie and Simone, I was the recipient of a few . . . distasteful suggestions . . . where my daughters' safety was concerned. I'm worried that, should the girls ever return to Ohio, those distasteful suggestions might very well become distasteful reality."

"But that was twenty years ago," Wyatt pointed out. "How can you be so sure those threats are still valid? If no one's tried anything by now, it seems unlikely that anything's going to happen."

"There's no statute of limitations on a threat," Luther said simply.

"And that threat would be? . . ." Wyatt asked.

Luther went on the prowl now, clearly feeling restless. "There was a bit of . . . trouble," he began, "with a business deal I made. The details aren't important," he hastily added when Wyatt opened his mouth to ask for that very thing. "Suffice it to say that I got involved with someone I shouldn't have. And when the deal went sour, that someone, who was very powerful, and very ruthless, decided I had deliberately cheated him out of a rather large sum of money."

"How large?" Wyatt asked.

"Very large," Luther told him.

"Define 'very.' "

"Quite."

"Define 'quite.' "

"Lots."

"Define 'lots.' "

"Big, big money."

"Define—"

"It isn't true, of course," Luther interjected, effectively ending, uh, whatever it was the two of them had been indulging in. "Things go wrong in business sometimes," he pointed out, "and for a variety of reasons. But this individual was certain that I was responsible for a significant loss that he suffered."

"Could you define 'significant'?" Wyatt tried again.

"No," Luther told him flat out this time.

"Then how about telling me who the individual is," Wyatt tried instead.

"It's immaterial now," Luther told him. "The individual died three years ago."

"Then what's the problem?"

"The problem is that his daughter took over his business after his death, and she made it clear after doing so that she was interested in . . . straightening out old accounts."

"I'm not sure I follow you, sir," Wyatt said.

"Luther, please," the older man corrected him.

But instead of conceding to the first-name-basis thing, Wyatt asked, "Who, exactly, is it that's threatening your family?"

Luther eyed him warily, as if he weren't sure he should even reveal the person's name. Finally, though, he said, "Twenty years ago, it was Dennis Portman."

Wyatt shook his head. "I'm not familiar with the name."

"He kept a low profile."

"And now it's his daughter managing his affairs?"

Luther nodded. "Alice Portman called me three years ago to 'talk about old times,' and remind me that I had an outstanding debt to the Portman family. She said her father had been willing to overlook the debt as long as my family and I stayed out of Ohio, and that she was willing to overlook the debt, provided we continued to stay away. But should any of us return, she said, she'd be obligated to make good on her father's original plan for my daughters."

"And that plan was what?" Wyatt asked. "Kidnap them? Kill them? What?"

Luther gazed thoughtfully down into his drink. "I took the girls and left Cincinnati twenty years ago because if I hadn't, Dennis made it clear that he would take them from me. I don't even want to think about what he would have done once he had them. The man was already half-crazy before the deal went bad. Afterward . . ." Luther shook his head slowly, as if he still couldn't believe what the other man had threatened to do.

"I managed to elude him for several years after leaving," he went on, "but, eventually, he found out we settled here in Santa Barbara. I paid him part of the money he felt I owed him, and as long as we stayed out of Ohio, he was content to maintain the status quo. But he made it clear that if I or the girls came back to Cincinnati, he'd . . ." Luther swallowed hard but didn't specify. "After he died, his daughter reiterated the terms. If any of us go back, then we'll be opening ourselves up to harm."

"I'm afraid I still don't understand all of this," Julian said.

Until his friend and partner had spoken up, Wyatt had honestly forgotten he was there. Funny how talk of another time, another place, could carry a person back to that destination so quickly, so completely. Wyatt gazed through the French doors again, out at the Pacific, now dark blue due to the sun's near departure, and he could scarcely believe he was thousands of miles away from home. For a moment, he'd been eighteen again, back in Cincinnati, and worried about Eve Van Dormer. Because someday she was going to bite off more than she could chew, and then she'd be in trouble, and he wouldn't be around to help her out, and then where would she be?

Her prick husband wouldn't let her.

Sounded like maybe Eve had already been there.

"Mr. Van Dormer," Wyatt said, moving uninvited toward a chair near the big desk and folding himself into it, "I'm a little confused myself. Maybe it would be better if you just started from the beginning and told us exactly what you need."

 *Two*

Eve Van Dormer really needed to get away for a while. Not so much to embark upon an extraordinary experience or astounding adventure. She didn't need hills or rills or breathtaking scenery. She just needed to get *away*. Away from Santa Barbara, away from her father's paranoia, away from her sister's mothering, away from the tragicomedy that her life had become.

As she stood on the wide balcony fronting her father's house—thinking that its nickname of The Keep was feeling way too appropriate these days—she gazed out at a last scrape of sunlight that hovered above the ocean. And she felt a soul-deep yearning for . . . something. She had no idea what. Just . . . something. Something more. Something different. Something that wasn't what her life had become.

One of her college literature professors had once told her there was a word for this type of feeling, a word to identify a person's homesickness for a place she had never visited before. But the term eluded her now. Evidently, it was buried too deeply in a long dormant part of her brain—the part that carried her memories of happier days spent as an undergrad English major at UCLA. They were days—memories—that seemed now to belong to someone else. And Eve supposed that, in a way, those days and memories did. Because they were part of her life that Edwin Walsh hadn't cooed and cajoled his way into, years that had been reasonably carefree, reasonably enjoyable, reasonably happy. And it had been a long time since anything in Eve's life had been reasonable.

Probably, she thought, that was because, these days, she didn't much recognize herself. She'd been robbed of who she was—of who she used to be, and of who she might have become. And even though she hadn't been anywhere close to Edwin Walsh for nearly three months, even though, God willing, she would never have cause to see him again, there were times when she didn't think she'd ever be out from under his thumb.

The sun dissolved completely into the ocean as the realization unrolled in her head, so Eve turned her back on both of them. Figuratively, that made her feel a little better. Literally, however, it left her gazing back at the bedroom whose open French doors she had wandered through some time ago. Simone's bedroom. So much more inviting than the guest room Eve had been occupying at the estate for the last few months, yet, somehow, so much more repelling, too.

Slowly, she made her way back through those doors, feeling as if she were passing through a time portal that spanned twenty years. The Laura Ashley wallpaper in a pale yellow stripe, the creamy lace coverlet and canopy on the bed, the floral hooked rug, the innumerable souvenirs from adolescence, all of it was reminiscent of Simone's bedroom back in Woodhaven.

She'd re-created it almost perfectly, immediately after the Van Dormers had taken possession of The Keep. There were even stuffed animals occupying the window seats and Madame Alexander dolls populating every available shelf, because Simone couldn't quite bring herself to pack up any of her loved ones in boxes and store them away. But she couldn't bring herself to put up a "free to good home" sign for any of them, either. So, like their owner, they sat where they had been sitting for two decades, waiting.

Eve knew it was because Simone still embraced a decades-old fantasy of marrying blond Brian Richie and having a house full of beautiful, blue-eyed daughters to whom she might pass her collections. This despite the fact that blond Brian Richie had married someone else shortly after graduating from Woodhaven High School. This despite the fact that blond Brian lived thousands of miles away. This despite the fact that blond Brian hadn't seen or spoken to Simone for nearly twenty years.

News had it that blond Brian was a widower now, and had been for nearly a year. He had three beautiful, blue-eyed—and motherless—daughters. And he would almost certainly be attending Woodhaven High School's twenty-year reunion in Cincinnati next week. Eve had no doubt that that was the primary reason why Simone wanted to go. Because, even after two decades, Simone was certain that blond Brian Richie, who had literally been the boy next door back in Woodhaven, was her destiny.

Eve sighed to herself as she made her way across

the room to where her sister sat curled up in a bent-wood rocker, reading. She tipped her head to note the title of the book and smiled. *My Friend Flicka.* Nope. Nothing in the room seemed changed from twenty years ago. But that was probably because very little in Simone had changed from twenty years ago, either. In many ways, she still seemed the fresh, innocent, naive seventeen-year-old she'd been the night their father had woken them from deep sleep and told them they had to leave. Now. Or else. Funny how Simone had managed to stay so much the same, while Eve had changed so utterly.

Then again, maybe that wasn't so funny, after all.

Simone looked up as Eve drew nearer. "Did Carmen find you?" she asked. "She said Daddy wants to see both of us in his study at seven-thirty." She spared a glance at the elegant gold watch encircling her delicate wrist. "It's almost that now."

Everything about Simone was elegant and delicate, Eve noted with no small admiration. With her pale blond hair, pale blue eyes, and pale ivory complexion, she was like a photographic negative to Eve. They were as unalike as two human beings could be, never mind twin sisters. And dressed in her cotton sweater set—pearl-buttoned and faint lavender in color—over slim, faded jeans and sandals, Simone was the epitome of fresh-scrubbed, golden California Girl.

Eve realized then that she'd been wrong a moment ago to peg her sister as unchanged. Because outwardly at least, Simone wore an entirely different shell from the one she had donned in high school. The years had softened and refined her appearance, and had brought a maturity and confidence to her that a person couldn't help but remark.

Blond Brian Richie was in for a surprise.

Eve gazed down at her own outfit, a shapeless, taupe tunic hanging untucked over even more shapeless taupe trousers. She'd swept her dark hair up into a simple French twist, but that had been hours ago, and now she could feel a few errant, escaped tendrils tickling her neck and cheeks. She knew she looked laggardly and dull, but she honestly didn't care. Laggardly and dull was pretty much how she felt these days.

"Carmen told me Daddy wants to see us," she replied to her sister's question. "But she didn't say anything about why."

Simone smiled. "Probably, he's going to try one more time to talk us out of going to Cincinnati."

"Probably," Eve agreed. "Or else he'll try one more time to sell us on that ridiculous idea of taking bodyguards with us."

"Oh, I don't know," Simone countered mildly. "I kind of liked the bodyguard idea. It was terribly romantic."

Eve chuckled. "You've been reading too many books."

"You talk like that's a problem."

"No, not a problem," Eve readily denied. "Just not very realistic. Not that I wouldn't enjoy it if life *were* more like books sometimes," she hastened to add.

Simone smiled, but there was something a little sad in her expression. She rose and closed her book, then placed it on the rocking chair cushion. She eyed it a little wistfully as she replied, "I wish that life was more like books *all* the time."

"Come on," Eve told her, tilting her head toward the bedroom door. There was no reason to stand around wishing for things that would never happen, after all.

"Daddy's waiting for us," she added. "And for some reason, I feel like we're in for a little surprise."

Eve's words came back to haunt her only moments later, because the little surprise she had suspected turned out to be a great, colossal shock. When she first strode into her father's office, she realized that yes, they were indeed going to revisit the bodyguard thing. That could be the only explanation for the big—very big—man standing near her father's desk. Tall, dark, and brooding, he was. Except for his eyes, which were an intriguing shade of light blue-gray that she could tell, even standing a good ten feet away from him, held a hint of speculation. Yep, a bodyguard, as they said in southern California, *fer shur*.

And, oh, look, she thought further when she detected the presence of another person in the room. The bodyguard had brought a friend for her sister. Well, wasn't that so nice? And wasn't that such a coincidence? And wasn't that so convenient? And wasn't that—

Wyatt Culver?

He spun around quickly, as if he'd heard her summon him, and only then did Eve realize that she had indeed spoken his name aloud. Judging by the expression on his face, he was no more prepared for her than she was for him, even though he'd obviously had some warning that she would be here. Because he was staring at her as if he couldn't quite believe she was real, as if she couldn't possibly be the same person he remembered from high school.

But she wasn't the only one who had changed. She recalled Wyatt as a lanky, cocky, eighteen-year-old boy, with longish dark blond hair and the most beautiful green eyes she'd ever seen. His hair was shorter now, darker, more brown than blond, really, and he held himself with more genuine confidence and less affected swagger. He had filled out quite a bit, but not an inch of it was fat—he'd just gotten larger . . . all over. Wider across the shoulders, broader at the chest, thicker around the forearms revealed beneath the rolled-back cuffs of his shirt. He was even a little taller than she recalled.

Only his eyes, she thought, with their beautiful mix of greens, looked the same. And the moment their gazes met, her heart began to hammer against her rib cage in a rapid, irregular riff. Some things, evidently, never changed.

Wyatt Culver. Of all people.

"Hey, Eve, long time, no see," he said by way of a greeting. Then he smiled in a way that was clearly phony and uncomfortable, and something inside of her twisted tight.

In hearing even that small utterance from him, she noted how much his voice had changed, too. It was deeper now, fuller, more self-assured. But, as had been the case before, the sound of it splashed heat throughout her midsection.

"Wyatt," she said softly, the single-word salutation all she could manage.

He opened his mouth to say something more, but her father intercepted, remarking, with an obviously forced joviality, "Well, it's good to see that everybody remembers everybody."

"Uh, not quite," the big, dark-haired, pale-eyed man near the desk interjected.

"Oh, right," her father said. "Sorry. Julian, these are

my daughters, Simone"—he gestured toward Simone—"and Eve." He dipped his head toward the man who wasn't Wyatt and said, "Simone and Evie, this is Julian Varga. He's Wyatt's partner."

"Partner in what?" Eve asked, directing the question to her father more than to Wyatt, even though the latter was a more appropriate recipient. She was still too shaken by his presence to actually speak more than a word—or to even spare another glance—in his general direction.

Nevertheless, it was Wyatt who answered. As he took a few oh-so-casual steps toward her, he said, "Julian and I are private investigators. We've been in business together for about four years now."

When Eve saw that Wyatt was drawing nearer, she strode toward the bar on the other side of the room and ducked behind it. She pretended it was because she wanted to pour herself a glass of wine, but really it was because she wanted to erect some kind of barrier, however inconsequential, between them. Anything that might keep him at a distance. She was afraid of what she might do if he got too close. Either hurl herself into his arms and try to shove her tongue down his throat, which really wasn't likely, or else run screaming in horror from the room—a much more conceivable scenario. Still, either way, she would end up looking kind of silly.

"Private investigators?" she asked as she reached for a bottle of Beaujolais. "Sounds interesting."

When she glanced up, she saw that Wyatt had stopped in the exact spot she had just vacated, and something inside her that was already coiled way too taut clenched tighter still. Oh, yes. A glass of wine was sounding very good. In fact, a *bottle* of wine was sounding very good. A great, big magnum ought to do nicely. For a start. Hastily, she uncorked the bottle—alas, not a magnum, but it would have to do—with her thoughts, and her gaze, dammit, focused entirely on Wyatt.

He focused his attention on her, too, homing in on her face, but his expression now was inscrutable. He could have been thinking about anything—about the night he had left her crying and half-dressed in the back of Stuart Turner's car, or about how he needed to remember to gas up on his way back to the airport. Eve told herself she didn't care what he was thinking about. But she knew she was lying through her mental teeth.

"It pays the bills," he said in response to her earlier comment.

"Do the two of you, by any chance, ever do any work as, oh, say . . . bodyguards?" she asked idly.

"Sometimes," he said.

Aha.

She turned her attention now to her father. "I thought we already talked about this, Daddy. Simone and I both agree that we don't need or want body-guards going with us to Cincinnati. Just because you're proposing someone we know this time, that's not going to change anything."

"Actually, I believe your sister was fine with the suggestion when I first mentioned it," her father countered.

"Only because she always does what you want her to," Eve said. The comment was offered without acrimony, as a statement of simple truth. Simone herself would concur.

And, in fact, she did. "If it would make Daddy feel more comfortable, Evie, I don't see the problem."

But Eve did. She intended to return to Cincinnati *alone*. She didn't mind going with Simone—Simone was her sister—but she adamantly refused to have anyone else accompany her, and she made that clear to her father.

"It isn't necessary," she reiterated. "If Simone wants to go along with the idea, fine. She can go along with it. In which case, I'll go to Ohio by myself. But I refuse to have a bodyguard."

"Not even Wyatt?" her father asked.

"Wait a minute," Wyatt interjected. "Bodyguard? Nobody said anything about being a bodyguard. I thought—"

But Eve's father cut him off before he finished. "Wyatt would be a good bodyguard, Evie."

Oh, wouldn't he? she thought before she could stop herself. "I won't have a bodyguard," she told her father again, even if, she realized, the response was intended more for Wyatt's ears. "Especially not him," she found herself adding.

"Evie, maybe you should listen to Daddy," Simone said, troubling her further.

Although Eve and Simone had never had the fast-and-true relationship that most twin sisters—or even most sisters, period—shared, they had never been adversaries, either. There had always existed between them an unspoken trust, a silent cooperation, and an invisible means of support, which neither sister had ever violated. When times had called for unity, the two of them had unified. When either had felt threatened, both had risen to defend. When one hurt, the other comforted. Even if they weren't the closest siblings in the world, they loved and respected each other, and each other's feelings. At least, they had respected each other's feelings until now.

"I think you should listen to what Daddy and Wyatt and Mr. Varga have to say before you decide," Simone added. "Daddy said someone threatened us if we go back to Cincinnati. Even if you don't take that threat seriously, it might not be a bad idea to have someone with you."

"And what about you?" Eve asked. "You don't take the threat seriously, either. Why would you agree to have a bodyguard lurking over you?"

Simone threw a hasty glance at Mr. Varga, clearly uncomfortable around the man. But she said, "No, I don't take the threat seriously. But if it will make Daddy sleep better at night—"

"Evie, I don't want you or Simone traveling any distance by yourselves right now," her father said in that no-nonsense voice that had left Eve quaking when she was a young girl.

Now, though, somehow, that tone of voice comforted her instead. These days, she knew her father only used it because he cared about what happened to her. Edwin had used a tone that was far worse, and for far more insidious reasons.

"Simone and I will both be fine," Eve told him wearily. "You're overreacting, just like you overreacted in bringing us all the way to California to begin with. It's been twenty years, Daddy. There's nothing dangerous waiting for us in Cincinnati."

But he ignored her protest. "I'll feel better knowing you and your sister are properly chaperoned."

"Properly chaperoned?" Eve echoed incredulously.

"We're grown women. You sound like we're going to the senior prom."

Oh, bad analogy, Eve. Really really *bad analogy.*

Wyatt obviously thought so, too, because when she braved a glance in his direction, she saw that he had squeezed his eyes shut and clenched his jaw tight, as if some searing pain were worming its way through his entire system.

And then, as if she hadn't already done enough damage, as if some demon had possessed her, Eve, to her own horror, heard herself adding, "And, hey, *nothing* happened at the prom, did it?"

She regretted the words the moment she uttered them. Why dig up memories of a night she wished she could forget? A night that Wyatt must certainly remember even less fondly than she? Who wanted to remember a night when some desperate, irrational girl begged you to make love to her, when that was absolutely the last thing you wanted to do? And who wanted to remember that she herself had been that girl?

Before Eve could mumble an apology that might take away the sting, Wyatt quickly countered, "Not that some people didn't try their damnedest to *make* something happen."

The heat of humiliation knifed through her at his remark, but she had no one but herself to blame for bringing it up. "Let's just forget it, all right?" she said softly. "I'm sorry I brought it up."

She wasn't sure, but she thought she heard him wince. All he said in reply, though, was, "So am I."

She dipped her chin downward, the best she could manage by way of an apology. "We won't mention it again, agreed?" *Especially*, she added to herself, *since I won't be seeing you anymore after tonight.*

Wyatt nodded curtly. "Agreed."

"Children, children," her father said mildly. "Do you think you could return to the present for a moment, and put high school behind you, where it belongs?"

Not likely, Eve thought. In spite of everything, a part of her would always be with Wyatt. Whether he wanted that part of her or not.

"I don't want Wyatt to be my bodyguard," she said again, this time with a little more conviction than before. Then, straightening her entire body, meeting her father's gaze levelly, she injected even more fortitude into her voice and added, "I *won't* have him as my bodyguard."

Her father eyed her curiously for a moment. Then he repeated, more adamantly this time, "Evie, it's not safe for you in Cincinnati. You need someone to keep an eye on you."

"I don't need anybody," she said. But she could tell that nobody in the room believed that any more than she believed it herself. "Now, if you'll excuse me, I've said my piece, and I have things to do. Wyatt," she added, tipping her head formally in his direction. But she couldn't quite bring herself to tell him good-bye. So she moved on to his companion and said, "Mr. Varga, have a good life."

"I intend to," Julian replied readily.

"Daddy," she continued, turning now to her father, "tomorrow night will be my last one here at the estate. When I get back from Cincinnati, I'll be moving out." Eve pivoted around to face her sister, who had, at some point, moved to stand next to the inimitable Mr. Varga—or perhaps Mr. Varga had moved to stand next to Simone. "Simone, I know we planned on flying back to Cincinnati together Sunday, but I need to prove a point. I'll be changing my plans and going alone. Just to show you, all of you," she clarified, arcing her gaze over each of them, "that I'll be perfectly fine, alone. *Alone*," she repeated more loudly. But the proclamation sounded nowhere near as brave or as noble as she had intended for it to sound.

And before anyone could contradict her—especially herself—she spun on her heel and left the room.

Wyatt watched Eve go with a twist of frustration wringing his gut and a bubble of admiration percolating around his heart. Damn. She'd always had a contrary effect like that on him. Evidently, there were some things that even the passage of twenty years couldn't change.

Twenty years had changed Eve, though.

He'd barely recognized her when he'd spun around to find her standing in Luther's study. She'd been so . . . so colorless. And she'd looked so tired. And she'd seemed so beaten down. Her father had indicated that her marriage had been a difficult, unhappy one, but Wyatt would never have guessed it would have left her looking—being?—like . . . like that.

Yeah, there'd been a fizzle of something when she'd stood up to her father there at the end. But nothing like the fire and fury that had blazed in her eyes and her soul when she was a kid. Gone, too, was the crackle of electricity that had simmered around her wherever she went. There had been a time when Eve Van Dormer wouldn't have been able to enter a room without setting every cell Wyatt possessed on red alert. But he hadn't noticed her arrival in the room tonight until she'd spoken his name aloud. And even then, when he'd turned to face her, there had been none of the blaze, none of the sparkle, none of the . . . the . . . the *passion* that had once defined her. Eve Van Dormer had always been bright lights and bottle rockets. But now . . .

Now someone had extinguished her fire. They might as well have tossed a blanket over the sun.

"Why don't you go talk to her, Simone?" Luther said abruptly to his other daughter. "God knows she won't listen to me."

Simone eyed her father with something akin to disbelief. "Evie's not going to listen to me, either," she said. "Not now. She's made up her own mind. And it's about time, I say. If you didn't hear it, Daddy, then I don't know what to tell you."

Luther looked puzzled. "Hear what?"

"Evie's going to go her own way on this," Simone told him. "You won't talk her out of it."

That comment left Luther silent, thoughtful. He turned his gaze down to his drink but said nothing more.

"Now if you'll excuse me, gentlemen," Simone added, turning her attention first to Wyatt, then briefly—whoa, *very* briefly, Wyatt noted—to Julian, "I have some things I need to do, too." She smiled a warm, genuinely pleased smile, and something in her expression indicated that she spoke from the heart when she said, "Wyatt, it was really nice seeing you again."

Then she threw a hasty—whoa, *very* hasty, Wyatt noted—glance at Julian and . . . blushed, strangely enough. But when she spoke to Julian, the honest emotion fled her voice, leaving it quiet and not a little nervous. All she said to him by way of a farewell was,

"Mr. Varga," and then the other Van Dormer sister disappeared, too.

After that, Wyatt was back where he'd begun earlier in the evening—standing in Luther Van Dormer's study, alongside Luther and Julian, feeling as if he'd just stepped in front of an oncoming express bus. And at the moment, he really didn't want to know what kind of traffic was coming up behind it.

Boy, the sisters Van Dormer had *both* seen their fair share of alterations. Eve's light had been eclipsed, and Simone's invisibility had disappeared. Then again, Wyatt thought, it probably wasn't possible for invisibility to disappear, was it? Invisibility was, by definition, not apparent, therefore, it couldn't *dis*appear, could it? So Simone had . . . what? he wondered. Appeared? That didn't exactly sound right either, but—

"Did you see that, Wyatt?" he vaguely heard Luther ask.

Still trying to figure out what was different about Simone, Wyatt replied with some distraction. "See what?" he asked.

"Evie just left in a huff."

"Yeah. So? What else is new?" Wyatt turned his attention back to Luther, leaving the quandary of the man's daughters for later. "Eve's been in a huff since the day I met her."

Luther shook his head. "No, she hasn't. She was never in a huff when she was married. Her prick husband wouldn't let her have any huffs."

There it was again, Wyatt noted. *Wouldn't let.* How could those words possibly be used in conjunction with Eve? Before he could ask for clarification, though, Luther continued.

"Simone is right," he said, smiling. "Evie just put her foot down. She's made up her mind, and she's not going to change it, no matter what anyone says."

Wyatt shrugged. "And that would be significant because . . . ?"

Luther's smile grew broader, making him look victorious for some reason. But all he said in response was, "I knew this would happen when I called you."

"Knew what would happen?" Wyatt asked.

"It's been a long damned time since Evie has shown this kind of gumption," Luther said. "And I can see only one reason for why it's come about now, today, this evening."

Not certain he wanted to know the answer to the question circling in his brain—not if the expression on Luther's face was any clue—Wyatt heard himself ask, "And, um, what reason would that be, sir?"

The other man's smile grew broader still, and Wyatt's body temperature dipped significantly in response. "You, Wyatt," Luther said. "You being here. That's what's put some spark, some life, back into Evie."

Wyatt gaped at Luther, having no idea what to say. Except maybe for "Huh?"

Luther nodded slowly, his blue eyes gleaming. He was clearly thinking about Wyatt, but what he said next was meant for his partner. "Julian," he said. "Why don't you go check on Simone? The two of you can map out your strategy for her travel to Ohio on Sunday. She all but said she'll agree to have you as her bodyguard. That's one bird, anyway. And I didn't even have to use a stone." He moved deftly over to his desk and pushed a button atop it. "I've called Carmen. She can show you to Simone's room."

"No problem, Mr. Van Dormer," Julian replied readily. In fact, Julian replied a little *too* readily, in Wyatt's opinion. Did the guy have to sound so happy about this assignment? This assignment they hadn't even formally accepted yet? As for Wyatt, to quote one of his personal heroes—Han Solo—he was getting a bad feeling about this . . .

Especially after the door clicked shut behind Julian and the housemaid/homicidal flamethrower, and Luther turned back to Wyatt, eyes sparkling with mischief. "So Evie has issued her edict, and won't let me hire you to be her bodyguard," he said. "Which comes as no surprise at all, because, as you may have gathered, it's a subject I've already covered with my daughters."

"I did rather get that impression, sir," Wyatt replied.

But Luther was clearly not bothered by Eve's recalcitrance. "That's okay," he said, the sparkle in his eyes growing more mischievous.

Uh-oh.

"Because now," Luther said, "we can go back and discuss that kidnapping idea."

 *Three*

"Yeah, let's do discuss that," Wyatt began eagerly, wanting to squelch the idea as soon as was humanly—or even inhumanly—possible. Call him unrealistic, but seeing as how Eve didn't want him as her bodyguard, he was fairly certain she wasn't going to accept him as her abductor, either. Just a shot in the dark, mind you, but still.

"Don't worry," Luther told him, "it will just be a little kidnapping."

"Define 'little,' " Wyatt said.

"Tiny," Luther told him with a vague flutter of one hand.

"Define 'tiny.' "

"Negligible."

"Define 'negligible.' "

"Not big at all."

"Define 'not big at all.' "

"It's nothing," Luther assured him.

"Then why are you smiling like that?" Wyatt demanded.

Luther's expression wavered not one iota. "Like what?" he asked mildly.

Wyatt battled an impulse to run screaming for his life. "For a minute there, you looked like Richard Nixon. It gave me the creeps. Even worse than when you said you want me to kidnap Eve, I mean."

Luther shrugged again, in that same no-nonchalance, evil Republican, trust-me fashion. "Oh, it won't be one of those ski mask, duct tape, trunk of the car kidnappings," he said casually. He arced a hand easily through the air, as if what he was saying were of no more significance than a list of plant-watering reminders for a house-sitter would be. "That would scare the bejeezus out of her, wouldn't it? We don't want to do that."

Well, gosh, Wyatt thought. That sure was a relief.

"No, what I have in mind," Luther went on, "is just a harmless little abduction."

"A harmless little abduction," Wyatt repeated. "Now that's a phrase you don't hear every day."

Luther ignored his sarcasm. "I have my reasons for wanting you to do this."

He enjoyed another, much larger, swallow of his drink, then paced restlessly to the French doors on the other side of the room, where he stopped to stare out at the night beyond. Wyatt followed his movements with his gaze, then noted the faint outline of a woman standing on the balcony outside, at the opposite end of the house. She was cast in darkness, but he knew, of course, that the woman was Eve.

Luther sighed heavily as he, too, gazed at the dark silhouette. "I blame myself sometimes for what happened with Evie. Her marriage and all, I mean."

"And what, exactly, happened to Eve with her marriage and all?" Wyatt asked.

For a moment Luther said nothing, only gazed out at his daughter. Finally, though, he spoke. "When Eve went down to LA for college," he began, "she was alone for the first time in her life. She hadn't had a chance yet to make friends here, and she was separated from her family. Simone stayed here at home and attended USC Santa Barbara, but Eve, of course, had to go her own way. Which wouldn't have been a problem, except that it came right on the heels of me bringing her across the country to an entirely new place, an entirely new life. Everything she'd ever had, everything that was familiar to her, was suddenly gone. She didn't know anyone, had no point of reference, no emotional or psychological compass."

Luther spun around now to look at Wyatt. "Although she'd never admit it," he continued, "I think she felt lost at UCLA. Her ex-husband, being the predator that he was, detected her sense of isolation and pounced on it."

"He was another student?" Wyatt guessed.

Luther shook his head. "One of her professors."

"Ah."

"He insinuated himself into her life, then made himself a big part of her existence while she was there, first as her professor, then, when Evie became a teaching assistant, as a colleague of sorts, then as . . . as something else entirely."

"A lover," Wyatt said, nearly choking on the word.

Luther shook his head. "No. What Edwin Walsh felt toward Evie wasn't love. It took her a long time to finally realize that. Edwin, the prick, did his best to keep her separated from her family and what few friends she'd managed to cultivate. He made her think that he, and only he, knew what was best for her, that only he could make her happy. It happened gradually, I'm sure, but what he did to her was a well-orchestrated maneuver on his part. I don't think Evie ever saw it coming, not until it was too late. But eventually, she did come to her senses. Eventually, she did see him for what he was."

"A prick," Wyatt concluded.

Luther didn't disagree.

What Wyatt wanted to ask next, he almost couldn't bring himself to put voice to. But he wanted, needed, to know. His gut tightened, heated, as he asked, "Did he ever . . . hurt her? Physically, I mean?"

When Luther glanced up this time, his expression was haunted, almost fearful. "I don't know, Wyatt," he said roughly. "I could never bring myself to . . . and Evie doesn't really . . ." He dropped his gaze back down to his now nearly empty drink. "I don't know."

Wyatt turned his attention to the French doors again, and saw that the figure out on the balcony had seated herself at the foot of a chaise lounge. For long moments he only gazed at her, feeling the insistent tug of something so strong, so visceral, so much a part of his essential makeup that even twenty years and two thousand miles hadn't been able to erase it. And somehow, he knew he'd be no more successful at battling that pull now than he had been before.

"Anyway," Luther continued, his voice softer now,

less ragged, "Evie's finally made her break from Edwin. But she hasn't shaken his hold. I don't know that she'll ever be completely free of him."

"What do you mean?" Wyatt asked.

Luther only shook his head slowly and said, "You saw her. You saw how she is now. She and Edwin separated more than a year ago, but she's still . . ." He sighed heavily and shook his head. "After the divorce was finalized three months ago, Simone went down to LA and convinced Evie to move up here to The Keep with us, because she needed to be with her family." He smiled, and there was obvious pride in the gesture. "Simone has her huffs, too, from time to time. She can be as formidable as Evie used to be, when she puts her mind to it."

This Wyatt found difficult to believe. Simone Van Dormer, for all the changes in her, still seemed much too nice and much too unassuming for her own good.

"Since Evie's moved back up here, Simone and I have tried our best to undo Edwin's influence, but . . ." He shrugged. "Evie is so unhappy, Wyatt. There's no animation, no excitement, no . . . no *joy* in her at all. She just seems so . . . so lost. She's not the bright, ebullient girl she used to be. And I don't know how to bring that Evie back again."

Wyatt hesitated a moment before asking dubiously, "And you think me being here could help?"

"What I know," Luther told him, "is that Evie was never more alive in her life than she was during the years she knew you."

"It was high school, Mr. Van Dormer," Wyatt pointed out. "She was young and beautiful and smart. Anything about that time could have made Eve happy."

The other man shook his head. "I'm not as dense as my girls—or you—like to think," he said. "It wasn't high school that made Evie happy back then. And going to her reunion next week isn't going to be what takes her back to what she used to be. Even if that's what Evie is thinking deep down. It'll take more than a weekend of reminiscing about old times to erase Edwin's handiwork."

Wyatt eyed the other man thoughtfully as he tipped back his own drink. Gee. Maybe Luther really wasn't as dense as his daughters—and Wyatt—thought he was.

Luther swirled the limp ice cubes around in his otherwise empty glass. "What has me worried even more, though," he continued, "is what might be waiting for both girls in Cincinnati. That's why I called you, Wyatt. I've kept tabs on several people over the years, and I knew you were a private investigator now—and that you're very good at what you do, too. I also knew that you and Julian had provided bodyguard services from time to time."

"Yeah, well, not that there's a *huge* call for bodyguards in Ohio," Wyatt said wryly. "Go figure. But yes, Julian and I have played the part on a few occasions. And yes," he added further, "we're very good at what we do."

Luther nodded. "Then you and your partner can keep the girls safe while they're in Cincinnati."

"And you want me to keep Eve safe by kidnapping her?" Wyatt asked skeptically. As much as he hated to return to the subject of Luther's harmless little abduction, he thought it might be prudent to conclude that particular business right now.

"If that's what it takes, then yes," Luther said. "I

want you to kidnap her. But you misunderstand my meaning when I ask you to kidnap her."

"Mr. Van Dormer—"

"Call me Luther, please," the other man said.

Wyatt eyed him warily but still couldn't quite bring himself to make that concession. "What you're asking me to do?"

"Yes?"

"Um, there are a few flaws in your logic, not the least of which is that if I *do* go along with your plan?"

"Yes?"

"I'd, uh . . . I'd be committing a felony. And last time I checked, felonies like kidnapping carried a mandatory sentence of something like twenty-five years to life. Now, that may not seem like much to you, because you, of course, would be here at your lovely home in Santa Barbara. But me, I'd be in a federal prison, and that's just not quite the same thing at all."

Luther eyed him intently. "You're making a joke, aren't you, Wyatt?"

"Actually, sir, I was striving for sarcasm."

"I see. Not to worry. You won't go to prison for this kidnapping."

"Yeah, well, you'll forgive me if I don't share your confidence on that score. And aside from the fact that, surprising as it may seem, I really don't want to be a party to terrorizing your daughter, things like, oh, kidnapping, felonies, federal prison, scaring the bejeezus out of innocent women, that kind of thing? They're just not really a part of my regular day, and I'd just as soon not pencil them in anytime soon. 'Kay?"

Luther gazed at Wyatt unflinchingly. "Please, Wyatt," he said. "I know you think I'm crazy. And I know you don't want to scare her or hurt her. I don't, either. That's just the point. And you still haven't heard my plan. But you have to do this. For me. For Evie. Please."

Wyatt returned the other man's gaze levelly, hooked his hands on his hips, and sighed with much apprehension. Well, hell, what would it hurt to listen to Luther's plan? he asked himself. Maybe he could point out enough problems with it that he would convince Luther of its lunacy. And maybe, somewhere along the line, Wyatt could convince Luther that Eve would be just fine on her own. Hey, while he was at it, maybe Wyatt could even convince himself of that, too.

He sighed heavily, strode toward the bar to refill his drink, and muttered, "All right, I'll listen to your plan. Tell me what it is you want me to do."

The evening breeze had ripened to a night wind while Eve was in the house, and now, as she stood on the dark balcony that cloaked the second floor of The Keep, the surly air dragged more than a few errant strands of hair from her formerly elegant twist. Each time the dark tresses strayed into her eyes, she brushed them absently away, over and over, until, finally, with much exasperation, she reached behind herself and plucked free the comb holding them in place. But this time, when her hair blew into her eyes, Eve didn't bother to push it away. Instead, she closed her eyes and let her hair dance wildly across her face, tangling and scurrying with the wind.

It was a surprisingly glorious sensation. She didn't normally wear her hair loose and hadn't for some time now. Edwin had always insisted that she wear it up instead. But feeling the long tresses cavorting with the damp, salt-tinted air stirred something soul-deep and nearly forgotten inside her. Impulsively, she threw her arms open wide and tilted her head backward, inhaling a great, gasping mouthful of air as she did. She held her breath for as long as she could, until she began to grow dizzy, then she released it in a rush and grabbed another one, pulling it even deeper into her lungs. She forced all thought to the furthest recesses of her brain, willed herself to think of nothing, nothing, nothing. And she succeeded, too—for nearly a full minute. Then . . .

Wyatt Culver.

Wyatt Culver.

Wyatt.

One image after another paraded through her head, each more poignant, more piercing than the one before it. She remembered his snug blue jeans and his cocky walk, and the way his T-shirts had stretched tight across his lean chest. She remembered the way he'd wrapped his mouth around her name when he'd uttered it, as if it had been a prayer and a promise and a prelude all at once. She remembered how he'd smelled of Ivory soap and boyish sweat and some other scent that was inherently his. And she remembered once, being pressed back against her locker as he'd kissed her, long and hard and deep, the hallway around them empty and silent, as empty and silent as the world might as well have been when she felt his body pressed against hers like that.

And when she realized she was a thirty-seven-year-old woman fantasizing about an eighteen-year-old boy, Eve collapsed onto a chaise lounge, pulled her legs up to her chest, folded her arms over her knees, and pressed her forehead to the back of her hand. And then, unable to help herself, she began to cry. Not great gasping sobs or horrible heaving wails. Just a steady stream of tears that came from twenty years of second thoughts, and what-ifs, and maybes.

She wasn't sure how long she sat there crying, the heedless wind enveloping her, the ceaseless song of the ocean serenading her. Eventually, though, the turbulence inside her began to ebb, and, little by little, she pulled herself back together. She'd become very good at that over the years, after all—pulling herself back together. There had been times when she'd even been able to convince herself—almost—that she'd never really fallen apart to begin with.

She palmed her eyes dry, then gazed over the balcony, toward the ocean and the night sky beyond. The Pacific looked black and limitless, bisected by a slender watery trail from the fat silver moon hovering just above the horizon. Santa Barbara was nothing at all like Cincinnati, but Eve couldn't quite shake the sensation that she had come full circle tonight. Or that, despite the path life had bumped her along, there were some things that would never, ever change.

She felt tears threatening again and directed her eyes skyward. Only darkness met her gaze, however. Stagnant, constant, immutable darkness. It comforted her not at all.

"Eve."

For some reason, she wasn't surprised to hear Wyatt call out her name. She'd known he wouldn't leave things as she'd left them in her father's study, because he wasn't one for surrendering the last word easily. Then again, neither was she. Or, at least, she hadn't been, once upon a time. Tonight, though, it really didn't matter which one of them got the last word. It wouldn't change anything, one way or another.

"Go away," she told him halfheartedly—for all the good it would do. He'd behave as he wanted to. He always had.

Just as she'd expected, he ignored her instruction. But she sensed, more than saw, him stride forward and fold himself into a nearby chair—there was no way, after all, that she was actually going to look at him.

"Why did you come out here?" she asked in spite of that. But the question came out so quietly that she wondered if he even heard it over the soft rumble of the wind and the waves.

From the corner of her eye—oh, all right, so she would look at him slantways, she conceded—she saw Wyatt lean back in the chair and stretch his long legs out before himself. And in the splash of lamplight that tumbled from the house behind them, she noted that he had loosened his tacky necktie so that it hung unfettered now around his neck.

She also noted that soft coils of dark hair, thicker than he'd had at eighteen, sprung from the elegant V of his open collar. And that the forearms he rested on the chair arms were more prominently sculpted than they had been two decades ago. She noticed how the fabric of his shirt strained against shoulders no boy of eighteen could have ever possessed, and that his finely chiseled features seemed more rugged than they had been years ago.

My, but the details a person could discover with a single sidelong glance, Eve thought. Then she realized that the reason for that was because, without meaning to, she had somehow allowed her sidelong glance to become a full-on examination. In fact, involuntarily, she had turned her entire body on the chaise lounge so that she might look upon him, as if he were the sun and she were a flower starved for light after a long eclipse. But instead of looking back at her, Wyatt gazed out at the dark ocean beyond.

"It was the damnedest thing," he said. "I was in your father's study just now, looking out at you, and suddenly, the strangest feeling came over me."

Although she told herself not to ask, Eve heard herself say, "What kind of feeling?"

He hesitated before replying, turning his gaze now to her. For a long moment, he only studied her face in silence. Then, very softly, he said, "I got the feeling that if I'd glanced down at my watch just then, all the hands would have been spinning backward."

She smiled a bit sadly. "Doesn't work that way, Wyatt. You can't go backward."

"You sound pretty sure about that," he said.

"That's because I *am* sure about that," she replied.

"I see. Well, you always did know everything, didn't you, Eve?"

She arched one eyebrow imperiously. "Why, yes. As a matter of fact, I did," she said playfully.

He smiled, but she couldn't quite tell if it was genuine or not. And all he said in response was, "Mm."

"So how are things in Cincinnati?" she asked. She told herself the question would lead to a nice, safe, bland change of subject, but after voicing it, she realized how much she honestly wanted to know the answer.

"Cincinnati's changed some," he said. "But Woodhaven is totally locked in a time warp. When you go back, you'll feel like nothing's changed at all."

"That would be nice," she said, smiling.

She wasn't lying. Eve missed Ohio, missed the massive oaks and maples, the rolling green hills, the indolent rippling of the muddy river, the warm Midwestern camaraderie. She missed seeing the trees stained with red and gold and orange in the autumn, missed watching everything burst out green in the spring. Southern California was beautiful, but nothing ever changed here—not outwardly, anyway. This wasn't where she belonged, she knew. Though, somehow, Ohio didn't quite feel like home anymore, either.

Suddenly, Eve felt displaced, rootless, as if she didn't belong anywhere at all. And she began to think that she might not ever find her way back to where she needed to be. Because she was beginning to suspect that that place—whatever it was—simply didn't exist anymore.

"I'm not going to go back to Ohio with you, Wyatt," she said suddenly, with surprising evenness. "I'm going to go alone."

His expression altered not at all. "You think so?"

She nodded. "I know so."

"Why is it so important that you go alone?"

Eve felt herself coloring, and her gaze skittered away from his. That, she thought, was none of his business. So she only told him, "It just is important, that's all."

He said nothing for a moment, then told her, "Your father thinks you need someone with you."

"It doesn't matter what my father thinks."

"Doesn't it?"

"No."

"You don't think anyone in Cincinnati's going to try to hurt you?"

"Of course not."

"How can you be so sure?"

She expelled an exasperated breath. "Why do you keep doing that?"

"Doing what?"

"Replying to all my statements with a question."

"Am I doing that?"

"Wyatt!"

He smiled at her then, and there was just the tiniest hint of the boy she remembered from high school in the gesture, the boy about whom she'd been fantasizing only a short time ago. Unable to help herself, Eve smiled back.

"You always could get a rise out of me," she said softly. "Doing nothing more than being within arm's reach."

"Yeah, well, I could say the same thing about you, you know."

He studied her with some intensity for a moment, and she wondered if he would try to revisit the past or stay here in the present. Part of her wanted very much to go backward in time with him, if only for one evening. Just to see if they both recalled it the same way. Then again, if they both recalled it the same way, what was the point in revisiting?

But when Wyatt finally spoke, it was to say, "Just this once, Eve, do what your father wants. Let him hire me in the capacity he wants to hire me."

Ah. So. The present it would be. Evidently Wyatt had no interest in exploring what had—and had not— happened between the two of them twenty years ago.

Eve studied him intently as she asked, "Why?" And

she honestly wasn't sure whether she was asking him in response to the statement he had made or to her own mental observation.

"Because it will be easier," he told her, clearly responding to the former. "Yeah, Luther's probably overreacting, but what difference does it make? It won't do you any harm to let me go with you back to Ohio. I have to go back, anyway," he pointed out with a grin. "Simone doesn't have a problem with Julian going back with her. So what's the big deal?"

The big deal, Eve thought, was that she had a point to make. For the first time in years, she was out from under anyone's thumb, and she needed to prove—to herself, as well as to her family—that she would be fine on her own. Alone. It would be too easy to succumb to her father's wants, too easy to let him make all the decisions on her behalf, just the way she'd let Edwin do for far too long. Eve wanted to go back to making her *own* decisions. *She* wanted to be the one in charge of her life. The way she had been a lifetime ago.

She wanted—needed—to go back to Ohio because that was the last place, the last time, she had been someone she could like and admire and respect. And she had to get there on her own steam, her own terms. She had to.

She *had* to.

"I won't go with you, Wyatt," she said quietly, firmly.

He eyed her intently, then nodded with what she could only liken to resolution. "Fine," he said shortly. "Then I guess there's nothing else to say."

"No, I guess there's not."

"So I'll just go to my room and see you in the morning."

Well, that certainly got her attention. "Don't you mean you'll just go to your *hotel*?" she asked.

He shook his head. "Your father was nice enough to invite me and Julian to stay here at The Keep for the weekend. A very accommodating guy, your father."

Says you, Eve thought. But she only replied, "It's his house. He can invite whoever he wants."

"So I guess I'll just be going back in," Wyatt said again. "To my room."

Eve nodded but remained silent.

"In fact, I think I'll be in the room across the hall from your room," he added, oh-so-matter-of-factly. "That's what your father said, anyway."

She expelled a resigned sigh. "Yeah, that's Daddy," she muttered. "Always planning."

Wyatt looked faintly puzzled. "What do you mean?"

But she only shook her head and said, "Forget it, Wyatt."

"Forget what?"

All of it, she wanted to say. Aloud, though, she told him, "Just never mind. Daddy's up to something is all. I mean, that's pretty obvious, isn't it?"

Wyatt smiled another one of those vaguely familiar, much too boyish, smiles. "I don't know. Is it?"

"There you go again, responding with a question."

"Am I? Gee, what was I thinking?"

In spite of herself, Eve smiled again. "Goodnight, Wyatt," she said.

He sighed heavily and pushed himself up from the chair. "Goodnight, Eve," he replied. "I'll see you in the morning."

Not if I see you first, she thought. *Not if I see you first.*

 *Four*

Julian Varga wasn't sure what to make of Simone Van Dormer's bedroom, but one thing about the place was absolutely certain—it gave him the creeps, big time. Here was a woman—or, more correctly, here was what Julian thought of as a *wo-man*—but her own private domain resembled a twelve-year-old girl's. Not that he knew much about twelve-year-old girls—or anything about them, for that matter—but he did know plenty about women. He knew even more about *wo-men*. And no woman—or *wo-man*—in her right mind lived in a bedroom like this, one full of dolls and stuffed animals and . . . and . . . and was that actually a canopy bed?

Creepy.

He wondered, for a moment, if maybe there was something a little, oh . . . *off* . . . with Simone Van Dormer, psychologically speaking. But neither Wyatt nor her father had alluded to anything like that, so Julian could only conclude that all of her mental faculties were working fine. Inevitably, that made him wonder about some of her other faculties, too, but he managed to rein in his wayward thoughts before they drifted into areas he'd be better off not contemplating. Not now. Not yet. Not until the two of them got to know each other better.

Not that he planned to get to know Simone Van Dormer any better than he had to in order to complete this job, Julian hastily reminded himself. Because it was beginning to look as if Simone Van Dormer, in spite of having lived life a good bit longer than he, had lived a life that was very sheltered.

Obviously she didn't have much experience with the outside world, certainly not as much as Julian had himself. If she still lived at home with her father at age thirty-seven, how savvy could she be? Hell, she still surrounded herself with dolls and stuffed animals and canopy beds and . . . and . . . and were those actually bunny slippers sticking out from under the bed?

Creepy.

Memo to myself, he thought dryly, *stay far, far away from Simone Van Dormer*. A woman as innocent and naive as she clearly was could only lead to trouble for a guy like Julian.

"This is, um, really nice," he lied as he took a step forward to enter the bedroom, sweeping a negligent hand toward the interior. Not that Simone had actually invited him to enter her bedroom, but Julian had learned a long time ago not to stand around waiting for things to happen. *Take action before action takes you.* That was rule number one in the Julian Varga universe. Rule number two was *Watch your back*. And rule number three . . .

Well, rule number three had to do with women like

Simone Van Dormer. Namely, to stay far, far away from them.

But Simone, too, had evidently learned a few things along the way, because before he could complete two steps, she moved deftly in front of him, bracing one hand on the door, the other on the jamb, in an obvious attempt to bar his way. Julian almost laughed out loud at her gesture. She couldn't be more than five-foot-six, a good nine inches shorter than he, and she probably weighed half as much as he did. Yet she clearly intended to hinder his progress with that slim, albeit luscious, body of hers. Well, wasn't that just the cutest thing?

Then again, he realized, he *had* halted the moment she stepped in front of him, hadn't he? So maybe she wasn't so ineffective after all.

"May I come in?" he asked belatedly, oozing courtesy as he fixed his gaze on her face.

How this woman could ever have been viewed as insignificant was beyond him. Her eyes were the color of a summer sky, though darkly lashed and as fathomless as the deepest part of the ocean. Her hair was like finely spun, white-gold silk, and he itched to sift the long tresses through his fingers. Her complexion was a flawless mix of ivory and roses, softer even than her hair appeared to be, and her voice . . .

"Why would you want to?" she replied curtly to his question.

Okay, so maybe her voice was a little clipped and cool right now, he conceded. But earlier, in her father's study, her voice had skimmed over him with the sensual slide of a lover's fingertips.

"Your, uh, your father seems to think we, ah, we should discuss our, um, our strategy for next week," he told her, cursing himself for the near-stammer. He'd conquered his stuttering when he was a teenager, and he wasn't about to go back to it now.

This was ridiculous. Julian never lost track of his thoughts, never allowed his focus to stray one inch from the task at hand. Unfortunately, he realized then that what he really wanted at hand right now was Simone Van Dormer. In fact, he wanted her at both hands. And at a few of his other body parts, as well.

Ooooh, this was not good.

"I don't think a strategy will be necessary," she told him, her grip tightening on the door, her entire body going rigid. "I'll write down my flight information for you, and you can meet me at the airport on Sunday. I'll see you then."

He smiled. "That's not quite going to do it, Miss Van Dormer. Your father wants me to shadow your every step once you leave his house."

Her lips, so full and luscious before, thinned into a tight line. "Then you can meet me at the front door on Sunday. I'll see you then."

"Actually, your father has invited Wyatt and me to spend the next couple of days here at The Keep. And the next couple of nights, too," he qualified meaning-fully—at least, it was meaningful to Julian. He had no idea if Simone would take his meaning. Then again, judging by her expression . . .

Oh, yeah. She definitely took his meaning. And she obviously didn't like it *at all*.

Hastily, Julian hurried on, "He wants us to stay here at the house until it's time for you and your sister to go back to Ohio. Presumably, this means he wants me to keep an eye on you around the clock, starting now."

"Don't presume anything about my father, Mr. Varga," she stated in a chilly voice. "Or about me."

She started to push the door closed, but Julian flattened his palm against it and pushed harder. For one brief moment, they warred for possession of a piece of sturdy mahogany, and he was frankly surprised at the strength she exerted in her effort to win. Ultimately, though, he was stronger than she, and with one final thrust, the door went flying back into the bedroom, crashing solidly against the wall.

"Thanks," Julian said blandly as he strode past her. Or, more correctly, shouldered his way past her. "Don't mind if I do."

He had no idea why he was behaving so rudely. This really wasn't like him at all. Normally, he was the most easygoing, unflappable guy on the planet. But the moment Simone Van Dormer had entered her father's study, looking so cool and fresh—and oh-so-unattainable—she'd made Julian's going anything but easy, and she'd flapped him more than he'd ever been flapped before.

As a result, he'd lost his center. And if there was one thing that Julian Varga absolutely could not tolerate, it was losing his center. He'd worked most of his life to find it, and once he'd found it, he'd embraced it completely. But with one look at Simone—*poof*. His center was gone. And there was no telling how far it had gotten, or when it would turn up.

Then again, she wasn't exactly behaving like the docile little flower he'd been led to believe she would be. The way Wyatt had been talking earlier, Julian had expected Simone Van Dormer to be Simone Van Doormat. Her own father had indicated she would go along with this bodyguard assignment quite willingly, because she always did what Daddy asked her to do. And although she hadn't openly challenged her father, she sure as hell wasn't making this easy for Julian. It was as if she had decided to hate him on sight, and he couldn't for the life of him figure out why. Hey, women generally loved him. Nowadays, anyway. Okay, sure, he was there at her father's insistence, and not her own, but that wasn't any reason for her to be so antagonistic.

"Maybe you don't mind, but I do," she said, true to form, as he made his way to the other side of the room, where French doors were thrown open wide to welcome in the salt-scented breeze.

It was exactly what Julian needed. A breath of fresh, clean, purifying air. Something to chase the scent of Simone Van Dormer from his system, the sweet, floral, innocent fragrance that threatened to intoxicate him. He inhaled a few deep breaths and counted slowly to ten, then made himself visualize a scene that would bring peace to his troubled mind. Yeah, here it came now.

He was visualizing a really good scene, a mental image of himself sitting out there on the beach as the sun dipped low above the horizon. Gradually, the imagined sight brought him some small peace of mind . . . until Simone Van Dormer invaded it. Wearing a bathing suit. A really skimpy one, too. In fact . . . Good God, was that a *thong* bikini she had on?

Julian snapped his eyes open again and spun around to face her. But even fully clothed, she was still a staggering distraction.

"Miss Van Dormer," he said softly, "I apologize for

this intrusion into your life, however brief it will ideally be. But we might as well take advantage of the next couple of days to get to know each other better, and outline our plans for your trip to Ohio. From what I understand, we'll be spending a week together once we get there, and—"

"We won't be together, Mr. Varga," she interrupted him.

He dipped his head forward in acknowledgment. "Not figuratively," he agreed.

"And not literally, either," she assured him.

"Not all the time, at any rate," he conceded. "But we will be spending quite a bit of time togeth—"

"Once we arrive at the hotel in Cincinnati," she interrupted him—again, "Evie and I will have the suite we've reserved, and you and Wyatt will have your own room on the same floor."

"Yes, but—"

"I may have agreed to go along with Daddy's ridiculous compulsion to hire a bodyguard, but I expect you to keep your physical distance from me."

"I understand your concern, Miss Van Dormer, but the very nature of our working relationship necessitates that I'll be—"

"And when it comes time for the reunion," she interrupted him—*again*, "wherein I will seldom be leaving the hotel, I'll expect you to remain in your room for the duration."

Julian arched his eyebrows in surprise, settled both hands on his hips, and told her, quite frankly, "Oh, I don't *think* so."

Her lips tightened into that flat line again, but her cheeks turned as pink as a rose. "While I'm attending my reunion next week," she said crisply, "I'm hoping to . . . renew an old friendship with someone. And I'd rather not have you hanging around, looming over me like King Kong, hindering that . . . renewal."

Julian forced a smile and did his best to ignore the King Kong remark. He did *not* loom, he assured himself, not on his worst day. And although he didn't mind being thought of as a wild animal, ape wouldn't have been in his top five choices.

"Renew an old friendship?" he repeated with much interest.

The stain on her cheeks went deep crimson, and something inside Julian twisted tight.

"Yes," she said. "I'm planning to look up a . . . an old friend."

"You're planning to hook up with an old boyfriend, you mean," he guessed.

She averted her gaze from his. "Not exactly."

"Then you're planning to attract the attention of someone you wish was an old boyfriend."

She said nothing in response to that assertion. Not that anything needed to be said.

Julian smiled, but the expression felt brittle. "I assure you, Miss Van Dormer, that I will in no way hinder your progress in that regard."

"I appreciate your assurance," she said softly. "But I'm not convinced that your very presence won't be a hindrance. I wish my father would reconsider this whole bodyguard thing. It's completely unnecessary."

"Is it?" Julian asked.

She nodded, but she wouldn't meet his gaze. "Believe me when I tell you that there's *nothing* in Cincinnati I can't handle."

Julian shrugged, hoping the action came off looking more careless than it felt. "Your father seems to be convinced there's a threat to you and your sister both."

She expelled a dubious sound. "He's just paranoid. He has been since Evie and I were children. I don't know where it comes from, but ever since our mother died, he's been like that. Maybe losing her just made him irrationally fearful that he'd lose us, too, I don't know."

"Sounds reasonable."

"Oh, please. There's nothing reasonable about my father."

"He seems okay to me," Julian replied honestly. Luther Van Dormer, for all his, um, quirks, did appear to be a genuinely devoted father and, hey, a nice guy to boot.

Simone said nothing for a long moment, just crossed her arms defensively over her midsection and gazed toward the open French doors. "He's changed a lot since we moved to Santa Barbara," she said.

Her admission surprised him. He wouldn't have thought she would volunteer any more personal information—about herself or her family—without major prodding. "In what way?"

She shrugged but still didn't look at Julian when she answered. "He was never exactly the most even-minded person, but ever since he moved us out here, he's been so fearful, so afraid there were people out to get him, that our family was in danger."

She seemed to realize then that she was delving too deeply into the personal—not that Julian minded—because she quickly, even anxiously, turned her attention back to him. The moment her gaze lit on his, however, she darted it away again, just as she had every time their gazes had connected that night—though, granted, those times had been few. And somehow, he knew the reason for both the darting and the infrequency was that every time it happened, she felt the same little sizzle of heat he did.

How very interesting, he thought. No, wait, he quickly backpedaled. It wasn't interesting at all. What it was was inconvenient. He didn't need to be feeling sizzles of heat for a woman who surrounded herself with dolls and stuffed animals and canopy beds and bunny slippers and . . . and . . . and was that actually a copy of *My Friend Flicka* on the rocking chair?

Creepy.

"Look, Miss Van Dormer, regardless of your father's convictions one way or another, he's hiring me and Wyatt to keep an eye on you and your sister."

"As if Evie is ever going to stand for something like that, now that she's rediscovering herself," Simone said, making absolutely no sense to Julian whatsoever.

"That's Wyatt's problem," he replied, disregarding her puzzling statement. "You're mine."

She arched her eyebrows coolly at that, and he squeezed his eyes shut tight. No matter how you translated that Freudian slip, it was remarkably difficult to explain. "Not that you're a problem," he quickly clarified.

"Nor am I yours," she said flatly.

"Hey, who said I wanted you?" he snapped back before he could stop himself. "I'm sorry," he immediately excused himself. He had to get a grip here. This was crazy. There was no rational reason for why he should be behaving so badly. "I apologize," he tried again. "That was uncalled for."

"Yeah, it was," she agreed. "But I guess I'm not

making it easy on you, am I? I apologize, too. Tensions are running high around here lately. Now if you don't mind, Mr. Varga," she hurried on, "I'd just as soon call it a night. If you and Wyatt are going to be staying here at The Keep for a couple of days, then we have plenty of time to, as you said, plan our strategy."

"No time like the present," Julian countered, wondering why he was so eager to prolong what was clearly an uncomfortable exchange for them both. She was right, after all. He and Wyatt would be here until Sunday. There was no reason he and Simone had to rush into things.

"I'm very tired," she told him, sounding in no way fatigued. Then she crossed quickly—and with wide-awake purpose—to her bedroom door in a clear indication that it was time for him to leave. "We can talk tomorrow."

Before obeying her command, Julian spared another glance around the bedroom, taking in the fluffy animals, the glassy-eyed dolls, the girlish furniture, the innocent literature. The room was definitely creepy. So why didn't Simone Van Dormer give him the creeps, too? Because it would have made things infinitely easier for Julian if she had. Then again, why take the easy route? Invariably, the difficult route was almost always the most rewarding. And usually the most fun, too.

Fun, he echoed to himself as he crossed the room to where Simone Van Dormer stood waiting for him to depart. Somehow, that wasn't a word he associated with her. She was much too serious and cool in demeanor to offer even the merest hint of fun. Then again, there were those bunny slippers peeking out from under her bed, he reminded himself. And he couldn't quite help thinking that loosening up Simone Van Dormer might be a pleasant way to pass the time. Gee, they would be spending a week together, after all.

And they *would* be together during that week, he promised himself adamantly. He didn't care what she said. Her father had hired him and Wyatt to look after the sisters Van Dormer. And Julian, for one, always took his work very seriously. If Luther wanted him to keep his daughter safe, then that was what Julian would do, whether Simone liked it or not. Just because she was hoping to hook up with an old boyfriend at her reunion next week, or whatever the hell the guy was, that didn't change Julian's plans.

"Fine," he said as he paused before her, not quite ready to go just yet—he would leave when *he* wanted to. "We can talk tomorrow."

"Or later," she corrected him.

"Tomorrow," he corrected her right back.

She narrowed her eyes at him, but, surprisingly, said, "Fine. Tomorrow."

"Until then, *Miss* Van Dormer."

"Until then, *Mr.* Varga."

Simone closed her bedroom door very firmly behind the infuriating *Mr.* Varga, and, just for safe measure, she twisted the lock on the knob, too. Then, just for safer measure, she leaned back against the door for a few moments, putting all of her weight—even if it was probably only half his own—against it. Then, just for safest measure, she grabbed a chair and shoved it resolutely under the knob. And *then*, just for safest measure of all, she took a few minutes to wrestle her dresser in front of the door.

There, she thought, once she'd completed the

maneuver, her breathing only marginally labored as a result. She decided to ignore the fact that what she'd just done was completely and totally irrational, and in no way like her. Just let Mr. Varga try to get past *that*.

Although why she would even think he'd *want* to try and get past that was beyond her. Not only had he just been anything but friendly but he was also little more than a boy, as far as she was concerned. And it wasn't like any man had ever tried to fight or finagle his way into her bedroom before. Not that she'd ever wanted a man to fight or finagle or anything else his way into her bedroom, in the first place. Oh, sure, she liked men as much as the next woman—they did have such quirky, amusing little habits, after all. But no man had ever captured her interest for any length of time.

Well, except for Blond Brian Richie, of course. But no other man. No way. Certainly not Julian Varga.

She conveniently disregarded the fact that she'd met him scarcely an hour ago, therefore he couldn't possibly have captured her interest for any length of time—well, no more than an hour, at any rate. But that was beside the point. The point was that Julian Varga would *not* capture her interest for any length of time. Because her interest was focused on one man, and one alone.

Blond Brian Richie.

She got goose bumps just thinking about him. She couldn't wait until she saw him again next weekend.

Blond Brian had lived next door to the Van Dormers in Woodhaven for as long as Simone could remember. And she couldn't recall a time when she hadn't been totally captivated by him. When they were kids, a more beautiful, more perfect boy had never existed. He was so smart. And so charming. And he had such lovely manners. He was, she had always thought back then, simply too good to be true.

And, of course, in the long run, that was exactly what he had turned out to be—too good to be true. Not that she'd ever had any hope that he would be hers the way she wanted him to be. Not any honest hope, anyway. Still, that hadn't kept her from embracing dreams of someday becoming Mrs. Blond Brian Richie, and having a house full of blue-eyed, golden-haired children. They were dreams she had held close the whole time she was growing up.

She'd never told anyone about her crush on Blond Brian, except Eve. And she'd only told Eve when they were in high school, and only then because Simone had thought her sister would understand. Because by then, Eve had had her own crush—on Wyatt Culver, a crush that Wyatt hadn't returned. Not the way Eve had wanted him to. Not the way he was supposed to. Not that Eve—or Wyatt, for that matter—had ever really understood what was, or should have been, between the two of them. Much the same way that Simone had never really understood what was, or should have been, between her and Blond Brian.

Within a week's time, though, she would be seeing Brian again. For the first time in twenty years. For the first time since she had so impulsively kissed him at the prom, shocking both of them. For the first time since he had kissed her back, shocking both of them even more. For the first time since—

Well. For the first time in a long, *long* time. Simone tried to envision how he would look now, with twenty years, three daughters, and the loss of a wife tacked on to his age. Somehow, she suspected he was more devastatingly handsome now than he had been then. And smarter. And more charming. And even better mannered. He had always been the kind of person upon whom Fortune smiled. But the more Simone tried to visualize Brian, the more scattered and indistinct the image became. In its place, the only image her mind's eye would form was of the dark and brooding Julian Varga.

Oh, swell. Just what she needed. She was finally ready to launch an operation she'd been planning for a long, long time, only to be thwarted at the last minute by the imposing menace of Julian Varga. His presence as her companion at the reunion would be misunderstood, and it would ruin everything she had planned with Brian.

Obviously, there was only one thing she could do. She would just have to ditch Julian Varga once she got to her reunion.

Simone sighed inwardly. Oh, sure. And that would be just *soooo* easy. Even knowing him such a short time, she could tell that the man took his work way too seriously and was smarter than the average bear, not to mention tenacious as all get-out. How could she expect to evade him for an hour, let alone an entire weekend?

Ah, well. She had a whole week to figure it out. And she would figure it out. She hadn't come all this way just to have her plans for Blond Brian Richie foiled by one guy. She would have her reunion with Brian. And it would end exactly the way it was supposed to, the way it should have ended a long time ago. It would.

It *would*.

 *Five*

Eve had no idea what possessed her to go looking for her senior yearbook immediately after waking the following morning. But, still dressed in her worn, white nightshirt and slouchy white socks, before she even ventured out of her bedroom to pour her first cup of coffee, she found herself ransacking the half-dozen boxes she had brought with her to The Keep. The boxes she hadn't bothered to unpack because surely she wouldn't be staying for more than a week, two at the *most*—which was what she had told herself three months ago when she'd stashed the boxes in the big walk-in closet in the guest bedroom. At the bottom of the third box, she hit pay dirt—the Woodhaven High School *Beehive*, 1981.

Now, she sat outside on the patio off the dining room, neglecting her first cup of coffee. She was still clad in her pajamas, her dark hair caught at the crown of her head in a not-so-tidy ponytail. The sun had crept up into the bright blue sky, but it hovered low in the east, so that the front of the house lay in shade. Across the street and a few hundred yards away, a small group of seagulls dive-bombed the beach for breakfast, crying out raucously with each endeavor.

But Eve scarcely heard them. Nor did she pay heed to the gentle, constant rush of the ocean surf, because she was too busy skimming her hand over the gold, leather-look vinyl that covered her yearbook. She traced her index finger slowly over the eight and the one that constituted her class year, and reflected that it seemed so long ago. So why, then, she thought, did it suddenly feel as if no time had passed at all?

She opened the yearbook immediately to the senior class portraits and fought a reluctant smile at the massive lapels of the mustard yellow tuxedoes the boys had been required—though not without substantial protest—to wear. The black velvet piping on the lapels was a mile wide, and huge black velvet bow ties grasped the boys' throats like rabid rain forest butterflies. The girls had been only a little luckier, having been tied into black velvet drapes that may or may not have hidden their bra straps, depending on the pose. Eve had been one of the fortunate ones. Simone, she recalled when she glimpsed her sister's photo next to her own, had not.

"Oh, God," she whispered with a wistful chuckle when she saw her picture. Had she ever been that young? That happy? That innocent? That handy with a curling iron? She read the list of credits beside her name—swim team, French club, yearbook staff, senior play—and then, at the bottom, her ambition: *To write the Great American Novel and be on* Dinah's Place. Of course, she would never achieve her ambition now, because *Dinah's Place* had been canceled a long time ago. Then again, so had a lot of other things, too.

Nudging the thought away, Eve zealously pushed the glossy pages backward, from the Vs toward the front of the alphabet. She remembered well the positioning of Wyatt's picture—left-hand page, bottom right corner—and that was where, not surprisingly, her gaze fell. Only Wyatt, she thought, could possibly make mustard yellow and a gigantic bow tie look good.

His hair—parted in the middle, she noted with a grin—was lighter and longer in his senior photo, an unruly wave and an utter lack of concern pushing one stray lock down over his forehead. His smile, naturally, was cocky and self-assured, as if he were more than ready to take on the world, hog-tie it, and thrust it high above his head as a personal trophy.

His own list of credits was about the same length as hers, but his ambition was infinitely more ambitious: *To climb Mt. McKinley, hike to the South Pole, sail solo across the Pacific, kayak down the Amazon, photograph the African veldt.* It had actually been much longer, she recalled with a smile. Having worked on the senior section of the yearbook herself, she'd had to cut Wyatt's ambition in half to make it fit.

He'd always had so much confidence, so much attitude, so much. . . . So much Wyatt. Back in high school, there had been occasions when Eve had felt as if she would explode with wanting him, even though, back then, she hadn't known what that sort of wanting really involved.

And there had been other times when she had wished Wyatt himself would explode—or, at the very least, go far away and never return. Hot and cold. Up and down. Her feelings for and reactions to him had been strong ones for a teenaged girl, and nigh on impossible for her to understand. Maybe if she'd met Wyatt now, when she was older, more mature, and less hormonal, more savvy about the ways of the world . . .

But that hadn't happened, she reminded herself. There was no point in sitting here, wondering What if? Especially since she was seeing him *now*, when she was older and more mature—and surely less hormonal, right?—not to mention more savvy in the ways of the world. And *now*, she was no more certain of her feelings for or reactions to him than she'd been twenty years ago.

Dammit, why, of all people, had her father called Wyatt?

"Good morning!"

She glanced up to find the object of her reflections striding through the French doors that led from the dining room to the patio, and she was surprisingly unsurprised by his appearance. In fact, so certain of his arrival had she been, she discovered, that she'd already formed an excuse to explain why she was looking at her high school yearbook.

No sooner had he reached tableside and opened his mouth, obviously to ask her about her find, than she looked him square in the eye and said, "I was trying to remember who in our graduating class was voted Most Likely to Wind Up in Federal Prison."

Wyatt closed his mouth slowly, his expression growing . . . well, the word *flummoxed* came to mind. Hmmm, Eve thought. Maybe he hadn't intended to ask her about the yearbook. Maybe he'd just been about to ask her if there was any more coffee. Maybe he hadn't been about to ask her anything at all. Maybe she just should have kept her mouth shut.

In spite of his puzzlement, however, and without missing a beat, he replied, "Mike Lindley. Remember? He got hauled in to juvie three times during our senior year. Once for vandalizing the Legion Post, once for attempted assault, and once for torching a Dumpster."

"That's right, I remember now," she said. "He was such a thug. Always picking fights and sabotaging events and acting like he was going to run people down in that beat-up Camaro of his. So what happened to him?" she finally asked. "*Is* he in federal prison?"

Wyatt shook his head, smiling. "Nah. He and his partner Stephen run a pastry shop and catering service called Sweet Memories. From what I hear, they're famous throughout southern Ohio for their marzipan."

"His, um, his partner Stephen?" she echoed.

He nodded. "They're partners in both the professional and the romantic sense."

She considered this bit of information for a moment, then said, "You know, that explains a lot." She eyed Wyatt thoughtfully. "So, do you stay in touch with many people from high school?"

He shrugged negligently. "Not really. But I hear things sometimes."

She watched as Wyatt pulled out the chair next to hers and folded himself into it. He'd obviously just showered, because his hair was still wet, pushed back from his forehead with careless fingers. He smelled clean and fresh and full of promise. He was dressed in loose-fitting khaki shorts and an even looser-fitting shirt decorated with myriad, minuscule, multicolored surfboards, and she had noted when she'd first set eyes on him that he was barefoot. It had, evidently, taken him all of twelve hours to become accustomed to California living. It didn't surprise her at all.

"So how do you spend *your* time these days?" she asked. Having skirted the past, she figured it was best now to return to the present. No sense going backward when one could make meaningless chitchat instead, right? "You have your own business—"

"With Julian," he added.

"Whom you met . . . where?" she asked.

Wyatt smiled cryptically. "In jail."

She emitted a single, surprised chuckle. "What?"

"It's a long story," he told her.

"I see," she replied. "Which means you don't want to tell me what you were doing in jail."

He smiled again but said nothing.

"Which leads me to believe you were arrested for something really stupid, like jaywalking or not curbing your dog."

Wyatt's gaze fell to his coffee as he ran the pad of his middle finger idly around the rim of his mug—around once, around twice, around three times—each slow turn more hypnotic than the one before. For some reason, Eve found the gesture to be profoundly arousing, and it sparked a heat deep inside her, in a place that hadn't felt warmth for a very long time. She closed her eyes briefly, inhaled a slow, steadying breath, then opened them again and pretended that her heart wasn't hurtling around in her chest like a runaway freight train.

"Yes, well," he said, "as much pride as I might take in being arrested for something really good, like, say, a string of cannibalistic torture-murders, you're right. It was something stupid."

Amid the heat rushing through her, Eve somehow found the wherewithal to remark, "Which you're not going to tell me about."

He smiled yet again but still said nothing. He also continued to circle his finger around the circumference of his cup, and with each smooth rotation, Eve's body temperature rose a few degrees more, and her heart rate accelerated a few more horsepower.

"All right then," she said softly. "Let's try another tack. You two jailbirds are private investigators, I think you said? Isn't that kind of ironic, seeing as how you've both done time?"

"Not really," he replied easily. "Two sides of the same coin, and all that. Plus, I think I understand the criminal mind *much* better, now that I've been on the inside. For nearly twenty-four hours, too."

"I see," she said. "So tell me more about this business you compassionate convicts run."

Wyatt glanced up at her then, curling his fingers into the handle of his mug, so that he could lift it to his lips for a sip. And something about seeing his mouth where his fingers had just moments ago been lingering only compounded the pressure and heat expanding in Eve's chest.

"Julian and I opened the business together shortly after we met," Wyatt said, "about four years ago. Even though he was only twenty-four at the time, Julian was already pretty well established in the field—he'd been doing it for about three years by then. But he was ready to branch out, and he was willing to take on a partner to do it."

"And you were qualified to become his partner because . . . ?"

Again Wyatt smiled, but this time there was something a little melancholy in it. "Over the years," he said, "I've become very good at looking for things."

"What kind of things?" she asked.

"All kinds of things," he replied.

"And have you found all the things you were looking for?"

"Not quite all of them, no."

Eve decided not to push him on that one. Something in his expression just forbade it. "So what were you doing before you landed in jail and met young Julian?" she asked instead.

"Most recently before that?"

She nodded.

"I was having a beer. Anchor Steam on draft."

She expelled a frustrated growl. "Come on, Wyatt. You know what I mean."

He, in turn, inhaled a deep breath, eyed her with much speculation for a moment, then told her, very evenly, very tersely, "I was in the navy."

Now this, Eve thought, was a total surprise. Although Wyatt had always had a wild hair, he had never been the kind of guy who would voluntarily undertake a lifestyle that included something like, oh, say, strict discipline. Structure. Hierarchy. She just couldn't see him submitting to any of those things.

"Last I heard," she said, "you wanted to join the staff of *National Geographic* as a photographer. You were planning to fine-tune your already sophisticated yearbook photography skills, and go to Ohio State to study geography."

"I did go to Ohio State to study geography," he told her. "For three whole semesters, in fact. And I've kept up with the photography over the years, as an avocation, if not a vocation." He grinned mischievously. "Comes in handy in my line of work."

"So what happened to your plans?"

He shrugged. "I don't know. I felt restless at Ohio State. Distracted. Couldn't focus on my studies. I could just never get into the college rhythm. So I quit."

"You never graduated?"

He shook his head. "I went to see my recruiter instead. I thought maybe I was just impatient to see the world. Joining the navy seemed like the quickest route to doing that. Plus, I figured I'd have no choice but to focus if I joined up. I thought maybe I wouldn't feel so distracted."

"And did that satisfy you?" she asked. "Being in the navy, I mean?"

"Not really," he said. "I saw a lot of the world while I was in, but I still couldn't focus. I still found myself feeling distracted, impatient."

"And now?" she asked. "Do you still feel impatient?"

He settled his attention on her face, his gaze flicking from her hair, to her eyes, to her cheeks, to her mouth, then back to her eyes again. "Yes," he said softly. "I still feel impatient."

Something in his voice, in his eyes, when he offered his admission sent a frisson of white-hot heat down Eve's spine. She closed her eyes for a moment, to wait for the sensation to pass. Then, when she realized it wasn't going to pass anytime soon, she opened her eyes again and asked, very quietly, "Why?"

"Why what?"

"Why do you still feel impatient?"

"Like I said, I still haven't found what I'm looking for," he said simply, without hesitation.

"And what is it, exactly, that you've been looking for?"

As readily as he had answered the rest of her questions, Wyatt declined to reply to this last one. He only continued to fix his attention on her face, so intently that Eve found it impossible to pull her gaze away from his. The morning breeze nudged a few strands of pale brown down over his forehead, and he lifted a negligent hand to push them out of his eyes. It was his left hand, she noticed idly, and he wore no jewelry on it at all.

He was single, she realized without doubt then. But it wasn't the absence of a wedding band that assured her of his marital status. No, it was something else entirely that indicated that.

In spite of her certainty, though, she asked, "Are you married? Any children? Or does your line of work, snooping on straying spouses and such, make a man want to stay single?"

He hesitated only a moment this time before replying, "No, that's not what's kept me single."

Eve decided it might be best not to ask for elaboration on that one. So she only followed up with, "Then you've never been married?"

"No."

She told herself her curiosity was merely idle, that she couldn't care less whether Wyatt Culver had attached himself to someone or not. Then she discovered that she was inordinately relieved by his negative response.

Nevertheless, she asked him, "Ever wanted to be married?"

He shrugged again, but there was something about the gesture that made it seem anything but careless. Again, she decided to parry instead of thrust.

But before she had the chance to ask anything more, he said, "I understand your own marriage wasn't exactly a happy one."

Eve's entire body went rigid at his remark. She told herself she shouldn't be surprised that he knew about the circumstances of her marriage. Her father was a talker, and hey, it wasn't like it was any big secret in the first place. But for some reason, she *didn't* want Wyatt to know about the circumstances of her marriage or her divorce. She didn't want him to be privy to that part of her life. She wasn't sure why, but there it was all the same. She didn't want him to view her as the woman she had become. She wanted to remain in his mind forever as a bright, spirited, seventeen-year-old hellion.

"You've been talking to Daddy," she said.

"Yes, I have," he admitted freely. "Was he lying to me?"

She wondered how much she should say, wondered how much she *could* say, without sounding like a whiner or a doormat or an idiot. Finally, she decided to simply tell him the truth. "No. Daddy wasn't lying to you. My marriage wasn't a happy one." There, she thought. That pretty much covered everything she needed to tell him.

"I see."

Somehow, Eve couldn't quite keep herself from contradicting him. "No, Wyatt, I doubt that you do," she said softly.

And, thankfully, he didn't challenge her.

"So I guess you have big plans for today, huh?" she

asked, shamelessly changing the subject. She added further, hopefully, "Like maybe you have a plane to catch?"

He shook his head. "No. No plane. When your father called me in Cincinnati and asked me and Julian to come out here for, um, a chat, he invited us to stay at The Keep for the whole weekend before accompanying you and Simone back to Ohio."

"Yes, but now that he won't be hiring you—"

"Who says he won't be hiring us?"

"Well, of course he's hired Mr. Varga," she allowed, "to keep an eye on Simone."

"And he's hired me, too."

"For what?" she asked. "I told him I don't want or need a bodyguard. What part of that statement didn't he understand?"

Wyatt's utterly content expression changed not one iota. "Your father understood just fine, Eve. But in spite of your objections, last night he hired me to complete a job. And I'm going to complete it to the very best of my abilities."

"But—"

"Anyway," he continued blithely, clearly unwilling to hear any more of her objections, "it's been a long time since either Julian or I have had a vacation. And neither of us has ever visited California before. We figured we'd just spend a couple of days taking in the local sights, catching some rays, maybe pick up a couple of lingerie models or aspiring starlets . . ." He sighed with much satisfaction. "Really, the possibilities are endless."

"Well, you and Mr. Varga have fun on your excellent adventure," she said as she leaned back in her chair and reached for her own coffee mug. Just to enhance his California experience, she added, "Dude."

Wyatt laughed. And his expression, when he did so, was dazzling. "Want to come with us?" he asked with undisguised enthusiasm.

Her smile fell, and she shook her head. "Thanks. No."

"Why not?"

She shrugged, but the gesture felt—and she was sure that it also looked—uncomfortable. "I just don't want to."

He studied her in silence for a moment. "You haven't set foot off of the estate since you got here, have you?"

She glanced down at her coffee, unable to meet his gaze any longer. "You've been talking to my father about that, too," she surmised.

"Actually, no. I haven't."

"Then it must have been Simone who told you."

"No, she's pretty tight-lipped when it comes to discussion of you."

"Ah."

"But you haven't left the estate since you got here, have you?" he asked again.

"No," she confessed reluctantly.

"Why not?"

She tossed off another one of those uncomfortable, unconvincing shrugs, then said, "There hasn't really been any cause for me to go out anywhere."

"Is that the only reason?"

"Of course. What other reason could there be?"

She figured he probably knew the answer to that as well as she did, but she hoped he would be polite enough not to mention it. And he was, too. Polite about that. What he wasn't polite about was his next question.

"What the hell did your ex-husband do to you to make you like this?"

Before she realized she was doing it, Eve pulled her legs up in front of her and wrapped her arms tightly around them, creating a snug—if utterly ineffective—little shield to keep the world away. "I'm not sure I know what you mean," she lied.

"The hell you don't," he countered roughly. "Look at you. You're timid, colorless, passionless."

And, oh, wasn't that just exactly what she wanted to hear? Eve thought. Especially from someone like Wyatt, someone who knew what she had been before.

"What the hell did he do to you?" he demanded again.

"It's none of your business, Wyatt," she said softly.

He inhaled a deep breath and released it slowly. And she could tell from the tone of his voice that it was costing him dearly to remain even-tempered when he asked, very bluntly, "Did he . . . did he ever hit you?"

For a long moment, Eve said nothing. Then, very softly, very evenly, she told him, "Only once."

"Only . . ."

But Wyatt didn't get out any more words than that one. And when he grew silent again, Eve braved a glance at him, only to find that he wasn't even looking at her. He was gazing out toward the ocean, where a trio of surfers was paddling out to meet the next wave. His expression, though, wasn't in keeping with the peaceful ocean vista. His cheeks were ruddy with his anger, his eyes were near slits, and his jaw was clenched tight.

"It's none of your business, Wyatt," she said again.

"It's about to become my business, Eve."

"Not if you leave right now."

"I'm not going anywhere," he said. "I have a job to do."

She nodded her resignation. He might think he had a job to do, and there was nothing wrong in letting him continue to think that. But Eve knew differently. She was going to go back to Ohio on her own speed, on her own terms.

On her own, period.

Still, she felt it only fair to warn him, "I'm not going to be a willing participant in my father's . . . whatever it is he's hired you to do."

Even though Wyatt still wasn't looking at her, she could tell that his expression remained impassive. "Gee, now there's a shocker," he said.

"Just so we're clear," she told him.

"Oh, we're clear," he assured her. "We are crystal clear."

He pushed back his chair and stood, still gazing at the blue Pacific sprawling to the western horizon. Eve allowed her own gaze to trail his, and she saw the surfers dipping and rising on the waves, obviously enjoying the ecstasy that comes with being so unencumbered. For some reason, a twinge of melancholy shook her upon witnessing their freedom. From this distance, it was easy to imagine the guys out there as young, unworried, and utterly lacking in professional responsibility or personal ordeal. No wonder they were having such a good time.

Was youth really as innocent and as wonderful and as carefree as she kept remembering it? she asked herself. And immediately, she told herself it couldn't possibly be like that. She remembered feeling overused and miserable on so many occasions when she was a teenager. How could those years have constituted a simpler, happier time, when they had generated so many hours of discontent and frustration? But it must have been a simpler, happier time, she told herself. It must have been. Because if it hadn't been, then what she was living now would someday be her good old days.

She turned and looked at Wyatt again and felt the pull of something ageless and timeless deep down in her soul. And somehow she couldn't help thinking that, old days or new, he would always be a part of them. So when, she wondered, would the good part come?

Six

Wyatt enjoyed a hefty quaff of his beer, thinking the smooth, malty coolness was a fitting punctuation mark to what had been a nearly perfect day. California, he had decided several hours ago—right around the time he'd been watching two women roller-blading down the sidewalk wearing little more than eight brief, and very strategically placed, triangles between them—was a damned nice place.

The sun had shone without interruption all day, the temperature had leveled off somewhere around seventy-four luscious degrees, the citizens were, to a person, outrageously attractive, and at every single place that he and Julian had visited they'd seemed to be constantly serenaded by the soft whisper of the ocean.

Life, he thought with a satisfied sigh as he set his beer back on the table, couldn't possibly get any better than this.

Then he glanced over at Julian's drink and realized

one minor flaw with his assertion. Generically, Wyatt was pretty sure the concoction was called a "fruit smoothie," which in itself was a sissy enough classification to make a *real* man avoid it like the plague. But this particular restaurant had decided to go one further in the sissy department and call their version of the drink a—Wyatt fought the urge to cup his hands protectively over that which made him a man—a *Frutitti*.

For God's sake, how could Julian drink something that was pastel in color and called a Frutitti? And in a public place, no less? Where the hell was his pride? His dignity? His testosterone? Man. You just never could tell with some people.

"So . . . how did you and Simone get on last night?" Wyatt asked his friend, hoping to generate something vaguely resembling a masculine exchange. People at other tables were beginning to stare.

When Wyatt had voiced the question, Julian had been chewing something green and leafy and in no way appealing, something with the word *alfalfa* in it, which Wyatt had been pretending not to notice, because maybe if he ignored it, it would just go away. Evidently, Julian had been in the process of swallowing it, too, because the moment Wyatt completed his question, Julian began to cough. Hard. And, boy, did that look unpleasant. Hacking up something that produced chlorophyll clearly was *not* an enjoyable experience.

To make matters worse, Julian reached for his— Wyatt squeezed his eyes shut tight so he wouldn't have to witness the ghastly spectacle—Frutitti, no doubt filling his mouth with the concoction in an effort to assuage his problem. When Wyatt opened his eyes again, it was to find that Julian had survived both the choking and the Frutitti, something about which, Wyatt realized, he had somewhat mixed feelings.

"I did *not* get it on with Simone last night," Julian gasped raggedly.

Wyatt smiled. "I didn't ask how well you *got it on* with her," he told his friend. "I asked how well you *got on* with her." His smile grew broader. "Interesting, though, the way you misunderstood that."

Instead of muttering a quick retort to the jab, Julian—oh, God, not *that*, Wyatt thought—blushed. Now he *knew* people at the other tables were beginning to stare.

"If you must know . . . " Julian began.

"Oh, I must."

"I didn't *get on* with her, either."

This Wyatt found surprising. Simone Van Dormer had always seemed like the kind of woman who could get along with just about anyone. Even guys who drank—Wyatt fought off another major wiggins—Frutittis. But, sympathetic to his partner's setback, he replied, "Bummer."

"That Simone Van Dormer is one angry woman," Julian announced.

Wyatt couldn't stop his jaw from dropping in astonishment. "Simone Van Dormer? Angry?" he repeated incredulously. "That's impossible. You must have said something to set her off."

"I did not," Julian replied indignantly. "She got set off the minute she came into her father's study last night. Before I even opened my mouth."

"Then you must have done something to offend her," Wyatt said. He tipped his head toward what was left of the other man's dinner. "Did you eat or drink anything in front of her? 'Cause God knows watching you consume that stuff has set me off a time or two."

Julian eyed the remnants of Wyatt's meal in return—he'd ordered French fries, mushrooms swimming in garlic butter, and a big ol' bloody steak. "You know, someday," he told Wyatt, "you're going to drop dead of a heart attack or Mad Cow Disease. And don't come crying to me when it happens."

All Wyatt offered in response was a bland look and a carelessly muttered, "Moo."

Julian shook his head slowly and returned his attention to whatever the hell it was on his plate. "Anyway, the woman is *not* going to make this easy. She views me as a liability, because she intends to look up an old boyfriend at her reunion next week."

Well, that little tidbit of information certainly got Wyatt's attention. "Simone doesn't have an old boyfriend," he said. "She never dated anybody at Woodhaven High."

"Then it's some guy she's looking to make a boyfriend now," Julian said. "Maybe you could enlighten me?"

Wyatt wasn't sure why Julian would care, but he said, "Got me. If she had a crush on someone, it could have been anybody. Not that anybody back then would have noticed her crush." Mainly, Wyatt thought to himself, because no one had noticed Simone.

Julian nodded. "Then maybe you could enlighten me about something else instead."

"And that would be?"

"You and Eve. What the hell is up with you two?"

That, Wyatt thought, was what he'd been afraid his friend was going to ask. So he replied with a question of his own. "Gee, why do you want to know?"

Julian eyed him levelly. "Because the minute she walked into her father's study last night, it felt like . . . like the air came alive or something. It was weird. What are you two, matter and antimatter? Can't you share the same space without there being some kind of massive cosmic disturbance?"

Actually, Wyatt thought, that did pretty much cover his whole entire relationship with Eve Van Dormer.

"Well, you know, Julian," he said, "there's nothing I'd like more than to accommodate your request— really, I would—but in order to enlighten you about me and Eve, then I'd have to know what the hell was going on between us back then myself."

"It was high school, Wyatt. How complicated could it be?"

Wyatt eyed Julian warily. "Did you go to high school, Julian?"

"Yeah."

"And you have to ask me a question like 'How complicated could it be?'"

"Yeah, okay. I see your point."

Wyatt inhaled a deep breath, gazed out at the ocean behind Julian, and realized how much he would miss the sight of the Pacific when he returned to Ohio. Barely twenty-four hours he'd spent in Santa Barbara, and he was ready to move here. The place was narcotic, addictive.

Much like Eve Van Dormer.

He sighed heavily as he turned his attention back to his companion. "I don't know what to tell you, Julian. There was some kind of strange attraction between me and Eve when we were teenagers, but we never dated. We didn't even run around in the same crowd. But every time we got within twenty feet of each other, it was like some kind of weird alarm went off for both of us, and I'm damned if I could ever figure out what the alarm signaled. There was just some kind of . . . connection between us. Sparks, fireworks, whatever you want to call it. To be honest, I think whatever was going on between us just scared and confused the hell out of both of us. Like maybe strong, adult emotions in two kids who just didn't have the capacity to understand or cope with them."

"So you guys never . . ."

"What?" Wyatt demanded caustically, knowing full well what the other man was asking but wanting to put off for as long as possible—preferably for all eternity—responding to the question.

With profound understatement, Julian clarified, "You never, um, kissed?"

Wyatt expelled another slow, restive breath. "Yeah, we did do that. Once." *Or twice*, he added to himself.

"And how did it turn out?"

It had actually been pretty life-altering, Wyatt recalled. He'd been cutting class one day, when Eve had evidently had to go out to her locker for something. He still wasn't sure what had come over him, but there she'd been, all alone, wearing this white, Victorian petticoat kind of dress. She'd just looked so . . . And she had smelled so . . . And Wyatt had felt so . . . And then, the next thing he knew, he was putting his hand on her shoulder, turning her around to face him. Her expression had been so . . . And her eyes had been so . . . And he'd felt so . . . And then, the next thing he knew, everything was different.

The moment his lips had touched hers, the two of them had connected on some primal, mystical level that had, as he'd just told Julian, confused and scared the hell out of him. But he hadn't been able to pull away from her, had realized at the very back part of his brain that what was happening between the two of them had gone completely beyond his control. Without even intending to, he'd moved his entire body forward, had opened his mouth wider, had filled her mouth with his tongue, had cupped one hand gently over her breast. He had kissed her for all he was worth. And in that moment, he had both possessed her and given himself to her completely.

He honestly had no memory now of how long they had remained embraced that way, perhaps seconds, perhaps centuries. But it had been an extraordinary kiss, even by adult standards. By teenaged standards, it had been . . . It had been . . .

Life-altering. That was the only way Wyatt could think to describe it. And when it had ended—he still couldn't remember if it had been Eve or he himself who had ended it—he had dropped his hands back to his sides and, without a word, turned and continued on his way down the hall.

"Eh, it was okay," he said now in response to Julian's question.

"Just okay?" his friend echoed dubiously. "You two had one okay kiss in high school, and twenty years later, when you're in a room together, you heat it up like a convection oven, just because of one okay kiss?"

"All right, so it went a little beyond the 'okay' stage," Wyatt conceded. "Especially the second time."

Julian said nothing, only studied him in a very speculative manner.

"All right, all right, I'll tell you," Wyatt finally said with much exasperation. "I can't stand it when you badger me this way. Even though I swore twenty years

ago that I would never, ever, not under any circumstances, speak—in any great detail, anyway—of that
night to *any*one."

Julian remained silent, still eyeing Wyatt with much
consideration.

"Oh, stop harassing me already," Wyatt told him. "I
said I'd tell you, and I will." He looked first left, then
right, then back at Julian. Then he lowered his voice,
and in an ominous tone, he whispered, "The second
time it happened was on . . . prom night."

Julian's expression remained impassive. But he ventured to ask, "And what, pray tell, happened on prom
night?"

Wyatt leaned back in his chair again, crossed his
arms over his midsection, and said, "You know,
twenty years after the fact, I'm still trying to figure it
out. It started off simply enough. I went to the prom
with Susan Gupton, who was actually more of a friend
to me than anything else. Eve went with Stuart Turner,
who she'd only been dating for a couple of months."

He paused for a moment before continuing. He
really had vowed twenty years ago to never discuss
that night with anyone. But somehow, he didn't mind
telling Julian what had happened. Maybe it was
because Julian was the best friend Wyatt had ever had.
Or maybe it was because Wyatt suspected there were
things in Julian's past that haunted him, too. Or maybe
it was just because Wyatt figured he was long past due
talking to someone—anyone—about what had happened that night. Someone like a shrink, for example,
he couldn't help thinking, but still. In a lot of ways,
Julian *was* Wyatt's shrink, or had at least played the
part from time to time. Julian did seem to have insight
into the human condition that most people didn't

have. And he didn't charge seventy-five bucks an hour, which was a definite plus.

"I couldn't keep my eyes off of her that night," Wyatt began again. "She was just so beautiful, you know? I'd never seen her that dressed up before. I kept gravitating toward her, wherever she was, without even realizing that I was following her around. And when I saw her go outside . . ." He shrugged. "I got curious. Or something. I followed her there, too."

"And?"

Wyatt scarcely heard Julian, because he had traveled two thousand miles and two decades from where the two men currently sat. In his mind's eye, he saw Eve Van Dormer wearing a rosy prom dress and looking like a Southern belle, her dark hair piled atop her head in a riot of curls, with a few errant, wispy strands uncoiling around her face and down her nape. He saw her exiting—alone—the ballroom of the Stanhope Hotel, the stately old luxury hotel in downtown Cincinnati where they'd held their prom, and he saw himself following after her as if it were the most natural reaction in the world.

"I never did find out why she went out to Stuart's car in the first place," he told Julian now. "But looking back, I honestly think she wanted me to follow her. She had the keys with her, and as soon as she unlocked the car door, she turned around and looked right at me, as if she'd known I was there all along.

"It was like that afternoon when I kissed her in the hall," Wyatt continued. "Kind of unreal. Like neither one of us had any control over what was happening, but at the same time, we both knew what we were doing. I remember saying her name, and I remember her saying, 'What?' And then I remember walking over to her and kissing her again. And the next thing I knew, she and I were in the backseat of Stuart's car, and the top of her dress was down around her waist, and her breast was in my mouth, and my pants were unfastened. And all I wanted, really, really, *really* badly, was to be inside her. I got her panties off, I got my pants down, I pushed the skirt of her dress up over her hips, and then . . ."

He couldn't quite bring himself to say what had happened—or rather had not happened—next. Somehow, though, the words came tumbling out anyway. "As much as I wanted to be inside of her," he said, "oh, my *God*, did I want to be inside of her . . ." He met his friend's gaze levelly now. "I couldn't get it up, Julian. I was completely turned on, randy as an eighteen-year-old kid can be . . . and I don't think I have to tell you how randy that is . . ."

"Nope," his friend assured him, "you don't have to tell me."

Wyatt sighed heavily. "In spite of how much I wanted to, I was physically unable to make love to her."

"You were impotent," Julian said.

Yeah, yeah, yeah, Wyatt thought. Leave it to Julian to fit into three words what had confused and confounded Wyatt for twenty years. He winced, squeezing his eyes shut tight. But he said, "Yeah. I was . . . what you just said."

When he finally opened his eyes again, he was grateful to see that Julian wasn't, in fact, holding his sides, doubled up with hysterical laughter over Wyatt's predicament. Instead, the other man only gazed back at him with much speculation, but he offered nothing in the way of analysis. Good thing

Wyatt wasn't paying him seventy-five bucks an hour, he couldn't help thinking.

"It had never happened to me before, and it hasn't happened since," Wyatt said, feeling defensive for no good reason he could name. "I'd had plenty of hard-ons before that night, usually, ironically, when I was thinking about Eve. Hell, I had a hard-on that day I kissed her in the hall. But that night, when I finally had the chance to make love to her, something I'd been wanting, whether consciously or not, to do for *years* . . ." He shook his head in complete mystification. "I couldn't do it. And to this day, I don't know why."

Julian continued to study him with much thought. Then, after a moment, he asked, "Do you think it would happen again? With Eve, I mean?"

Wyatt wished he could vehemently reply that hell, no, it would never happen again, not just because he was way, *way* too manly to *ever* succumb to something like im . . . impo . . . impote . . . um, *that*, ever again, but also because he had absolutely no intention of ever trying anything like that with Eve ever again, not that she was inviting him to try anything with her anyway, so there was that to consider, which actually kind of sucked now that he thought more about it, and . . . and . . . and . . .

And what was the question again?

Oh, yeah. Would it happen again with Eve?

He remembered how she had looked when he'd pushed himself away from her that night, how confused and frightened she'd been. When he'd finally admitted to himself what was going on, he'd panicked. He'd been too confused and embarrassed and humiliated to explain to her what was happening—or, rather, what was *not* happening. He'd been ashamed to admit that his member was as limp as a wet sock, had been terrified that she would laugh at him when she found out.

So he'd reacted without thinking. He'd pulled himself away from her, had exited the car, had turned his back on her quite literally. He'd said nothing as he'd jerked up his pants and tucked in his shirt and refastened his belt. And he'd remained silent when he'd reached back into the car for his jacket.

He'd had no choice but to look at her then, though. And what he'd seen had twisted something hot and sharp inside him. Eve was crying and clutching the top of her dress to her chest. And she was begging him to please not go. She was asking over and over what was the matter, what had she done wrong, whatever it was, she was sorry and she'd try harder, and please, Wyatt, don't go, don't leave me here alone.

And Wyatt, God help him, simply had not known what to do. So he'd turned without a word and walked away from her.

A week later, she'd been gone, and any chance he might have had to try and explain or apologize was gone with her. Neither of them had seen the other again, until last night. And last night, he'd realized he still hated himself as much today as he had twenty years ago for what he had done.

Julian's question echoed through his head once more. *Would it happen again with Eve?* Wyatt wondered. He was more than a little troubled to hear himself answer aloud, "I have no idea."

One thing was certain, though. He sure as hell wasn't going to put himself into a position with her where he might find out. Nuh-uh. No way. No how.

"So then why did Luther give you a fat lip?" Julian

asked. "Because you *didn't* have sex with his daughter?"

Wyatt gazed down into his beer. "Because he thought I tried to assault her," he said.

"What?" Julian asked.

"Luther came to my house just before midnight," Wyatt told him, "while my parents were still, thankfully, out celebrating their anniversary. Between his screaming at the top of his lungs and the subsequent punch in the mouth, I was able to conclude that whatever Eve had told her father, it wasn't the whole story. But I didn't feel like I was in any position to defend myself. Hell, I deserved a rap in the mouth. And then some.

"But at least I found out that Eve made it home all right, no thanks to me. Brian Richie, boy next door and all-around great guy, found her crying in Stuart's car, saw me leaving the scene, and naturally assumed the worst. So he took Eve home. And he also told Luther that I assaulted her. Then he went back to the prom and told the entire senior class that I had assaulted her."

"Great guy," Julian said dryly.

"Yes, well, didn't I just say that he was?"

As a result of Brian's jumping to conclusions, Wyatt had become the official black eye of the Woodhaven High School Class of '81. And even though he'd heard from a couple of friends that Eve had done her best to stop the gossip, Wyatt had been banned from the graduation ceremonies and ostracized by pretty much everyone in the class.

And hell, he hadn't even cared about any of that. Because after what he'd done to Eve, he'd figured he **deserved every punishment in the book. In leaving her** alone that night, he had behaved abominably. And to this day, he had no idea what he might say or do that would come close to making up for the shabby way he'd treated her. But he'd been eighteen years old. He'd been mortified by what had happened. And ashamed. He'd been so ashamed of himself. Not just for being unable to perform sexually, but for being unable to explain why it had happened—to her or to himself.

Julian said nothing more, only reached for his Frutitti and enjoyed a healthy swig. This time Wyatt didn't cringe at the other man's action. Hell, at least Julian had never been im . . . impo . . . impote . . . um, *that*. Drinking a Frutitti was nothing compared to a man's inability to perform. Even if that man had only been a boy when it happened.

"We should go," Julian finally said. "I have to get up early tomorrow. I'm going to need my sleep if I have to face *Miss* Simone Van Dormer again."

Wyatt nodded and did his best to forget about the past and focus on the present instead. Julian wasn't the only one who was going to have to get up early in the morning to cope with one of the Van Dormer women. So he tossed back what was left of his beer, enjoyed one final glimpse of the blue, blue Pacific, and sighed heavily.

"Yeah, I know the feeling," he told his friend. "I have a pretty complicated job I need to do tomorrow myself."

Eve couldn't believe her success in eluding Wyatt for the rest of the weekend. Although she went out of her way to avoid seeing him at The Keep, she was surprised by how well she managed it. He must not be very good at whatever her father had hired him to do, she decided smugly. Because on Sunday morning, she showered and dressed in a loose-fitting, sleeveless white sheath and sandals, packed her luggage into her car, said good-bye to her father and Simone, and drove off into the sunrise all by herself. And Wyatt, the big chump, was nowhere in sight for any of it.

Her triumph, however, was short-lived, concluding as it did at the end of her father's driveway. As she'd told Wyatt the day before, Eve hadn't left the estate since she'd arrived there three months ago. And, as she'd told Wyatt, she'd assured herself that was only because there hadn't been any reason for her to leave. She hadn't had a job for years, and what few friends she'd managed to cultivate before getting involved with Edwin she had neglected after her marriage. And that, of course, would be because Edwin had discouraged her from having a life that didn't totally revolve around him.

Eve told herself now that her hesitation was silly, that beyond the gate to her father's estate lay a wealth of experiences she had missed for far too long. Beyond the gate lay adventure, excitement, maybe even romance. Well, okay, probably not romance, because she had no intention of getting involved with anyone until she'd—for lack of a better phrase—"found herself" again. And that search, she was certain, would be a long and complicated one.

But beyond that gate lay life, she thought. And life was something she hadn't had to call her own for a very long time. So what was stopping her? Why was she so reluctant to move forward? Why did she want to turn her car around, drive back up to the house, and hide under her bed for a long, long time?

Tamping down the fear that threatened to foil her, Eve pressed her thumb against the button on the gate release that was fastened to the visor. And she watched with her heart pumping madly as that last obstruction between her and the world—between her and her future—slowly eased aside. Then, very carefully, she urged her foot down on the accelerator. One final tremor of panic shook her as she cleared the gate, but once she was on the other side, she felt as if nothing in the world could stop her.

When she entered long-term parking at the airport, she grabbed the first parking place she found, then scrambled to gather her things. But just as she slammed the trunk of her car, the hairs on the back of her neck pricked up. And not in one of those *Ooo-that's-so-spooky* kind of ways, either. No, they shot up as straight as Fascist soldiers marching before Mussolini.

Telling herself that there was nothing amiss, Eve slipped her tote bag neatly over the metal pull handle of her garment bag, and then slung her smaller cosmetic bag on top of that. After tipping the trio of bags to a comfortable angle, she took her first step toward freedom, pulling her luggage along for the trip. And she did her best to shake off another sensation that she was being watched.

She completed two more steps before she felt the presence of another person coming up behind her, much too quickly and much too close. By the time she started to spin around, though, in an effort to identify the oncoming person's intent, she already understood exactly what that person's intent was—to drag her, presumably kicking and screaming, toward a waiting van, whose engine suddenly bellowed to life like the thrumming of a dragon's roar. What Eve *wasn't* able to figure out was the identity of the person. But it was most definitely a *him*. Of that, she was certain, thanks to the size of the arms wrapped around her throat and waist, and the strength with which he used those arms to pull her backward. Although she tried to free herself from the vicious embrace, she was helpless to even ease the man's hold on her. Instead, she could only struggle fruitlessly as he dragged her backward, toward the van and whatever loathsome destination lay beyond.

Eve had always hated being wrong about something. But this time, it was especially odious.

Instinctively, she drove her heel down onto the man's foot as hard as she could and was surprised when the maneuver actually worked. In fact, the man turned loose of her so quickly that it was almost as if he'd been physically ripped from her by a third party. Spinning around, Eve realized that was exactly what had happened. Because Wyatt Culver was tangled up with her would-be abductor, doing his best—and it was definitely some very good *best*—to overpower the thug.

She should have known he'd insist on having the last word about this. Then again, all things considered, she didn't really mind so much letting him have it this time.

Before she could even think what she should do, Wyatt dispatched her assailant—who, Eve realized now that she got a good look at him, was a complete stranger—with a series of well-placed blows to the man's head, face, and, um, privates. In response, the man gripped that part of his anatomy that most men considered exceedingly important and stumbled back to the van. As he climbed in, the driver gunned the

engine and sped off with a bone-chilling squeal of
tires.

The next thing Eve knew, Wyatt was grabbing her
hand and tugging her along behind him. He scooped
up her luggage as they passed it, pulling it jerkily
across the pavement as they fled toward a big, ruby
red SUV whose engine was also rumbling like an
angry beast, and whose driver's side door had been
flung open.

"Get in," Wyatt instructed her unnecessarily as he
pushed her toward the open door. He went around to
the back of the vehicle, and in one swift, deft maneuver, heaved open the hatch, tossed her bags carelessly
inside, and slammed the door shut once again. Just as
she landed in the passenger seat, he climbed in on the
driver's side, throwing the big truck into drive before
he'd even closed the door.

"Holy cow," Eve said as he took a corner much too
quickly, hurling her against the passenger side door.
Hastily she clipped her seat belt into place and shoved
down the lock with her fist. "What the hell was that
about?"

Wyatt was still breathing much too hard to reply
with any amount of coherence, but what eventually
came   out   sounded   like,   "Can't . . . beleevt.
Sumbitch . . . tried . . . catnip . . . you." Strangely, he
sounded even more outraged about it than she felt
herself.

"We should call the police," she said.

"Yeah, we sure as hell should call somebody," he
agreed.

"The police," she repeated, thinking his response
was a little odd. "We should call the police."

But instead of replying, Wyatt only clamped his jaw tight and tried to breathe levelly.

"Did you get a license plate number on the van?" she asked, chastising herself for not thinking to do that. Then again, she *had* had other things on her mind at the time.

"No," he told her. "I'm sorry, but I didn't. I was too focused on what was happening to you."

"Jeez, Wyatt, you don't have to apologize for that," she told him.

He said nothing in response, only glanced at her briefly, then straight ahead again.

"I think we should call the police," she said once more.

He expelled a ragged breath. "Just . . . let me take care of it, okay?"

Eve opened her mouth to object, but something in his expression forbade her to say anything. Instead, she, too, gazed out the windshield. It had started to drizzle, and Wyatt had turned on the windshield wipers. As she watched their laconic to-and-fro, it occurred to her that she moved in much the same way these days—back and forth, back and forth, never quite making it to one side or the other. And no matter how hard she tried to brush away the things that obscured her vision, those things just kept coming right back again, making visibility a problem.

She and Wyatt both remained quiet for some time after that, until they were a few miles away from the airport. Even then, Eve only broke the silence because she couldn't stand the fact that Wyatt hadn't uttered the obvious by now.

"So?" she said softly. "Aren't you going to say, 'I

told you so'? I figured those would be the first words out of your mouth when you saw what was happening back there."

He shook his head but kept his gaze fixed on the road, because the rain was coming down full force now. "No, the first words out of my mouth were—" He threw her another hasty glance, then shifted uncomfortably in his seat. "Well, they weren't exactly fit to repeat. Something along the lines of, 'Hey, that matriarch-fricking poopoo-head is stealing Eve. If I get my gosh-darned hands on him, I'll punt his gosh-darned tushie right up his gosh-darned proboscis.' I have a job to do, after all."

Eve nodded, resigned now to her fate. Suddenly, having her body guarded by Wyatt didn't seem like such a terrible thing, even if her father was the one who was responsible for it. Even if Wyatt was only doing it because he was getting paid to. In fact, her body didn't seem to mind the realization, either, because every single cell she possessed was currently humming with anticipation at the prospect.

"Gee, I guess this makes you my bodyguard, after all," she said, leaning back in her seat, "just like my father wanted."

A few moments passed before Wyatt replied, obviously with more than a little reluctance. "Um, actually, bodyguard wasn't *exactly* the position your father ultimately hired me to fill."

Eve narrowed her eyes at him in confusion. "It wasn't?"

He shook his head but said nothing more to elaborate.

"Then . . . if you're not going to be my bodyguard," she said, "what *exactly* are you going to be?"

His voice was peppered with something akin to pride, something even akin to glee, when he told her, "I'm your kidnapper, Eve. I'm your kidnapper."

"You're my *what*?"

Ooo, Eve didn't sound happy about this new development *at all*, Wyatt thought as he tried to balance his attention between the rainy highway before him and the stormy woman beside him.

"I'm your kidnapper," he reiterated. But when he braved a glance in Eve's direction, he found that her tone of voice had only hinted at her mood. Because she was currently gazing back at him the way one might gaze at a cockroach. A dead cockroach. A dead cockroach who was belly up on the kitchen counter. With an empty egg sac lying beside it. And its newly sprung offspring—all twelve dozen of them—zooming into an open bag of Oreos nearby.

"My . . . kidnapper," she repeated in a flat voice that offered absolutely no indication as to what she might be thinking. Not that the dead, spawning cockroach expression didn't tell Wyatt pretty much everything he needed to know. And then some.

"Yup," he told her. "Your kidnapper."

"Then, um, who was that guy back there at the airport?"

"No idea," he replied honestly. Though, actually, he did have his suspicions. "I thought maybe you might have known him."

"Nope," she said. "No idea. I can't think of anyone who would want to have me kidnapped. Oh, wait a minute, yes I can," she immediately corrected herself, punctuating the admission with a merry snap of her fingers. "My father. My own flesh and blood. But then, he'd hire some pathetic, brown-nosing little lackey to kidnap me, wouldn't he?"

"Hey, I resent that," Wyatt retorted. "I am *not* little. I grew a full two inches in height after graduation. I've officially hit the six-foot mark. So there."

"I cannot believe my father hired you to kidnap me," she muttered as she slumped back in her seat and crossed her arms over her chest. "Still, I guess I should be grateful," she added ungratefully. "You foiled that other attempt. So now I don't have to worry about being kidnapped for real."

Oh, oh, oh, Wyatt thought, he was going to have to be soooo careful about how he continued. "Um, actually, yes, you do have to worry about that," he told her.

"Why?"

"Because your father hired me to kidnap you," he said. "I'm sorry. I thought you got that part."

She eyed him narrowly again. "Are you trying to tell me that this"—she arced both hands around the cab of the Expedition—"is a kidnapping?"

He nodded. "I'm afraid so."

"I thought it was a rescue."

"No, what I did back there at the airport, that was a rescue," he said. "Really. This, now, is most definitely a kidnapping."

"But—"

"I don't know what to tell you, Eve," Wyatt interrupted. "What can I say? You're my prisoner."

"I'm your what?"

Despite the even timbre of her voice, Wyatt could tell that she was starting to get pretty mad. Boy, and after all he'd done for her, too. He'd saved her from a kidnapping. A *real*, honest-to-God kidnapping. And now she was ticked off, just because he was perpetrating a little faux kidnapping instead.

Women. Who could understand them?

He sighed heavily, trying to figure out the best way to go about this. "Look," he began, striving for a lightness he didn't quite feel. "Your father has been worried about you—"

"Well, yeah, I guess so," she interjected, "what with that impending kidnapping he arranged for me and all."

"He thinks you've forgotten how to enjoy life," Wyatt continued, ignoring her interjection. "He thinks there's no joy in you. No passion. No life. And you know what, Eve? He's right."

Well, that, Wyatt noted, finally shut her up. When he braved a glance in her direction this time, he saw her gazing back at him with her mouth hanging open, her eyes wide, as if someone had just whacked her across the face with a big, wet fish. Turning his attention back to the highway, he reached over and gently pushed her chin back up, until her mouth was closed.

"I don't know all the stuff that happened to you when you were married," he continued, his voice—among other things—softening, his attention still fixed on the highway ahead of them. "But your father told me it was unhappy. That *you* were unhappy. And now that it's over, he wants you to be happy again. That's what this kidnapping is all about."

"He thinks it will make me happy to be kidnapped?" she asked dubiously. "By you?"

"Beats a sharp stick in the eye," Wyatt quipped.

Eve said nothing in response to that. And he decided it might be prudent not to ask her to.

"Look," he continued, "he just wants me to . . . to . . . to show you a good time." Even as he put voice to them, Wyatt knew the words weren't quite appropriate. But he had no idea how else to describe what Luther had asked him to do. "He wants me to make sure you have fun between now and the weekend, on the way back to Cincinnati."

He waited a moment to see if that announcement would register with Eve the way it was supposed to. *Tick, tick, tick,* the seconds crept by. *Tick, tick, tick,* a few more followed. *Tick, tick, tick,* they just kept going and going and going . . . Until he heard Eve groan, long and lusty and low. And he knew then that, yup, she'd finally figured it out.

"Are you trying to tell me that we're going to *drive* all the way back to Cincinnati?" she asked.

"Yup."

"Do you know how *far* it is from Santa Barbara to Cincinnati?"

"Yup."

"Do you realize how *long* it will take us to get there?"

"Yup."

"And you're going to do it anyway?"

"Yup."

"Oh, no . . ."

"Oh, yup." He threw her the most dazzling smile in his arsenal. "It's not a pretty job, Eve," he conceded, "but somebody's gotta do it."

"And since Daddy hired you . . ."

"Yup. That somebody is me."

"Oh, God . . ."

She sounded a little nauseous as she pleaded for

divine intervention, but really, all things considered, Wyatt thought, her reaction was surprisingly good.

"Don't worry," he told her. "I have a plan. And I have a map. In fact, I have a whole bunch of maps. It'll be fun, Eve. An adventure. And how long has it been since you've had an adventure, hmm?"

"Oh, God . . ."

This time when he braved a glance in her direction, it was to find that she had buried her face in her hands and was turning her head from side to side, muttering, *Oh, God, oh, God, oh, oh, oh, my God,* over and over again. So Wyatt did the logical thing—he reached for the radio dial. She'd be okay with it in a little while, he told himself. He was—almost—sure of it.

He spun the dial over static and commercials, then halted abruptly when he heard an announcer fairly shouting, "—and we've got an all-eighties weekend for you here!"

"All *right,*" Wyatt replied to the disembodied voice. "Did you hear that, Eve? All eighties. The music of our youth."

"*Oh, God . . .*"

"Next up," said the announcer over the opening bars of a familiar song, "Dexy's Midnight Runners with 'Come on, Eileen.' "

Wyatt smiled. "Oh, oh, I love this song. This'll cheer you up. This is a *great* song."

He waited for another moan of *Oh, God,* but Eve surprised him by actually speaking. Okay, so maybe she was actually grumbling, he amended. It was a start.

"Yeah, you would think that," she grumbled. "It's a song about a guy who's trying to get a girl to have sex with him."

"And the reason that would preclude this from being a good song would be . . . ?" he asked.

But all she said in response was, "Only you, Wyatt. Only you."

He decided not to ask her to elaborate on that, because they were words he'd always wanted to hear Eve Van Dormer utter in his presence. Okay, so maybe he'd imagined the situation just a tad differently. Like maybe, for instance, he'd pictured the two of them enjoying some kind of postcoital euphoria, lying with their arms and legs—and maybe a few other body parts—entangled . . . and not with him having just, you know, kidnapped her, and her being totally, you know, pissed off at him.

Details, details. Sheesh.

"This song," he said, "contains some of the best lyrics ever written."

Eve gazed at him blandly, but she sounded almost interested when she said, "Oh?"

He nodded. "The part at the end, that talks about how all the people in their neighborhood are all boring and drab and resigned to their fates. But then the singer goes on to say that that will *never* happen to him and the girl he's singing to, because they're too young and clever. I love that part. It just so perfectly describes the way kids think at that age. They're too young and clever to ever get caught in a trap like the ones adults create for themselves."

Eve expelled a sound that wasn't exactly polite. "Yeah, that's the arrogance of youth for you," she said impassively.

This time Wyatt was the one to gape. "Arrogance?" he echoed. "Why is it so arrogant for a teenager to assume he'll be happy as an adult?"

Her lips parted fractionally, as if she intended to respond, but no words ever emerged. Instead, after a moment, she closed her mouth again, held his gaze for another second or two, then turned to look out the window at the swiftly passing scenery.

Wyatt in turn spun the other dial—the volume dial—until music filled the cab of the big SUV. He had his work cut out for him, he realized. Luther Van Dormer had definitely been right about one thing. Eve surely did need kidnapping.

And Wyatt Culver was just the guy to do it.

The rain was coming down full force by the time Wyatt spied a pay phone in the parking lot of a restaurant on the ocean side of the road. Immediately, he spun the steering wheel to the right and pulled alongside it, then turned to Eve, who had spent most of the last half-hour staring out the windshield and saying nothing.

"I need to make a phone call," he said unnecessarily.

She glanced over at him, and he was relieved to see that her face wasn't quite as pale as it had been thirty minutes ago. It was a good sign. Now if he could just do something about that dead cockroach expression . . .

"The police?" she asked.

"Yeah," he lied. And he hoped like hell she would forgive him when all was said and done.

She looked like she was going to ask him something else, but she must have changed her mind, because she only nodded silently. Wyatt freed his seat belt and leapt down from the SUV, ducking under the rain as well as he could as he covered the scant distance to the phone booth. Once inside, he withdrew from his wallet the business card Luther Van Dormer had given him that morning. On the back was a list of phone numbers, all belonging to Luther—his home phone, his work phone, his cell phone, his private line that nobody, but nobody got, unless they were of vital significance. It was that last number that Wyatt dialed first. Luther must have been waiting by the phone, because he answered before the second ring was finished.

"Van Dormer," he said gruffly.

"It's Wyatt. Do you have something you want to tell me?" he asked without preamble. "Something I'm sure you *meant* to tell me before I left? Something you surely *forgot* to tell me this morning?"

The other man hesitated a moment before replying, "Like what?"

"Oh, gee, I don't know," Wyatt said sarcastically. "Like maybe that you hired someone *else* to kidnap your daughter, in addition to myself? And that maybe it wasn't the same *kind* of kidnapping you wanted me to perform?"

There was a moment of silence from the other end of the line, then he heard Luther chuckle, albeit a bit nervously. "Wasn't that a brilliant idea?" the other man asked.

Wyatt bristled, his fingers curling more tightly over the receiver. "Oh, it was something, all right."

Luther said, "I figured if Evie thought there was a real threat to her, she'd be more inclined to go with you. And, more importantly, to stay close to you."

Wyatt bit back a few very colorful expletives. "And you didn't think about something like that scaring the bejeezus out of her?" *And me?* he wanted to add.

"She was never in any danger," Luther said. "Those two men were people who work for me. Two of my vice presidents. They've known me for years."

"That must have been some Christmas bonus you promised them," Wyatt muttered.

"Actually, it was some stock options," Luther told him. "Excellent ones, I might add. Plus, they just feel a personal obligation to me."

Wyatt rolled his eyes heavenward and prayed for patience.

"They had no intention of hurting her," Luther added.

"Yeah, well, Eve didn't know that," Wyatt pointed out. "And *I* sure as hell didn't know it, either."

"If you'd known," Luther said, "you wouldn't have reacted realistically to the threat, and then Evie would have known something was amiss. I had to do it this way."

Vaguely, Wyatt found himself contemplating that deep end business again where Luther Van Dormer was concerned, and he modified it to a gaping, black abyss. Because surely no man in his right mind would make such plans. Not that anyone had ever accused Luther Van Dormer of being in his right mind. Still, no one had ever really considered the fact that he might honestly lose it, either.

Wyatt sighed heavily. "Are there going to be any more surprises like this one that I should know about? Any more 'harmless little abductions' during the rest of the trip?"

"Mmm . . . could be," Luther said. "I don't want Evie to get complacent."

"Think you could let me in on the precise agenda?" Wyatt asked. Though, unfortunately, he already pretty much knew the answer to that question.

"As I said, Wyatt, if you knew about my plans in

advance, you wouldn't react in a realistic fashion. I need to have the element of surprise on my side."

Actually, Wyatt thought, what Luther Van Dormer needed was some heavy-duty psychoanalysis, followed, hopefully, by some massive and prolonged sedation.

"Let me do this my way, Mr. Van Dormer," Wyatt said in the best no-nonsense voice he could manage. "Promise me there won't be any more of these phony attempts to abduct her. Promise me you won't interfere in any way for the rest of the trip."

"But—"

"It's not necessary, Mr. Van Dormer," Wyatt said. "I can handle this myself."

But instead of replying to that statement, Luther only said, "Please, Wyatt. How many times do I have to ask you to call me Luther?"

Wyatt inhaled a deep breath and released it slowly. "It's not necessary . . . Luther. So promise me there won't be any more of these staged dangers for the trip."

The other man was silent for a moment, then he said, "All right. I promise to leave both of you alone."

"Thank you."

"But you, in turn, have to promise me something, Wyatt."

"Anything," he said.

There was a short, pregnant pause from the other end of the line, followed by a very softly offered, "Make Evie happy again."

Wyatt closed his eyes and swallowed hard. Oh, there was nothing he'd like more than to make Eve Van Dormer happy. Unfortunately, he was beginning to suspect that he was the one who had initially set her off on the course to her current unhappiness—twenty years ago, when he had rejected her so flagrantly, without an explanation.

"I'll do my best," he told Luther.

Somehow, though, he didn't think that would be nearly enough.

 *Seven*

As much as Julian had enjoyed his brief sojourn in the lovely fantasy land known as Santa Barbara, he was relieved when the plane touched down at the Cincinnati airport, even if he *was* still saddled with *Miss* Simone Van Dormer. In fact, he was so happy to be back on his own home turf that there was only one thing that could have improved his mood: if, at some point during the flight, the exit door near *Miss* Simone Van Dormer had accidentally blown open and *Miss* Simone Van Dormer had accidentally been sucked out of the cabin and hurled down onto one of the many states over which they'd flown. Alas, however, that hadn't happened. No, Julian had arrived back on his home turf with *Miss* Simone Van Dormer, and he would be here with *Miss* Simone Van Dormer until the princess returned to her magic kingdom on the West Coast in one week.

Julian was already counting down the minutes.

Tragically, however, there were still many, *many* thousands of minutes between now and then, and for those, he had no choice but to stay close to *Miss* Simone Van Dormer. He spared a glance at her now, standing beside him at the baggage carousel, tapping her foot impatiently as she awaited the arrival of her luggage. She was wearing a short-sleeved dress, the delicate fabric of which was pale yellow and spattered with little pink rosebuds. It was a deceptively innocent-looking garment that hugged her curves in a way that was likewise deceptively revealing.

Or maybe not so deceptively revealing, Julian amended with a not-so-quick double take. Because *Miss* Simone Van Dormer was standing in the light in such a way that made it possible for him to discern the hazy outline of her legs and fanny beneath the thin fabric, and the scant swell of one breast. And in a fit of hormonally charged astonishment, he realized she wasn't wearing a stitch of underwear beneath that dress. And then he remembered that he'd been sitting right next to her—*right next to her*—for more than four hours on the plane. And she hadn't been wearing a stitch of underwear then, either. And Julian hadn't noticed.

Man, he was slipping.

He decided then that, under other circumstances, being stuck with *Miss* Simone Van Dormer for a full week might not be such a bad thing. Circumstances such as, oh . . . Julian didn't know. Like maybe if, for instance, she wasn't coming back here to look up some guy—some guy other than Julian—with whom she was hoping to arrange a romantic interlude.

Oh, yeah. And also if, for instance, they didn't hate each other's guts.

He had no idea *why* they hated each other's guts, only that they did. He knew that because, in the more than four hours they had spent on the plane—wherein she hadn't been wearing a stitch of underwear, he couldn't help recalling—they'd spoken *maybe* five words to each other. And each of those words had been chillier than the one that preceded it.

"Do you *mind*?" she said now as she reached past him to grab the tapestry-design Pullman he had been about to snag from the baggage carousel himself. So much for trying to do something nice for *Miss* Simone Van Dormer. "My father didn't hire you to be my valet. Just my . . . you know."

"*Body*guard," Julian replied crisply, intentionally putting the emphasis on the first two syllables of the word, because he'd discovered over the weekend that it really pissed her off when he did that.

Sure enough, at hearing him say it in such a way again, her lips thinned into a tight line. Also, at hearing him say it that way, her elbow found its way into his gut. Although he was absolutely, positively certain it had just been an accident on her part. Not. He grunted at the contact, even though the impact was laughably light. Well, sort of laughably light anyway. Man, where had she learned to elbow a gut like a pro?

"After we pick up the rental car," she began . . . as she set the heavy suitcase down on his foot—hard. "Oops. Sorry," she said without a trace of apology. Nor did she do anything to remove the onerous piece of luggage from his foot.

"Do *you* mind?" Julian asked this time. Very politely, too, if he did say so himself.

She looked at him vaguely. "Do I mind . . . ?"

"Um, removing your valise from my tootsies?" he

clarified. Very politely, too, if he did say so himself.

"Oh, gosh. Of course. I didn't realize."

"No, of course you didn't," he replied. Very politely, too, if he did say so himself.

She offered him a watery smile as she removed the offending suitcase from his toes, but she didn't finish whatever she had been about to say. Instead, without warning, she lunged forward to claim a fat garment bag, and it was only at the last possible moment that Julian managed to get out of her way. Otherwise, he might have ended up winning a free trip around the baggage carousel himself.

She was a damned good lunger, he'd give her that. She must have taken lessons somewhere. Only after she had claimed the last piece of luggage from her arsenal—one of those metal briefcases most often used by terrorists and assassins, he couldn't help noting—did she finally finish the instructions she had started earlier.

"After we pick up the rental car," she began again—and Julian hastily took a step backward, lest she again punctuate the sentiment the same way she had before—"there's someplace I need to go right away."

"The hotel?" he asked hopefully.

"Woodhaven," she said.

The boyfriend, Julian guessed. Now that she was back in town, she didn't want to waste any time finding the guy. "Can't that wait?" he asked anyway, telling himself it was only because it was getting late, and he was getting tired, and he wanted to be at the hotel, all settled in. It wasn't because—

Well, it wasn't because of anything else.

"No," she said succinctly. "It can't."

"Fine," he replied, just as tersely.

She turned and started off, her purse slung over one

shoulder, her garment bag hanging over the other, her briefcase clutched in one hand, her Pullman trundling along behind her. And with every step she took, Julian simply could not help but note that glaring absence of underwear.

Boy, could he not help it. *Miss* Simone Van Dormer, underwearless. Who would have ever guessed?

He told himself to do the gentlemanly thing and offer to carry her bags—not to mention stop ogling her fanny—but he got the distinct impression that if he offered to do so, she'd reply with some caustic retort about being able to handle her belongings just fine by herself, thankyouverymuch. So he didn't do the gentlemanly thing and offer to carry her bags. And since he wasn't going to be gentlemanly about that, he decided he wasn't going to be gentlemanly about the other thing, either. He just kept right on ogling her fanny. Hey, no sense being rash.

Before she went too far, though, he cleared his throat indelicately to get her attention. "Oh, Miss Van Dor-mer," he sang out in his very best *yoo-hoo* voice, hoping it annoyed her as much as it did him.

She spun back around, her expression indicating that yes, as a matter of fact, it did indeed annoy her that much.

"*My* luggage?" he said pointedly. "*I* still have a garment bag to collect."

She rolled her eyes and expelled another one of those impatient, put-upon sounds that she had obviously mastered some time ago, her entire body drooping as she did. And somehow, Julian knew she would have reacted exactly the same way if he'd just told her that the reason she needed to wait for him was that he had just gone into full cardiac arrest.

Unable to help himself, he snapped, "Don't worry. Your boyfriend isn't going anywhere."

Miss Simone Van Dormer gazed back at him as if he were something gross and stinky she'd just discovered on the bottom of her shoe. "As I've told you on a number of occasions, *Mr.* Varga, the person I'm hoping to encounter at the reunion is *not* my boyfriend."

"Not yet," Julian conceded. "And if you act too desperate, he ain't gonna be, either. Trust me—guys don't respect desperate girls. They will, however, take great advantage of them whenever they can."

"Oh, my. How shocking. I never would have guessed that about your gender," she replied blandly. "Your gender is, after all, so seldom on the make. Look, do me a favor," she said further, before Julian had a chance to comment on that last sarcastic part of her statement. Not that he had any idea what he'd intended to say. It wasn't like he disagreed with her. "Just forget I ever mentioned that I came back here to see someone, all right?" she asked.

Gladly, Julian thought. Still, he wasn't sure he'd be able to accommodate her request. Or, rather, her decree. Whatever. He'd been hired to protect her, after all. And that meant he had to be on top of her . . . on top of *things*, he quickly corrected himself. He had to be on top of *things*. Hoo-boy. What a mess *that* could have made, to get those two mixed up.

Anyway, it would be helpful to know what was going on in that wily, beautiful head of hers—the one attached to the body that wasn't wearing a stitch of underwear, he couldn't help thinking further. Really. He couldn't help it. Honest. Unfortunately, he was beginning to realize that knowing what *Miss* Simone **Van Dormer was thinking at any given moment was a** near impossibility. She was too cool, too calm, too focused. Much like he was himself, he reflected.

He was spared having to reply to her request . . . her decree . . . whatever . . . not to mention his own strange thoughts, because his garment bag finally spilled onto the luggage carousel, and he abandoned his other bags—not to mention *Miss* Simone Van Dormer—to collect it. When he returned, he stooped to gather the rest of his belongings, and, noting again her assassin briefcase, his curiosity got the better of him.

Telling himself he was just making idle conversation, he asked, "What is it you do for a living, anyway?"

When he stood, he saw that she was smiling now, a smile that was surprisingly soft and sentimental and serene. It nearly took his breath away.

"I'm a, uh, a teacher," she said.

"Really?" he asked.

Her smile grew broader. "You sound surprised, Mr. Varga."

"No," he lied. "Just . . . I don't know. I never realized teachers—" *walked around without a stitch of underwear on*, he finished to himself. Probably, that wasn't a good thing to say out loud. Not if he wanted to keep the conversation idle. Not if he wanted to keep her elbow out of his gut.

"You never realized teachers what?" she prodded. Her smile now led him to believe that *she* knew exactly what *he* was thinking about. And, worse, she found his thoughts to be very amusing. And, gee, there was nothing a guy liked more than to know he *amused* a woman who wasn't wearing a stitch of underwear.

"I never realized teachers, um . . . flew first class," he finally finished lamely.

"Only on special occasions," she told him with another one of those knowing grins.

Julian tried really hard to keep his thoughts blank. "What, um, what do you teach?" *When you're standing at the front of the classroom without a stitch of underwear on?*

Now her eyes got into the act, he noted, the pale blue irises practically sparkling with mischief. Ooo, he hated it when women's eyes did that.

"Mm, political science," she told him.

Oh, well, Julian thought. That totally explained the not-a-stitch-of-underwear thing. But there'd been something in her voice when she'd spoken that had made him think she taught a different kind of political science than he'd studied when he was in college. "So then you teach at a university level?" he asked.

"More like post-grad," she told him.

He nodded, wondering for a moment why she would make such a distinction, then decided not to dwell on it. Probably, there were academic nuances at work here that would elude and confound him. Not that he really cared, anyway. He'd never been one for academics. In any form.

"Political science. I see. That sounds, uh, fascinating," he lied again.

"It can be," she told him. "Under the right circumstances."

Well, yeah, he thought. Like if the teacher wasn't wearing a stitch of underwear.

And would he never get off that riff? There *were* other things to think about, he reminded himself. Now, if he could just remember what they were . . .

"The rental car," *Miss* Simone Van Dormer reminded him then, thereby verifying that she did indeed pick up on every thought he had running through his head. Which could potentially pose a problem over the next several days. Especially if the not-a-stitch-of-underwear thing was something she did—or, rather, didn't do—often.

"Right," Julian said. "The, uh, the rental car."

"And then Woodhaven," she decreed.

"Right. Woodhaven. And then the hotel," he reminded her.

She nodded. "Then the hotel."

Woodhaven hadn't changed at all in the last twenty years.

Simone made the observation without surprise as she gazed through the passenger window of the big, luxury sedan that she had rented and asked *Mr.* Varga to drive, so that she herself could enjoy the sights of home—even if it was from under cover of darkness. And although *Mr.* Varga had seemed surprised by her request that he take the wheel, he had readily accepted. This in spite of the fact that her father had hired him to be not her chauffeur but her *body*guard.

Dammit. Now she was thinking about him that way, too. And the last thing she needed to be emphasizing where *Mr.* Julian Varga was concerned was either of their bodies. She had an infinitely more important body she needed to be thinking about now that she was back in Cincinnati. Blond Brian Richie's body. And, hey, that wasn't such a bad body to be focusing on. Bodies didn't come much more beautifully formed than Brian's.

Inescapably, her gaze wandered toward the driver's side of the car—or, more specifically, to the driver himself. Okay, so *Mr.* Varga had a pretty decent body, too.

All right, all right . . . so he had a *spectacular* body, she amended reluctantly. One she'd scarcely been able to keep her eyes off of, ever since she'd opened her bedroom door at The Keep that morning to find him standing on the other side. His broad shoulders strained against a black blazer, and a crisp white T-shirt stretched taut over the impressive chest beneath, delineating every delicious cord of muscle and sinew he possessed.

Not that she could see those luscious delineations now, in the dark car, but she could remember them. Oh, boy, could she remember them. She could also remember how his faded jeans had hugged his trim hips and thighs, and lovingly cupped his . . .

Well, Simone hadn't allowed herself to inspect him any further than that. She'd been too afraid of what she might do as a result of that inspection. Besides, his eyes had been what attracted her notice more than any of his other qualities, so unearthly was their color. Gray, surely, she told herself now as she recalled them, a common enough tint for the human eye. Or, perhaps, blue, likewise not unusual to find on a person. But she didn't think she'd ever seen quite that particular hue of gray *or* blue on another human being before. On wild wolves, maybe, but never a human being.

Still, as attractive as *Mr.* Varga was, he wasn't Brian Richie. Therefore, he wasn't someone she needed—or wanted, for that matter—to have on her mind.

"Turn left at the next stop sign," she directed him, pulling her thoughts back to the matter at hand.

"This is the neighborhood where you and your sister grew up?" he asked as he made the requested turn.

Simone nodded. "In fact, this was our street."

"Nice," he remarked with vast understatement.

She didn't disagree with him. Woodhaven *in toto* ran the gamut of the economic spectrum, from crowded, broken-down urban dwellings on the south end, to plain, brick ranch houses skirting the western edge, to spacious, showy mansions scarcely two miles away in the north. It was past those last that Simone and her companion currently drove. Her family on both sides had been wealthy for several generations, and although it had never once occurred to Simone to apologize for her financial circumstances, she suddenly felt the need to make excuses.

"My father worked very hard," she said impulsively, "for as long as I can remember. It's not like this was all just handed to him."

Mr. Varga hesitated a moment before asking, "Wasn't it?"

"Well, yeah, okay, maybe it was handed to him," she backpedaled diffidently. "But he worked hard to keep it. He still does."

"And just what is it your father does for a living, anyway?" Julian asked.

"He, uh . . . he's a businessman," Simone said, feeling reluctant, for some reason, to discuss her father's profession.

"What kind of business?"

"He's a real estate developer."

Mr. Varga nodded knowingly. "Ah. Well, that would explain the potential for shady business deals."

She narrowed her eyes at him. "What shady business deals?"

Even in the darkness, she could see his cheeks darken with a flush. A man like him, blushing, she marveled. Who would've thought?

"Wyatt and your father mentioned something that

happened here twenty years ago, when you and your family—"

"Left town under cover of darkness," Simone finished for him. She'd realized some time ago how notorious the circumstances of their departure must have been in Woodhaven. She suspected their disappearance had spawned much debate and speculation among the local gossips. None of it in any way accurate, she was sure.

"That's how Wyatt described it, yes," *Mr.* Varga confirmed.

She sighed heavily. "Daddy never did explain that to my or Evie's liking. But I'm certain he overreacted to something."

"How can you be certain about that?"

"Because Daddy has always been paranoid, that's how," Simone said. "And getting back to what we were talking about earlier, he's always worked very hard to maintain our lifestyle," she hurried on before her companion could question her further. She wanted to move the conversation back to what had generated it in the first place, and depart from a topic she'd just as soon not discuss with the mysterious *Mr.* Varga.

"And my parents were always big time into philanthropy, too," she added for good measure. Though she still didn't know why she was expending so much energy defending herself and her family to a man she couldn't care less about. She couldn't. Really. It was true. "My father contributed heavily to the Cincinnati arts scene, and there's a scholarship named after my mother. And when Evie and I were kids, every year at Christmas and Thanksgiving, we volunteered at several different—"

"Miss Van Dormer." His voice, so low and level—

and, oh, God, so utterly sensuous—cut through the darkness.

Simone battled a ripple of awareness that settled somewhere deep inside her against her wishes. "What?" she asked softly.

He continued to gaze straight ahead as he said, "You don't have to defend yourself to me."

"Don't I?"

This time, he threw her a look that was very intent. "No. You don't."

Simone told herself to let it go, that neither of them needed to say any more on the subject. In spite of that, she heard herself tell him, "Because, it's funny—I get the distinct impression that you do resent me for some reason."

He hesitated a weighty moment before replying, "Not for your social standing, I don't."

She hesitated not at all. "Then you do admit that you resent me."

"I didn't say that."

"You didn't have to."

He said nothing in response to that—neither agreed nor disagreed with her assertion—and Simone decided it might be best not to press the issue any further. No sense having verified exactly what she suspected. That Mr. Julian Varga hated her guts. Of course, after the way she'd been treating him this weekend, she could hardly blame him. But she couldn't help it. He put her on edge whenever he came within fifty feet of her. And she'd always reacted badly to people who put her on edge.

There was just something about him that, put simply, rubbed her the wrong way. Some mysterious quality in him spoke to something equally baffling in her, and those two strange somethings had been bickering for the last forty-eight hours. Simone really wished that, whatever those somethings were, they would just shut up.

"There," she said, pointing toward the house where she and Evie had spent their childhood. She smiled as it came into view. "Pull over to the curb for a minute."

"Yes, ma'am, *Miss* Van Dormer," he replied crisply.

"Please," she added belatedly, apologetically.

That seemed to placate him some, because his voice was a bit less chilly when he asked, "This was your house?"

"Yeah," she replied, her smile returning when she switched her attention back to it.

The big Tudor looked smaller than Simone recalled, but the trees scattered about the large lot were all bigger and more expansive. The shutters of the house were beige now, where before they had been dark brown, and the front door was painted green, instead of the dark red it had been when the Van Dormers had claimed the residence. Other than that, though, little about the house had changed. On the outside, at any rate. A stark, angular halogen light burned in the window of the living room, where before had been a whimsical Tiffany lamp. Another light was on upstairs, in what had been Simone's bedroom. Heavy-looking drapes framed that window now, obscuring much of the mullioned glass, where she had hung lace curtains herself. She'd always thought them, like the rest of the house, very romantic.

It really was a wonderful house. She only now realized how very much she missed it.

"I wonder who lives there now?" she said. "I hope it's someone with kids. It was a great house to be a kid in. Lots of trees to climb, lots of yard to run around in. Evie and I used to put up a tent in the backyard in the summer, and sleep outside. In the winter, there was always so much snow. Enough for a whole army of snowmen. It was wonderful."

"Sounds like."

So caught up in her memories had she become that Simone had almost forgotten Mr. Varga was with her. Almost. Now, she turned her attention away from the house to look at him instead. His face was half-shadowed, half-lit by the yellowish glow from a street-lamp on the corner, and she found his appearance then to be strangely appropriate. Light or dark, which was he? she wondered. Maybe this week she'd find out.

Then she reminded herself that it didn't matter what Mr. Varga was, because he wasn't the man she had come here for. The man she had come here for was far more important to her well-being and peace of mind, and much less difficult to figure out. And imminently more attainable, too, she was certain. Something about Mr. Varga just prohibited further inspection. Blond Brian Richie, though . . .

Ah. Now there was a far more approachable specimen.

"Could you drive down a little bit further?" she asked. "Just to the next house? But pull around the corner, and park across the street. Please," she added, before he had a chance to plague her with another one of his cool retorts.

He seemed surprised by her request—or maybe it was the "please" that had surprised him, she couldn't help thinking—but he did as she instructed. As the sedan crept forward, Simone turned her attention to the big, Federal-style house next door to the one where she had grown up. The Richie house. Brian's house. He had moved to Mount Airy after he'd married and had lived there for thirteen years. But he had come back home to this house after his father's death a couple of years ago to care for his mother and finish raising his family. Although, at sixty, his mother was in excellent health, she still lived here with him—Simone had checked—and so did all three of his daughters. The oldest, Stephanie, though, was headed to Miami University in Oxford in the fall—Simone had checked that, too.

When the car rounded the corner, Mr. Varga parked it across the street, where there were no streetlamps to reveal their presence. The Richies' house had changed even less than the Van Dormers', and, as had been the case at the Van Dormers', the current residents—at least some of them—were home. It was full dark by now, making it easy to see into the rooms that were lit. And in the den on the side of the house stood a young girl of perhaps twelve or thirteen, along with a man Simone knew must be Brian. She couldn't discern his features from this distance, but he appeared to be as slim—and as blond—as he had been in high school. As she watched, he withdrew his wallet from his back pocket and pulled something—presumably money—from inside. Then he handed it to the girl—his middle daughter, Anna, Simone deduced—who jumped up and down quite gleefully, then sped from the room.

A generous father, Simone thought. Why was she not surprised? He was a man, she was certain, who would put family first, who had probably spoiled his girls every chance he got.

For a moment, Simone indulged in a little fantasy, wondering how it might have been if things had turned out differently. If she had been the one to marry Brian, as she'd always hoped she would. If she had been the one to give him three beautiful daughters. If she had been the one who was living in that house with him now.

Don't do it, she told herself. *Don't even think about what might have been.*

She made herself forget the past and focus on what actually *was*. To think about the weekend that lay ahead, and her plans for how things would unfold between her and Brian then. And remembering that, Simone felt better. About herself. About Brian. About what might, or might not, have been.

"Looks like Mr. Right got married," Julian Varga said from the seat beside her.

"Yes," Simone told him. "He did. Two years after graduating from high school. His girlfriend was pregnant at the time."

"Ouch," Julian said. "That had to put a crimp in his plans for the future."

"Not really," she said. "They'd planned to get married anyway. Childhood sweethearts, and all that. He and his wife dated all through high school."

"So then . . . isn't *Mrs*. Right going to put a crimp in *your* plans for next weekend?" Julian asked.

"Mrs. Right is dead," Simone said plainly.

"Oh."

"She died almost a year ago. A boating accident."

"Oh." He sounded distinctly uncomfortable. "Gee, I guess I should say I'm sorry, but this does sort of put you in a pretty good spot, huh?"

Oh, if he only knew, Simone thought. "Well, certainly it gives me an additional reason to . . . look Brian up."

"Brian," Julian repeated. "Now there's a nice, upright, forthright, do-right kind of name for you. A real all-American, too-good-to-be-true kind of name, Brian."

"That was always the kind of guy he was, too," she concurred, still gazing at the man beyond the window of the house across the street. "All-American. Too good to be true. He was a total sweetheart in high school."

"But you two never dated?"

"No."

"That's right. He had a girlfriend."

"Though she attended a different school," Simone said idly.

"Ah. So . . . did you know him well?"

"Not really."

"Then how do you know . . ."

Simone finally pulled her gaze away from Brian and returned it to the man seated across from her. "How do I know what?"

"How can you be so confident that things are going to work out the way you want them to this weekend?"

"I just am," she told him. "I've been planning this for a long time."

"I see."

Well, she doubted that. But she wasn't about to outline for Julian her plans for Brian Richie. Those plans were much too private. And they were none of Julian's business.

"We can go now," she told him instead. And it struck her as odd that at some point over the last few minutes, she had begun to think of him as Julian, instead of *Mr.* Varga.

"To the hotel?" he asked hopefully.

She nodded. "To the hotel."

He shifted the car into drive and eased away from the curb. "Excellent," he said quietly.

Simone found herself smiling, thinking she couldn't quite disagree.

Pulling away from the curb, Julian had to battle the same creepy sensation that had washed over him the first time he'd been alone with Simone Van Dormer. As he'd watched her watching her beloved Brian, something had come over her expression that had given him a major wiggins. A look of intent, maybe. Of conviction. Something almost predatory. Like she was utterly determined to land this guy and make him her own personal love slave. Whether he liked it or not.

Creepy.

And depressing, too, in a way. There was just something kind of sad about a woman who'd been saving herself for two decades for some guy she hadn't even ever dated. Waiting around for twenty years for some opportunity to arise that might allow her to fit herself into his life. And now that the guy's wife was dead, that opportunity had come at last.

Creepy. Really creepy.

Not that Julian thought for a moment that Simone had ever sat around hoping this guy's wife would buy the farm. She was way too polite for something like that. But the whole scenario just didn't set well with him. Something about it was just really . . . well, creepy.

He pushed the uncomfortable sensation away and focused on retracing their route until he'd found his way back to I-71 South, which would take them back through downtown. The Woodhaven High School reunion would be taking place at the historic Stanhope Hotel, Simone had told him, the same site where they had staged their senior prom twenty years ago—and when had he started thinking of her as Simone, instead of *Miss* Simone Van Dormer? Julian wondered idly.

She had booked a suite at the Stanhope for herself and her sister to share, adjoining rooms on the same floor for him and Wyatt. But, although she didn't quite know it yet, her plans—and reservations—were about to change. Not the suite of rooms part, but the room-*mate* part.

Julian was still trying to figure out how, exactly, he was going to explain it to her when Simone herself offered the perfect opening.

"I want to make sure Evie has a good time here this week," she said out of the blue, as if she'd once again sensed his thoughts. "I think she needs it, and I think she's earned it."

Oops, Julian thought. Considering what Wyatt had told him this morning, that, um, that was going to be something of a problem. But gee, how to tell Simone that.

Finally, he decided on "That, um, that's going to be something of a problem." Hey, why beat around the bush?

He glanced over to find that she had narrowed her eyes at him, very carefully and very suspiciously. Then, likewise carefully and suspiciously, she asked, "Why is that going to be a problem?"

"Oh, look, is this our exit already?" Julian said with much relief when he saw the sign ahead.

He prevented any further discussion by assuring her that he had to concentrate really, really hard for the rest of the trip, because he wasn't familiar with this

part of town—even though his and Wyatt's office was
only about six blocks from the hotel, but hey, Simone
didn't have to know that, did she?—then maneuvered
his way vigilantly beneath the dark green awning that
spanned the hotel's main entrance. After handing the
keys to the valet and overseeing the removal of their
luggage from the trunk, Julian turned to Simone and
found that she was still studying him in that careful,
suspicious way.

Uh-oh.

"We, uh, we better follow our luggage," he told her
as the bellman began to roll away the dolly upon
which he had heaped their bags. "You never know
where it might end up."

Simone curled her fingers lightly over the bellman's
upper arm to halt his progress. "If you could just take
that inside and park it by the reception desk, we'll
catch up with you in a minute."

There was no way any right-thinking man would
contradict that tone of voice, Julian knew. And there
was no way any right-thinking bellman would contradict the twenty-dollar bill Simone pressed into his
hand by way of a punctuation mark to her command.
As he wheeled away their things, simultaneously tugging anxiously at his collar and humming happily as
he went, Julian remained stuck firmly in place, bracing
himself for what he was certain would come next.

"What did you mean back there when you said that
my making sure Evie has a good time this week might
be something of a problem?" Simone demanded again
in a deceptively quiet voice.

He glanced down at his watch and saw that it was
nearly nine-thirty P.M., eastern time. Nearly six-thirty
back on the West Coast. By now, Wyatt and Eve would

be hundreds of miles away from Santa Barbara. He couldn't say for certain exactly where they were—jeez, he hoped Wyatt could—but, surely, by now, they were well under way on the trip that Luther had hired Wyatt to make with his daughter. Therefore, even if Julian told Simone what had happened, there was little she would be able to do about it now.

He hoped.

"Well, see, Eve is going to be arriving in Cincinnati via a, um, a different route than originally planned," Julian said.

Simone looked at him the same way she might observe a slug upon whom she had just dumped salt. "By what route, exactly," she said, "will Evie *be* arriving in Cincinnati?" Her voice was low and level, but there was a clear menace in her tone.

"Oh, probably I-71 North," Julian told her. "That would make the most sense."

"I-71 North," Simone repeated.

He nodded.

"I'm guessing that means she probably won't be arriving in an airplane."

"No, probably not," he concurred. "I think the highway department frowns on that kind of thing. Not to mention it could really wreak havoc with rush hour on a Friday . . . if she makes it by rush hour on Friday, I mean, which, if you knew all the circumstances, you'd realize is a big, *big* if. And rush hour is bad enough already, what with all the construction and everything. I mean, do you think they'll *ever* finish that stretch of highway between Florence and—"

"She's *driving* to Cincinnati?" Simone interrupted.

Julian nodded.

"From Santa Barbara?"

Another nod.

"Surely, she's not doing that alone."

"No, not alone," he affirmed. "Wyatt's with her."

Simone gaped at him for a moment, then groaned. "Oh, *no*. Oh, why was I so afraid you were going to say that?"

"Hey, Eve is perfectly safe with Wyatt," Julian retorted, offended on behalf of his friend. "He'll make sure she gets back to Cincinnati okay."

"No, you don't understand," Simone told him.

"What? What don't I understand?"

She expelled an impatient sound. "When Wyatt and Eve get together . . ."

"What?"

"Stuff just . . . I don't know how to describe it," she said helplessly. "There's a great disturbance in the Force, Obi-Wan Kenobi. That's all there is to it. There's no way they'll make the trip without something . . . I don't know . . . *combusting*."

Julian nodded. Hadn't he told Wyatt yesterday that he'd sensed something of that nature himself when he'd seen the two of them together? Not so much a *great* disturbance in the Force, but something had definitely shifted and changed in their collective reality.

"They'll be fine," Julian said.

Though, for some reason, he didn't feel quite as certain about that as he had a moment ago. Because, suddenly, he had the oddest sensation that either Wyatt or Eve would do something rash. And knowing Wyatt as well as he did, Julian would bet good money on the Y chromosome.

Simone clearly did not believe his assertion any more than he did himself, because as she turned to make her way toward the hotel entrance to catch up with their luggage, she muttered, "I just hope they don't kill each other by week's end."

Julian remembered then that he hadn't finished telling her about the change in plans where her room accommodations—or, more correctly, her room*mate*—was concerned. And he found himself hoping there wasn't going to be a death at this end, either.

"Oh, Miss Van Dormer," he said, hastening his step to catch up with her. "There's something I forgot to tell you . . ."

 *Eight*

"Good evening, Flagstaff! We're coming up on eleven o'clock in the P.M., and we're winding up our awesome eighties weekend on this bee-yoo-tiful Sunday night! Next up, The Pretenders! The 'Middle of the Road' is tryin' to get Chrissie Hynde! But hey, ain't that the way it is for all of us?"

Eve awoke with a start, instinctively recoiling at the disembodied voice that had jerked her into reluctant consciousness. She tried to ignore it, but the rabid echo reverberated in her head, bounced off every last brain cell she possessed, then embedded itself at the front of her cranium with a blinding slash of awareness. Oh, man. She hated it when that happened.

Resigned to her fate, she pried open first one eye, then the other, and immediately discovered that she had no idea where she was. For a moment, she felt dazed and disoriented, wondered why she wasn't in her bed at The Keep, or in the bed she had occupied during her brief life alone in her LA apartment, or even in her bed at the house she had shared with Edwin for so many years.

Why, instead, was there a splendid night sky above her, spattered with too many stars to ever count? Stars that were so bright and so beautiful, it looked as if someone had scattered a fistful of diamonds into the lap of a black velvet gown. Why was there a cool, gentle breeze caressing her face? And why was her body being rocked gently to and fro, a motion that encouraged her to close her eyes again and go right back to sleep?

But if she closed her eyes and went back to sleep, she thought, she wouldn't be able to see that amazing sky, wouldn't feel that sweet breeze stroking her face. If she closed her eyes and went back to sleep, she'd start dreaming. Dreaming about darkness and compliance and apprehension. There was no way she would go back to her dreams. Not when reality looked and felt like this.

Eve remembered then where she was. With Wyatt, her kidnapper, who had been paid by her father to show her a good time. And although the success of that "good time" business was up for grabs at the moment, he seemed to be succeeding pretty well on the kidnapping front. She just wished she knew where the two of them were going. Not so much geographically—she had some idea of their topographic route. No, she was much more concerned about their other route—the one they had been traveling twenty years ago when they'd been separated by such a drastic detour. Just where exactly was that one supposed to lead them, now that they were back on the road again?

Eve decided for now that she wouldn't think about it. Wyatt had cranked open the moon roof, hence the beautiful sky and cool night wind, and he had turned the radio knob to the left, so that the music wasn't playing quite so loudly now. He still didn't know she was awake, she realized. So she remained as motionless as she could to perpetuate his condition. And she watched him as he drove.

The wind rushing in from the open driver's side window tousled his hair with much affection, and his face was bathed in the pale, bluish-green light emanating from the dashboard. He'd grown so handsome over the years. But she still hadn't quite jibed the man of thirty-eight with the boy of eighteen. The two blurred and combined in her head, and she couldn't quite distinguish one from the other. In many ways, they were two distinct and very different individuals. But in other ways, they were one and the same person. Nevertheless, she couldn't quite shake her conviction that the Wyatt of twenty years ago lived only in her memories, and that the Wyatt of today was someone she knew not at all.

Ah, the remnants of sleep, she thought. She'd never been able to think clearly upon waking. And she had no idea at the moment how long she had slept. The last thing she remembered was stopping for gas in Ludlow, and, a little while before that, for dinner at a minuscule roadside diner—Merle and Wylene's, it had been called. She'd blissfully stuffed herself with chicken 'n' dumplins and root beer that had been served up in a frosted mug—Wyatt had insisted on ordering for them both, connoisseur that he was of fine dining—then she had toddled back to the SUV. It had been a long time since she'd eaten that much in one sitting, she thought now. She couldn't remember the last time she'd had a genuine appetite.

After Ludlow, there had been only a long, solemn stretch of highway bisecting the graceful desert terrain. She'd watched the sky behind them from her side-view mirror as it became stained with splashes of orange and purple and pink during the sun's slow descent toward the western horizon. She smiled inwardly now as she remembered. She'd always wanted to see the Mojave Desert, but until today, that wish had gone unfulfilled. Although she'd lived in California for twenty years, she hadn't actually visited much of the southwest. First she'd been too focused on her university studies to get away for any kind of traveling, and then—

Well, then there had been Edwin. And Edwin had discouraged all the traveling she'd wanted to do. He'd discouraged anything that might have broadened her horizons, or added to her bank of knowledge, or just plain made her happy. Edwin had insisted on being Eve's horizon in every direction. He'd demanded that her bank of knowledge be drawn exclusively on him. He'd decreed that he and he alone would claim responsibility for her happiness. And, God help her, that was what Eve had allowed him to do. She wasn't sure she'd ever be able to forgive herself for that.

But that life was gone, she reminded herself. And this life was here now. She just wished she could identify exactly what this life, *here now*, was.

She turned her gaze upward again and sighed silently. Right now, she thought, life was this spectacular stretch of night sky. It was a cool breeze redolent of darkness and desert. It was a song on the radio about aging and maturing that was filled with raucous, youthful, electric guitar. It was a boy-turned-man who straddled her long-ago past and her newly discovered present, a man whose smile, as he drove, was contented and sure.

Life *here now*, Eve decided, actually wasn't too bad.

She studied Wyatt again through the darkness, fighting the urge to say thank you to him. She fought it because, if she told him that, he wouldn't have understood what she was thanking him for, and he would have asked her to explain. And Eve just didn't think she could manage that right now.

So she settled on, "Where are we?" instead. It was as good a question as any. And my goodness, but it had so many potential answers, too.

He looked surprised when he glanced over at her, but he smiled. "Well, good evening, Sleeping Beauty," he said quietly.

She noticed then that a shadow of beard darkened his cheeks, the only indication she could discern that they'd spent the entire day—and then some—on the road. How could he possibly look and sound so chipper—and Eve had really never cared for chipper *at all*—after driving for . . .

She glanced at the dashboard clock and expelled a soft sound of disbelief. "Is it really going on ten o'clock?" she asked, sitting up.

"Going on eleven, local time," he corrected her.

Nearly twelve hours he'd been sitting in that seat, she marveled, with little reprieve. And he looked as if he didn't mind sitting there for a good many more.

"Aren't you getting tired?" she asked.

He launched himself into as much of a full-body stretch as he could, seeing as how he was operating heavy machinery to the tune of seventy-plus miles an hour. Eve tried not to notice how his entire body seemed to expand in response to the action. She should feel overwhelmed by a man that big, she thought. But there was nothing about Wyatt that intimidated her.

Confused her, yes. Bothered her, sure. But of all the strange, conflicting responses she'd had to him over the years, fear had never been among them. Not fear for her safety, at any rate. She'd been more afraid of her own responses to him than she had been of anything Wyatt might say or do.

"I guess I am starting to feel the brunt of the day," he said when he relaxed again.

"How come you didn't stop before now?"

He shrugged. "I hadn't intended to drive this far today, but there's nowhere much to stop once you get out of Barstow. I thought we could spend the night in Needles, but you fell asleep just before we got there, so I kept driving." He smiled, still gazing out at the black ribbon of highway that bled into the darkness ahead. "Then I thought we could stop in Kingman, but you were still asleep. And you looked so peaceful, I didn't want to wake you."

"You could have wakened me," she said. "I didn't need the sleep that bad."

"Coulda fooled me."

She was about to repeat her question regarding their whereabouts when a highway sign appeared to announce that Flagstaff was less than thirty miles away.

"We should stop here," she said, confident that Wyatt would follow her thoughts. "It shouldn't be too hard to find a hotel in a city this size."

"Grab that Triple-A guide in the side pocket of the passenger door and see if you can find something."

Eve nodded as she reached for the guide. "I'll use my cell phone to make a reservation." She did, and within moments they had adjoining rooms booked at the Canyon Vista Motor Lodge. "I didn't realize we were getting close to the Grand Canyon," she said as she tucked the guide back into the side pocket of the passenger door. "Have you ever seen it?"

He shook his head.

"Me, neither. Too bad we'll have to miss it."

"Says who?"

She hesitated a moment. "Well, we're going to have to get up early tomorrow to drive, aren't we? I mean, we do have a long way to go to get to Ohio."

Wyatt grinned. "We have all week to get to Ohio," he pointed out with much nonchalance. "We could sleep in tomorrow morning, then maybe find a Denny's and have a Grand Slam Breakfast. Hey, how long has it been since you've had one of those, huh, Eve? Then," he hurried on, not waiting for an answer, "we could head for the Grand Canyon for the day."

For some reason, Eve couldn't quite muster the enthusiasm he seemed to be feeling himself. "Um, why?" she asked.

"Um, because it will be fun," he told her.

"But—"

"A good time, Eve. That's what I'm supposed to show you this week, remember?"

Yeah, because he was being paid to, she couldn't help recalling. "Wyatt, you don't have to take my father at his word about that."

"Sure, I do."

"Just because he's paying you to—"

"Eve, I'm not just doing this because he's paying me to."

"Then why?"

Instead of answering her, he threw her another one of those disarming little grins that had always so, well, disarmed her. This one was no different.

"We'll have fun," he told her. "Wait and see."

She nibbled her lip thoughtfully for a moment, telling herself she should discourage this. She really did want to get back to Cincinnati. She'd been looking forward to spending the week there with Simone before the reunion, doing all the things and visiting all the places they'd loved to do and visit as teenagers. And she'd been looking forward to spending some time alone, too. She'd wanted to drive around the entire metropolitan area and see how things had changed, and how they had remained the same. She'd wanted to immerse herself in a past where she had been reasonably happy, and forget about a present that held little appeal.

She wanted to go home, Eve realized. She wanted to go *home*.

"Wyatt . . ." she began to object.

But nothing more than his name left her mouth, because she really had no idea what to say. For some reason, at that moment, getting back to Cincinnati—going home—didn't seem quite as important as it had a few days, or even a few hours, ago. Because, suddenly, being here with Wyatt somehow filled that need. For now, anyway. She was sure it wouldn't last. But, for now, it was enough.

"Just promise me," she finally said, "that you won't make me ride to the bottom on one of those donkeys."

He smiled. "Don't worry, Eve. I have our itinerary all planned."

The Canyon Vista Motor Lodge offered neither a vista of the canyon nor much of a lodge, Wyatt couldn't help but note as he tossed his duffel bag onto the bed in his room. What it *did* offer was a vista of a Bob

Evans restaurant next door, and what might charitably be called "vintage" 1950s decor, right down to the orange chenille bedspread tossed over the double bed, and the little orange-and-brown pompoms trimming the faded shade of a tiled lamp on the nowhere-near-convincing-walnut-veneer dresser. A painting of the Grand Canyon—surely *not* paint-by-number, in spite of its appearance, he told himself—hung over the bed, and a rotary phone—did anybody even remember how to use one of those things?—squatted on the nowhere-near-convincing-walnut-veneer nightstand beside it.

The tiny room also provided a total lack of peace and quiet, seeing as how it was situated right next to the pool. The pool where what was evidently the entire youth group of the Burning Bush Baptist Church of Clovis, New Mexico—if the gaily painted school bus parked nearby was any indication—appeared to be holding the national semifinals of the Marco Polo Invitational. Wyatt couldn't quite conjure the irritation he figured he should probably feel about the noise level, though. The kids were just having too much fun to bear them any grudge.

The only *good* thing about his room, he thought, was that it adjoined Eve's—which, as far as Wyatt was concerned, was a very good thing indeed. Especially since the two doors that did the actual adjoining currently stood wide open, and Eve hadn't objected at all when he'd insisted they stay that way.

He still wasn't entirely sure why she was going along with this excursion as willingly as she had been. He'd expected her to fight him every mile on the road, had anticipated a long, meandering monologue about how ridiculous her father's "kidnapping" scheme was, and about how contemptible Wyatt's involvement in it was, and about how inconvenient the trip would be in preventing her from getting to where she really wanted to be—namely, Cincinnati. He'd anticipated her being on her cell phone, making an airline reservation from the next city large enough to have an airport. He had thought she would try to give him the slip every time they made a stop for gas or food or lodging. At the very least, he had expected to be run off the road and beaten senseless by an angry truck driver, because Eve had surreptitiously held up a home-made sign in the window that said, Help! I'm being kidnapped by a moron! Dial 911!

But none of those things had happened. Not even the sign. Eve had been surprisingly compliant, for the duration. Yet for all her cooperation, Wyatt was irritated as hell. Because *compliant* was the last thing he'd ever figured Eve Van Dormer would grow up to be. A Marine Corps drill instructor, certainly. A breeder of killer Dobermans, no doubt. Owner of a piranha farm, yeah, sure. A favorite of the WWF's weekly "Smackdown!" series, absolutely. But not compliant. Never that.

When he realized he'd heard nothing from the other room for the last several minutes, he called, "Everything okay in there . . . ? Eve?" he tried again when he received no reply. Once again, though, silence was his only response. Hmmm . . .

Maybe he'd been a little premature in thinking she had become compliant. Maybe she'd just been trying to lull him into one of those false senses of security he'd read so much about, so that she could make her move. Maybe she was outside hot-wiring the Expedition right now. Or maybe she was already speeding toward the airport to catch a plane.

Wyatt strode quickly into the other room, ready to scoop her up and tie her to a chair, if he needed to. She *was* going to let him show her a good time, dammit, whether she liked it or not. Though, now that he thought more about it, he supposed that maybe being tied to a chair wasn't her idea of a good time—even if he himself had rather enjoyed such a fantasy from time to time. But that was beside the point, because right now he had to find out where Eve was. And as he strode purposefully into the room, he found that, just as he had suspected, she was indeed—

Sleeping.

Oh. Well. That was okay then.

Man, she hadn't even unpacked her bags yet, he noted. And she hadn't even bothered to take off her sandals. She looked as if she had just slid the chain into its slot on the door, then had turned around to fall face first onto the bed. She lay on her stomach, her hair spilling from its careless ponytail, one hand curled into a loose fist by her face, the other arm slung in an arc over the top of her head. One leg was bent slightly, the soft white fabric of her dress riding just above that knee, the rest of the garment draping over her frame.

He realized then how thin she was. Much too thin, really. She wore such baggy clothes, he hadn't noticed it before, but with her dress veiling her body the way it was now . . . He wondered how long it had been since she'd had a big enough appetite to enjoy a decent meal.

Then he remembered their dinner at Merle and Wylene's earlier. She had put away her entire—and very generous—serving of chicken 'n' dumplins, then

the last of Wyatt's to boot. Plus fried apples and corn-
on-the-cob, and for dessert, a big ol' slice of chess pie,
piled high with meringue. He smiled now at the recollection. So maybe she was eating better today than she
had for a while. And maybe her father hadn't been so
crazy to suggest this trip after all.

And maybe, just maybe, Wyatt really could show
her a good time for the next few days. Hey, it was the
least he could do, with or without being paid by her
father. He owed her.

Sighing softly, he moved to turn off the lamp near
the bed, so that she might sleep through the night. As
an afterthought, he carefully removed her sandals and
set them on the floor, amazed that she didn't stir once
during the process. Then he adjusted the air conditioner and pulled a lightweight blanket from the shelf
above the alcove designated for hanging clothes—the
Canyon Vista Motor Lodge didn't offer anything as
sophisticated as a closet—and settled the cover carefully over her lower half. And then Wyatt told himself
to leave, to go back to his own room without looking
back and ready himself for bed. Hell, he needed to get
some sleep, too.

But something prohibited him from doing that. For
some reason, he was suddenly overcome by the feeling
that there was something else—something very
important—that he needed to do before he could call it
a night. Unfortunately, he had no idea what that something very important might be.

He watched Eve as she slept, observing the way one
wayward length of hair near her mouth danced with
every soft breath she exhaled. Not sure why he did it,
Wyatt nudged the errant tress back over her shoulder.
And then, even more uncertain why he did it, he bent

and, after one small hesitation, brushed his lips lightly over her cheek—her soft, warm, delicate cheek. But she didn't stir in response to that, either, save a soft sough of sound that may or may not have been the result of his touch.

"Goodnight, Eve," he whispered as he reluctantly drew away. "Have sweet dreams."

Then, still feeling disjointed and confused and incomplete, he strode quietly back to his own room, wishing he could figure out just what the hell else it was that he was supposed to do.

He awoke with a jerk several hours later and wrenched himself out of his bed, only to discover that his room was dark and silent and empty, save himself. A slice of light from the yellow bug lamp outside slipped in through a gap in the drawn curtains, enough so that he could see the outline of every piece of furniture in the room. Nothing was amiss. No intruder had ransacked the place or taken him hostage. He wondered what had roused him, and why it had startled him so.

Immediately, his gaze lit on the open door between his own room and Eve's, and, heedless of the fact that he wore nothing but a pair of briefs, he made his way toward it. Peeking through, he found her room, too, was lit just well enough to distinguish that it was also dark and silent, and empty, save—

Save nothing. Eve wasn't in—or on—her bed.

Wyatt was fighting off a heart attack when he heard a sound from outside, the soft splash of water and the flapping recoil of fiberglass, as if someone had just pushed off a diving board and into a pool. Eve. He was sure of it. Swimming had always been the way she'd relieved pent-up energy. He knew that because, in high school, he had worked at the indoor pool facility where the Woodhaven swim team had practiced three times a week, rain or shine. And there had been weeks when Eve Van Dormer was there a lot more than three times, her sleek, slim body knifing effortlessly through the pool, water sluicing elegantly over her smooth skin, her suit clinging wetly to every last luscious inch of her.

He'd asked her about it once, why she spent so much time at the pool, swimming and swimming and swimming, as if to stop would spell certain doom. She had told him it was because she needed to alleviate stress, to burn off excess energy. He'd replied that he could think of another, much more enjoyable, way to do that, and he'd be glad to act as her instructor in the activity. She'd retorted that it was ironic, her coming to the pool to relieve the pressures of life, seeing as how Wyatt was one of those prime pressures, and he worked at the pool. But she hadn't stopped coming. She hadn't stopped swimming. She hadn't stopped being sleek and elegant and wet.

Judging from the sounds he heard outside, she was all of those things again.

Sparing only enough time to tug a pair of blue jeans over his briefs, Wyatt scooped up his hotel key and the keys to the Expedition and made his way outside. Just as he'd suspected, Eve was in the water, arcing her arms gracefully over her head as she pulled her body—her sleek, elegant, wet body—from one end of the pool to the other. For one heart-stopping moment, Wyatt thought she was naked—the lights in the pool played some very erotic tricks on the ol' eyes. Then he realized she was wearing a beige, one-piece swimsuit, and his circulation kicked in again, though it wasn't nearly as level as it had been a few minutes ago. Nor was his body temperature nearly as cool.

With her face in the water, she hadn't detected his presence yet. As quietly as he could, his attention never veering from the woman in the pool, Wyatt made his way to the Expedition and unlocked the back. Then he pushed aside a few odds and ends until he found what he was looking for—a bottle of very good Scotch and a case of very fine wine. He pocketed a corkscrew and scrounged up a couple of plastic cups, then retraced his steps to the pool. But the gate was locked, the sign affixed to it stating in capital letters, POOL CLOSED AFTER ELEVEN P.M. NO EXCEPTIONS.

He glanced down at his watch, which he'd reset for mountain time upon arriving at the motel. Three-fourteen A.M. Ah, hell. Like he'd never broken a rule before. And anyway, no one had *ever* accused Wyatt Culver of being exceptional. So, since he wasn't an exception, it was obviously okay for him to go right on in to the pool, wasn't it?

There. How was that for justification?

In spite of his corrupt, though effective, philosophizing, the moment Eve came up for air on his side of the pool, he called out softly, "Pool's closed, miss."

Her face was etched with surprise when she glanced up to find him there. Then she smiled, an unexpected, conspiratorial little grin that made something inside Wyatt pop and fizz. Funny, he thought—he hadn't even opened the wine yet. And it wasn't a sparkling varietal, anyway. So what was with the pop and fizz?

"But the fence is short," she countered just as quietly. "Climb on over."

"There's no lifeguard on duty," he pointed out. "You could be taking your life in your hands." But he wasted no time in vaulting first one leg, then the other, over the squat, chain-link fence. Once he'd cleared the obstruction, he strode toward one of the plastic tables near where Eve had stopped, setting down his booty for her inspection.

From her position in the pool, Eve eyed Wyatt carefully, marking the way the pool lights caused faint ripples of white to dance over his naked chest, and the way the top button of his jeans winked playfully in the light. The top button that was unfastened, she couldn't help but register, as if he'd been in a hurry when he'd put them on.

It didn't matter if there was a lifeguard on duty or not, she thought. It wasn't the water that was dangerous.

"I don't think they allow alcoholic beverages out here at the pool," she told him, nodding toward the two bottles he had set on the table.

"I guess you read that on the same sign that said the pool is closed after eleven o'clock, no exceptions, didn't you?" he asked.

"That would be where I learned about it, yes."

"I see." He pulled a corkscrew from his pocket and went to work on the wine. "I recall that you prefer red."

"You remembered," she said, striving for a playful, coquettish tone of voice that was in no way keeping with the tumult of emotion pitching through her. "I'm flattered."

"Yes, well, this particular vintage isn't quite down to our teenaged standards," he said as he began to wrestle the cork free, "but Cella Lambrusco and Yago Sangria aren't as easy to find as they used to be. And I don't have any 7 UP to mix with it, anyway, which, as I recall, was the way you preferred your wine back then."

"Well, I was a connoisseur, you know," she pointed out. "Most kids back then weren't drinking wine at all."

"Mm," he said noncommittally. "I hate to tell you this, but you weren't, either. And, tonight," he hurried on before she could correct his assertion—not that there was any way you could correct that assertion— "you're just going to have to make do with a nice California Merlot that's dry without being playful and robust without being overwhelming. Deal with it."

"Oh, if I must."

He poured a generous serving into one of the plastic cups and brought it to her poolside, where, after pulling her upper body out of the water and resting her arms on the concrete, Eve gratefully accepted it. It was indeed a nice California Merlot, she realized with one sip. Very smooth going down. But something inside her kind of wished Wyatt *had* found a bottle of Lambrusco and another of 7 UP, even if she would no doubt have paid for it—severely—in the morning.

"Wyatt," she began as she watched him splash a couple of fingers of her father's favorite brand of Scotch into the other glass, smiling when she realized whence he had pilfered his stash, "do you ever think about high school?"

He finished pouring his drink before he answered, then pulled a plastic chair to the edge of the pool and seated himself. "Not often," he said. "I wasn't one of those people who had their entire identity as a human being tied up in their senior class social standing. Nor, do I recall, were you."

That was true, Eve conceded. Although she had been a member of several clubs and active in sports at Woodhaven High, she'd never much run around with the "in" crowd. At her school, there had been the Preps, the Jocks, the Nerds, the Punks, and the Hoods, and Eve had moved pretty freely among all of them. As had Wyatt, she remembered now.

Her very best friend had been Amy Maguire, but Eve's move across the country had effectively put an end to that friendship—after they'd settled in Santa Barbara, her father had forbidden her and Simone to have any contact with anyone from back home. Still, Amy Maguire had been surprisingly easy to get over, Eve recalled. Indicating that she must not have been such an intimate friend after all.

No, the only person Eve had continued to think about for a long time after high school was Wyatt. For years, she had replayed that travesty of a prom night, wondering about what she might have done differently that would have resulted in a more agreeable outcome. She had thought things were going nicely between the two of them that night. They had come so close to—

Well. They had come so close. And then Wyatt had just . . . walked away. As a seventeen-year-old girl, she had been devastated by his rejection. But as a thirty-seven-year-old woman, she knew there were worse things in life than being left crying and untouched in the backseat of a car.

"Do *you* ever think about high school?" he asked this time.

She shook her head. "Not really. At least, I didn't until the invitation to the reunion arrived. But lately—" She stopped herself before continuing, unwilling to reveal just how heavily such memories *had* been winding through her head over the last few months. Mostly, though, she was unwilling to reveal how many of them had focused on Wyatt.

"Lately?" he spurred.

"Nothing," she said before sipping her wine. "Never mind."

"So how did the reunion committee find you?" he asked. "God knows nobody else in Woodhaven knew where you went."

"Actually, they found Simone," she told him. "She went back to Cincinnati last fall for a couple of weeks—something that had to do with her job—and she ran into Michelle Kaden somewhere while she was there. Well, Michelle Kaden is Michelle Somebody-Else now, but she was on the reunion committee and putting together the guest list. Evidently, she was delighted to see Simone—everyone thought we'd both dropped off the face of the Earth."

Wyatt said nothing in response to that for a moment, only leaned back in his chair and sipped carefully from his cup, his eyes never leaving Eve's. "It was worse than that," he said softly. "It was like you'd just disappeared from the universe. And there was a big, gaping black hole left in your wake."

Eve found it impossible to pull her gaze away from his, so amazed was she that he would offer such a candid admission. And as she studied him, something inside her stirred to life that hadn't been active for some time. In fact, whatever the feeling was had lain fallow for so long, she couldn't quite put her finger on what, precisely, it was. But it was a good feeling, that much she knew. A feeling she had experienced before at some point, because it was kind of familiar, in a way.

She waited a minute, to see if it would grow stronger. And after a minute, it did.

Mischief, that was it. That was what she was experiencing. A much delayed, too long dormant feeling of mischief. Of amusement. Of . . . of fun.

Tipping back her cup, she drained it of the last several swallows of wine, then extended it toward Wyatt. "Refill?" she asked lightly. "Please?"

He seemed a bit surprised that she would be making such a request so soon, but he rose to accommodate it just the same. Eve waited patiently, still half submerged, as he poured her another round. And she smiled her gratitude when he returned and hunkered down at the edge of the pool to hand it to her. But when she reached up to take the wine from him, instead of curling her fingers around the cup, she circled them deftly around his wrist instead. And before he had a chance to determine her intention, she tugged hard, pulling him headfirst, wine and blue jeans and all, into the water.

He was sputtering when he broke the surface, blustering about how matriarch-fricking cold the water was, his hand still clenched around the plastic cup, his expression one of stark and intense . . . She smiled. Fun. It was an expression of stark and intense fun.

Well, well, well, she thought. For the first time since she'd seen him standing in her father's study two nights ago, she and Wyatt were on the same wavelength.

"I cannot *believe* you're out here swimming in water this cold," he gasped.

"And I cannot *believe* you spilled my wine," she retorted, feigning—but not too hard—outrage. She was pretty sure her grin was going to spoil the image, anyway. "That's going to cost you," she threatened him. "Severely."

Where Wyatt had been treading water, now he stood up, tossing back his wet hair in exactly the same way teenaged boys do, something that sent a little thrill of excitement spiraling through Eve's entire body. The water level halted just below his chest, but tiny droplets clung to the dark hair, catching the pool lights as if they were tiny diamonds. Thin rivulets streamed off his shoulders and meandered down his biceps—those broad, solid shoulders, and those dense, prominent biceps. Wyatt had clearly pumped some iron since high school, she thought idly, watching the indolent movement of the water as it wound over his body. And she couldn't help wondering what it would be like to let her fingers wander along the same path.

Belatedly, she realized she never should have started this . . . this . . . this whatever it was . . . with him. She never should have started this, because she was beginning to suspect that this was something she wasn't prepared to finish. Judging by the expression on Wyatt's face, though, he clearly *did* intend to finish this. Only *this*, to him, was obviously not what *this* was to her. At least, she didn't think she had intended for this to be what he was starting to make of this. If, in fact, he was making this into what she suspected he was making this into.

Or something like that. Um, what was the question again? She couldn't quite remember now . . .

And the reason she couldn't quite remember was that she was much too focused on the way one rivulet of water in particular was winding its way over his shoulder, to disappear in the dark hair scattered across his chest, just begging a woman's fingertip to follow it, and—

"I'm going to pay severely?" he repeated lightly, scattering her thoughts—some. "Promises, promises, Eve." He smiled. "Come and get me, then. I dare you."

Oh, he would do that, she thought. He knew she'd never been able to resist a dare. At least, she hadn't been able to resist a dare when she was in high school. Not when Wyatt Culver was the one issuing it. Now, however . . .

She smiled, too. She still couldn't resist a dare, she realized. Not when Wyatt Culver was the one issuing it.

"You dare me?" she asked.

He nodded. "Yeah, I dare you. In fact, I double dare you."

"Ooo, you're pushing it, Wyatt."

"Am I?"

"You know I never turn down a dare," she reminded him. "Never mind a double dare."

He pretended to stifle a yawn. "I'm waaaiiiting . . ."

As much as Eve wanted to go over and dunk him, she hesitated. She wasn't sure why. For one long moment, she only stood where she was, watching Wyatt, and wishing . . .

She sighed heavily to herself. Wishing for too many things that would never come true. The mischief that had briefly visited her suddenly fled, and any sense of fun she might have experienced went with it. She held up her hands, flattening them and positioning them into a T, the internationally recognized signal for *time-out*.

And she said, "Game over, Wyatt. Never mind. Forget I said anything."

He eyed her for a minute with much consideration. Then, softly, he said, "There are some things, Eve, I can never forget." He took a few steps forward, the water purling behind him as he drew closer. "And this, I'm afraid, is going to be one of them. You started something here. Now we're just going to have to finish it."

He halted when scarcely a ripple of water lay between them, his wet body towering over hers by a good eight inches. Instinctively, she pushed herself backward, only to find that she was trapped by the unforgiving concrete wall of the pool. She glanced hastily to her right, but Wyatt anticipated her move by dropping a hand to the pool's edge, his arm preventing her escape in that direction. On her left, only inches away, was the pool ladder, thereby making any escape in that direction iffy.

As Wyatt gazed down at her, he lifted his free hand to run his fingers through his hair, slicking it back from his forehead. Eve's mouth went dry at the way the muscles in his arm bunched and relaxed with the motion, and, when her gaze again found his, she caught her breath at the gleam of intent that darkened his eyes.

For one curt, lunatic moment, she thought he was going to kiss her. And, as if he read her thoughts, he slowly reached toward her. This time, he dragged his fingers lightly through her wet hair, and the scrape of his fingertips over her scalp was almost unbearable in its exquisite tenderness. Eve's eyes fluttered closed, and her lips parted slightly, but somehow, she still couldn't quite get enough air. She sensed, more than saw, Wyatt's deliberate move toward her, but she knew he was leaning in, slowly, slowly, oh, so slowly.

And just when she didn't think she'd be able to stand the anticipation any longer, just when she was sure she would die if he didn't pull her into his arms, the fingers in her hair went taut, his head moved closer to hers, and finally, finally, he . . .

. . . dunked her.

One minute, Eve was standing still, heart racing, prepared for—even anticipating—the touch of his lips against hers, and the next, she was taking on more water than the *Titanic*. Which, she supposed, would make Wyatt the iceberg. Somehow, the analogy seemed perfectly right.

"You . . . you . . . you . . ." she sputtered as she shot back out of the water.

But she could think of no word that was suitable to label him for what he had just done. So she spat out the last remnants of water—unmindful of how unladylike the gesture was—and swiped her hands over her eyes to clear her vision. But that only left her looking at Wyatt, and seeing a smug, smarmy little grin curling his lips.

"Oh, now you're *really* going to pay," she vowed. Screw her earlier trepidation. This was war.

"Yeah, yeah, yeah," he replied, clearly unbothered by her threat. "Like I said, Eve. Promises, promises."

This time, not one scrap of timidity hindered her as she formed her intent. This time, she wasn't about to back down. This time, Wyatt would pay. She just hoped, you know, he didn't retaliate by dunking her again. She took a few steps forward, but just as she got within arm's reach of him, Wyatt ducked under the water and swam to the other end of the pool.

His efforts, Eve knew, would be fruitless. She'd

always been able to swim rings around him—literally.
Which, now that she thought about it, was a very good
idea. She waited until she saw him about to surface at
the deep end of the pool, then she dove down into the
water as far as she could go. She swam quickly along
the bottom, completing two full circles beneath him
without surfacing, hoping to confuse him. And
although he pushed the upper part of his body out of
the water, before he managed to get his bearings she
swam up beneath him and grabbed both of his ankles.
Then she jerked down on them as hard as she could,
yanking him back under the water.

Once again, Wyatt was the one to end up sputtering
as he broke the surface, but when Eve came up for air,
she heard his laughter mingling with his affront. And
his smile this time . . .

Oh, my.

His smile this time was frisky and happy and affectionate. And although Eve told herself she should have
seen it coming, she was totally unprepared when
Wyatt knifed through the water toward her and settled
his hands on her waist.

She reacted without thinking, curling her fingers
over his slick, wet shoulders. The water was too deep
where they were for either of them to touch bottom,
and their legs got tangled as they both tried to tread
water. The brush of wet denim against her bare legs
was an utterly erotic sensation. Even more so was how,
in their efforts to stay afloat, their torsos bumped
repeatedly, rubbing gently and seductively against
each other. Every touch seemed more intimate than
the one that preceded it, creating a delicious friction.
Heat shot through her in a spiral of wanting unlike
anything she had felt since . . . since . . .

Since the Woodhaven High School prom, 1981. And look how that had turned out.

Upon forming the memory, Eve instinctively tried to push away from Wyatt, but he looped one arm around her waist to prevent her flight. With the other arm, he side-stroked toward the center of the pool, pulling her alongside him for the ride, until he reached a place where he could stand with his head out of the water—but where it was still too deep for Eve to do the same. She had no choice but to cling to him, to hold on to him or risk drowning. Not that Wyatt would ever let her drown, she knew. And not that she necessarily wanted to let go of him in the first place. Not now. Not yet. Not until she was confident that she could stand on her own two feet without sinking.

For a moment, he said nothing, only curled his fingers intently around her rib cage, resting his thumbs just beneath her breasts, to hold her in place before him. Her eyes were on a level with his, and the clarity of the water undulating around them made his seem even greener than usual somehow, gave them a luster of yearning she was certain she must be imagining. Then she thought, no, she wasn't imagining it at all. What she saw in his eyes was simply a reflection of the longing she knew must show in her own.

"I'd say that little stunt you pulled makes us even," he murmured, his voice a soft caress that washed over her more fluidly than the water did.

"Actually, I think I'm still one up on you," she countered.

She was amazed to hear her voice emerge on such a level timbre, because *level* was the last thing she felt at the moment. His fingers lay so surely over her, so intimately, so possessively. And his body grazed hers with such tenure. She wanted nothing more than to cup her hand around his nape, to thread her fingers through his hair, to—

"You're still one up on me?" he echoed quietly, dispelling her fantasy. "Just how do you figure that?"

"First, I pulled you in, and then I dunked you," she said softly, her voice sounding as shallow as her mind felt at the moment. "You just dunked me. So it's still two to one. I'm ahead."

"Mm," he replied evenly, his gaze still fixed on hers. But he said nothing more for a moment, only raked one thumb lightly down over her ribs, then back up again with aching idleness. "Gee," he finally said, his voice mimicking the soft stroke of his thumb across the taut fabric of her bathing suit, "then I guess I'll just have to even the score another way, won't I?"

Before she had a chance to ask him how he planned to do that, Wyatt showed her—by dipping his head deftly toward hers and covering her mouth with his.

It wasn't a passionate, hungry kiss, but she felt the pull of his desire as keenly as she felt her own. Slowly, tenderly, he brushed his mouth over hers, once, twice, three times, before dragging the tip of his tongue along the plump curve of her lower lip. Somewhere inside Eve, someplace down so deep and so dark that she'd forgotten anything was there, something roused and grew warm that had been cold for much too long. Slowly, the ember sparked, gradually, it flamed, and little by little, that flame flickered into fire. She curled the fingers of one hand around his nape and threaded the others through his wet hair. And then she tilted her head to the side, just a bit, enough to facilitate his exploration.

It was, evidently, all the encouragement Wyatt needed.

Because the moment she offered him even that tiny bit of reassurance, he pressed his mouth to hers again, more insistently this time, claiming her as if . . . Well, as if she were his for the taking. And as Eve melted into the kiss, she realized she couldn't quite deny that she wasn't. His for the taking. His for whatever he wanted. His for however long he wanted her. Because suddenly—or maybe it wasn't so sudden at all—Eve wanted to take Wyatt, too.

Then even that hazy, indistinct concept evaporated, to be replaced by memories of another time, another place, and a feeling very much like this one. Eve felt as if she were seventeen again and had just encountered Wyatt Culver in a deserted hallway at Woodhaven High, and he had kissed her, deeply, wantonly, with an almost drugging effect. He had cupped his hand gently over her breast that day, the first time she had ever allowed a boy such a liberty. And with that simple touch, such heat, such need had shot through her . . .

Now that episode folded over into this one, and Eve let herself go with it, flow with it, let the woman and the girl join together as one. And, oh, how the woman and girl reacted. Passion gusted in her chest, blasting warmth throughout her body, hastening her heart rate to a dizzying pace. In that moment, she *was* seventeen again, and nothing of her adult life corrupted what she had been at that tender age. There was only Wyatt, and the way he made her feel—the way he'd always made her feel. And there was heat. And there was hunger. And there was freedom to do whatever she wanted to do.

Reflexively, she tightened her hands on his shoulders and wound her legs around his thighs. She crowded her body against his, *opened* her body against his, and, with one slow, swaying motion, dragged herself up and over his torso, then down again, the erotic friction of having him against her almost more than she could abide. Wyatt growled something incoherent against her mouth, then dropped both hands to her bottom, tucking his fingers beneath the tight fabric of her suit, curling them against her taut flesh.

Eve gasped in response to the intimate touch, and he took advantage of her reaction by intensifying their kiss. He filled her mouth with his tongue, tasting her as thoroughly as he could, and she opened herself wider, inviting him to explore her more deeply still. The hands gripping her fanny tensed fiercely, sending a shock of fire straight to her belly. Eve pulled herself closer, rubbed her body languidly against his, and fought for possession of their kiss.

And then, just when the stakes were about as high as they could be without tumbling, just when she was beginning to believe that yes, maybe she and Wyatt could go back to where they'd fallen off track and start anew, just when she felt as if there was some hope for . . . Well, just when she felt as if there was some hope, Wyatt pushed her away.

Or maybe he pulled himself away—Eve wasn't entirely sure. In any event, when he released her and turned his back on her, she slipped down below the water, because she had nothing to hold on to for support, nothing to keep her from falling.

Immediately, she swept her arms down and pushed herself back to the surface, then swam alone as far as she needed to go in order to find sure footing. Wyatt began to swim, too, she noted, passing her without heed, until he reached the shallow end of the pool and pushed himself out. Water sluiced over his body, washing over his bare back and arms, puddling in a dark stain at his feet. But he kept his back turned to her, dragged his hands through his hair, holding them there, as if he didn't know what else to use them for.

And all Eve could do was think, *Not again. Please, Wyatt. Don't do this to me again.*

"Wyatt?" she called out softly, almost fearfully.

He went absolutely rigid at her appeal, his back stiffening, his head erect, his hands curling into fists as he dropped them to his sides. But he didn't turn around to look at her.

"Wyatt?" she tried again, more softly this time, more fearfully.

She thought he would leave then, without once looking back, just as he had left her that night twenty years ago. And indeed, he did take a single, silent step away from her, toward the gate. But he'd barely completed that step when he must have reconsidered, because slowly, he turned back around. His expression, though, offered no indication of what he might be feeling or thinking. Eve held her breath as she waited to hear what he would say, because she couldn't find her own voice to speak to him again.

He hooked his hands loosely on his hips and met her gaze, then told her, "That, um . . . That shouldn't have happened. I'm sorry. I had no right to . . . to . . ."

She squeezed her eyes shut tight, not wanting to hear any more. Maybe it would have been better if he *had* just walked silently away, she thought. Because the last thing she wanted to hear was that he was sorry.

"Don't," she told him. "Don't say another word."

"Eve, I—"

"Don't," she said again, more firmly this time.

"But you don't—"

"Don't you dare apologize to me. And don't even try to explain." Somehow, she managed to look him right in the eye when she added, "We'll just pretend this didn't happen. And you'll just stay away from me for the rest of the trip."

He inhaled a deep breath and expelled it slowly, but he never took his eyes off her face. "That's going to be a bit difficult, don't you think?" he asked. "The Expedition's not that big, and I promised your father—"

"That you'd show me a good time?" she finished sarcastically. "Thanks, Wyatt, but if this is the way you plan to go about it, don't bother."

"What I was going to say," he told her pointedly, "is that I promised your father I'd stay close to you. That I'd keep you safe."

"Fine," she conceded. "Stay close. Keep me *safe*. Just don't . . . don't . . ." Eve, too, curled her fingers into impotent fists, frustrated that she couldn't put into words the upheaval of emotion winding through her.

"Don't what?" he finally asked, his voice softening some. And, for some reason, that softening only made her that much angrier.

Instead of answering him, Eve turned her back on Wyatt this time. She took a few deep breaths to level off her ragged heart rate, then plunged back into the water as deeply as she could. And then she began to swim. Back and forth and back again, from one end of the pool to the other, over and over and over, until, finally, Wyatt left.

It was a good way to alleviate stress, she told herself, a good way to burn off excess energy.

Only when she didn't have the strength to continue

did she finally stop to rest. She was panting when she pulled herself out of the pool, near the table where Wyatt had set their drinks earlier. As she toweled herself off, she noticed that the light was still on in his room. And she noticed, too, that he'd taken the bottle of Scotch with him.

 *Nine*

The caustic *thump* for which Wyatt had been listening all morning—ever since he'd heard the slamming of Eve's door last night—was punctuated by an unbroken, and seemingly endless, echo of that thump. An echo that scored his brain with all the keenness of a knife blade being dragged just beneath his scalp. He sighed raggedly and tried not to look at the almost half-empty bottle of forty-two-year-old Scotch that sat on the nightstand near his head. He'd been so certain that liquor that fine and that old and that mellow would have the good manners and decency not to give him a hangover. Especially since he'd never quite fallen asleep.

My, but the lessons one learned as one traveled through life. You couldn't even trust premium Scotch to behave itself.

Now, hungover in spite of his complete lack of shut-eye—actually, that wasn't quite true, because he had, in fact, shut his eyes, but with the room spinning and lurching the way it had been, he'd been forced to open them again, but that really hadn't stopped the spinning and lurching, either, because it had just gone on and on and on, until he'd thought the bed would twirl right out the door and up into hyperspace, where the absence of oxygen would no doubt complete the job that the Scotch hadn't been able to accomplish, and . . . and . . . and . . .

Um, where was he? Oh, yeah.

Now, hungover in spite of his lack of slumber, every little sound Eve made in the room next door was amplified to an astronomic extent.

He knew exactly when she had awakened, because her telephone had rung with what Wyatt had guessed was a wake-up call—as shrilly as a mean drunk belting out "Misty"—at a few minutes after seven. He knew exactly when she had showered, because the water had come on in her bathroom—the water whistling through the pipes like all seven dwarfs performing "Wipe Out"—just before seven-thirty. And he knew exactly when she had finished packing her weekender, because the zipper had whisked down its track—buzzing like fifty billion hornets—shortly after eight. And he knew exactly when the taxi arrived, too, because the driver laid on the horn with all his might, bellowing louder than a pack of elephants on a crack cocaine high.

And he just barely managed to make it outside before Eve finished hauling her bags out of the Expedition, clearly intending to shove them into the waiting cab.

And, oh, *boy* was that sun bright when he opened his hotel room door . . .

"Eve," he called out weakly as he staggered over the threshold.

He was immediately forced to lift a hand to cover his eyes, because if he hadn't, the glaring sunlight would have burned out his retinas. Blindly, he extended his other hand forward and began to make his way, well, not exactly forward, but definitely in her general direction. He hoped. Unfortunately, just as he drew near, his bare foot made contact with a sharp piece of gravel—a really, *really* sharp piece of gravel—and he stumbled to his knees on the pavement, barely five feet away from her.

Well, hell. That wasn't going to do much to promote the I'm-the-one-in-charge-here-and-don't-you-forget-it speech that he was about to give her, was it?

Somehow, he found the means to shove himself back up to standing, and he was fairly sure he was almost convincingly nonchalant when he brushed a hand over his blue jeans and his green East Beach, Santa Barbara T-shirt. This time, instead of having to cover his eyes, Wyatt found that he could effectively squint—sort of—against the light. In doing so, he could just discern Eve's outline as she stood at the foot of the big Expedition, holding up the hatch with one hand. And she looked like she was . . . she was . . .

Wow. She looked incredible. Wyatt would bet good money that she had no idea just how transparent that dress was. Suddenly, his focus was very good indeed, and he was able to determine a few other details, as well. Like how she had her dark hair pulled into a ponytail high atop her head and bound with some gauzy material the same pale yellow as her sleeveless dress. And like how her face wasn't quite as pale this morning as it had been yesterday afternoon. And like how her brown eyes weren't quite as shadowed as they had been before.

And like how she looked very, *very* mad.

Before he could even open his mouth to get a word out—not that he had any idea what to say, except maybe "Ouch, my foot"—she stated, in no uncertain terms, "I'm flying to Cincinnati this morning, Wyatt. Don't try to stop me."

He sighed heavily. "Eve, we have to talk."

"I've already talked. Obviously you're not listening. So let me reiterate. I'm flying to Cincinnati this morning, Wyatt. Don't try to stop me."

He bit back a growl of discontent. "Fine. You've talked. Now it's my turn. Listen closely." He settled his hands on his hips and leaned his body forward as far as he dared—just shy of swinging distance. "You are *not* flying to Cincinnati this morning, Eve. I *will* stop you."

Instead of replying to Wyatt, she turned to the cabby, who had stepped out of his car and was approaching the couple. "You can start putting these bags in the trunk, please," she told him.

Wyatt, too, turned to the oncoming cabby. "Put any of those bags in the trunk," he told the man, "and I'll see to it personally that you're charged with aiding and abetting a felon."

"What?"

Surprisingly, the exclamation came not from the cabby but from Eve. Which, Wyatt supposed upon further reflection, maybe wasn't so surprising, after all. Nevertheless, he continued to focus on the other man as he spoke.

"This woman is wanted in five states for committing a string of nefarious felonies."

The cabby stopped dead in his tracks, his mouth

dropping open in astonishment. He glanced at Eve—
Wyatt could tell immediately that he was surprised by
the transparency of her dress, too; someone really
should throw a rug over her—then back at Wyatt.

"You'd never know it to look at her, would you?"
Wyatt asked. "She seems so innocent, doesn't she? But
I assure you, she's responsible for crimes so depraved,
so vile, so . . . you know . . . nefarious, that I can't even
begin to tell you about them, because I swore a
solemn oath of silence to the FBI's ultra-secret Special
Nefarious Crimes Unit, of which I am a card-carrying
member."

"If you're a card-carrying member," Eve said
blandly, "then why don't you show us your card?"

"I can't. I told you—it's ultra-secret," Wyatt replied.
Hastily, because the cabby didn't appear to believe
him—go figure—he added, "If I described for you the
crimes that she's committed, you'd never be able to
live your life happily again. You might even have to be
institutionalized, once you got knowledge like that
stuck in your head. I mean, what she did to those innocent little chipmunks . . ." He shuddered for effect.
"No warm-blooded animal should have to go through
that, you know? She's pure evil, man. You don't want
to get too close."

"Wyatt . . ." The warning in Eve's voice was quite,
quite clear, but he didn't back down an inch. Why
should he? She was totally harmless.

Obviously, the cabby was beginning to doubt that,
though, because he took a step backward, toward his
car. For one brief moment, Wyatt thought he was
going to reconsider, was going to risk the same fate as
the chipmunks, just to get his fare. But something
must have given him second thoughts—better safe

than sorry, after all—and he completed another step back to his car. Then another. And another. And another. And then he was gunning the engine to life and lurching out of the parking lot with tires squealing and without a backward glance.

Which left Wyatt alone with pure—and nefarious— evil, he thought, turning his attention back to Eve. And gosh, she was awful cute. He hated to say it, but she was beautiful when she was angry.

"What those innocent little chipmunks suffered," she said evenly, "is *nothing* compared to what I'm going to do to you. You want nefarious, Wyatt . . ."

He wiggled his eyebrows playfully. At least, he hoped it was playful. And he hoped it was a wiggle. His head was still kind of numb from the Scotch. "Don't keep me waiting too long," he told her.

She narrowed her eyes at him but said nothing. Too busy plotting, he supposed.

Without further comment, he made his way—more carefully this time, to avoid really, *really* sharp gravel— toward her luggage and, one by one, tossed each piece back into the Expedition. Then he slammed the hatch shut, locked it, and turned around to meet her gaze again.

"I have to shower and pack, and then we can go," he said.

"Fine," she retorted shortly. "Shower and pack."

"And while I'm showering, you can sit in the bathroom with me and sing 'Oh, Susannah' at the top of your lungs."

"I beg your pardon?"

He rubbed a hand restlessly over his face. "Funnily enough, Eve, I don't trust you not to go running off with the first Tom, Dick or Cabby who comes along, the minute I turn my back on you. Go figure."

She gaped at him. "*You* don't trust *me*? That's a laugh."

He gaped right back. "Oh, and what have I done that might make you mistrust me?" he demanded.

"Gee, let me think a minute," she said. "Well, there is that kidnapping business, for one."

Oh, fine. She would bring that up again. But all he said was, "Don't tell me you're going to hold a little thing like kidnapping against me."

"And the reason I shouldn't hold that against you would be . . . ?"

"Oh, come on. What's a little abduction between friends?"

"We are not friends."

Well, he certainly couldn't argue with her there. He couldn't say what, exactly, they were, but *friends* sure didn't feel like the right word to use for whatever it was. In spite of that, he asked, "Then what are we?"

She hesitated before answering him. For some reason, he took that to be a good sign. Until she finally told him, "Archenemies, Wyatt. That's what we are. Antagonists, adversaries, antitheses—"

"I get the picture," he interrupted.

"Oh, hey, I'm not even out of the As yet," she assured him. "Good thing we have a long drive ahead of us."

"Okay, okay," he finally relented. "You don't have to sing 'Oh, Susannah' if you don't want to. If you'd rather perform something from the Beatles songbook, that would probably be better anyway. For both of us."

She expelled an impatient sound. "I'm not going to sit in your bathroom and sing to you while you shower, Wyatt."

He shrugged. "Suits me. I just hope you don't mind

being stuck with one stinky guy in one very small truck cab for the rest of the day."

She eyed him thoughtfully for a moment. "Okay, fine. I'll sing." Then she smiled, a cruel, relentless little smile. "I just hope you like Barry Manilow."

Ooo, that was *so* harsh, Wyatt thought. Still, he supposed he had it coming. "If you must," he muttered distastefully.

"I must."

"Fine."

"And one more thing, Wyatt."

"What's that?"

"We are *not* going to visit the Grand Canyon today. The sooner we get to Cincinnati, the better."

That, of course, was what he'd been afraid she would say. Not that he was looking forward to a donkey ride down into the canyon in his current condition, anyway. In fact, he'd pretty much felt like he was riding a donkey—or something equally bristly, bad-tempered, and unpleasant—since he'd rolled out of bed that morning. And he was fairly certain that the real thing wouldn't come close to making him feel as twitchy and queasy as he did right now.

But before he could say anything in response to Eve's assertion—either agreeing or disagreeing with it—she continued, "From here on out, we're not stopping for anything except sleep and food. You want to show me a good time, Wyatt? Then get me back to Cincinnati. And then, when we get there, you can leave me *alone*."

For some reason, hearing the song "Mandy" being screamed at the top of Eve's lungs reminded Wyatt way too much of what had happened in the wee hours of that morning. Probably, he thought, it was the pain factor. Listening to her screeching right now was almost—but not quite—as agonizing as the feelings that had plagued him upon returning to his room after their . . . whatever it had been . . . out in the pool.

He still couldn't figure out what had come over him to make him kiss her the way he had. She had just looked so beautiful and tempting, and she had felt so good to touch, and he simply had not been able to help himself. And after that first, experimental contact, after that initial brush of his lips against hers, he hadn't been able to stop himself. She'd tasted sweet and fresh and innocent, just as she had tasted that day in the hallway of Woodhaven High School twenty years ago. And Wyatt had reacted exactly the same way he had back then.

Well, okay, not *exactly* the same way, he admitted reluctantly. And that was where the agonizing part came in. Because as he had deepened the kiss, as Eve had opened herself so freely to him, as she had returned his passion with equal fire, and equal demand, he'd felt his heart rate skyrocket and his good sense plummet. And he'd felt heat and need and hunger, and a riot of other emotions too tentative and elusive to name. Unfortunately, what he hadn't felt was . . .

Well. He hadn't felt any kind of . . . physical action below the waist.

He'd tried to tell himself it was because the water was so matriarch-fricking cold. He'd tried to remind himself that sometimes it took a while for a man to . . . you know. Get fired up. Even though it had never taken him a while before—except for prom night, anyway. But he hadn't succeeded in convincing himself that either of those things was responsible for his appalling state of non-arousal. In fact, the moment Wyatt had realized what was happening again—or, more correctly, what *wasn't* happening again—he'd just . . . panicked. And panicking had done nothing to help rectify the situation. In fact, panicking had only compounded the problem. Especially since it had been that panic that had caused him to turn away from Eve.

He squeezed his eyes shut tight and ground his teeth together hard. Not because Eve had executed an unsuccessful segue from "Mandy" to "Copa Cabana" just then, but because Wyatt remembered all too well the expression on her face when he had pushed her away the night before. It had been the same expression she'd had on her face on prom night. And her voice last night when she'd called out his name had been every bit as plaintive as it had that other night.

For twenty years, the mournful echo of her voice had rolled around in his head, calling out to him as it had when he'd walked away from Stuart Tucker's car that night. Last night, that memory had stopped being a memory—it had become a reality once again. And Wyatt was no better equipped to deal with her anguish today than he had been then. When she'd uttered his name last night, he'd been hurtled two decades back in time, feeling like the confused eighteen-year-old boy who hadn't known what he was supposed to do. It had been bad enough being that boy once. He sure as hell didn't want to be him again. Especially not when he was a thirty-eight-year-old man who ought to know—and feel—better.

But that was exactly how Eve had made him feel last night. And that was why he had turned his back on her—both literally and figuratively.

Oh, God. How could he ever offer her an adequate apology for that? He hadn't even been able to explain his actions for what had happened that first time—not that Eve had ever asked for an explanation, then or now, something that still kind of surprised him. But even if he somehow managed to explain that first episode—"I was a stupid kid, Eve, what can I say?"— how could he excuse his behavior for this more recent one? "I was a stupid adult, Eve, what can I say?"

Somehow, he didn't think that would be quite satisfactory. Not for what he had done to her twenty years ago, and certainly not for what he had done to her last night.

So Wyatt said nothing at all. Hell, what could he say that wouldn't make things worse than they already were? Not that Eve wanted to talk to him anyway. Not that he could blame her for that.

He blew out an exasperated breath as he ducked his head under the shower again, feeling grateful that the rush of water overrode Eve's new segue from "Copa Cabana" to "Could This Be the Magic?" One thing was certain, he decided right then. There was no way he could allow himself to get as close to her again as he had last night. But there was no way he could leave her alone. Not along the way. And not once they arrived in Cincinnati, either. He still wasn't convinced of Luther's insistence that Eve was in danger back in Ohio, but Wyatt didn't want to take any chances. Then again, when he got right down to it, that wasn't why he wanted to stay close to Eve anyway.

It was going to be a long trip home.

Eve's tension eased a little once they left the Canyon Vista Motor Lodge, partly because she had convinced

Wyatt to let her drive—something she hoped would take her mind off other things—but mostly because he fell asleep in the passenger seat before they'd even cleared the Flagstaff city limits. Still, it was only when she heard a soft snore erupt from his side of the SUV, when she knew he was fully unconscious, that she was finally, finally, able to relax.

Until she remembered—yet again—what had happened during the night.

For perhaps the hundredth time, she tried to convince herself that her embrace with Wyatt in the pool had been nothing but a dream. A wild, wanton—and okay, wet—dream, to be sure, but a dream nonetheless. Unfortunately, she was no more able to convince herself of that now, in the broad light of day, than she'd been able to convince herself of it under cover of darkness in the wee hours of the morning.

Wyatt *had* kissed her last night. He had settled his hands on her waist, he had pulled her close, he had bent his head to hers, and he had kissed her. *He* had done all those things. Actively. Purposefully. Intentionally. Certainly Eve had been a willing participant, but *he* had been the one who had instigated everything. And *he* had been the one who had ended it, too. And just as before, none of it made any sense.

But then, that was Wyatt, she thought. If ever there was a senseless human being . . .

She glanced over at him, finding him slumped beneath his seat belt, his eyes closed, his dark lashes spanning the shadows beneath. He'd crossed his arms over his chest, had stretched his legs out before him as far as the cab of the SUV would allow, had leaned his head against the window. He smelled like Ivory soap and men's shampoo and Wyatt. She smiled. Even after twenty years, something of his scent was familiar to her.

And he wasn't senseless, she told herself. In spite of everything, she still thought he was a good guy. He was just a good guy she couldn't figure out.

He looked so harmless when he was asleep, she thought, reluctantly returning her attention to the highway. He looked like some regular guy who wouldn't intentionally hurt anyone to save his life. And probably, he hadn't *intended* to hurt her, she conceded. But the realization of that offered nothing to ease the pain of what had happened last night.

One thing was certain, though. Eve would *not* put herself in the position of being rejected by him again. Clearly, Wyatt was no more able to figure out what had always burned up the air between them than Eve was. Clearly, they both confounded and confused each other now as badly as they had before. Clearly, there was no more point in pursuing their bizarre relationship today than there had been back in high school.

Clearly, the situation was as hopeless now as it had been back then.

Eve drove in silence for some time emptying her mind, becoming fascinated by the speed and elegance with which the white wisps of cloud scooted across the blue, blue sky. The landscape was striking in its simplicity, the black ribbon of highway bisecting high desert plains that were studded by magnificent, rocky plateaus. It was unlike any panorama she had ever seen before, and she drank it in thirstily, as if she might never see anything like it again. She'd noted on the map earlier that they would be passing through a petrified forest further ahead, and she anticipated the sight with the same sort of enchantment that would enthrall a child.

Thirty-seven years old, she thought. And she could still get excited over something like scenery. All in all, she decided with a smile, that wasn't such a bad thing. Maybe there was hope for her yet.

She drove without incident, her mind wandering freely over things of no consequence at all, recalling half-remembered snatches of her life in Cincinnati, wondering how much the place had changed, curious as to how Simone was faring with the inimitable Mr. Julian Varga. That last, especially, was a burr of curiosity that wedged itself into her brain. Although her sister would never have admitted it, to Eve or anyone else, Simone the unruffled had been more than a little agitated by Mr. Varga back in Santa Barbara. And Mr. Varga, who seemed to be equally unruffled, had been no less bothered by Simone.

By week's end, Eve thought with a smile, the two of them were probably going to be pretty ruffled.

She heard Wyatt stirring then, and she spared a glance at him, only to find that he was awake. His eyes were heavy-lidded, at half-mast even, but his gaze was trained levelly on her. Eve pretended not to notice, pretended not to be affected, and went back to driving in silence.

"What are you thinking about?" he asked softly.

"I'm wondering how much longer 'til we get there," she lied.

"It won't be today," he told her.

"Well, I did sort of figure that."

"You might as well try to enjoy the ride."

"I would, if the company weren't so disagreeable."

He said nothing in response to that, although she sensed that he wanted to. In an effort to keep him from talking about something she didn't want to talk about, she quickly pitched into a different line of questioning. "So what's the story with you and Julian Varga?"

"Why do you want to know?"

She shrugged, feigning nonchalance. "You said you met him in jail. He's currently with my sister. I want to be sure she's safe with him."

"No worries there," Wyatt promised her. "Julian is the most trustworthy guy I've ever met."

"And you meet a lot of trustworthy people in jail, do you?" she asked pointedly.

"Actually, Julian is the only person I've ever met in jail."

"Gee, that's quite the testimonial for Mr. Varga," Eve said dryly. "Not to mention for you yourself."

Wyatt expelled a resigned sigh. "Look, I've known Julian for four years, Eve. He's a good guy."

"Then what was he doing in jail?" she asked. "For that matter, what were *you* doing in jail? Not that I can't hazard a few guesses."

"And none of your guesses would come close to the truth," he said indignantly. "For your information, I was only in jail because I, um . . . sent a chair through a barroom window. Accidentally," he tacked on as an obvious afterthought.

"Mm," Eve said without looking over at him. "Actually, that's not so far from one of my guesses at all. Except that I figured there would have been someone sitting in the chair when it went through the window."

"There was no one sitting in the chair when I sent it through the window. Accidentally, I mean."

"No?"

"No. The guy fell out of the chair before I picked it up."

"And did he have any help falling out of the chair?" she asked sweetly.

"Maybe. A little."

"Like maybe he was pushed?"

"Maybe."

"By someone's fist perhaps?"

"Could be. My memory's not so clear."

"I see."

"Hey, the guy had been bothering one of the waitresses, shoving her around," Wyatt said. "He deserved to accidentally fall out of a chair after maybe being pushed a little by perhaps someone's fist. If his friend hadn't, you know, beat the hell out of me just then, I would've sent the guy through the window, too, right after his chair."

Eve decided not to comment on that. Not just because she didn't want to think about anyone beating the hell out of Wyatt, but because she didn't want to think of him defending another woman's honor—a stranger, no less—when he'd pretty much walked away from hers.

"And why was Mr. Varga in jail?" she asked instead. "Was he part of the scuffle?"

"Actually, it wasn't so much a scuffle as it was a vicious, bloody fistfight," Wyatt told her.

"But you were going to tell me what Mr. Varga was doing in jail, weren't you?" Eve asked again.

"Right," Wyatt concurred. "I forgot. Julian was in

jail because a judge found him in contempt of court and had him put there until he was . . . um, less contemptible, I guess."

"Oh. Well. That's . . . interesting."

"He refused to testify against some woman friend of his who'd been charged with her husband's murder," Wyatt clarified.

Like that clarified anything, Eve thought. "A woman friend," she repeated dubiously. "Accused of her husband's murder. That, uh, that doesn't sound good, Wyatt."

"Julian knew she was innocent, but I guess things did look bad for her at that point," Wyatt agreed. "Anyway, she wound up going free the very next day, because some other evidence came to light that made it clear her husband's business partner committed the crime. And then they let Julian out of jail."

"And what happened to the woman friend?"

"I don't know. But she didn't take up with Julian, if that's what you're asking."

"That's what I'm asking."

She heard Wyatt chuckle. "Julian doesn't have a wife and kids stashed somewhere, in case you're worried that Simone will lose her heart to some two-timing jerk."

"Actually, I'm not worried about that," Eve said. Simone, after all, was saving herself for Blond Brian Richie. "I just want to make sure the guy has scruples, that's all."

"Oh, scruples. Listen, Julian is the safest, most decent guy I know. He's big on taking care of himself and other people. He doesn't sleep around. He eats all that healthy crap and works out regularly. He rarely drinks, he doesn't smoke, he doesn't raise hell."

"So how did the two of you get to be friends?" she asked. "It doesn't sound like you have a lot in common. I mean, when was the last time *you* were in a gym?"

"Hey, I've been in a gym recently," he retorted petulantly. "A couple of years ago, as a matter of fact. I was there to pick up my girlfriend."

Eve's knowing smile fell. "Oh."

Well, what had she expected? she asked herself. She didn't honestly think Wyatt had been celibate all these years, did she? Of course there would have been women in his life—probably quite a few of them. He was a handsome, charming, eligible man who could make people laugh. What woman wouldn't be drawn to him?

"It was a long time ago," he said, as if he were picking up on her thoughts. Then, of course, she realized he was speaking about Julian. "I can't remember what got me and Julian started talking that night, but we realized we had some friends in common. One thing led to another, and within a few months, we were going into business together."

"He's from Cincinnati originally then?" Eve asked, genuinely curious about the man now. She'd sensed the strange friction between Julian and Simone back in Santa Barbara, but when she'd asked her sister about it, Simone had deftly changed the subject. Eve hadn't pried any further. She'd learned when they were kids that once Simone clammed up, she didn't open again until she was ready—if she ever opened again at all.

"You know, I don't really know where he grew up," Wyatt said thoughtfully, sounding a little surprised, as if he just now realized he didn't have that information. "I'm not even sure he has any family. Or where he went to college. Or even if he *did* go to college. Julian doesn't talk about himself a lot."

"Sounds like he doesn't talk about himself at all," Eve observed.

"Hm. I guess he doesn't." Once again Wyatt's voice was thoughtful, edged with surprise.

"Yet you claim you know him well."

"I do know him well."

"But—"

"I know what's important about Julian, Eve. And Simone is perfectly safe with him. Trust me."

Oh, sure. Like she was dumb enough to do *that*.

Still, something told her that her sister was indeed in good hands with Julian Varga. Eve just hoped his presence didn't cramp Simone's style when it came time for her to bag Blond Brian. That could create some turbulence. To put it mildly.

Neither of them said a word after that, and after a while, Eve heard another one of those soft, muffled snores, indicating that Wyatt had drifted back to sleep. She wondered if he'd slept any more last night than she had. Probably neither one of them was fit to drive any great distance today. Might not hurt to stop early for the night. Of course, that would just make their arrival in Cincinnati take that much longer . . .

She bit back a yawn and drove on in silence until she just couldn't stand the quiet any longer. Switching on the radio, she left the volume low, then spun the dial slowly until she heard the pull of a DJ's mellow voice.

"Comin' up in just a few minutes, we've got an oldie

but goodie from Pat Benatar. 'We Belong Together.' Hope you stay with us. 'Cause we've got a totally eighties Monday comin' atcha."

Stifling a groan, Eve spun the dial again. And she wondered how long until they got there.

Ten

Julian rattled open the sports section of the *Cincinnati Enquirer*, set his orange juice back down on the table, and watched unobtrusively as Simone Van Dormer daintily lifted her teacup for a sip of decaffeinated green tea. And more than anything in the whole, wide world, he wanted to calmly stand, calmly circle the table, and calmly pull her out of her chair. Then he wanted to calmly slip her robe from her shoulders and calmly tug her nightgown up over her head. Then he wanted to calmly bend her forward over the table, calmly unzip his pants, and not-so-calmly have his way with her naked body from behind. Over and over and over again, as many times as he could.

He squeezed his eyes shut tight and tried to expel the graphic vision from his brain. But the more he tried to erase it, the more vivid it became. He could almost feel the lush plumpness of her breast filling one hand, her nipple caught between index and middle fingers as he pressed himself harder against her. He could practically taste the sweet heat of her naked flesh as he dragged the tip of his tongue over her bare back and shoulder. He could almost smell the heavy, narcotic scent of her unrepentant response as he fingered the damp folds of flesh between her legs. And he could practically hear her panting his name, begging him to *please, please, please, Julian, please don't ever stop* as he thrust himself into her, over and over and over again, as many times as he could.

Why he should keep experiencing such a fantasy— and with such clarity, too—was beyond him. It wasn't like she'd offered even the tiniest bit of encouragement, or even the tiniest bit of interest, for that matter. On the contrary, she'd barely acknowledged his presence since their arrival at the hotel Sunday night. And even if she had offered some vague indication that she might be responsive to partaking in such an activity with him—hah, what a laugh—it wasn't like he would ever do it.

Hell, he wasn't sure he even *liked* her. He couldn't understand it. It had been a long damned time since he'd experienced such an immediate and intense physical reaction to a woman. These days, Julian wasn't like most men, a fact of which he was proud. He wanted—needed—some kind of emotional commitment from a woman before he would even consider becoming sexually involved with her. He was no longer the type to engage in idle sex simply because his body happened to demand it. Nowadays, his body didn't demand it until after his mind, his spirit, and his psyche did.

All right, so it hadn't always been that way, he conceded reluctantly. There had been a time in his life, years ago, when he'd been almost insatiable when it had come to women. There had been a reason for that, he had to admit now, though not a very good one. But he'd been unable to resist the rampant temptation that had suddenly surrounded him after being all but invisible to the opposite sex for so long. By the time Julian entered his twenties, he'd been smart, good-looking, and randy as hell. And he'd been the shy, quiet type at first, too, making him a package that many women evidently found impossible to resist. So Julian hadn't bothered to resist, either. He'd taken them up on whatever they'd had to offer.

And oh, how some women had offered. And oh, how he'd taken those women. Over and over and over again, as many times as he could.

But those days were over, he reminded himself now. He'd had his fun, and he'd gotten more than he'd bargained for in the process. These days, he was in control of his life, his libido, himself. At least he had been. Until Simone Van Dormer had come along. And with Simone Van Dormer . . .

He wanted her *now*. Physically. Primitively. Profoundly.

He wondered how she felt about sex herself, whether she shared his current opinion of its sanctity, or if she could blithely copulate with whomever she might find attractive. He wondered how many lovers she'd had, or if she'd had any at all. He wondered if she was as pure and innocent as so many things about her suggested, or if her purity and innocence were just a facade.

He recalled her bedroom back at The Keep, with its girlish furnishings and accessories, recalled how she favored fashions of pastel colors and tiny flower prints. And he recalled, too, that she wore no under-wear beneath those fashions, something that kind of played havoc with the pure and innocent thing. Nevertheless, there was something about her that gave her the appearance of being untouched. Untried. Untainted.

And realizing that just stimulated Julian's bent-over-the-table fantasy again, with all the velocity and ferocity of a massive steam engine speeding through a damp, dark tunnel. Over and over and over again, as many times as it could.

He forced the image away and strove for cleaner, purer thoughts. But instead of cleanliness and purity, he found himself reflecting upon how the last thirty-six hours had been pure hell. Simone had barely spoken a word to him since they'd checked in—or, to pinpoint the time more accurately, since he had told her of the change in sleeping arrangements, whether she liked it or not. And his back hurt like hell from having to occupy the sofa-sleeper in the main salon of their suite. *Their* suite? he echoed dubiously to himself. Oh, there was no question that this was *her* suite. *He* was an interloper here. And she hadn't let him forget it.

She sipped her tea again, then set it down to turn the page of the main section of the paper, which she had claimed without preamble—or without asking—the moment it had arrived with their breakfast. And she appeared to be intent on reading, Julian noted, every last word of every last article printed there.

He folded up the sports section and slapped it down on the table with more force than he had intended. Simone, he noticed, noticed. She glanced over the top of the newspaper for one brief, frosty moment, then she glanced back down again.

Wow, he thought. That was the most attention she'd paid him since their arrival. She must be coming around.

Between them lay the remnants of their breakfast—fresh fruit, fresh breads, freshly squeezed orange juice, fresh tea. He supposed he should be grateful they had *some*thing in common—namely, a concern for their own health and well-being. Like Julian, Simone didn't smoke, didn't drink, and she'd visited the health club adjacent to the hotel yesterday afternoon. Beyond those qualities, however, they seemed to be miles apart.

Although he himself had showered and dressed nearly an hour ago after running two miles on the track in the adjacent health club, Simone still sat contentedly in her nightgown and robe, a matching set of garments made of chaste white cotton trimmed with chaste white lace, a fabric that draped itself over every last luscious inch of her. Her hair was fastened in a loose knot atop her head, held in place by some invisible means of support, a few errant, wispy strands framing her face and lingering over her nape. Her feet were bare, her toenails painted lavender, something that Julian found to be very, *very* sexy.

To a casual observer, they might be a happily married couple enjoying breakfast in their excessively costly hotel suite. Except, of course, for the fact that the temperature around them hovered somewhere between the witch's, um, bosom setting and the ninth circle of hell setting. Oh, but, hey, other than that . . .

"I'll be going out today," she said suddenly, her gaze still fixed on the newspaper.

It was a fairly monumental event, as far as Julian was concerned. She'd spoken *five* whole words to him.

In a row. And *two* of them had even been polysyllabic. She was definitely coming around.

"Where?" he asked.

"Woodhaven."

Well, now, there was an answer he hadn't expected at all. "May I ask why?"

"You may."

When nothing more was forthcoming, he swallowed an expletive and ground out, "Why?"

"You'll find out when we get there."

Gosh, Julian couldn't wait. He was just quivering with curiosity thinking about it. "You sure I won't be a millstone around your neck?" he asked sarcastically.

"Oh, I don't doubt for a moment that you'll be a millstone around my neck," she promptly replied. "But I also don't doubt for a moment that you'll be staying with me all day like some rancid piece of meat I might have consumed for dinner last night. So I have no choice but to take you with me, have I? I might as well make the best of it."

And this is the best she can make of it? Julian wondered.

"Gee, Miss Van Dormer," he said blandly, "keep sweet-talking me like that, and I'm going to start thinking you've got a big ol' crush on me."

She closed the main section, folded it neatly, and placed it on the table. "That's highly unlikely," she said without looking at him.

He smacked his forehead lightly. "Oh, that's right. You're all keen to replace some guy's dead wife, whom he's loved since childhood. I keep forgetting that."

Wow. That got her attention. She stood up so quickly that her chair went toppling backward. But she ignored it, choosing to focus on Julian instead. "You have no idea what I'm keen to do, *Mr.* Varga."

So they were back to that emphatic *Mr.* business again, were they? Hey, that suited Julian just fine. "Judging by your expression and tone of voice, *Miss Van Dormer*," he said, "at the moment, you're keen on murdering someone." And he'd lay good odds that he knew just who that someone was.

She smiled coolly. "Well, well, well. Maybe you do have an idea after all."

And something about the way she said that made every hair he possessed stand right on end. The lady was good at issuing threats. He'd certainly give her that.

"I'll be ready to leave in twenty minutes," she ordained as she turned toward the circular stairs that led up to her bedroom. "Bring the car around, Mr. Varga, will you?"

It was only with great restraint that Julian kept himself from picking up a butter spreader and flinging it at her retreating back. Nevertheless, he couldn't keep himself from muttering, not quite under his breath, "Yes, Your Majesty. Whatever you say."

Simone called herself every nasty epithet she could think of as she plucked the last of the bobby pins from her hair and remembered how badly she had just treated Julian. Then she awarded herself a few more bad names while she dragged a brush—using more force than was necessary—through the tangled tresses. Then she invented a few new names to apply to herself as she tugged a sleeveless, pale lavender sheath over her otherwise naked body. And then she added one or two more disagreeable designations to her person as she slipped her feet into sandals. She concluded by assuring herself she was a Very Mean Person—the

most heinous accusation she could hurl at anyone—
because that was exactly how she felt.

But she didn't know of any other way to act around
Julian. There was just something about him that—she
might as well admit it—scared her. From that first
night in her father's study, he'd roused feelings in her
she hadn't understood, feelings that had startled her,
frightened her, because they'd been so immediate, and
so intense, and had seemed to hit her blindside. She
was attracted to him, certainly, that much she knew.
But there was something about the attraction that she
didn't understand, because it was like nothing she had
ever experienced before.

And he'd rattled her when she'd first run into him
that morning, in a way that had left her feeling oddly
off-kilter ever since. Only once before in her life had
Simone been rattled, and she hadn't liked it then,
either. That was twice in one lifetime. There was no
way she was going to allow this rattling business to
become a habit.

She inhaled a shaky breath and closed her eyes,
struggling to find her center of serenity, the one deep
inside her that she had cultivated all of her adult life.
But that center eluded her now. In its place, she found
the memory of Julian Varga, the way she had seen him
when she'd gone down for breakfast that morning.
Again, she felt rattled. Again, she felt confused. Again,
she felt frightened.

She had expected to be alone when she'd gone
downstairs, even though that part of the suite had
been half-lit. It had been so early, after all, and Julian
had spent nearly two hours at the adjacent health club
before breakfast yesterday morning. But today, he'd
returned earlier for some reason. And when Simone

had rounded the curve in the curling stairway, she'd seen him emerging amid a plume of steam from the bathroom, like some great ocean god about to part the seas. He'd been stripped to the waist, still damp from his shower, his only adornment a thick, white towel knotted loosely on one hip.

He hadn't sensed her presence, and Simone had found it impossible to drag her gaze away from him. Instead, she had backed up a few steps so that she could peek around the curve of the stairwell, and she had watched him. Intently.

Unaware that he was being spied upon, Julian had strode to the bureau to withdraw a pair of blue jeans and a crew neck shirt the color of a pewter coin, along with a pair of briefs and socks. He'd strolled to the television set and palmed the remote control, turned it on, adjusted the volume, and pushed the channel button until he located CNN. His body had moved leisurely, gracefully, as if there were a symphony playing somewhere that only Julian could hear. Muscles had purled poetically in his back, his shoulders, his forearms, his legs.

Simone had never seen a man move that way, so confidently, so casually, so elegantly. And she had never observed one moving about without clothing to hinder his progress. The play of easy, self-assured motion had fascinated her. She'd been captivated by the simplicity and facility of it. And she'd liked it that a man could feel so comfortable in his own skin. She'd liked it even more that she could feel comfortable watching him. And just as those revelations had formed in her head, Julian had—

Well. He had unhitched the towel from his waist

and tossed it carelessly aside. And, fully naked, he had turned around to put on his clothes.

Simone closed her eyes now as heat washed over her again, recalling her brief glimpse of his body, completely naked, offering a view of full frontal—and full backal—nudity. He had been glorious in his nakedness, more beautiful than anything she had ever seen. So beautiful that she had scarcely been able to tolerate the sight. She had scrambled back up the stairs to her own room as quickly as she could, and she'd fled to her bathroom, locking the door, leaning back against it to catch her breath. Her reaction to Julian had been so fierce and unexpected, and her heart had raced so rapidly, that she'd grown dizzy from the rush of blood. And rattled. Good God, she'd been rattled.

She still wasn't sure if she'd ever feel steady again. Certainly she wouldn't as long as the vision of Julian Varga—naked Julian Varga—was tumbling around in her brain. And she was fairly certain that vision was going to remain a permanent fixture in her head, whether she liked it or not. Strangely, though, she found that she did like it. In fact, she rather liked it a lot.

And, likewise strangely, she rather liked the coil of excitement that scrolled through her body upon recalling that vision. She even liked the way her body grew warm and damp at the recollection, in places she hadn't known could experience such change. Whatever it was that Julian Varga made her feel—and Simone was still hard-pressed to identify what, precisely, that was—it wasn't, on second thought, such a terrible thing. Not as terrible as she might have thought it would be.

Though it most definitely played havoc with her plans for Blond Brian Richie.

Which, now that she thought more about it, might be the true root of her foul temper this morning. Her plans weren't going according to plan. And if there was one thing Simone disliked intensely—even more than losing her center of serenity—it was having her plans not go according to plan.

She sighed heavily. She would just have to focus more intently on the real reason she had returned to Cincinnati. For Brian. She could not—would not—let anything interfere with that. Not even a Greek-god piece of artwork named Julian Varga, who made her body respond in ways she had never thought it could respond.

Brian, she repeated adamantly to herself. Not Julian. Her focus now was trained intently on the former. So with one final, fortifying breath, Simone headed downstairs to meet the latter. And she tried not to think about what an exceptional *body* her *guard* had.

Julian wasn't surprised to discover that Simone Van Dormer knew where Brian Richie worked, in one of downtown Cincinnati's older, sophisticated high-rises. What did surprise him was that she knew Brian would leave that building at precisely twelve, noon. What surprised him even more was that she knew he would drive north on I-75 in his silver Jaguar sedan, to meet an associate for lunch at a bustling eatery in Sharonville. But that was exactly what Brian—and, consequently, Julian and Simone—did.

Even more surprisingly, Simone asked Julian to hang back a bit as they drove, to give Brian a good lead that would enable him to meet his associate and get settled at his table before she and Julian arrived on the scene. And she told him not to worry—that they, like Brian, had a reservation for lunch, thereby guaranteeing them a table. A table, however, wasn't what concerned Julian at the moment. What did concern him was how Simone Van Dormer seemed to be taking on all the qualities of a stalker.

His curiosity finally got the better of him as he pulled the big Town Car into one of the few parking spots left at the restaurant. Before Simone had a chance to open the door and get out, Julian turned toward her, stretching his arm along the back of the seat, resting it lightly on her shoulder, to prevent her flight. The moment his fingers made contact with her bare skin, however, she angled her body away from his touch without comment. Her expression, however, was inquisitive.

He pretended not to notice her withdrawal and asked, "How did you know Brian Richie would be coming here?"

"I have my ways," she told him.

"And they would include . . . ?"

She eyed him levelly. "I may not have lived in Cincinnati for a long time, Mr. Varga, but that doesn't mean I don't still have friends here."

"And one of those friends works with Brian Richie?"

"You could say that."

"Or I could say something else?"

"We have a reservation," she reminded him pointedly, opening her door to get out.

Julian relented—for now—and followed her to the entrance, trying really, really hard not to let his gaze rove over the tasty curves of her naked-beneath-the-thin-fabric-of-that-dress fanny. Or, at least, trying really, really hard to make sure she didn't *catch* him letting his gaze rove over the tasty curves of her naked-beneath-the-thin-fabric-of-that-dress fanny. Whatever. In any case, neither of them spoke to the other again until they had been seated at their table, a table that was located—surprise, surprise—only two tables away from the blond, the blue-eyed, the All-American . . . Brian.

Damn the man.

Julian pretended to study the menu their server unfolded in front of him, but his attention was trained fully on Simone, who was seated—what a shocker—facing Brian Richie. He'd expected her to be focused on Brian, but so far she hadn't even spared a glance in the man's direction. It made no sense. For all the trouble she'd gone to to ensure the proper arrangements, she acted like she couldn't care less about the object of her affections. Or, rather, the object of her stalking. Whatever.

That wasn't, however, the case with the stalkee, as became evident almost immediately.

Because no sooner had Julian observed Simone's lack of interest in Brian Richie than Brian Richie himself appeared at their table. In fact, so swift and intense was the man's appearance that it frankly gave Julian the creeps.

Gee. Nice to know Brian and Simone had something in common.

"Simone?" the other man asked in a voice of obviously delighted surprise. "Simone Van Dormer? Is that you?"

Instead of turning his attention to Brian, Julian watched Simone's reaction. Had he not known better, he would have thought she honestly didn't recognize the man she had traveled two thousand miles to see. For a moment, she only gazed at him with her brow furrowed, as if she were struggling very hard to identify who he was. Then, finally, her expression cleared, and she smiled.

"Brian Richie," she said, sounding as if she were genuinely—and pleasantly—astonished to see him. "Well, my goodness. What a surprise."

"I could say the same thing myself," he rejoined easily, his own smile dazzling—and not a little smarmy, Julian thought. "My God, how long has it been?" he asked. He immediately answered his own question, though. "Twenty years, isn't it?"

"Almost to the day," she agreed. She closed her menu, curled her fingers beneath her chin, and gave him her full, undivided attention.

Damn the woman.

"That's right," he said with another one of those oily grins. "The last time we saw each other was the night of the senior prom, wasn't it? Your family moved shortly after that."

"You remember our last meeting," she murmured. "I'm flattered."

This time Brian's smile was less smarmy and more . . . Julian ground his teeth together hard. Lascivious, that's what his smile was now.

Damn the man.

"Remember it?" he echoed incredulously. "How could I forget? We had a good time that night, didn't we, Simone?"

"The best," she concurred softly.

A *very* meaningful silence followed—at least, Julian figured it was meaningful to *them*, even if he himself had no idea what it meant—until he began to grow uncomfortable with it and cleared his throat. Cleared it very meaningfully, too, by God.

"Oh," Simone said, snapping out of her seeming trance. "Brian, I'd like you to meet my, um, my cousin. Percy," she added mischievously. "Percy . . . Lipschitz."

Even Brian seemed surprised by the name, but ever the good-mannered boy—the putz, Julian thought—he extended his hand toward Julian with a warm smile. "Mr. Lipschitz," he said by way of a greeting.

Reluctantly, Julian took the proffered hand. And he tried not to notice how good-looking and well-mannered and congenial and blond and blue-eyed the other man was.

Damn him.

"Please," Julian said. "Call me"—he eyed Simone venomously—"Percy."

Brian shook his hand, then turned his attention quickly back to Simone. "I don't remember you having any cousins here in town named Lipschitz," he said.

And was that *suspicion* Julian saw crossing the other man's face? Or was Julian merely transferring his own feelings over to Brian Richie?

"Percy lives up in Dayton," Simone said. "He drove down to meet me when he heard I was going to be in town. His mother was my mother's cousin. Miriam Wentworth Lipschitz. Of the Toledo Wentworths."

"And the Toledo Lipschitzes," Julian threw in for good measure.

"Ah. I see."

But Julian could tell that the other man didn't see at all. Brian *was* suspicious of something. Julian sensed it. Of course, Brian was probably just wondering if Julian was actually Simone's cousin, or perhaps a more intimate acquaintance. A more intimate acquaintance who was also ten years younger than he was, so there. Brian was probably also wondering what Simone had on under that seemingly innocent little lavender dress of hers. And Julian was feeling just mean enough at the moment to tell him.

Oh, by the way, Brian, Simone doesn't have on a stitch of underwear beneath that dress. Bet you're just dying to know how I know that, aren't you? Well, nyah, nyah, nyah, nyah, nyah. I'm not going to tell you.

Oh, yeah. That would have put a new spin on things.

"I guess you're back in town for the class reunion, aren't you?" Brian asked now, returning his attention to Simone and dismissing Julian with all the interest one might display for a crouton in the salad.

"Among other things," Simone told him.

Oh, go ahead, Simone, Julian thought. *Tell him what other things you're back in town for. I dare you.*

"Well, I'd love to get together with you while you're here," Brian said. "Besides at the reunion, I mean. We can talk about . . . old times."

Simone smiled that peaceful, self-contained little smile again. "I'd like that, Brian," she said softly. "I'd like that very much."

He smiled back, a decidedly less peaceful, more salacious smile. "Do you have any plans this evening?" he asked.

Jeez, Brian, can you be any more obvious? Julian thought. *Show some restraint, man. You'll give our gender a bad name.*

"Oh, I'm sorry," Simone said, much to Julian's amazement. As convincing as her phony aplomb was, he hadn't thought she would prolong for a moment a tryst with her beloved Brian. "I can't tonight. I have plans."

"Then what are you doing tomorrow night?" Brian asked without missing a beat.

Down, boy, Julian thought. But he supposed he really couldn't blame the other man for his, um, enthusiasm. Had circumstances been different—different in the sense that Julian actually *liked* Simone Van Dormer, for instance—he probably would have been reacting the same way himself. Except that he probably wouldn't be drooling *quite* as much as Brian was.

"I can't tomorrow, either," Simone said, surprising Julian again. But she offered no reason for declining.

"Thursday then," Brian said insistently. He smiled a very oily smile, then added, "You know, I never did get to show you my family's boathouse on the river the way I'd planned to do when we were in high school. I'd love to show it to you now. It's nice and secluded. The perfect place for . . ." He glanced surreptitiously at Julian, then back at Simone. "For what the two of us might have shared, had you and your family not moved away so suddenly," he concluded.

She hesitated, pretending to think about whether or not she might be available. "Thursday might be doable," she finally told him. She didn't even spare Julian the tiniest bit of interest as she further replied, "I think I could make it then. What exactly did you have in mind?"

The other man's smile now was downright lecherous. So much so that Julian just about launched himself out of his chair to feed the guy something that most definitely was not on the menu—namely, his fist.

"Oh, I don't know . . . *exactly*," Brian said in

response to Simone's question. "As I mentioned, maybe we can . . . revisit old times. Where are you staying? I'll pick you up at seven on Thursday."

This time Simone was the one whose smile was radiant. "I'm in the Rivermont Suite at the Stanhope. I'll be ready for you on Thursday at seven."

But there was something in her voice when she spoke that made all those hairs on Julian's neck go jumping to attention again. And there was something in Brian Richie's eyes that made his blood run a little cold.

Creepy. *Really* creepy.

Forget Luther Van Dormer's nebulous, twenty-year-old threat, Julian thought. As long as Brian Richie was around, Julian wasn't going to let Simone Van Dormer out of his sight.

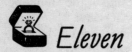 *Eleven*

"Hey, Tulsa! It's a bright, gorgeous Wednesday afternoon. An excellent eighties adventure Wednesday, if you're just tuning in, and we've got some great classics lined up for you. Right now, a tune from one of my favorite bands, the Plimsouls. They're 'A Million Miles Away.' "

Boy, they weren't the only ones who were a million miles away, Wyatt thought as he lowered the volume on the song. He glanced over at the passenger side of the Expedition—or, more specifically, at the *passenger* of the Expedition—and sighed to himself. So far, this trip hadn't gone quite the way he'd anticipated. He'd figured that, by now, Eve would have cast off the manacles of oppression and would be dancing in celebration of her newfound spiritual liberation. He'd figured that she would have abandoned the darkness to make merry in the light. He'd figured she would have thumbed her nose at the recent past and embraced the future for all it was worth. At the very least, he'd figured she would be having a reasonably good time.

But she wasn't having a good time. Not really. Not the way she was supposed to be.

They'd spent Monday night in Santa Fe, having ended up there because Eve had pulled a Bugs Bunny during one of her stints at the wheel, taking a wrong toin at Albacoiky. As wrong toins went, though, that had been a good one. But as quaint and as splendid as Santa Fe had been, neither he nor Eve had been able to enjoy it as well as they might have under other circumstances.

Circumstances like, oh . . . Wyatt didn't know . . . like maybe if he *hadn't* abducted her and forced her to drive cross-country with him whether she liked it or not, because her father was paying him a bundle of money to do it. Or circumstances like, oh . . . gee . . . like maybe if he *hadn't* kissed her in the pool that first night on the road, and *hadn't* worked them both into a frenzy of sexual need, and then *hadn't* coldly rejected her in much the same way as he had on prom night.

But in circumstances other than those, they might be having a really good time right now. Maybe. Possibly. Perhaps. Hey, it could happen. In an alternate universe somewhere.

Anyway, they'd both been pretty beat by the time they'd hit Santa Fe, due to a lack of sleep—among other things—on Sunday. In spite of that, Wyatt had coaxed and cajoled Eve into taking in some of the sights, and they had strolled along Canyon Road, enjoying the galleries, the studios, and the shops. Once or twice he had glanced over to find her fascinated by some brightly painted piece of pottery or artwork, or a resplendent native garment in a shop window. And, better still, once or twice he had seen her smile.

Not at him, necessarily, he reluctantly conceded, but just . . . because. Which, now that he thought about it, was actually better than having her smile at him. Because those smiles had seemed to come about for no reason other than that Eve felt good about something, if only for a moment.

Still, over all, she hadn't quite seemed happy on this trip. And Wyatt hadn't quite known what to do to change that. He still didn't. But he was working on it.

On Tuesday, they'd taken their time driving and had opted to spend the night in Amarillo. And once again, Wyatt had coaxed and cajoled Eve into visiting a few places beyond their motel room. Cadillac Ranch, for instance—he had insisted—and a historic section of Route 66 populated by antique galleries, specialty shops, and cafés. Dinner, however, had been at what he now considered to be the single greatest find in all of America, the Big Texan Steak Ranch and Opry. And *oh*, how he had wished Julian could have been there. Talk about your *moos* . . .

Eve's favorite place in Amarillo, though—not that she would admit it—had been the Wonderland Park amusement park. Wyatt knew it was her favorite place because he'd caught her smiling a full *four times* while they were there—once with her teeth actually showing. And even though he hadn't been able to coax or cajole her onto the Texas Tornado, which had looked like a truly bitchin' roller coaster, she had at least conceded to let him win her a big ol' hot pink teddy bear, one who was wearing a perpetual expression of total surprise. Currently, it sat in the back seat of the Expedition, taking up way more room than it deserved, but Wyatt didn't care, because he'd won it for Eve, and something about that just made him feel really, really happy inside, even if such a happy feeling still eluded her. He was working on that. He was. Any time now, she ought to start coming around.

So far, he'd contented himself with the knowledge that he was at least keeping half of the promise he'd made to Luther Van Dormer. Although the *good* part was still in question thanks to the infrequency of Eve's smiles, Wyatt was definitely showing her a *time*. And he secretly vowed that, before they reached Cincinnati, he'd have succeeded on the *good* front, too. Yeah, four days after beginning their trek across America, he felt like they were finally on their way.

Four days after beginning their trek, they were also very tired. Although Eve had slept a little bit better than Wyatt had over the last couple of nights, she'd been forced to expend an inordinate amount of energy nurturing that grudge against him that she seemed intent on nurturing, all because of a harmless little kidnapping. Okay, okay, and a not-so-harmless, not-so-little rejection, too, he admitted. Nobody was perfect.

As a result, they were both starting to skirt the edges of exhaustion. And that, he was certain, was the only reason why neither of them had seemed to speak more than a handful of words to each other over the last few days. As for why they hadn't seemed to speak a word to each other today, well . . .

Sleep debt, he told himself. Yeah, that was it. It was just going to take a while for them to catch up and return to being their old, usual, perky selves.

For now, though, Wyatt wasn't feeling *too* bad, even if Eve, sitting over there in the passenger side with a grim expression clouding her features, did still look a bit, um, tired. Although he'd had his way every night where adjoining rooms—and open doors—were concerned, she had been extra careful to avoid visual contact once they'd arrived at the motels where they'd spent those nights.

Thankfully, Wyatt's hearing was as sharp as that of a nervous gazelle grazing on a lion-infested veldt. Otherwise, he might have been afraid Eve would try to give him the slip. Fortunately for him, though, he'd picked up every aural nuance of movement that had occurred in her room, from the rattling of the air conditioner to the whisper of a nightgown gliding down over her skin.

Okay, so maybe he'd just imagined that last bit of aural nuance. Oh, *boy*, had he imagined it. Several times, in fact. He'd still known where she was at every minute of every day they'd been together.

Well, okay, *almost* every minute of every day. Just because she'd slipped out of her room and into his while he was sleeping Monday night, and had filched the Expedition keys from his blue jeans pocket, and had driven fifteen miles to find a Dunkin' Donuts, and had sat there jawing with the locals for forty-five minutes, and then had gone to a midnight movie with the waitress after her shift ended, that didn't mean anything.

It hadn't happened a second time.

Because that second time, on Tuesday night, Eve had only made it as far as the motel exit before Wyatt had caught up with her, panting and sweating from his run, and had jumped into the passenger seat to join her on her adventure. Which, on that night, happened to be jawing with the locals at a place called Bonita's

Pie Kitchen for an hour and a half, then going roller-skating with the short-order cook after his shift ended.

Yessir, you had to get up pret-ty early in the morning to fool Wyatt Culver. More than once. That was for sure.

Now, even though they still had several hours of daylight ahead of them, Tulsa seemed like a good place to stop for the night. He *would* show Eve a good time this time. It would be *him* doing it. Not a waitress. Not a short-order cook. Not a bag of doughnuts. *He* would. Wyatt Culver. Whether Eve liked it or not.

"Oh, quick, take this exit," she piped up suddenly from the passenger side, showing more animation than he'd seen her show in the last four days—except when she was around waitresses and short-order cooks and bags of doughnuts, anyway.

So excited was he by this sudden excitement that he obeyed without asking why, then turned as she also directed him at the base of the exit.

"There!" she cried, jabbing her finger at the passenger side window. "Take me there."

Wyatt trailed his gaze in the direction toward which she was pointing and saw a big, sprawling shopping mall.

"The mall?" he asked, surprised. "You want to go shopping?"

"I haven't been inside a mall in ages," she said. "I used to love to go to the mall. Back before—"

She halted abruptly without finishing the sentence, not that the sentence really needed finishing. So much for showing her a good time, Wyatt thought. But, by God, if Eve wanted to go to the mall, then that was by God what they would do. With a quick glance into his rear- and side-view mirrors, he spun the steering wheel to the right, toward the mall. Then he cruised the lot until he found a parking space near a main entrance.

"Shop 'til you drop, Eve," he said as he thrust the Expedition into park and switched off the ignition. But his order fell on deaf ears. Actually, his order fell on no ears. Because the moment the vehicle had come to a stop, Eve had hopped down and headed for the mall.

Oh, *fine*, he complained to himself. *He* always listened to *her* edicts, but *she* totally disregarded *his*. Man, that was just like Eve to ignore him and do whatever she damn well—

Hey, wait a minute, he thought, backpedaling. That really *was* just like Eve to ignore him and do whatever she damn well pleased. He smiled as he unhooked his seat belt and pushed open the door.

Oh, yeah. They were *definitely* making progress.

Boy, women and malls, he thought as he watched her flee with glee toward the entrance. They must have shared some common geologic element that just immediately bonded them. Before he lost sight of her, Wyatt, too, jumped out of the Expedition, then had to jog to catch up with her. The soft breeze caught her dress and danced it above her knees, and he realized she was wearing something that was vividly colored for a change—a loose-fitting sundress thing she'd purchased in Santa Fe. It had skinny straps that tied at the shoulders, and the floral print fabric boasted a bright splash of virtually every color in the spectrum. Likewise for the first time she'd left her hair unbound, and it tumbled past her shoulders, between her shoulder blades, nearly the same length it had been when they were in high school.

Wyatt considered both developments to be Very

Good Signs. Coupled with the ignoring-him-to-do-what-she-damn-well-pleased thing, he saw great potential for their sojourn in Tulsa.

"Eve! Wait up!" he called when she reached the entrance.

But either not hearing him or choosing not to hear him—which was probably more accurate—she strode in ahead of him without a backward glance. By the time Wyatt finally made it into the mall, she was—surprise, surprise—gone. For some reason, though, the realization didn't alarm him as much as it might have a few days ago. In spite of her grudge and her midnight forays in search of pastry, Eve had offered no indication that she wanted to dump Wyatt and continue on her way alone. And in spite of the physical distance she kept between them, it hadn't escaped his notice that, every night, before she went to bed, she passed in front of their adjoining doors and glanced into his room, to make sure he was there.

There was still some fear in her—that much was obvious. Though whether that fear was left over from her marriage or a result of something else entirely, Wyatt couldn't say. And he sensed something else in her, too, mixed with the fear, something that made her stick close to him. But he wasn't sure he could identify quite what that something else was.

In any case, he didn't worry about her running off without him. Even if he didn't know where she was at the moment, he'd bet good money that she had him in her sights.

Directly in front of him was a big department store, its beaming lights and colorful fashions beckoning. It was a woman magnet, plain and simple, and that was the direction Wyatt chose to follow. Within moments, he had located Eve, and he smiled when he noted what had made her pause. Prom gowns. Hundreds of them. In soft pastels and sophisticated darks and exuberant brights, waiting for the arrival of excited, delighted, giggling teenaged girls who might want to buy them for that special night.

And also, he couldn't help thinking as he watched Eve, for wistful, sentimental adult women who might want to look at them and wish things had turned out differently.

Wyatt wasn't sure how long he stood there observing her, noting how she grazed her fingers over the supple, delicate fabrics, how she held one up before herself—an elegant, rather revealing, midnight blue number, made out of some sparkling, shimmery fabric . . . man, they'd *never* made prom gowns like that in '81—to see if it might fit. Eventually, though, she must have sensed his presence, because she glanced up from the gown she held before herself to find him staring at her.

Immediately, her dark eyes went wide, and she blushed profusely. Then, guiltily, she hung the dress back on the rack and pretended she hadn't been completely captivated by it.

"You should buy it," Wyatt said impulsively, taking a few steps forward to join her.

"Oh, please," she retorted, sounding nervous. "Not only is it meant for a teenage girl, but I have no place to wear something like that. Besides, I have a prom gown. Somewhere."

For some reason—he had no idea why, honestly—he found himself telling her, "I know. I remember it. It was pink, and you had it pushed off your shoulders. It had all this lacy stuff there around the top, and there were like ... tiers ... all down the skirt, with more lacy stuff on the bottom. I don't think I ever saw you looking more beautiful than you did that night."

She'd dropped her gaze to the floor the moment he had started talking, but where before her cheeks had blazed with color, now her face was pale. He waited for her to make some flip comment, to offer some sarcastic remark that would put him in his place, because he'd just spoken of the unspeakable.

But all she said, very softly, was, "I thought you looked pretty wonderful, too, that night. Even with your lapels that spread wider than a mile, and a crushed velvet bow tie the size of Rhode Island."

She'd clearly meant for the comment to be humorous. Funny, though, how neither one of them laughed.

"I'm sorry," he said suddenly, softly. Though, in truth, he honestly wasn't sure what he was apologizing for. Maybe for what had happened that night, maybe for not apologizing sooner. Or maybe it was because he still couldn't quite explain things, still couldn't quite understand them.

Eve didn't really seem to be too sure, either, because she only nodded her head once, quickly, then began to walk toward the store's entrance.

Wyatt strode after her, catching up in just a few steps. "So . . . you hungry?" he asked as they went.

"I could eat," she told him, still looking at the floor.

"Food court okay? I'm not sure I have it in me to look around for a decent restaurant." He forced a smile. "Besides, The Big Texan Steak Ranch and Opry is going to be one tough act to follow."

She did smile at that, albeit a bit halfheartedly. It was better than nothing.

"Food court's fine," she said. "Then can we find a

hotel? I'm really tired. I don't want to go sight-seeing tonight."

For some reason, Wyatt didn't, either, so he didn't argue with her on that count. Instead he only nodded silently and extended his hand toward the interior of the mall. And, without looking at him even once, Eve turned and walked that way.

It rained that night. Not a languid, romantic little cloudburst that pit-pit-pittered and pat-pat-pattered on the roof but a full-blown, angrily gusting thunderstorm. It roared in just past midnight, waking Eve from what had only been a moderately restful sleep anyway. Still, she had been dreaming, good dreams for a change, too. One minute she was standing on a sunset-tinted beach in Santa Barbara, the breeze lifting her hair from her neck and face, watching as Wyatt rose half-naked and glistening from the surf and strode intently toward her. Then the next minute, a brutal crack of thunder was jolting her awake, with a startle factor powerful enough to topple her out of bed.

For a moment, she couldn't remember who or where or what she was, and in that moment, she panicked. Because in that moment, Eve honestly didn't *know* who or where or what she was. She couldn't get her bearings at all.

Wyatt?

She thought his name just scrolled through her head, and only then because she had been dreaming of him. She didn't realize she'd consciously called out to him—not until he was crouching beside the bed, beside her, curling his hand gently around her upper arm. Still a bit dazed and a lot confused, she looked up at him, but in the darkness, all she could distinguish was a masculine outline. And in that peculiar, capricious moment, she was suddenly uncertain about everything—everything except that there was a man crouching over her, touching her, murmuring soft, unintelligible words to her.

Edwin.

She hadn't intended to voice that name, either, but she must have, because the man standing over her— Wyatt? Edwin?—went momentarily rigid.

And, then, just as suddenly, he relaxed. "It's me, Eve," he said softly. "It's Wyatt. It's okay."

"Oh. Wyatt."

She did consciously speak his name aloud this time, and in doing so, she must have uttered the magic word that broke the odd spell that had visited her. Because the moment she murmured Wyatt's name, Eve began to feel more certain of her surroundings, more certain of her situation, more certain of herself.

She let him help her up from the floor, let him sit her down on the edge of the bed, let him sit himself down beside her, let him switch on the bedside lamp. She was vaguely conscious of the fact that she was wearing her pajamas—a cream-colored silk combination of short-sleeved shirt and boxers—but somehow, the knowledge of that didn't concern her. What did worry her was the fact that Wyatt had once again obviously been in a hurry when he'd dressed and had donned only a pair of blue jeans before coming to her aid.

Now she became *very* aware of his closeness—not to mention his half-nakedness—and of the way his bare arm brushed along hers when he folded his body down beside her, the way the heat of his skin seemed to seep into her own. She noticed how his biceps flexed and relaxed as he lifted a hand to run his fingers through his unruly hair, remarked the subtle arc of muscle in his forearm when he dropped his hand back into his lap. And when she forced her gaze higher, when she looked at his face, she saw in his eyes concern for her well-being . . . and something else, too, something that looked very much like affection, which she hoped she only imagined.

Because any affection Wyatt might potentially feel for her was actually, she was certain, leftover affection for the vibrant, sassy girl he recalled from their youth. And she was a girl who existed nowhere now but in his memories. Whatever Wyatt might feel for Eve now . . . Well. She didn't want to think about what he might feel for her now. Because she was confident it wasn't what she suspected she was feeling for him. And what she was feeling for him, although it may have started off as leftover affection, too, was fast growing into something else entirely. Something that had nothing to do with two teenagers. Something that was, most assuredly, adult in nature. Something she was in no way certain that she could even trust.

Another vicious clap of thunder clamored overhead, virtually shaking the motel, and literally shaking Eve. Despite the ambivalence of the emotions churning through her, she was unable—or perhaps unwilling—to help herself when she leaned into Wyatt, tucking her head into the curve created by his neck and shoulder. She inhaled a great lungful of his soapy, masculine scent, and after pulling even that small part of him inside herself, she felt less troubled. In that moment, it was almost as if Wyatt Culver became the antidote to everything that had ever been wrong in her life.

But how could that be? she wondered even as she settled back against the arm he'd wrapped around her waist. Wyatt himself was a part of that wrongness. Wasn't he? His rejection of her when they were teenagers had, in many ways, been the beginning of the downturn her life had taken. Nothing had gone right after that night. Nothing. Not that she blamed Wyatt for what had happened to her during her marriage—Eve accepted full responsibility for that. But something about that night at the prom had generated something inside her, something that had steered her down a path of one bad mistake after another.

Or perhaps, she conceded, what had happened that night had only triggered something inside her that had been there all along. Either way, that night with Wyatt had been a major turning point in her life. And what had followed, without him, had been no life at all.

Now, though, somehow, with Wyatt, things felt right again. She'd done everything she could to keep her distance from him on this trip—mentally and emotionally, if not physically. She hadn't wanted to risk putting herself in another position where he might push her—or pull himself—away again. But now, for some reason, all she wanted was to have him close.

"Were you having a nightmare?" he asked, scattering her ruminations.

She shook her head, trying not to notice how warm and fragrant was his skin, how strong and vital was the arm circled loosely around her waist, how velvety and soothing was the voice that murmured so close to her ear. Tenderness. That was what Wyatt was showing her. And it had been a long, long time since anyone had treated Eve tenderly.

"No," she told him. "I was actually having a very nice dream. I was dreaming about—" She halted abruptly when she recalled that she had been dreaming about him.

"About what?" he asked.

"About . . . Santa Barbara," she said. It wasn't a lie—not really. She had been dreaming of Santa Barbara. And of so much more, too.

"Then it was a good dream," he said.

"Yes. It was."

"Do you want to talk about it?"

She shook her head. "Not about the dream, no."

"But you do want to talk about something?"

Overhead, thunder rumbled maliciously again, and then, as if cued by the monstrous sound, the light beside the bed flickered once, twice, three times, then went out completely. In the darkness, unconsciously, Eve crowded her body closer to Wyatt's.

And then, very quietly, she said, "Yes. I want to talk."

But instead of launching into conversation, she couldn't remember exactly what it was she wanted to say. She only knew she didn't want Wyatt to leave. Not yet. Not while it was so dark inside. And not while there was a storm seething outside. She hated storms. Truly hated them. And she didn't want to be alone for this one.

Wyatt didn't seem to be bothered—or even surprised—by her conflicting signals, first telling him she wanted to talk, then speaking not a word. Instead, he only sat beside her, letting her curl her body into his. He made no demands, asked no questions, required nothing of her except that she take whatever she needed from him. Eve sighed softly and closed her eyes, and for the smallest of moments, she could almost convince herself that everything was going to be all right.

Then another smack of thunder made her jerk her eyes open, made her entire body lurch forward, made Wyatt tighten his grip and rein her back in.

"Are you okay?" he asked.

She shook her head. "I hate storms. They've always scared me to death, ever since I was a kid."

He expelled a soft, incredulous sound. "You? I didn't think you were afraid of anything when we were kids," he said. "Nothing ever seemed to scare you. I was in complete awe of your self-confidence and your strength. There was nobody in Woodhaven who even came close to you."

Eve, too, murmured a soft sound in response to his statement, but hers was one of resignation. "Oh, Wyatt," she said. "*Everything* scared me back then. Couldn't you tell? And if nobody came close, it was because I didn't want anybody to get close. I didn't want anyone to see what a phony I was."

Of course, that wasn't entirely true, she knew. There was one person she had always wished would come closer. But the only times he had . . . Well. Somehow, she'd repelled him right back again, hadn't she?

"That's why I acted the way I did back then," she told him, only now beginning to understand how true that was. "I was bluffing. I bluffed my way through my entire teenage life, and I kept on bluffing after high school was over."

She inhaled a deep breath and released it slowly, and was grateful for the darkness in the room. Somehow, the darkness evened things up between the two of them. The darkness made it harder for her to distinguish between the Eve and Wyatt of her memories and the Eve and Wyatt of today. And strangely, somehow, that made all the difference.

"You were a good bluffer, then," he said, his soft voice parting the darkness. "I sure never suspected."

"I kept thinking," she continued, "that maybe if I pretended to be strong and brave, then eventually I *would* be strong and brave. I kept hoping that nobody would ever see me for who and what I really was." She hesitated only a moment, then said, "There were some days, though, when I hoped that maybe, eventually, somebody would."

She squeezed her eyes shut tight against the tears that threatened. "And you know, as luck would have it, eventually, someone did come along who saw me for who and what I really was. Someone—" She halted abruptly, unwilling to say any more.

Wyatt, however, evidently didn't share her reluctance. "That someone was Edwin, wasn't it?"

She nodded. A long pause followed, neither of them speaking a word. Rain smacked against the window, thunder grumbled overhead, and wind shushed past the door, fast enough to rattle the metal casing on the bug light outside.

Finally, though, very softly, Wyatt asked the question he'd asked in Santa Barbara, the one she had found it so difficult to answer. "What did he do to you, Eve?"

"It wasn't what he did to me," she told him. "It was what I *let* him do."

"I don't understand."

In an effort to explain—to him *and* to herself, she supposed—she said, "I first met Edwin when I was a sophomore in college. He taught a survey course in

European literature that I took. I sort of developed a crush on him in that class. Even though he was so much older than me . . ." She chuckled wryly at that. "So much older," she said again. "He was the same age then that I am now. Oh, yeah. So much older."

Wyatt said nothing, but she felt the arm around her waist tighten a bit. The touch was reassuring, though. And it helped her say the rest of what she had to say.

"Edwin was very attractive," she continued, "in that bookish, English professor kind of way that so many young women find attractive. And he was very smart and very charming." She shrugged. "He just seemed so . . . so nice. And I could tell he liked me, too, even then. We didn't actually start dating, though, until the last part of my senior year. I asked him to be my advisor on my independent study paper, and we ended up working fairly closely together. One afternoon in his office, one thing led to another, and he kissed me. After that, we started dating. And then later . . ."

Wyatt's voice belied nothing of what he might be thinking when he said, "Later?"

The storm outside seemed to pick up steam, the wind hurtling faster, the rain thrashing harder, the thunder booming overhead now like a howitzer. Had the circumstances been different, Eve might have managed a smile at how appropriately the weather outside the motel reflected the tempest simmering inside her. Except that the storm was much more confident than she.

"It probably started even before we got married," she began again, "while he was directing my master's thesis. Edwin would correct my opinions and redraw my conclusions for me in my paper, and I naturally deferred to him because he was my instructor, and I thought he knew more about the material than I did. Looking back, though, I think my opinions and conclusions were perfectly good ones. But every time Edwin told me I'd done something wrong, I took him at his word, and revised my work to his specifications. I re-created it in his image.

"After we married," she continued, "it wasn't just my academic work Edwin took exception to. He thought I should dress differently, now that I was the wife of a professor—ditch the batik skirts and tank tops in favor of less extravagant colors and more conservative styles. And he thought my language was inappropriate for my new position as his wife—it was too slangy, and I swore a time or two. Basically, he thought it was time I acted like a grown-up—his idea of a grown-up, at any rate. So I started dressing and speaking and acting the way he told me to dress and speak and act."

"Sounds like he was no fun at all," Wyatt said softly. "Sounds like you should have ditched the jerk at the get-go."

She sighed wearily. "You have to understand, Wyatt, all this stuff didn't just happen overnight. From the time I got involved with him until the time I left him, nearly fifteen years passed. *Fifteen years*," she repeated more adamantly. "His wearing me down was so gradual. And he wasn't a bully about it. Not at first, anyway. He was always very pleasant when he told me I was ugly. And he was always very polite when he told me I was stupid."

Wyatt was silent for a moment. Then, "So when did he become a bully?" he asked.

"What do you mean?"

"You said he wasn't a bully about it 'at first,' " Wyatt pointed out.

The realization that she had indeed said that surprised Eve. Although Edwin had certainly been a bully, she had never consciously labeled him as one before now, not even in her thoughts. A bit bemused by her sudden insight, she could only stammer, "I, um, I'm not . . . I mean, I don't—"

"You said he . . . h-hit . . . you once," Wyatt interrupted, stumbling over the one word as if he had trouble voicing it. "When did that happen?"

Eve swallowed with some difficulty when she recalled the episode. "The last night we were together," she said. "By then, I was practically a Stepford Wife, doing everything Edwin told me to do, behaving exactly as he wanted me to behave, always putting his needs and his desires before my own." She expelled a morose sound. "By that point, I don't think I even had any needs or desires anymore. But that last night . . ." She shook her head, still not sure what had happened that night to make her act the way she had.

"What?" Wyatt asked. "What happened that night?"

"We were supposed to have dinner guests—the head of the English department and her husband. And I wasn't feeling very good. I just . . . I was tired," she said simply. "I was so, so tired. And when Edwin came home, I asked him if we could postpone the dinner, because I just didn't think I could do it that night. And he started in telling me how useless I was, because I'd never been able to do one of those dinners right. And he told me if I messed it up, I'd just look like the idiot that I was. And on and on and on." She inhaled a deep breath and released it slowly. "And then I did the most unforgivable thing I could possibly do."

"And what was that?" Wyatt asked, his voice cool now, angry.

"I took exception," she said softly. "I told Edwin I *wasn't* an idiot and I *wasn't* useless. And then he . . . For a minute, he only looked at me as if he couldn't believe I'd just contradicted him. And then . . . then he doubled his fist and he . . . he hit me. Hard enough to knock me down."

"Oh, Eve . . ."

"He meant for it to put me in my place," she interrupted quietly, with a calmness that surprised her. In many ways, what had happened that night seemed as if it had happened to another woman entirely. Over the last few months—and, more particularly, the last few days—Eve had begun to feel as if that whole chapter of her life was complete fiction. As if it had never occurred. As if it were all a bad dream from which she had finally awoken. And now that it was over, she wanted to start trying to forget it.

"But instead of putting me in my place," she added quickly, unwilling to hear the pity she knew would lace Wyatt's voice, "ironically, it made everything come completely clear to me. What kind of man Edwin really was. What he had done to me. What I had allowed him to turn me into. I can't explain how or why it happened," she added before he had a chance to ask. "Maybe it will never make sense to anyone who hasn't been through something like that. But day by day, he chipped away at my self-esteem, a little here, a little there, year after year, until I really, truly believed he was just trying to help me improve myself. That he was doing these things for my own good. That I would be nothing without him. It never occurred to me that he just wanted someone to control, someone who would do his bidding as if he were God Almighty. Someone he could push around so that he would feel better about himself. But that was what it was."

Wyatt said nothing for a moment, as if he were trying to digest all this information about her life. Finally, though, he admitted, "You're right. I don't understand it, Eve. But maybe it's not important that I do, you know?"

She crumpled a little bit inside at his words. "But I need for you to understand it," she told him. "It's really important to me that you understand, Wyatt."

"But . . . why?"

"Because I was hoping you could explain it to me."

"Oh, Eve . . ." he said again.

But there wasn't so much pity in his voice when he said it this time, she noticed, as there was . . . something else. Something much warmer and much fiercer, something much more intense and much more resolute.

The last thing Eve expected Wyatt to do was kiss her, but the first thing she felt after voicing her confession, her confusion, was the press of his mouth against hers. It was a gentle kiss, an innocent kiss, a kiss of reassurance between friends. As was the second kiss. And the third. And even, to some extent, the fourth. Eventually, though, the kisses became less innocent, less reassuring. Gradually, they built into something that was more demanding, more needful.

Without even thinking about what she was doing, Eve lifted her hands to curl her fingers in his hair, then tilted her head to the other side to facilitate their mutual exploration. And when she did . . . Ah, it was so sweet. *He* was so sweet. She'd never really thought to use such an adjective in relation to Wyatt Culver, but suddenly the word fit him perfectly. He *was* sweet. Sweet to taste, sweet to touch, sweet to smell, sweet to hold. So what else could she do but taste him again? And again. And again.

She wasn't sure how long they sat there that way, mouths joined, fingertips grazing each other's faces, fingers skimming through each other's hair. But for the longest time, that was all they did. It was almost as if they were rediscovering long-forgotten ground, giving themselves time to become reacquainted. But how could that be, she wondered vaguely, when they'd never really known each other to begin with?

And then she understood. They were moving slow now because they *were* getting to know each other. Something about that reassured her, heartened her, made her feel bolder. So she pushed her body forward, closer to his, and parted her lips to allow him inside.

Immediately, he responded, filling her mouth with his tongue, roping one arm around her waist to press her body flush against his own, tangling the fingers of the other hand more earnestly in her hair. Heat exploded in her belly at the urgency of his actions, at the sheer possessiveness in his embrace. He wanted her—there could be no doubt. And heaven help her, she wanted him, too.

The warmth of his bare chest seeped through the thin silk of her pajama top, generating an answering heat inside her. The denim of his jeans scraped along the skin of her thighs, creating a delicious friction that roused yet another incendiary response. Eve found herself trying to get closer to him, wanting, needing, to feel his weight and the press of his body on hers. So she tipped herself backward, until the cool sheets of the bed pillowed her descent, and Wyatt, warm, hard Wyatt, covered her.

He wasted no time after that. He wedged one leg between both of hers, bending his knee so that his thigh was pressed deliberately against that most intimate, most sensitive part of her. The shock wave that shuddered through Eve at the contact nearly tore her apart. What reeled her back in was the light skim of his fingertips over her rib cage, strumming up and down, up and down, up and down, along her bare skin, igniting a string of little fires along the way. She opened her hands over his naked back, reveling in the dance of muscles and sinew she encountered beneath her fingertips. He was heat and satin and tempered steel, strength and power and finesse. And he was hers. If she wanted him. And Eve discovered, not much to her surprise, that she wanted him very much indeed.

He murmured her name as he dragged damp, open-mouthed kisses along the slender column of her throat, then moved his hand from her ribs to the neckline of her pajama top. Deftly, hastily, he flicked open the uppermost button, then nosed aside the fabric to trace her collarbone with the tip of his tongue. One by one, the rest of the buttons followed, and as he dispatched each, his oral exploration expanded. Eve went limp when he cupped a hand beneath one of her breasts and pushed it upward, into his waiting mouth. And she arced a hand over her head like a drunken ballerina when he sucked her deep inside.

With his free hand, he palmed the sensitive peak of her other breast, then captured her nipple and rolled the swollen bud gently between thumb and forefinger.

In spite of the darkness, she closed her eyes so that she might experience more purely the intoxicating rush of desire that surged through her. She scooted the hand on his back down some, to the waistband of his jeans and beyond. Dipping her fingers beneath the heavy fabric, she cupped what she could of his taut buttocks and pushed him against her. He thrust his entire body forward, and she felt the heavy ripeness of his shaft swell against her thigh.

Oh, Wyatt . . .

She didn't realize she had spoken his name aloud, but she must have, because he lifted himself from her damp breast, braced himself on his elbows, and gazed down into her face. She couldn't discern his expression in the darkness, but she could hear the ragged rhythm of his breathing, could feel the heat of his body hovering over hers, could sense the tension coiled tightly within him. He twined his fingers in her hair, brushing it back from her forehead, then bent to skim his lips over hers again.

She thought he was going to say something, and perhaps he had intended to do just that. But instead of speaking, he lowered himself down to her again, angling his body alongside hers. He curved one arm over her head, and with his other, nudged aside the fabric of her pajama top. Then he flattened a hand over her torso and steered his fingers skillfully to the waistband of her boxers.

Eve responded in kind, moving her hand to the buttons of his jeans, pushing each through its fastening one by one. When she tucked her hand inside, she felt his hard member pushing against the fabric of his briefs, proud and demanding. As he buried his fingers in the moist curls between her legs, Eve gasped and opened her legs wider, then dexterously dipped her own hand beneath his briefs. He was hot and unyielding in her palm, bigger than she would have guessed. Not that she had much to compare him to—no one but . her ex-husband—but somehow she sensed that Wyatt wasn't like most men.

She must have murmured something incoherent at the realization, because Wyatt pushed his fingers lower, deeper, plowing her tender flesh, penetrating her with one long middle finger. His breathing was almost harsh now, fraying, as if he was having trouble maintaining control. She rolled her hand over the hard head of his shaft and felt the steamy heat of his response film her skin. All they had to do, she thought, was shed what little clothing they wore, then they could join in the most basic, most primal way that a man and woman could join.

"Eve," he said, his voice uneven and uncultured and . . . uncertain.

Something in his tone when he said her name whipped her back through time twenty years, to the backseat of a car, where they had been engaged in an activity very much like this one. Oh, they'd been too inexperienced and too clumsy to get quite as far then as they had now, but Eve knew what that tone of voice meant.

Wyatt was about to pull away from her again. Somehow, she just knew it. So, quickly, before he had the chance to retreat, she rolled away from him, and scrambled to the opposite side of the bed. She leapt up, turned her back, and rearranged her clothes as well as she could. Even in the darkness, she sensed how much her action surprised Wyatt. Perhaps as much as it surprised her. But there was no way she was going to let him get her worked up and then leave her again. She wasn't sure she could stand it if he did.

So, very, very softly, she told him, "This time I'm the one who puts a stop to it, Wyatt. This time, I'm the one who walks away."

For a moment, only taut silence was her reply. Then she heard him exhale, a slow, shaky breath that seemed to go on forever. For a long time, he said nothing. His gradually slowing respiration was the only indication she had that he was even in the room.

Then, finally, he said, "Okay. I guess I deserve that."

"I'm not doing it because it's what you deserve," she told him, emphasizing the "you" just the slightest bit.

She heard him shift on the bed, the mattress squeaking under his weight. When she turned back around, she could discern just enough of him in the darkness to know that he nodded—nodded as if he understood, she thought. And maybe, in some strange, vague way, he did.

"My father hired you to get me safely to my reunion," she reminded him. "Not to . . . not to . . ." She expelled an impatient breath, unsure what to say. Finally, she decided on, "Not for this."

"Your father hired me to show you a good time," he immediately reminded her back. "As well as keep you out of danger."

"Well, you're not doing your job on either count," she told him. But she knew neither one of them really believed that.

Wyatt, however, was decent enough not to call her on the lie. Instead, he rose from the bed and slowly made his way back toward the connecting doors. He hesitated before returning to his room, however, and spun back around to face her. And even though the darkness and common sense forbade such a thing, she thought he could see right through her.

"I'll get you to the reunion, Eve," he vowed before he left. "I promise you that, if nothing else. I will get us where we need to be."

Twelve

On Thursday morning, as Julian sipped his orange juice, read the *Enquirer*, and entertained his daily erotic fantasy about Simone—she was straddling him on the sofa this time, her plump breast filling his mouth, his long fingers creasing the firm globes of her bottom as she moved up and down atop him—he remembered suddenly that it was his turn to run an errand today. But he waited until he had finished his juice—not to mention his fantasy—before saying anything about it.

"I need to run by my apartment for a few minutes," he announced as he and Simone were—in his mind, at least—basking in the aftermath of their loving. Then he grimaced inwardly at his own wording. What the two of them had just enjoyed in his mind *wasn't* loving, he told himself. It was a pure, elemental, physical response to a primal, animal instinct.

And, *boy*, had it been satisfying.

She glanced up at his declaration, her face etched

with curious surprise. Then she smiled, a small, almost shy little smile that held none of the edge he might have expected earlier in the week. Over the last couple of days, as they'd spent more time together—and learned to stay out of each other's way, he couldn't help thinking, too—they'd entered into a kind of vague truce, tolerating each other more easily, even warming to each other at times.

Naturally, Julian couldn't help thinking that Simone's sunnier disposition had come about because she'd finally achieved contact with her beloved—and very blond—Brian. Somehow, though, he suspected there was a little more to it than just that. And part of him couldn't help hoping that maybe, just maybe, Julian himself had something to do with her improved mood. Because he was beginning to think that maybe, just maybe, Simone herself had had something to do with his. And speaking for himself, he was grateful for the reprieve. Resenting Simone Van Dormer had become tiresome. Especially since he'd never quite been able to pinpoint where the resentment had come from in the first place. And especially since he wasn't the kind of man who resented anyone. Not anymore, anyway.

"What is it?" he said in response to her curious expression.

"It's just that I keep forgetting you live here in town," she said.

"Where have you been thinking I live?"

She shrugged. "I don't know, I guess I just haven't thought about it at all."

Oh, and didn't *that* just make him feel *so* much better, Julian thought. There was nothing a man liked to hear more from a beautiful woman to whom he'd just made love in his mind—or, rather, with whom he'd just had an elemental response to a primitive instinct in his mind—than that she didn't think about him at all. If she kept this up, he was really going to get a big head.

His reaction must have shown on his face, because Simone laughed at him, lightly, with faint amusement.

Ooo, inspiring light laughter and faint amusement in a beautiful woman was even better than having her not think about him, Julian thought wryly. And he should know. He'd spent most of his adolescence either faintly amusing people or being thought about not at all.

"I just meant . . ." she began. Then she gave up trying to explain. "Never mind. Whereabouts do you live?" she asked instead.

"Here in the city," he told her. He tried to forget about the faint amusement and the not thinking about him at all, but he didn't do a very good job of forgetting about either. "Not far from the hotel, as a matter of fact," he added.

She narrowed her eyes at him. "The night we arrived, you said you had to concentrate on your driving because you weren't familiar with this area."

"The night we arrived," he said, "I was lying."

She arched her delicate eyebrows in surprise. "Oh, there's a shocker," she said mildly. "A man lying to a woman. Color me astonished."

"You know a lot about men lying to women?" he asked, his interest piqued, even though he'd sworn to himself he was *not* interested in Simone Van Dormer. Liked her, okay. Interested? No way.

"I know enough," she said.

Julian couldn't imagine any man lying to a woman

like her. Not just because she seemed like the kind of woman who would see right through a lie, but because . . . Well, hell, look at her. Why would anyone lie to a woman who was beautiful and smart and fiery and not wearing a stitch of underwear? A man would have to be crazy to lie to a woman like that.

He sighed heavily and decided it might be best to change the subject. "Look, after the last several days, I'm inclined to agree with you that your father is just paranoid and that there's no threat to you and your sister here in town. But I'm still reluctant to leave you alone, if for no other reason than I promised your father I wouldn't. I mean, it's one thing for me to run next door to the gym while you're still asleep, but I'm not comfortable leaving you here alone on the hotel premises entirely. Do you mind coming with me to my place? As I said, I won't be long."

Instead of answering his question, she backpedaled to the first part of his statement instead. "You agree with me that Daddy was wrong about there being any danger here?"

He nodded. "I haven't sensed any threat to you at all since we got here," he said. *Well, except for that jerk, Brian Richie,* he added to himself. *And the only real danger there is being smarmied to death.* "No one's tried to contact you, and I haven't noticed anyone suspicious hanging around. When I've spoken to your father on the phone this week, he says he's heard nothing more from whoever threatened you to begin with." He eyed her levelly and asked, quite frankly, "Does Luther have a history of . . ." He paused. "How can I put this delicately?"

"Mental illness?" Simone supplied helpfully. "Delusions? Paranoid schizophrenia? Feelings of being persecuted? Voices in his head? That kind of thing?"

Julian bit the inside of his jaw for a moment. "Um, yeah. That, delicately, would be what I meant."

She chuckled wryly. "My father's not the most level-headed man in the world," she conceded, "but he's not mentally ill, either. Yes, he has some odd ideas, and yes, he's a little paranoid, but . . ." She tossed off another one of those casual shrugs. "I'm not worried about anyone hurting me or Evie, either, Julian. But if it would make you feel better, I'll stay close to you today."

Oh, he really liked the sound of that. Not just the way she called him Julian now, and the way his name rolled so naturally off her tongue, but the way she said she'd stay with him. He liked that part very much. Probably more than he should.

"Thanks," he said. "I'll make it brief."

"What do you have to do?" she asked.

He grinned sheepishly. "I have to water my plants."

Simone had never known a man to voluntarily keep plants. Nor had she ever known a man to be as tidy as she discovered Julian Varga was upon entering his home. Then again, she hadn't really been privy to any man's private life, had she? So how could she possibly know if they were generally plant-keepers or tidy or anything else?

Julian's apartment, though, was immaculate, and surprisingly homey. It was on the second story of an old apartment building, its hardwood floors gleaming like sun-drenched honey, its walls painted a creamy beige. Area rugs were scattered over much of the floor, and the furnishings were old, but comfortable. Framed poster art decorated the walls, Art Deco advertisements in French for coffees and wines and Parisian cafés. Along the windows spanning the far wall, numerous plants spilled and sprang from various containers ranging in size from enormous clay urns to small terra-cotta pots. Other than the plants, though, there were few accessories, and even fewer personal touches. But the effect overall was one of Continental sophistication and cultivated warmth.

Julian fit here, she decided. With his black hair and pale eyes, wearing dark trousers and a loose-fitting white T-shirt and finely woven blazer in shades of gray, he looked very European, very suave, very debonair. Very handsome. Simone had tried to match the mood of her attire to his, had thrown on a breezy, flowered cotton dress in soft pastels, and she had tossed a pale blue sweater over her shoulders. But she still felt plain and unremarkable beside him. In no way was she European or suave or debonair.

He was so different from her, she thought. He was so worldly, so accomplished. So self-contained. No wonder they had yet to make a solid connection. She would bet he'd had scores of girlfriends in the past, perhaps had scores in his present, as well. In high school, he had probably been the most sought-after boy—the jock, the brain, and the class president all rolled into one. She was certain he hadn't faded into the woodwork as she had. Not that Simone had ever really minded being invisible. She'd rather liked the freedom of movement that had come with it.

"You have a nice place," she told him once they were inside and he'd closed the door behind them.

"You sound surprised," he countered.

She shook her head. "No, I just didn't know what to expect, that's all."

"Because you don't think about me at all," he said.

His words, she was amazed to discover, were tinted with something akin to injury, as if she had hurt his feelings when she'd said what she had earlier. She hadn't meant for her remark to be interpreted the way he'd evidently interpreted it. She'd actually given Julian Varga plenty of thought over the last several days. In fact, there had been times when she couldn't think of anything else. She just couldn't put voice to any of those thoughts, certainly not to his face. He might get the wrong idea about her. He might think she cared for him. He might think she liked him— beyond a casual, friendly sort of way, at any rate. He might even think she wanted him. And that wasn't the case at all. No way.

So instead of commenting on his comment, Simone said nothing, and Julian went about the motions of a man who's returned home after a long absence. He sifted idly through a pile of mail on the coffee table, checked the messages on his answering machine, booted up a sophisticated-looking laptop that sat on the kitchen counter. And he also watered his plants. His neighbor had taken care of it the first part of the week, he'd explained on the way over, but she'd had to go out of town herself on Tuesday, by which time Julian had known he'd be back in Cincinnati. He told Simone to make herself at home as he went about his various tasks, and she, naturally curious, took him at his word. As he checked his e-mail and went about his other chores, she explored the living room, then the kitchen, then the dining room, then points beyond.

Next was what appeared to be his office, which, like

the rest of the apartment, was all comfortable furnishings and minimal decoration. Here, though, she found a few personal mementos that were lacking elsewhere in his home—the books (mostly nonfiction), the CDs (an eclectic assortment of jazz and R&B), the Dilbert comic strips taped to the computer terminal and bulletin board, the Batman mouse pad. And, she couldn't help noticing, more plants. Lots and lots of plants.

"I like an oxygen rich environment," Julian said from behind her, even as she formed the observation.

She spun around to see him armed with a watering can, and something about the incongruity of such a large, masculine man cradling such a small, feminine object was very, *very* sexy.

How strange, Simone thought. It had been a long time since she'd found a man sexy. Well, a man other than Brian, anyway. But she'd been a girl when she'd first evaluated Brian, and Brian had been a boy—what did she know about real men? And when had she stopped viewing Julian as an obstacle to her plans with Brian, and begun seeing him as, well, an attractive man she might like to get to know better? Not that she had any intention of getting to know him better. He wasn't the kind of man she should know better. He was nearly a decade her junior, had obviously been around the block a time or two—so to speak—and she had virtually nothing in common with him.

Still, he was very attractive. And interesting. And sexy.

As he went about the motions of tending to his jungle, Simone scanned an assortment of framed photographs that lined the tops of his bookcases. On the first bookcase, there was a picture of Julian and Wyatt holding up some dead fish, and another of Julian with his arm around a *very* attractive brunette—though, on second glance, Simone couldn't help thinking the brunette's nose was just a *smidgen* on the large side. Then there was a photo featuring an older couple she suspected were Julian's parents, and one with two very young boys, nephews, perhaps. Other pictures featured an assortment of people whose identities Simone couldn't possibly identify, so she turned her attention to the next bookcase, where the photographs appeared to be older ones—from a couple of decades ago, even. But none of these pictures appeared to include Julian, unless he was the one boy who appeared in several of them, which Simone found highly unlikely, because the boy was so . . .

Startled by what she saw upon further inspection, she picked up one photo in particular and turned to Julian. "Is this you?" she asked.

He paused in his plant watering long enough to glance over his shoulder. "Yeah, that's me," he said blandly as he went back to his task.

"The boy in the middle?" she asked further, still not trusting her eyes. "The, um, the, uh, the ah . . ."

"The fat kid," Julian finished for her without looking back. "Yeah, that was me. That was who I was the whole time I was growing up—the fat kid. The fat kid with a stutter, in fact. The fat kid with a stutter named Julian, who inspired laughter and merriment in many people. After I graduated from high school, I decided I was tired of being the fat kid with a stutter named Julian. I didn't really want to change my name—I was sort of attached to it by then—but I did make some changes in the way I lived. I started eating better, started working out, read more, that kind of thing.

Conquered the stutter with the help of a good doctor and continuous deep meditation. Julian the man is a much happier person than Julian the kid ever was. Of course, there were some rather weird years in between the two, but . . ." He shrugged. "It was a necessary phase."

His voice was only slightly tinged with rancor as he offered his summation, but even so, Simone could tell he still bore a little resentment toward the labels people had assigned him when he was a child. She supposed she couldn't blame him. People could be so thoughtless sometimes. So insensitive. So cruel. She replaced the photo in its original position and silently cursed anyone who had ever made Julian Varga feel like less of a person on the inside just because he had been more of a person on the outside.

"What kind of weird years were in between?" she heard herself ask him. Though, truly, she hadn't intended to pry. His comment had simply been too intriguing to ignore.

He continued to water his plants, pinching off a few dead leaves here and there as he spoke. "It took me a couple of years to lose the weight and tone up. But once I did, a very strange thing happened to me."

"What?"

"Women began to, um, notice me."

Simone couldn't quite halt the chuckle that escaped her at his remark, so surprised did he sound by the realization. Of course women would notice him when he looked the way he did. In a word, Duh. A lot of them would probably betray their country, or, at the very least, give up chocolate for a month, just to have a meaningful—or better yet, a not so meaningful—conversation with him.

"What's so funny?" he asked, turning fully around now to look at her.

"You," she said. "You standing there sounding so surprised that women would notice you."

"Why shouldn't that surprise me?" he asked.

Oops, Simone thought. She'd sort of dug herself in on that one, hadn't she? Now he was going to know that she herself thought he was attractive. And that, she was sure, would only lead to trouble. "Well, um, it just, uh . . . It shouldn't be surprising, that's all," she finally told him.

He set the watering can down on the windowsill and turned toward her, his eyes fixed intently on hers. "No?" he asked.

She shook her head. "No."

"Why not?"

But she wasn't about to answer that question. Not honestly anyway. She wasn't about to tell him what a hunka hunka burnin' love he was. "What, a nice-looking boy like you?" she replied vaguely instead. "Of course they'd notice."

He took a few slow, deliberate strides toward her, halting when only a few inches separated them. " 'Nice-looking boy'?" he echoed. "You talk to me like I'm still a kid, Simone."

She swallowed hard at the way he voiced her name and the way his eyes seemed to grow darker when he said it. "You are still a kid," she told him.

He took another measured step forward, effectively closing what little distance was left between them. Simone told herself to take a step backward in response, to retreat far enough that he wouldn't be able to touch her, wouldn't be able to hurt her. But she knew he wouldn't hurt her. She was fairly certain he wouldn't even touch her. Not unless she touched him first. And she wasn't about to do that.

"I don't feel like a kid," he assured her. "Especially not when I'm around you."

Oh, dear. This was really *not* a good path to travel. And just when had this path opened up, anyway? she wondered. It hadn't been that long ago that the two of them had been fuming and snapping at each other like . . . like . . . Well, like two sexually frustrated people who couldn't understand their responses to each other.

Hmm . . .

"Julian . . ." Simone began cautiously. "I don't think—"

"But then," he interrupted her suddenly, "we were talking about my weird, in-between years, weren't we?"

She relaxed a bit, relieved by the change of subject. "Yes. We were."

"Those were the years of my sexual awakening, when I couldn't get enough of women," he told her bluntly.

Okay, so maybe she wasn't so relieved by the change of subject after all.

"For the first time in my life," he continued before she could stop him, "women were paying attention to me, where before, if they'd noticed me at all, it was to recoil. Suddenly, instead of recoiling, they were coming close. *Very* close. And I, being the kind of man that I was then—namely horny as hell—took full advantage of each and every one of them, in as many ways as I possibly could."

Something sparked hot in the pit of Simone's stomach, and as much as she wished she could say it was fear and revulsion, she had no choice but to admit that it was actually a surprisingly intense fascination. Julian clearly claimed a vast store of sexual knowledge, where she herself claimed almost none. And although she'd never really been overly interested in such things before, somehow, with Julian, her curiosity—among other things—was much aroused.

In spite of that, she protested, "Julian, this is really none of my—"

"You asked," he reminded her.

"Yeah, but—"

"Okay, if you don't want to talk about it, we won't talk about it," he said agreeably.

Well, it wasn't *that*, Simone thought. She *was* kind of, sort of interested in hearing, oh, one or two details, anyway. Still, all things considered, maybe they'd be better off sticking to less volatile subject matter. So she scrambled for anything that might change the topic and put them on more stable ground.

"So then I take it your childhood wasn't especially wonderful," she said.

Oh, well done, Simone, she congratulated herself. This subject matter ought to cheer things right up.

Julian eyed her in silence for a long moment, his expression offering no clue as to what he might be thinking. Finally, though, he said, "No, it wasn't. My adolescence was even worse."

Simone nodded. "Teenagers can be vicious," she agreed.

"Yes, they can."

Neither of them commented on that. Probably because no comment was necessary.

"But in hindsight," Julian told her, "I'm grateful for the experiences I had in high school."

She glanced up at him in surprise. "Really? Why?"

He hesitated a moment, then said, "When you're one of the social outcasts in high school, you see things other people don't. You notice things about your classmates they might not even know about themselves." He eyed her intently. "It's a trait that stays with you, too, when you become an adult. Comes in handy in my line of work. And at other times."

Simone narrowed her eyes at him. The conversation seemed to have turned to her own personal issues somehow, but she couldn't quite put her finger on what he'd said to make it so. "What do you mean?" she asked.

He studied her thoughtfully for a moment more, then settled his hands on his hips. "Like from the minute you laid eyes on Brian Richie, when we were sitting in the car outside his house that first night, I knew there was more going on with you and him than you were letting on."

Simone schooled her features into as bland an expression as she could manage. "Oh?" she asked, feigning disinterest.

He nodded. "And when we saw him at the restaurant that day, I could sense then that you wanted to find him for reasons other than the ones you'd described."

She licked her lips, her mouth suddenly feeling dry. "I, um, I-I don't know what you mean."

"I'm not sure I do, either," he said thoughtfully. "I just know that whatever reason you came back here for Brian, it isn't because you want to start a romance with him. Not a healthy kind of romance, anyway."

This time Simone was the one to hesitate before speaking. Then she amazed herself by admitting, "No, that's not the reason I came back for him."

"And I sense something in Brian," Julian continued, "that's kind of . . ."

"Off?" she supplied helpfully.

He shook his head. "Evil."

"Ah. Well. I see that you really do have an insight into people that others lack," she said.

"You want to talk about it?" he asked.

Simone arced her gaze around the room, at the warm touches and personal mementos and photographs of smiling people. It was a nice room. A happy room. A room—and an apartment, in fact—that she realized she'd like very much to see again. There was no way she would taint this warm space with descriptions of her past. No way she would bring badness into what was very much a good place.

So Simone, too, shook her head in response to Julian's question. But instead of telling him that no, she didn't want to talk about it, what she heard herself say was, "Not here."

Julian surprised her at lunch by ordering a bottle of wine with their room service, but he must have taken a good look at her and thought she needed it. And at the moment, Simone wasn't sure she could disagree. Or perhaps he'd ordered it because he was the one who needed it, she reconsidered as she watched him tug the cork free. There was a turbulence in his expression she'd never seen before, and a bright fury in his eyes he didn't bother to mask. He'd always seemed so calm and imperturbable before, even on those occasions when the two of them had been at odds. Now something simmered just below his surface that she wasn't sure it would be wise to provoke.

She waited until he returned to the table and poured himself a glass of wine, shaking her head when he held the bottle silently over her glass. But he didn't sample his right away, only twirled the glass carefully in his hand, watching the ruby liquid sheet on the sides before swirling back down again. Neither of them even looked at their food, lunch being for both of them, she was sure, just a pretense.

In spite of that, Simone pushed the food around on her plate a bit and even managed to swallow a few bites before she finally gave up pretending.

"Evie always jokes that I'm the good twin, and she's the evil twin," she said by way of a beginning. "But the fact is, I've always been more like the invisible twin. At least, I was in high school."

Strangely, Julian didn't seem at all surprised by her sudden declaration. He simply glanced up from where he'd been pushing his own food around on his plate and said, "Oh?"

She nodded. "Evie had enough spirit and passion and presence for two people, so I always kind of faded into the background. Not that I minded," she added honestly. "I actually liked being invisible. I liked it that I didn't have to act a certain way because that was what people expected of me. I liked sitting on the sidelines and watching everybody else, seeing how they behaved, listening to what they said. I learned a lot. As you said, the social outcasts are privy to observations and information that other people might not notice."

Julian studied her thoughtfully. "I wish I'd been invisible in high school."

She smiled. "I would have seen you."

He smiled back. "I wouldn't have minded if *you* saw me." Then he obviously grew uncomfortable with the change of subject, because he backtracked, "But we were talking about you."

"I didn't have a date to the prom," she told him, jumping track again.

He seemed surprised. "No one asked you?"

"Robby Duggins did," she said.

"But he was a geek?"

"Actually, he was a very nice boy. Cute, too."

"So why didn't you go with him?"

"Because I was saving myself for someone else."

"Brian Richie."

She nodded.

Julian looked thoughtful for a moment. "But I thought he had a girlfriend from way back when."

"He did."

"Didn't you assume he would take her?"

"Oh, I knew he would take her," she readily admitted.

"Then why . . . ?" He didn't finish his question, but Simone knew perfectly well what he was asking.

"I had plans for Brian," she said, "even back then. A plan for prom night in particular." She met Julian's gaze levelly. "I planned to seduce Brian Richie on prom night, because I wanted to give him my virginity before we both went off to college. Even though I knew he and his girlfriend were planning to get married, I just . . ." She shrugged. "I convinced myself when I was in ninth grade that Brian was my one and only, that someday he and I would be together somehow. And I wanted my first time to be with him."

Julian said nothing in response to that, only eyed her silently, his expression so intent she could almost see the thoughts circling through his brain. She just couldn't quite discern what those thoughts were about.

"I volunteered to be in charge of the punch table," she began again. "I figured that, at some point, Brian would come up to the punch table, and I could ask him if I could talk to him privately, and then we could step outside where I could tell him what I wanted. To go someplace where the two of us could be alone, so that we could make love, and he could be my first. And then, I thought, we could go do just that."

"And how did the plan go?"

Simone inhaled another deep breath and released it slowly. "It went perfectly. At first. Brian did come to the punch table, and he did accompany me outside, and I did tell him that I wanted him to be my first. That part went just fine."

"So what went wrong?" Julian asked softly.

Simone swallowed hard. "It was the um, the making love part. We, uh, we didn't share the same vision for that."

"What happened?"

Julian's voice was even softer now, but somehow also edgier than it had been before. When Simone looked at him, she had to bite back a gasp at the sheer menace in his expression. He knew what was coming next, she thought. He knew Brian better than she had.

"I would have made love with him that night, Julian," she said. "I would have. I wanted to. And I was ready. I wanted to lose my virginity that night, and I wanted to give it to Brian." She inhaled a shaky breath. "But not the way he took it from me. I didn't want it like that."

Julian studied her for a moment in silence, his expression suddenly impassive, his eyes now unreadable. Then, very quietly, he said, "He raped you. Is that what you're trying to say?"

She nodded and moved her gaze to the floor. "It started off okay. When I kissed him that first time, he was obviously surprised, but he returned the kiss right away. Very tenderly, too, initially. But then he . . . he . . ." She inhaled a deep breath, released it slowly. "He turned ugly. He turned into a total stranger. The Brian Richie I'd always known—the one I'd always thought I'd known—he was a nice guy. But that night . . ."

"That night, he showed his true colors," Julian guessed.

She nodded again. "After I kissed him that first time, he smiled at me, and for a minute, I honestly thought he was going to tell me he'd always had a crush on me, the way I'd had one on him. For a minute, I was so happy, like this dream I'd had for four years was about to come true, and that he'd tell me he loved me, that he'd never loved anyone but me, and that he'd break up with his girlfriend and start dating me. Then he leaned forward and kissed me again. But it turned very quickly from gentle into something else. Something hungry and demanding and . . . and . . ." She glanced up to look at him, then quickly looked away. "And . . . mean."

"Simone, you don't have to tell me this if you don't want—"

"I do want to," she told him, surprised to realize it. "I think it's important that you know this about me,

Julian. I don't know why, but—" She halted abruptly, unsure what to say. Then she went on, "I know you've felt wary around me since that first night at my father's house—"

"Simone, it's not what you—"

"I know I've given you the creeps sometimes," she added, knowing it was true, unwilling to hear him deny it. "And if you know what happened that night, you'll understand. It will explain why I'm . . . It's why I . . . It's why . . ."

"It's why your bedroom back at The Keep is the way it is," he finished for her with surprising understanding.

"Yes," she told him.

"It's why you keep your dolls and toys so close at hand."

"Yes."

"It's why you sleep in a canopy bed and read books like *My Friend Flicka*."

"Yes."

"Because that's what you did before you went to high school."

"Yes."

"Before you decided Brian Richie was your one and only."

"Yes."

His eyes, with their unearthly color, had gone dark with something as he spoke, something Simone didn't think she should ask him about right now. So, not sure why she did it, she confessed the rest.

"And it's why I don't . . ." She glanced away again, unable to meet his gaze. "It's why I don't . . . wear underwear. I know you've been curious about that."

For a moment, dead silence met her ears. Then,

obviously uncomfortable with this new route the conversation had taken, Julian stammered, "Well, I, uh, I, ah . . ."

"I've seen the way you look at me, Julian," she interjected. "I know you've noticed. And I know you've wondered why. That night that Brian . . . That night that he . . ." She inhaled another deep breath and released it just as slowly. "We went out to the parking garage, to his car. I thought we could just talk out there, and then make up some excuse to leave the prom separately, and meet up again someplace else. A hotel maybe, or something. I really didn't think that far ahead.

"But once we were in his car," she continued, "and I told him what I wanted, and then kissed him . . . Well, after that, Brian didn't want to wait. I guess he figured I was fair game. I guess he figured I got what was coming to me. And he, um . . ."

Her voice trailed off because she really didn't want to go into any great detail about what had happened that night. "I tried to fight him," she said, "tried to tell him that wasn't how I meant for it to be. But he was way bigger than me, and I guess he didn't listen, or he just didn't care, or he thought no meant yes, and that was how I wanted it. He, um . . . at one point, he just . . . he tore off my underwear. So hard that the elastic in my panties burned my leg, and the hooks in my bra cut my back. I haven't been able to stand the feel of underwear against my skin since then. I just don't like it. It's too—"

She hesitated before saying any more, thinking she'd said enough. But when she finally braved a glance at Julian she began to think that maybe she'd actually said too much. Because he looked like he wanted to kill someone just then. And the way Simone felt, she wasn't inclined to stop him.

"How, um, h-how did you get ho-home that night?" Julian asked her. The slight stammer was her only indication of just how enraged he was.

She forced a wry smile that was in no way happy. "Brian drove me home afterward."

Julian arched one dark brow in disbelief. "H-he what?"

"He drove me home," she repeated. "Just like we'd been on a date or something. He drove me right to my house, leaned over me and pushed the door open, then kissed me goodnight. As I got out, he told me he'd call me. He said his father kept a boathouse on the river that was nice and secluded, and that next time, we could meet there for our fun. Then he drove away. I snuck in the back door, and I took a shower, and I went to bed, and I tried to pretend that nothing had happened. Later that night, Brian came back to the house, only this time he was bringing Evie home. And he was a hero then."

"Oh, Simone . . ."

"I never told anyone what happened," she said, concluding her story. "Not even Evie. Not until now, Julian. Not until you. I was too scared, too ashamed."

"You had nothing to be ashamed of, Simone," he said adamantly. "You didn't do anything wrong."

"A lot of people would have said I had it coming," she said.

"Yeah, well, a lot of people are asses," he pointed out.

She didn't argue with him. Instead, she told him the rest of what she needed to tell him. "I did come back to the reunion to find Brian, but not for the reason everyone thinks. Evie's so sure I've been carrying a torch for him all these years. She thinks I want to marry him. And Daddy has no idea what happened on prom night."

"If he did," Julian began.

"He'd kill Brian," Simone finished calmly.

"Yeah, well, at this point, he'd have to get in line."

She hesitated only a moment before saying, "So will you."

Well, that certainly got his attention. He eyed her warily. "You don't mean to tell me you came back here to—"

"Kill Brian?" she asked calmly.

Julian nodded. Not so calmly.

"As much as I've fantasized about such a thing over the last twenty years, no," she said. "That's not why I came back. But I did come back for Brian. I did come back for him."

"But how . . . ?"

Julian let the question linger unfinished, either because he wasn't sure how to phrase it, or because he didn't want a response. In either event, Simone didn't answer him. Instead, she turned her attention to the bottle of wine from which he'd poured only one glass, still untouched, the half-empty—or perhaps it was half-full—one that sat before him.

And although Simone hadn't touched alcohol for twenty years—it would have violated the innocence of the lifestyle she'd struggled so hard to preserve—she asked Julian, "Will you pour me a glass, too?"

She was, after all, over twenty-one, she thought. Perhaps it was time she started acting like it.

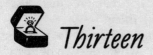 *Thirteen*

"Good evening, St. Louis! If you're just tuning in on your ride home from work, we've had a totally eighties Thursday here for you today. Next up, A Flock of Seagulls and their big hit, 'I Ran (So Far Away).'"

Wyatt switched off the radio, thinking he should probably be doing exactly what the song suggested. Instead, he braved a glance at Eve, who was seated on the passenger side of the Expedition, looking surprisingly—and no doubt deceptively—calm.

And he said, "Okay, so I never told you exactly *whose* reunion I would get you to, did I?"

In return, she threw him a look that was . . . Woo. He'd had no idea a woman's eyes could be that chillingly evil. Any minute now, her head was going to start spinning around, and then that *Exorcist* pea soup thing would almost certainly follow. He suddenly wished he'd had the foresight to pack a crucifix and some holy water and a rogue priest. Or, at the very least, some Saltines.

"Well, did I?" he demanded. "No, I did not. I distinctly remember saying, 'I'll get you to *the* reunion.' Not *'your'* reunion. Not *'our'* reunion. Just *'the'* reunion. What does that say up there?"

He pointed at the sign rising high from the middle of the Holiday Inn parking lot, where the two of them were currently sitting. It was backlit by a breathtaking sunset that stained the western sky with streaks of pink and orange and purple, but the beauty of the sight obviously eluded Eve. Mainly because she wasn't looking at it, Wyatt noted. And that would be because of the aforementioned evil eye that she was still casting upon him.

Still, she must have noticed it when they'd first driven up, because she said, very coolly, "I'll grant you that that sign up there does indeed say Welcome Class of '81."

"Which is total serendipity if you ask me," Wyatt interjected quickly while he had the chance—because it was going to be hard to talk around the fat lip that he was pretty sure would be coming any time now.

"Class of '81," she continued, her tone of voice plummeting the temperature another forty degrees, "Doheny High School," she finished. "Not Woodhaven High School. Doheny High School. Color me curious, Wyatt, but I don't think we know anyone who attended Doheny High School in St. Louis, Missouri."

He feigned thought for a moment. "Doheny . . . Doheny . . . Doheny . . . Nope, you're right. I don't believe we know anyone who attended Doheny High School in St. Louis, Missouri. But ya know, Eve, I'd lay good odds that the kids at Doheny High School had experiences that were pret-ty similar to ours at Wood-haven."

"You think so?"

"You bet."

She eyed him thoughtfully. "So you figure that, right now, somewhere in that Holiday Inn, there's a woman who's seething mad at one of her male classmates?"

He nodded magnanimously. "Oh, hey, you can count on it."

"Do you think she's ready to kill him?"

"I believe she might be, yes."

"Do you think she'll succeed before the night is through?"

This time Wyatt shook his head. "Nah. Not as long as he doesn't turn his back on her."

She bared her teeth in something that did sort of resemble a smile—the kind of smile a crocodile bestows on an aquatic mammal that it's about to turn into breakfast, for example. "If I were him," she said pointedly, "I wouldn't be so confident."

"If you were him, I wouldn't have gotten into that car with you on prom night. I mean, I'm an open-minded guy, Eve, but . . . That's just not my thang."

She inhaled slowly, deeply, and he wondered if she would take him to task—or, you know, rip out a major organ with her bare hands—because he had spoken of the unspeakable yet again. And a not-so-little part of him was actually hoping she would. Take him to task, anyway—he wasn't quite ready to surrender an organ. But for the last couple of days, Wyatt had deliberately been pushing his luck—along with Eve's buttons—precisely because he did want to get a rise out of her.

They were a day's drive from Cincinnati. Their reunion officially began tomorrow. His time was running out. If he was going to rouse that old righteous indignation in her, he was going to have to do it soon.

And for a moment, it looked as if he had indeed roused her righteous indignation to the point where she would, well, go for his jugular, if not for his spleen. But that moment passed before she attacked. Slowly, her flashing eyes dulled, and gradually, her ramrod-straight back crumpled.

And very, very softly, she said, "I want to go home, Wyatt. Now. I want to be in Ohio, where I'm supposed to be. I want to see my old neighborhood, I want to see my sister, and I want to see my former classmates." She lifted her head and met his gaze levelly. "And I need a break from you."

In spite of the knife edge he felt twisting in his gut in response to the last part of her statement, Wyatt tried to make light of her comment. "Oh, now, you know that's not entirely true, Eve. There are plenty of people from high school I bet you'd just as soon not see again. Stephanie Dewitt, for instance. I remember you putting peas in her shoes at lunch one day. And she's the kind to hold a grudge, too. She may very well turn up at our reunion with a whole case of Del Monte that has your name on it."

Eve said nothing, only continued to gaze at him in that flat, lifeless way that was somehow even scarier than the *Exorcist* look she'd given him before.

"And teachers," he added for good measure. "What if some of our old teachers are there? What if one of them is Mr. Durst, the English teacher? Remember him, Eve? You couldn't stand him because he was so freakin' literal all the time." Wyatt forced a smile he was nowhere close to feeling. "Remember? Ending sentences with a preposition was something with which up he would not put?"

Her shoulders rose and fell with her silent sigh. "I want to go home, Wyatt."

He softened at her tone. "I know you do, Eve. So do I, for that matter. But we're not going to get there today. We have to spend the night somewhere. Might as well be here."

"But—"

"We're so close. A day's drive, no more. I'll get you where you want and need to be, I promise you."

"You also promised me you'd get me to our reunion."

"*The* reunion," he corrected her. "I never specified exactly whose."

She inhaled another one of those slow, deep breaths and released it carefully. "Tomorrow. You will get us to Cincinnati by dinnertime tomorrow."

"No worries, Eve," he assured her with as much false bravado as he could rouse. "Like I said. I'll get us where we need to be. And I'll get us there when we need to be there."

She didn't look anywhere near convinced, but Wyatt was fully confident himself. At least, he was pretty confident. Sort of confident, at any rate. Kind of. In a way.

Hey, at least they'd made it this far.

"Dinnertime tomorrow," she reiterated. "I mean it, Wyatt. If this car isn't tooling down I-64 East bright and early tomorrow morning, then I'm striking out on my own."

Something about the way she said that made him smile. Because she'd said it as if she meant it. And somehow, he believed that she did. She *would* strike out alone on her own tomorrow if he didn't hold up his end of the bargain. He was sure of that. She sounded confident, independent. In spite of the shadows that still smudged her eyes, in spite of the tight lines that still bracketed her not-quite-smiling mouth, in spite of the way she still slumped her shoulders sometimes . . .

He remembered again the way she had pushed herself away from him the night before, the way she had asserted that *she* would be the one to walk away this time. He wondered what had made her put the brakes on things, just when they were about to—

Well. Just when they were about to. Because he had been more than ready to himself. He smiled again when he recalled just how ready. Oh, yeah. Mr. Happy had been *very* happy last night. In fact, Wyatt didn't think he could recall Mr. Happy *ever* being quite as happy as he had been the night before. Certainly *Wyatt* had never been as happy as he had been the night before. Hell, he'd been happier than Mr. Happy. And Mr. Happy had been pretty damned happy.

He still had no idea why everything had functioned fully last night—oh, boy had it been full—when it had failed to perform before. One of life's great mysteries, he supposed. Or perhaps one of testosterone's great mysteries—of which there were many, Wyatt knew. Maybe, twenty years ago, he'd just been too intimidated by Eve—by her confidence, by her passion, by her strength—to be able to perform. And maybe, back then, he'd just been too scared of the intensity of their responses to each other. Hell, maybe that had still been the problem the other night—he'd been too anxious and uncertain about so many things. Though, mind you, that water in the pool *had* been awfully matriarch-fricking cold.

But last night, he'd seen Eve more vulnerable than he'd ever seen her before. And he'd understood, for the first time, that, back in high school, she'd been just as scared of and unsure about things as he had been. And he'd realized that, these days, too, she was just as anxious and uncertain about things as he was. Last night, he'd seen Eve for what she really was. Not an awesome, adolescent tower of power. Not a carefully created feminine ideal. Not a perfect, well-preserved memory. She was a woman, a human being. With hopes and dreams, and frailties and fears, and hurts and setbacks, just like his. And that had suddenly made everything all right.

Until she had pulled away.

Wyatt still wasn't sure what had made her do that, but she'd no doubt had her reasons. She'd made it clear that she hadn't done it because *he* deserved it, but she'd made it equally clear that maybe it was because she had. She'd taken the initiative in the situation, regardless of her motives. She'd done what *she* wanted, what *she* needed, to do.

She was getting closer, he thought. Maybe not to the Eve she'd been twenty years ago, but to the Eve she'd always had the potential to be. Little by little, she was starting to recapture the *essence* of the girl she once was, the girl who might very well have eventually grown into a strong, sassy, confident woman, had fate not intervened in the form of Edwin Walsh and prevented it.

She was almost there, he thought. And he couldn't

help wondering what it was going to take for her to make it all the way home.

"Oh, come on, Eve, it'll be fun."

Wyatt gazed expectantly at his companion as he awaited her reply, but she didn't really look like she wanted to reply. And, truth be told, she'd hardly spoken a word to him since they'd arrived in their respective rooms. She'd opened the adjoining door politely when Wyatt had knocked, but she hadn't invited him in. Not that he'd expected her to. But even a casually offered "Don't you dare come in here, you big jerk" or something like that would have been appreciated.

"Let me get this straight," she said suddenly, surprising him. Not so much because she had spoken, but because the words *You big jerk* hadn't been among the ones she'd chosen to use. "You want to go downstairs and crash the reunion for the Doheny High School class of '81?"

He nodded eagerly, then reiterated, "It'll be fun."

"They'll throw us out," she said.

"No, they won't," he countered. "Nobody recognizes anybody at these things. We'll just go down there and snag a couple of leftover name tags and walk right in."

"What if the owners of those name tags show up and take exception to the impostors who have usurped their places?"

"Not a problem," he said confidently. "I did some checking. This reunion has been going on all week. It started on Sunday. Anybody who was planning to come would already be here. All the name tags that are left belong to the no-shows."

She narrowed her eyes at him. "And how would you know there are any name tags left?"

He smiled, then reached into his jacket pocket and withdrew two of the tags in question. "Like I said. I did some checking."

"Oh, Wyatt."

"There was a table outside the banquet room down there that must have had twenty or thirty of these things left on it. Nobody was tending to them, so they've obviously abandoned any hope of the owners showing up. Therefore, nobody will mind that I took the liberty of procuring a couple for me and you." He thrust one toward her. "You're Bitsy Stuckey."

Eve rolled her eyes. "Oh, great. What kind of a name is Bitsy Stuckey? It's way too perky. She sounds like the head of the pep club, the captain of the cheerleading squad, and the president of Future Homemakers of America, all rolled into one. She was probably a whiz in home ec."

Wyatt smiled proudly as he held up his own name tag. "And I'm Stanley Morganstern. He sounds like the head of the chess club, the captain of the math team, and the president of Future Computer Geeks of America, all rolled into one. He probably got stuffed into somebody's locker on a regular basis."

Eve tried to hand her name tag back to Wyatt. "We cannot do this," she stated adamantly. "At worst, it violates some kind of law, and we'll wind up in jail. At best, it's a grave social faux pas, and we'll wind up peeling potatoes in Martha Stewart's kitchen."

Wyatt ignored her extended hand and pinned his own name tag to the breast pocket of his blazer, the same blazer he had worn that first night in Santa Barbara. In fact, his whole outfit was the same, right down to the necktie with the hand-painted hula dancer. They were the only dress-up clothes he had.

"Come on, Eve," he cajoled again lightly. "What else are we going to do tonight, huh?"

He hoped he had injected the question with just enough licentiousness to trouble her. Evidently, he had succeeded, because her eyes went wide, and she blushed most becomingly.

"Uuuummmm," she said, stringing the comment out over several time zones. "I, uh . . . Actually . . . Well . . . Maybe we could stay in our room and watch a movie."

"Good idea," Wyatt concurred. "I missed *Red Hot Coeds in Knee Socks* when it was out in theaters. But it's on one of the cable channels tonight."

"I, um, I was thinking more along the lines of something like *Sense and Sensibility*. I never did get to see that when it was out. Even though he was an English professor, Edwin knew it was something I'd enjoy, so he wouldn't let—"

She cut herself off before completing the sentence. But instead of sounding wounded and timid and fearful when she made a reference to her ex-husband, this time Eve sounded angry and sarcastic and loaded for bear. Silently, Wyatt sent up a cheer.

And then he gaped at her, comically, he hoped, to lighten the mood. "*Sense and Sensibility?*" he asked incredulously. "Well, where the hell is the fun in that? *Red Hot Coeds in Knee Socks* would be a much better choice, if you ask me."

"I don't recall asking you."

"Good. Because I'd much rather go to this reunion."

She opened her mouth to object again, but Wyatt cut her off.

"It'll be a good time, Eve. You told me I haven't

shown you one of those yet. Give me a chance to make good on my promise to your father."

"Why? So you can collect your paycheck?" she asked, again with the anger, again with the sarcasm, again with the loaded for bear. Wyatt grinned at the realization. Oh, yeah. She was definitely coming along nicely.

He shook his head. "No, Eve, not because of that."

"Then why?"

He grinned at her. "So I can see you smile."

She blushed again, even more becomingly than before. But all she said was, "Oh."

Very slowly, she pulled her hand back in toward herself, and she gazed down at the name tag she still held. "Bitsy Stuckey," she read aloud. "She sounds like she was a nice girl in high school. Popular. Perky. Fun. She was probably happy."

"You were a nice girl, too, Eve," Wyatt assured her. "You were popular. Even if you don't want to admit it, you were perky. And boy, were you fun."

She could be happy, too, he thought, with the right motivation. And maybe, just maybe, he could help in that regard.

She nodded but said nothing in response to his comment. Instead, she spun around, but not before he caught the glitter of something shiny in her eyes. "Just give me a minute to change my clothes," she told him, her voice coming out a little shaky.

"No problem," he told her.

And for the first time since leaving Santa Barbara, Wyatt felt like that might just be true.

Eve couldn't imagine what had possessed her to let Wyatt talk her into crashing someone else's twenty-year reunion. But she had changed into a sapphire-colored, off-the-shoulder cocktail dress, a bit of whimsy she had purchased shortly before moving from LA, to wear to her own reunion, if not this one. Even though, back then, she'd wondered if she would ever be able to find the nerve to put it on. Now, as she stood in the cavernous banquet room of the Holiday Inn, waiting for Wyatt to return with her champagne cocktail, wearing a name tag that identified her as Bitsy Stuckey, Eve had to admit that she did indeed feel strangely nervy. Strangely . . . good.

It was kind of nice pretending to be someone else for a change. Someone whose history she could totally fabricate and control. Someone who, she had decided, had been cheerful and well-liked and carefree in high school, and who had gone on to marry a fine, upstanding young man named Jerry whom she met in her Intro to Philosophy class in college. Jerry now worked as an attorney for the ACLU, and Bitsy was a stay-at-home mom who sold Avon on the side. They had three lovely children—Heather, Jessica, and J J (short for Jerry Junior)—and a dog named Skip. All in all, she decided, Bitsy had a pretty nice life, with no ugly memories to clutter it up.

Wyatt, on the other hand, had decided that Stanley Morganstern had moved down to Miami after college, had made a fortune after starting his own software company, and then had lost it all in a hazy, month-long blitz of wine, women, and song. Now he sold hot tubs for a living and was married to a Miami Dolphins cheerleader named Lacy. He had three legitimate children with Lacy—Boris, Natasha, and Chip—and one illegitimate son—Clarence—by a former girlfriend named Barbi with an "i."

Some people, Eve thought, just had no ambition at all.

"Bitsy! Bitsy Stuckey! I was hoping you'd show up!"

Eve was startled to discover that it wasn't Wyatt who had offered the—rather loud—exclamation but a total stranger. A man, specifically. A balding man, more specifically. A pudgy, balding man, even more specifically. A pudgy, balding man in glasses who came to a stop much, *much* too close for Eve's comfort. As he halted, he bent forward a bit, and appeared to focus intently on her . . . breasts?

Well, of course, that was where she'd pinned her name tag—sort of—Eve thought, but still. Surely, it didn't take *that* long to read the words Bitsy Stuckey.

She injected a delight into her voice that she was nowhere close to feeling and said, "Why, hello there . . . um . . ."

She squinted at the man's name tag, but before she had a chance to read the words printed there, he slapped a hand over them. "Guess who," he said.

She smiled as becomingly as she could and said, "Come on. Give me a hint."

He smiled back, not so much becomingly, though, as . . . lecherously? Hmmm. "You want a hint, baby?" he asked. Oh, yes. That was definitely lechery. "I'll give you a hint," he told her. "Homecoming. Sophomore year. The backseat of Ryan Thurmond's Chevette. You gave me a lube job it took me three days to get over."

Oh, dear, Eve thought. Maybe Bitsy Stuckey hadn't been such a nice girl in high school after all.

"Funny, though," he added thoughtfully. "I remember you being a redhead."

Before she had a chance to comment—not that she

had any idea what to say—another man approached.

"Did I hear someone say Bitsy Stuckey?" he asked—rather lecherously, too, if she wasn't mistaken.

Eve was starting to get a bad feeling about this.

"Why, Bitsy," the newcomer said to her. Or, rather, he said to her breasts. "You look incredible. But don't I recall you being a blond? Oh, hell, what does it matter?" He, too, slapped a hand over his name tag. "Guess who I am?"

Eve knew better than to ask for a hint this time.

"Let me give you a hint," he said. "Junior prom. Under the bleachers behind the football field. You showed me and Donny Coogan a defensive position we'd never used on the field before. Hey, did those grass stains ever come out of your dress?"

Oh, my, Eve thought. Bitsy really got around.

"Why, Bitsy," yet another member of the Doheny High School class of '81 said upon approach, having clearly overheard the, um, the conversation—for lack of a better word.

This time, however, the newcomer was a woman, much to Eve's relief. Then again, she thought, the woman was probably the angry wife of someone for whom Bitsy had performed a great feat of derring-do. Bitsy was probably about to receive the verbal thrashing of a lifetime. Eve steeled herself for battle.

But the woman only smiled. Oh, no. Lecherously. "Remember me?" she asked in a smooth voice, covering her name tag. "Okay, here's a hint. Sandy Stein's slumber party the summer of eighty. You gave me a whole new definition for the word *manicure*."

Oh, yeah. Bitsy definitely got around, Eve thought. She quickly reevaluated her assessment of the Bitsy Stuckey of today. She was thrice-divorced from men who had names like Mack and Stony and Moose, and she worked as a stripper at a club called Monty's Girls Galore, with the professional name Bits O'Honey. She had an X-rated tattoo of some Disney character etched on her backside, she watched *Cops* and *Jerry Springer* religiously, and she took her Jack Daniels straight up. Her favorite thing to do on a Saturday afternoon was to water the begonias outside her trailer—and then pass out in them.

"Um, if you'll all excuse me," Eve said suddenly, "I really need to go find my date . . ."

"Oh, don't rush off," the lube job complained.

"You just got here," the defensive position protested.

"We can talk about old times," the manicure pleaded.

Eve shook her head resolutely. "No, really, I have to look for, um . . . Stanley."

At the mention of that last word, each one of her companions' faces went absolutely white, and, as one, they took a giant step backward.

"Stanley?" the lube job echoed shallowly.

"Morganstern?" the defensive position cried.

"Stanley Morganstern?" the manicure exclaimed.

Eve nodded. "Ye-es . . ."

The lube job shook his head slowly in disbelief. "I can't believe that sonofabitch would show his face here," he muttered.

"Not after all the things he did," the defensive position concurred.

"Imagine the nerve," the manicure said.

Yep. Eve was definitely getting a bad feeling about this.

"Oh, look, I think I see him over there," she lied,

extricating herself from the crowd with as much aplomb as she could—which, under the circumstances, wasn't very much aplomb at all. "It was lovely seeing you all again," she lied further. And not just the part about seeing them again was a lie. It hadn't been lovely, either. "There's nothing like reliving old memories to give a person a nice, warm feeling inside, is there?"

That, finally, seemed to rouse her companions from their bleak humors.

"Seeing you again, Bitsy, has roused a very warm feeling inside me," the lube job said with a wink.

"I'm warm," the defensive position concurred with a leer.

"It does seem overly hot in here, doesn't it?" the manicure agreed with an ogle.

Definitely time to go, Eve decided. Amid assurances that all of them would see more of her this weekend—which, in hindsight, she decided probably wasn't the best phrase to use—Eve fled as quickly as she could.

She found Wyatt a few minutes later standing near the bar, holding her champagne cocktail in one hand, a beer in the other, and a trio of men at bay—barely. She approached cautiously, having seen firsthand that the Doheny High School class of '81 could be formidable foes.

"Look, guys, there's been a misunderstanding," she heard Wyatt say as she drew nearer. "If I . . . you know . . . beat the hell out of you on a regular basis twenty years ago, I apologize most sincerely. I'm a reformed man now, I'm tellin' ya. A man of the cloth. Yeah, that's it. Father Stanley, that's me."

"Father Stanley?" one of the men said. "Gee, that's interesting, because I remember going to your bar mitzvah. My mother made me."

"Ah, yeah," Wyatt said. "Well, see, there's a really funny story attached to that."

The second man cracked his knuckles rather ominously. "I remember a funny story," he said. "It started with you calling me a 'panty-wearing geek boy,' and ended with you dunking my head in the toilet in the bathroom. Remember that, Stanley? I sure as hell do. And I'm not a foot shorter and a hundred pounds lighter than you anymore."

On the contrary, Eve noted, the man topped Wyatt by several inches and had a good fifty pounds on him. Amazing what those second puberties could do for a person.

"Look, I'm sorry," Wyatt said again. "It was an accident."

"How about when you put my head in the vise in shop class and said you were going to turn me into panty-wearing geek boy hash?" the third man asked. "Was that an accident, too, Stanley? 'Cause, you know what? I could accidentally kick your ass tonight, if you're not careful."

"Oh, Stanley!" Eve called out cheerily, bracing herself for what might come once she joined the fray. "My goodness, I've been looking all over for you," she added as she shouldered her way gently between two of the men. "I didn't realize you'd run into some of your old friends."

"Uh, yeah," Wyatt said, looking relieved to see her. "Hey, guys," he added quickly, "you remember Bitsy Stuckey, don't you?"

Each of the men turned from Wyatt to Eve, their expressions quickly changing from malevolent to . . . oh, dammit . . . lecherous.

"Bitsy!" the first man said. "Last time I saw you was

at Tony Carmichael's wedding. Yeah, that was a real religious experience I had with you in the confessional."

Oh, did Bitsy have no shame? Eve wondered. She waited for the two other men to relive their past encounters with Bitsy—the first had apparently opened her sluice gates near the banks of the Mississippi, and the second had evidently gotten some hot monkey lovin' at the St. Louis Zoo—then looped her arm through Wyatt's.

"Yes, well, I do so love to reminisce," she said, "but Stanley and I are an item now. We're very happy together."

"You and *Father* Stanley?" the first man asked skeptically.

Oops. Eve had forgotten about that.

The second man jabbed the first in the ribs with a knowing elbow. "Guess you're not the only one who has fond memories of that confessional," he piped up.

"Yeah, no wonder Stanley converted," the third man agreed.

The three men shared a few guffaws at their crass jokes—not that Eve hadn't set herself and Wyatt up for them, she had to admit—then quickly sobered.

"You better watch your ass for the rest of the week, Father Stanley," the leader of the pack said. "We're not in high school anymore ya know."

Oh, no one had ever pegged the situation more accurately than that, Eve thought.

She sighed heavily. It was going to be a long night.

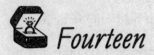 *Fourteen*

Oh, man, what a long night.

Wyatt expelled an exhausted, exasperated breath as he fell backward onto his bed. He wrestled his necktie free of his collar as he went, then thrust the accessory to the floor and unfastened the top three buttons beneath his collar. He'd had no idea how fatiguing it could be to fend off a pack of angry former panty-wearing geek boys. A pack of angry former panty-wearing geek boys who were now big enough—and mad enough—to kick his ass from here to kingdom come. And hell, he wasn't even the one who deserved it. If he ever got his hands on that bastard Stanley Morganstern . . .

Oy.

All he wanted right now was a long, hot shower and a pair of clean, cool sheets to lie between. And maybe a soft, fragrant woman to go with. Yeah, that was the ticket. Unfortunately, the only place he was likely to find such a woman right now was in his dreams. Or in his fantasies. Or in his memories.

Gee, where was Bitsy Stuckey when you needed her?

"Wyatt?"

For a moment, he thought he'd only imagined the soft sound of his name, but when he lifted his head, he saw Eve framed by the doorway that connected his room to hers. She was still wearing that heart-stopping little number she'd had on at the reception tonight— talk about your devil with a blue dress, blue dress, blue dress, devil with a blue dress on—and it had the same effect on him now that it had when he'd first gotten a glimpse of her wearing it.

Heat. Lots of it. And it all pooled in that very special place where he'd been so relieved—and triumphant— to feel it collecting last night. Just looking at Eve in that dress made him go hard. Really hard. And, oh, *man*, did that feel good. What would feel even better would be—

Never mind. Best not to think about such things. It would only lead to trouble.

"Yeah?" he asked. "What's up?" He bit back a wince after voicing the question, wishing he'd chosen another way to express the sentiment. Then again, considering the thoughts currently parading through his head, he supposed he should be relieved his remark had been as innocent as it was.

"Can I ask you a question?" she said.

"Sure," he told her. Anything to alleviate his current state of arousal, he thought to himself.

For a moment, though, she said nothing, only continued to gaze at him from her position in the doorway, standing not quite in her own room, and not quite in his. Then she said, "Being down at that reunion tonight made me think."

Oh, yeah, he'd just bet it had. Being down in that reunion had put more than a few thoughts in Wyatt's head tonight, too. And not all of them had been about high school, either. No, several of them had been about the here-and-now. But the really good ones had been about the night ahead.

But then, he was probably getting ahead of himself there.

"Made you think about what?" he asked.

She shrugged lightly. "Just that . . . All this time, I've been thinking about how much has changed over the years. How much *I've* changed over the years."

"Yeah?" Wyatt replied. "Well, it happens to the best of us, Eve. You can't stop change from coming."

"But in a way, you can," she said. "Don't you see? To those people down there, Bitsy Stuckey and Stanley Morganstern are always going to be the way they were in high school. I mean, Bitsy could be some big wheel on Wall Street right now with a multi-million dollar portfolio, and Stanley could be a devoted, loving husband and father who coaches his son's Little League team and spends time as a scout leader. They may very well have made one hundred and eighty degree changes in personality since they were in high school. But to their classmates Bitsy will always be the class slut, and Stanley will always be the class bully. Even if they'd come to the reunion, no one would have looked past what they used to be. No one would have forgotten that."

"So what's your point?" Wyatt asked.

She scrunched up her shoulders again and let them drop. "I'm not sure," she said. "Just that maybe, as much as we think we change, there's a part of us that other people, at least, will keep with them forever. Good or bad."

Wyatt still wasn't sure where she was going with her observations. Nevertheless, he responded, "I guess you're right."

"And that maybe, because that part of us stays with someone else, even if we don't see it in ourselves anymore, it's still alive in us in a way. It's still real."

Wyatt considered that for a moment, then nodded, understanding a little better what she meant. Regardless of how we evaluated ourselves these days, there were people out there in the world who remembered us as someone else entirely. Sometimes that might not be such a good thing, especially if we'd made vast improvements to ourselves and our lives. But sometimes, it could be reassuring to realize that somewhere, in someone's mind, we would be seventeen or eighteen forever.

Eve, too, remained thoughtful for a moment more, then she fixed her gaze intently on Wyatt. "And being down at that reunion tonight made me think about something else, too," she said.

"And what might that be?" he asked.

"Prom night," she said succinctly.

So now she was speaking of the unspeakable, too, Wyatt thought. And not so deep down inside, it occurred to him that it was about damned time they confronted this.

"So what's the question you wanted to ask me?" he said.

She hesitated for a moment, as if she was having second thoughts about whatever she wanted to say. Finally, though, she asked, "Why did you ... why did you leave me that night?"

Heat seared Wyatt's belly as she completed the question, even though he'd known full well it was coming. In fact, he was surprised she hadn't posed the question before now. Like maybe even that first night in Santa Barbara. Then again, he could have taken the initiative himself and explained things that night, couldn't he? But no, he'd pretty much decided that what had happened twenty years ago was dead and buried, and not especially pertinent to their experiences of today.

Yeah, right, he thought now. What had happened twenty years ago had defined life for both of them to this point. Eve had felt lousy enough about herself after that night that she'd ended up in an unhappy relationship with a man who had treated her badly. And Wyatt had felt lousy enough about himself that he'd never been able to commit to any woman for more than a brief, superficial affaire. He'd never gotten over Eve Van Dormer. And maybe, he thought, just maybe, she hadn't quite gotten over him, either.

She deserved to know the truth about what had happened to him that night, he thought. Hell, she'd deserved to know it twenty years ago, too, but she'd disappeared without a trace before he'd had the chance to explain. Now, though, he could explain. Because now they were mature adults, right? Now, they could discuss this in a mature, adult fashion. Now, he could tell her he'd been im ... impo ... impote ... you know ... that night, without fear of her laughing at him. Now, she might even understand. And hey, maybe if she understood, then she could explain it to Wyatt.

He jackknifed into a full sitting position, dropping his hands between his knees, weaving his fingers loosely together. Eve leaned her body to the right, until her shoulder connected with the doorjamb, all settled in for the explanation. She'd removed her shoes and stockings, he noted, and her feet were bare. Something about that made him smile, because in that moment, she seemed so young.

"Prom night," he said. He blew out a long, thoughtful breath. "That was a long time ago."

"Seems like yesterday in a lot of ways," she said.

He couldn't really disagree. "Yeah, I guess it does."

"So why did you leave me that night?"

Gee, nothing like cutting right to the chase, he thought. Then again, what was the point of prolonging something that had already been twenty years in coming?

"I didn't want to leave that night," he told her honestly. "I wanted to make love to you." He expelled an incredulous sound. "Man, what an understatement that is. I wanted you so much. So much. When I realized what was going to happen between us, when I knew you wanted it, too . . . God, Eve, something just exploded in me that night. There was *so much* need, *so much* wanting, *so much* passion for you. I thought I would die from it."

"Then, why . . . ?"

He suddenly smiled, a slow, ponderous smile. Because suddenly, out of nowhere, Wyatt himself began to understand. "I think, maybe . . ." He shrugged. It suddenly seemed so clear. "I think it was because there was *so much* need, *so much* wanting, *so much* passion for you, that's why."

She shook her head slowly. "I don't understand."

"You scared the hell outta me when we were in high school," he said frankly. "I was so crazy about you, but I didn't know why. I wanted you so much, but I didn't know why. I . . ." *Might as well admit it*, he thought. "I loved you, Eve, so much. But I didn't know why. And that night, when I finally had the chance to show you just how much I wanted you, just how much I loved you . . ." He shook his head, mystified. "I guess I was just overwhelmed by you, and my feelings for you, and my reaction to you. And I became totally intimidated by the thought of making love to you. And I couldn't do it."

"But why couldn't you?" she asked again. "If you wanted me and . . . and . . . If you felt the way you did, why didn't you make love to me? Why did you walk away?"

"When I say I couldn't do it, Eve," he said softly, "I mean just that. *I couldn't do it.* I physically could not do it. I couldn't get it . . . I wasn't able to . . ." Man, where was Julian to articulate the damned word when he needed him? Wyatt thought. "That night, I was im . . . impo . . . impote . . ."

"Impotent?" she asked.

Okay, so maybe he didn't need Julian after all. Not when he had Eve. "Yeah, that," he said, surprised by his lack of embarrassment and humiliation. Because Eve wasn't laughing at him. She wasn't even smiling. Probably because there was nothing funny about any of it. "I was impotent that night," Wyatt reiterated calmly. "It was humiliating. I didn't understand it. I was ashamed. And I was afraid that if you found out, you'd laugh at me. And I just couldn't stand the thought of you thinking less of me. Of you thinking I was weak. Not when you were so strong."

"Oh, Wyatt."

"I was a stupid kid, Eve," he said with profound understatement. "I panicked. I know that doesn't even come close to explaining or excusing what I did, but there you have it. I was eighteen years old, and I didn't know what to do. I'd never made love to anyone before that night. You would have been my first. And I was terrified by what happened—or didn't happen. So I bolted. I guess I had it at the back of my mind that I could try and explain it later. But a week later you were gone, and I had no idea where you were, and any chance I might have had to explain or apologize was gone with you."

She said nothing, only continued to study him in silence, and he wished like hell he could tell what she was thinking. While she was trying to figure it out, though, he figured he had one more thing he had to explain.

"It happened that night in Santa Fe, too, in the pool," he told her. "As I was kissing you, even though I wanted you . . ." He blew out an exasperated sound. "Nothing . . . nothing happened. Below the waist, I mean. Up here," he added, pointing to his head, "and here," he continued, pointing now to his heart, "I was more than ready. But . . ." He shrugged. "I don't know, maybe I just didn't give it enough time, maybe the water was too cold, maybe I still wasn't ready, but . . . I panicked that night, too. I tried to explain. At least, I think I did. But you wouldn't let me. Still, it was my fault. And I'm sorry."

Now her expression changed from thoughtful to confused. "But last night, you were . . ."

"Oh, it didn't happen last night," he agreed quite happily. "Nossirree. Last night, everything worked *juuust fiiine.*"

"Then why were you going to stop?"

Her question surprised him. "Stop? I wasn't going to stop last night. I was all systems go. You were the one who stopped."

"But that was only because I thought you were about to . . ." Her voice trailed off before she completed the statement.

"I had no intention of stopping last night," he told her. "I was totally ready."

"But why last night and not before?"

He shrugged, no less puzzled by that than she. "I don't know," he said honestly. "Like I said, maybe in Santa Fe the pool water was just too cold for me to . . . you know." He sighed heavily before admitting, "And maybe, too, in Santa Fe, you still scared the hell outta me."

She gaped at that, her eyes going wide. "*I*? Scared *you*?" she asked incredulously.

He nodded. "You're one hell of a strong woman, Eve. You may not think so, but you are. Look what you went through with your prick husband, but you didn't let it defeat you."

She met his gaze levelly, her dark eyes turbulent. "Yes, I did let it defeat me. I stayed with him for fifteen years."

"No, you didn't let it," he insisted. "Because after fifteen years of that, look where you are now."

"I've left him," she said.

"Yep."

"And now I'm here."

"Yep."

"With you."

He nodded again.

"Just like old times," she said softly.

This time Wyatt shook his head. "No. Not like old times at all. This week with you, Eve, it's been *much* better than old times."

She studied him in silence for several moments more before asking, "That night at the prom would have been your first time?"

"Yes," he admitted readily. "It would have."

"It would have been my first time, too," she told him.

Somehow, he found the revelation in no way surprising.

"So then you really did want me that night?" she asked again, even though Wyatt figured he'd more than answered that question.

"Yeah, Eve," he said anyway. "I really did want you."

She nodded slowly, thoughtfully, then asked, "Do you think it would have lasted? You and me, I mean, if we had gotten together that night?"

"Well, there was that small matter of your family disappearing a week later," Wyatt reminded her, "so . . ."

"I wouldn't have gone with Daddy and Simone if you and I had made love that night," she told him. "Or else I would have come back as soon as I could."

"You wouldn't have had to," Wyatt said. "I would have come after you, if you'd told me where you were."

"I'd have told you."

"Then I'd have come."

"So do you think we would have stayed together, if we'd made love that night?" she asked again. "Would we have started dating? And even if we'd started dating, would we have lasted, or would we eventually have broken up? Or do you think that, if we'd made love, in the morning we would have just pretended it never happened, the way we did with that kiss in the hall? Would we have both gone off to college in the fall, and then continued with our lives, with that knowledge of our first, and last, time together being nothing but a fond memory?"

"That's too many questions," he said. "And there's no way we'll ever know the answer to any of them. And maybe we shouldn't try to second-guess it all, anyway. It'd just make us crazy to sit around wondering what if." This time he was the one to hesitate a moment before telling her, very softly, "But you know, Eve, we could still have a first time together. If you wanted to. And in the morning, we could see where it takes us."

Immediately, Wyatt regretted putting voice to that last part of his statement. Not because he hadn't meant it, but because he was afraid he'd pushed too far, too soon. They were just beginning to find their way back to some common ground, he reminded himself. He shouldn't try to steer them down a path that was still way too unfamiliar, and way too overgrown with stuff they still needed to clear. He didn't want to risk them losing their way on that path again. Last time it happened, it had taken way too long for them to find their way back. And even though they'd found their way back now, they still had to clear a whole new route. A new route, he reminded himself, that was totally uncharted.

He thought Eve must have agreed with him, because she continued to gaze at him in silence for a moment more, altering her pose not at all.

He opened his mouth to take back his final words, when suddenly she asked, "Wyatt?"

"Yeah?"

"Can I ask you another question?"

"Sure."

"Could you, um . . . Could you help me with my zipper? I was having trouble a little while ago getting it down."

And something about her tone when she said it made something inside Wyatt start humming like a finely strung wire.

"Would you mind giving me a hand?" she asked again.

Oh, would he mind giving her a hand? he echoed to himself. And wasn't that just the question of the century? Hell, she could have any body part she wanted, as far as he was concerned. But his voice was the picture of coolness when he replied, "Sure. Come on over here."

She pushed herself away from the doorjamb and strode toward him, slowly, cautiously, as if she weren't quite certain of what she was about to do. Well, that made two of them, Wyatt thought. 'Cause he sure as hell didn't know how to act at the moment, either.

Probably, he thought as she came to a halt in front of him and pivoted slowly around to give him her back, it would be best if he let her lead. Probably, he thought further as he reached the zipper and tugged it downward, it would be best if he just took his cues from her.

Probably, he thought further still as the supple blue fabric separated to reveal her bare back and the merest scraps of sapphire brassiere and panties, it would be best if he held himself in check until she gave him a clear signal of what she wanted.

Then he totally ignored each of those *probably*s and leaned forward to press his open mouth to the silky flesh just above her bottom.

He heard her gasp as he completed the action, but she didn't pull away. So he pushed the zipper down to its base and tucked his hands inside the softly parting fabric, placing one on each of her hips. He could barely distinguish where the satin of her panties ended and the velvet of her skin began, so he cupped his palms over her more possessively in an effort to find out. Then he dragged his open mouth up along the elegant line of her spine, drawing his hands up over her waist and rib cage as he went. With one deft move, he pushed the dress from her shoulders, skimming his fingers down over her arms as he helped the garment along, until it puddled in a pool of rich blue at her feet.

He moved one hand to her dark hair so that he might push the silky curtain aside, to allow himself further exploration. But Eve beat him to it, reaching behind herself, curling her hands under her hair to lift it high atop her head, so that nothing hindered his progress. Wyatt stood slowly, leaving another trail of faint kisses as he went, along her spine, between her shoulder blades, behind her neck, releasing the back clasp of her bra as he passed it. As he helped that garment, too, to the floor—over one arm at a time as Eve moved first one way, then the other—he pushed his hands forward to cup them gently over her breasts. Her nipples went hard against his palms as he filled his hands with her sweet heat, but the rest of her was soft and heavy and warm. Never had he felt such exquisite loveliness, such keen perfection. And never had he wanted a woman the way he wanted Eve.

She arched her body forward, pushing her breasts more completely into his hands, uttering a sound that was ripe with passion. "Promise me you won't stop tonight, Wyatt," she said. "Promise me you won't stop until . . . not until this is finished."

"I promise I won't stop," he vowed as he pressed a kiss to the silky flesh of her shoulder. "I will never, ever, stop." Because if Wyatt had his way, then whatever it was that was burning up the air between them was never going to be finished.

"Part of me feels like we should pretend we're teenagers again," Eve said as she leaned her body back against his. "But I honestly don't want to go back to the way we used to be. I want to be here with you now, the way we are. I want our first time together to be the way we are now. Let's start from here and go forward. And maybe . . ."

She never finished whatever she had intended to say, and Wyatt didn't ask her to. Probably because he was already pretty sure what she had been about to say. He was sure, because he felt the same way, too.

She spun around to face him and circled her arms around his neck, pushed herself up on tiptoe, and covered his mouth with hers. A wild heat surged through him as he returned her kiss, deeply, resolutely, possessively. He tried not to think about what had come before. He tried not to think about what might—or might not—lay ahead. He thought only of this night, this moment, with Eve. He thought about how sweet and lush she felt in his arms, about how fresh and luscious she smelled, about how very badly he needed her, about how very much he wanted her. They were here together now, he told himself. And that, for the moment, was all that mattered.

Eve still couldn't quite remember the precise point in the evening where the time-space continuum had shifted, where the past and present had folded in on each other and had seemed to become the same. At the moment, though, she didn't care. Because at the moment, she was feeling such a delicious mix of emotion and sensation. When Wyatt touched her the way he did, she responded with both the innocence of the girl she had once been and with the experience of the woman she had become. She was no stranger to the sex act, having been married as long as she had. But what she felt with Wyatt went beyond an act, and it certainly went beyond sex. What she felt with Wyatt was new and exciting, and so very different from what she had experienced with . . .

She couldn't even bring herself to think her ex-husband's name now. Because he was as out of place here as . . . as . . . Well. He was part of the past, she told herself. And Wyatt was her present. Wyatt might perhaps be her future, too, but right now, she wouldn't let herself think that far ahead.

So she enjoyed that moment, and the moment that followed it, and the one that followed after that. And the moments strung together, one by one, a blur of hazy, delicious sensations and newly blossoming emotions. There was Wyatt. There was Eve. There was fire. There was need. There was . . . Oh. So much more than she had ever imagined there could be.

The scrape of his shirt against her bare breasts was an acute and sensuous torture, and acting on instinct alone, she rubbed her body languidly against his. Wyatt spanned his open hands over her naked back, rushing his fingers up and down her spine, cupping them over her satin-clad fanny, pushing her into the heated cradle of his pelvis. She felt him surge against her, ripe and ready, eager to please. She dropped a hand to that part of him, palming the hard ridge through his trousers, rousing a growl of anticipation from what sounded like a very deep place inside him. His hands abandoned her back momentarily, long enough to unfasten his belt and fly, then they circled her waist again and pulled her close once more, in a silent bid that she should finish the job he had begun.

Eve turned her attention first to the buttons of his shirt, plucking them through their fastenings as quickly as she could. Then she shoved the garment off his shoulders and tugged free his T-shirt from his trousers, pulling it over his head until it, too, landed in a careless heap on the floor. Then, finally, they stood naked torso to naked torso.

He was glorious, she thought as she drank in her fill of him, flattening her hands to skim them over his shoulders, his abdomen, his arms. Dark hair spanned his chest and arrowed down to disappear into the waistband of his trousers, over a flat belly and truly spectacular abs. His shoulders and arms were a range of richly defined musculature, and she took her time tracing a fingertip over each of the solid curves.

As a boy, he'd been adorable, she thought. But as a man, he was awesome. She lifted her gaze to his, and what she saw in his eyes nearly stopped her heart. Raw hunger. Very much like her own. More than two decades in the making.

She cupped his jaw in her hand, and he closed his

eyes, tilting his head to lean into her touch. She threaded her fingers through his hair, lifted her other hand to his shoulder, and pushed herself up on tiptoe again to kiss him. This time, Wyatt met her halfway, roping an arm around her waist to pull her closer still. As their mouths met, he spun her slowly around and down, until they lay side by side on his bed.

For a long, long time, they only explored each other's bodies, languidly, thoroughly, rediscovering territory they'd barely covered before, and finding new regions to claim. Wyatt slipped his hands beneath her panties, cupping his hands intently over her derriere to mold her against himself. Eve, in turn, pushed his trousers aside and over his hips, found his taut buttocks beneath his briefs, and palmed the firm muscles, urging him closer still. He bucked his pelvis against hers, once, twice, three times, the rubbing of their clothing over their sensitive flesh making that delectable friction all the more arousing. Then, in one frantic move, Wyatt skimmed his pants and briefs off, and rolled Eve onto her back to settle himself between her legs.

He felt glorious positioned there, the hard, heavy length of his entire body pressing against her own. He braced himself on forearms that he'd folded on each side of her head, and tangled great handfuls of her hair in each fist. For a long moment, he only gazed down at her face, his eyes dark with wanting, his lips parted to facilitate his ragged respiration. With each deep, quick breath he took, his chest pressed harder against her naked torso, tantalizing her, tempting her, torturing her.

He dipped his head to hers for a lengthy, thorough kiss, exploring her mouth intimately, possessively, with his tongue. Eve responded by opening her hands over his bare back, curling her fingers into his heated flesh before urging them lower, to his firm hips and buttocks, then up to his back again. Wyatt moved his head to her neck, burying his face in the delicate curve where her neck met her shoulder, brushing soft, butterfly kisses over her tender flesh. She tilted her head back against the mattress to give him freer access, and he immediately took advantage, tasting the divot at the base of her throat before turning his oral attentions to her collarbone, her breastbone, a few of her ribs, and, finally, finally, her breast.

After dragging the tip of his tongue leisurely along the plump lower curve, he grasped the soft globe firmly in one hand and pushed upward, filling his mouth with as much of her as he could. He sucked her hard inside as his fingers gently squeezed her flesh, the damp heat of his tongue pressing over the distended peak, generating a fire in her belly she knew wouldn't be extinguished anytime soon. She thrust a hand into his hair and held him where he was, silently demanding that he increase his ministrations.

He complied enthusiastically, cupping his hand over her other breast, palming it with much affection before catching the taut nipple between his thumb and forefinger. He rolled the tight bud gently, then shifted his mouth from one breast to the other, sucking even harder this time in his effort to consume her. He let his free hand wander downward, over her flat belly and points beyond, then slipped it deftly beneath the waistband of her panties and between her legs.

Instinctively, Eve opened herself to his touch, bending her knee as she moved one leg further aside. As Wyatt pulled her breast more deeply into his mouth, he pushed his fingers into her damp curls, furrowing her, parting her, exploring her with one knowing touch after another. She cried out as he inserted one long, confident finger inside her, then withdrew it slowly to slide it in more deeply still. Again and again he penetrated her that way, until Eve thought she would go mad with wanting him. Then his thumb found the stiff nub of her clitoris and pressed gently, and she thought she would rip apart at the seams.

"Oh, Wyatt," she gasped. "Please make love to me."

"Not yet," he said roughly as he withdrew his hand from her panties again. "But these, I'm afraid," he added as he fingered the elastic, "have got to go."

"Okay," she immediately acquiesced. She smiled at him as she reached for the garment in question.

"Ah, ah, ah," he said softly, circling sure fingers around her wrist to stop her. "Allow me."

"Well, all right," she murmured breathlessly as she relaxed back against the mattress. She arced her hands high over her head, crossing her wrists. "If you must."

This time Wyatt was the one to smile. "You are so beautiful," he said, his gaze roving hungrily over every inch of her. His eyes locked with hers again as he curled his fingers gently over her neck, guiding his fingertips along the line of her jaw. "So very beautiful," he repeated reverently.

He skimmed his hand slowly downward again, more tenderly, less urgently this time, over the small divot at the base of her throat, along each collarbone, down against her breastbone, moving sideways to circle first one dark aureole, then the other. Then down further still, over her torso, into her navel, pausing only for a moment at the waistband of her panties. He glanced at her face one last time, as if asking permission, and Eve nodded eagerly, silently. She lifted her hips as he tugged the garment over them, then relaxed again as he drew the scrap of fabric down over her thighs, her knees, her calves, her feet.

He was practically kneeling before her by the time he completed the action, and he seemed in no hurry to rejoin her on the bed. Eve felt his fingers circle first one ankle, then the other, felt the soft brush of his mouth along the inside of first one calf, then the other. Heat rocketed from her toes to her belly and beyond, and she murmured a soft sound of contentment as she closed her eyes. Wyatt kissed her knees and the insides of her thighs, urging her legs further apart as he ascended. Then she felt his hands moving higher still, felt his thumbs pressing close to that most sensitive part of her once again. With a gentle push, he opened her legs wide, and this time she felt the butterfly soft flick of his tongue as he tasted her dewy center.

Fire shot through her at the contact, and she sucked in her breath at the intensity of the heat. She'd never felt such . . . No one had ever . . . This was the first time anyone had . . .

Oh, Wyatt.

She didn't realize she'd gasped his name aloud until she heard his soft chuckle. Before she could voice a protest—not that she was absolutely certain she even wanted to protest—he tasted her again, more deeply this time, more thoroughly, and she found that she couldn't speak at all. She could only feel, could only react, could only savor the wild tumult of sensation that was wheeling through her. Wyatt must have understood her condition, because he took complete advantage of it, dipping his head eagerly toward her again. He laved her with the flat of his tongue, tantalized her with its tip, then, just when she thought she would die from the fever that shuddered through her, he opened his mouth and devoured her.

She cried out at the relentless rush of her response, a response that seemed to last forever. And she was nearly insensate with her need for him by the time Wyatt moved his body up alongside hers. Somehow, though, she found the strength to reach for him, and when he came to her, she pulled him close. His entire body was damp with perspiration, both hers and his own, and redolent of the musky scent of her release. When she moved her hand down to grip his hard shaft in sure fingers, she discovered he had donned a condom at some point before returning to her, and she gazed at him with hazy curiosity.

"What can I say?" he asked sheepishly. "I never leave home without one. It was in my wallet, in my trousers, on the floor."

"You get lucky that often, do you?" she asked roughly, breathlessly, the realization touching her words with melancholy.

He shook his head. "No, I don't," he said with much certainty. "Only tonight, Eve. Only with you do I feel lucky."

She smiled at that, telling herself she should be thankful for his foresight, because she certainly hadn't come prepared herself. Then again, she didn't think she could have ever been prepared for Wyatt. She hadn't been prepared twenty years ago, and she wasn't prepared tonight. That didn't mean, however, that she wasn't ready for him.

"Make love to me," she told him again. "Now, Wyatt. I want to feel you inside me. I've waited for so long."

It was all the encouragement he needed. Once again, he settled himself between her legs, propping himself up on his elbows, one on each side of her head. He bent to kiss her as he drove himself deep inside her, pushing his tongue into her mouth with the same possessive purpose with which he penetrated her body. Eve opened to him willingly, welcomed him inside, curling her legs over his thighs, her arms over his shoulders, locking him inside herself. She thrust her hips upward as he drove himself down, and he shoved a pillow beneath her bottom to intensify their joining.

Again and again they claimed each other, each moving more deeply and giving more freely with every coupling, until, as one, they cried out in their completion. And then, as one, they clung to each other, until the last of the aftershocks had ebbed.

A long time later, they lay entwined in the darkness, their arms and legs so tangled it was virtually impossible to tell where one body ended and the other began. Never in her life had anything felt more good, more right for Eve. Being here with Wyatt this way ... It was as if she'd found a piece of herself that had been missing for far too long. He'd been inside her physically now, and, even more important, he was inside her spiritually and emotionally, too.

She told herself she should be frightened by the totality of her response to him, but instead, she felt utterly content. Because she remembered what he had said earlier, what had been circling through her head the whole time they were making love.

"Wyatt?" she said softly.

"Hmmm?" he replied, every bit as quietly.

"Earlier tonight, when we were talking about ... about before, you said ..."

But she couldn't quite bring herself to repeat the words out loud now. Once she'd heard them, she'd buried them deep inside herself, and now she was reluctant to pull them back out again and release them so soon.

Still, she tried again. "Earlier tonight, you said that . . . You told me that, back then, you . . ."

"That I loved you?" he finished for her, clearly already knowing what was going through her mind, through her heart.

"Yes," she said, so quietly this time that even she almost didn't hear it. She strove for a bit more fortitude when she continued, "You said that you loved me."

There was a moment of silence when she thought she could almost hear their heartbeats thrumming in time. Then, "I still do," he told her. "If that's what you were wondering."

She expelled a slow, shaky breath she hadn't even been aware she was holding. "I was wondering," she admitted.

He, too, released a long pent-up breath, twining a length of her hair around his finger. "I have always loved you, Eve. As much as I tried to tell myself I didn't . . . I never stopped," he told her. "But it's different now, somehow. I just . . . I guess the love I felt for you when I was a kid has matured and grown up along with me. Because now . . ."

"Now . . . ?" she urged him cautiously.

He turned to look at her, smiling, tracing her jaw with the finger that had captured her hair. "It's stronger, for one thing," he said. "I would have sworn that wasn't possible, but it is. And it's not as hard to understand as it was before. And it's not as uncertain, either."

She smiled back, her entire body humming with happiness. "Good," she told him, tightening her arms around him as she snuggled closer. "Because you should feel certain."

She felt his smile broaden as he pressed a chaste kiss to her forehead. "And why is that?" he asked.

"Because I love you, too," she told him. "I always have. I never stopped. And it's stronger now than it's ever been before."

He inhaled deeply and tucked her head into the curve of his shoulder and neck, resting his cheek on her crown. "Oh, Eve," he said. "It's been such a long road to get here."

She nodded. "And we still have a ways to go."

"A day's drive," he told her. "No more than that."

"I wasn't talking about Cincinnati," she said.

"Neither was I."

She leaned her head back and eyed him curiously, but he said nothing more. He only dipped his head to hers and covered her mouth with his, a sweet, innocent kiss that gradually built to something more—something that was in no way innocent, yet still very, *very* sweet.

And as Eve lost herself to that kiss, lost herself to Wyatt, lost herself to everything that was left to come, she still couldn't help wondering how much longer 'til they got there.

 *Fifteen*

At precisely 6:46 P.M. on Thursday evening, the knock that was supposed to come at seven o'clock sharp sounded on the door to Simone's suite. And Julian couldn't help thinking that Brian Richie was an impatient little prick.

Julian had promised Simone that he would make himself scarce tonight, had promised her he'd be gone—or at least be hiding in the closet—by the time Brian arrived. And he'd been frankly amazed that she had believed him. Now, he heard water shut off upstairs and realized she hadn't heard the knock of the early bird who was really just a worm.

This, he thought as he reached for the doorknob, *is going to be very enjoyable.*

"Why, Brian," he said when he opened the door to the malignant little maggot. "It's so good to see you again."

Brian's smile—another one of those smarmy, wiggins-provoking smiles—fell a bit when he saw Julian standing there, instead of Simone, the object of his . . . whatever it was that revolting rapist scumbags like him felt. "Uh, Percy, isn't it?" he asked.

Julian tried not to wince. But his voice was level when he replied, "Yeah. That's me."

"Where's Simone?"

"She's still getting ready."

The putrid little pig nodded thoughtfully. "Strange, you being here at her suite this way when she's expecting me."

Julian shrugged. "Not really."

"Oh?"

But instead of clarifying, Julian decided to let the slimy little swine draw his own conclusions. "Can I get you something while you're waiting?" he asked. "Beer? Wine? Coffee?" *Belladonna? Hemlock? Rat poison?*

"No, thanks," the vile little vermin replied with an obsequious smile. "I'll just wait for Simone."

Julian figured he had ten minutes, at most, to take care of business before Simone came down. Which was absolutely no problem. He'd done a lot of damage in a lot fewer than ten minutes in his day. Those weird, in-between years he'd described for Simone hadn't been weird only because he was discovering his sexual self. No, with all his newly developed muscles, Julian had discovered his macho self, as well. And his macho self had been one angry sonofabitch, no question there. At least until his macho self had swilled enough Bourbon and knocked enough heads to get it all out of his system. A rancid little rat like Brian Richie was going to prove no contest at all.

Julian cracked his knuckles with much affection.

Brian Richie, he noticed, noticed.

And so, evidently, did Simone as she rounded the curve in the stairs, because Julian heard her . . . snarl?—yep, that was definitely a snarl—ever so softly under her breath. Dammit. She was early, too. Now he'd never be able to beat the hell out of Brian before she intervened. Why couldn't people show up at the designated time anymore? How incredibly impolite. Where was Emily Post when you needed her?

When he turned to face Simone, the explanation he'd so meticulously planned to offer about why he was going to pound her date into a bloody pulp fled his brain completely. Because Simone Van Dormer looked more delicious than he'd ever seen her look before. And that was saying something. Her long, pale hair was wound up the back of her head and gathered in a little knot at her crown, and only now did he realize just how incredibly sexy her neck was. Her shoulders were bare, save the thin straps of her dress, a dress that was the color of cotton candy and just about as substantial. The neck scooped low, the hem fell high, and, as always, she wasn't wearing a stitch of underwear beneath it. And although Julian told himself it was just his imagination, he swore he could faintly make out the perfect, quarter-sized circles surrounding her nipples. His shaft went stiff as a pike as a result.

"Jul . . . uh . . . Percy?" she asked curiously—and not a little snarlingly. "What are you doing here? I thought you were going to go on that sunset bird-watching tour with the boys?"

Oh, great. So it wasn't enough she had to name him Percy Lipschitz? he thought. Now she was going to make him a bird-watcher, too?

"It got canceled," he told her. "The guys decided to take in a Reds game instead. And you know how I feel about all that unnecessary violence in baseball."

She narrowed her eyes at him. "Then how about taking in a movie?" she asked. "Because Brian and I have plans to go—"

"Sounds great," Julian interrupted before she could finish. He smiled first at her, then at the revolting little rodent who'd come calling. "Just let me get my wallet. I'd love to come with you guys. Thanks for inviting me along."

"Well, what was I supposed to do?" he asked Simone several hours later as she paced the length of their suite and grumbled incoherent—though, he was certain, insulting—words under her breath. "Let you go out alone with that squalid little snake? Who knows what he might have tried to do to you? Hell, what he might have *done* to you? In case you've forgotten, Simone, I'm your *body*guard. Whether you like it or not."

She halted on the other side of the room, narrowed her eyes at him, and stated, quite coherently now, "I can take care of myself, Julian."

"Oh, sure. Like you did on prom night?" He hadn't intended to be mean by bringing up something so painful, but Simone was in dire need of a reality check. "He's still twice your size, and twice your weight. He could easily overpower you the way he did before. And I've been hired by your father to make sure nothing like that happens, even if Luther thinks the real threat lies elsewhere. Don't even expect me to let you out of my sight with that sleazy little scumbag Brian sniffing around."

"Things are different now," she told him. "I know what Brian is, and I'm prepared this time."

"Yeah, that's what concerns me," Julian told her. "This preparation you've been preparing for so long. Just what the hell do you have planned for the guy? You said you didn't want to kill him, but that doesn't keep the murderous gleam out of your eyes whenever his name comes up. I need to know what's going on, Simone."

"No, you don't," she countered. "It's none of your business."

"I've made it my business."

"And I'm telling you it's not. When Brian and I go to the reception together tomorrow night—"

"I'll be right there with you," Julian assured her.

All night long he'd had to watch while that turgid little toad cozied up to Simone, pressing his body against hers every chance he got, running his hands over every inch of her he could reach in polite society. Julian's own hands had been clenched into perpetual fists, and it had taken every ounce of willpower he possessed not to plant one square into Brian's jaw. Or his nose. Or his eye. Or some other vulnerable body part—Julian wasn't particular. Worse, he'd had to watch while Simone pretended to be interested in the slimy little slug, gifting the insidious little insect with the kind of smile she'd never offered Julian, laughing at the contemptible little cretin's stupid jokes, holding the despicable little deadbeat's hand.

And all the while, Julian had tried to figure out what was going through her mind, and what she had planned for the odious little obscenity. But she'd seemed like a woman who was genuinely delighted by her company, a woman who was honestly having a good time, a woman who was halfway in love with the man who had, twenty years ago, robbed her of herself and of her soul. That creepy sensation had washed over Julian again, and not just because of Brian Richie's presence. Simone was up to something—he was sure of it. But for the life of him, Julian couldn't figure out what it was.

Now, as she glared at him, she shifted her shoulders back in challenge and fisted her hands on her hips. And she clearly didn't realize what the gesture did to her dress, how it pulled the fabric taut over her torso, outlining distinctly the generous curve of each breast. Julian squeezed his eyes shut tight so he wouldn't see how lovely, how perfect she was. And he wished with all his heart that she hadn't had to suffer the experience she'd had to suffer at the hands of that scabrous little sleazebucket Brian Richie. Because there was nothing he wanted more at the moment than to pull her into his arms and show her just how fine it could be between a man and a woman.

"You're ruining everything," she said softly. "If you don't let me do this my way, Julian, it's all going to be for nothing."

"Just tell me what you're going to do," he pleaded.

She shook her head. "Let me do this my way. I have to do it my way."

"I can't let you do that, Simone. I'm worried about you."

She narrowed her eyes at that, drawing her mouth into a tight line. "What? You think the pathetic little rape victim can't get past the need for revenge?"

He nodded vigorously. "Yeah, as a matter of fact, that's exactly what I think."

"I'm over what happened, Julian," she stated adamantly. "I've been over it for a long time."

"Simone, back in Santa Barbara, you live your life the way a thirteen-year-old girl lives. Trust me. You're not over it."

She said nothing to that at first, only eyed him with a speculation he couldn't begin to comprehend. "Trust *me*, Julian," she finally said softly. "Trust that I know what I'm doing."

"Yeah, you're very knowledgeable about this stuff, aren't you?" he asked cynically.

"I know enough," she assured him.

He took a few deliberate steps toward her, his gaze fixed on hers, stopping only when a few scant inches of air separated them. "Have you ever even kissed a man, Simone?" he asked suddenly, softly.

Her lips parted fractionally, and two bright spots of pink tinted her cheeks. "What's that got to do with anything?"

"Have you?" he asked.

"I don't see what this—"

"You said you know what you're doing," he interrupted her. "And you said you're over what happened. I interpret that to mean that you've put the episode behind you, and that you've gotten on with your life."

"That's true," she said. "I have."

But her voice lacked the conviction that might have swayed him to believe her. Instead, ever since she'd started defending herself, she'd been speaking quietly, mechanically, as if what she was saying was something she'd memorized years ago and repeated automatically by rote.

"Then, if you've gotten on with your life, you must have had at least a few romantic relationships over the last twenty years," he surmised.

Now she said nothing, only gazed at him in silence.

"I mean," he continued, "you're a beautiful, intelligent, charming woman. Surely there have been plenty of men who've been interested in you. Men who've asked you out."

She swallowed, he noted, with some difficulty. "Yes," she told him. "There have been. A few."

"And surely you've been interested in at least a few of them, too," Julian further speculated.

"Maybe," she conceded. "One or two."

"So then you must have accepted when they asked you out." Although Julian knew where he was going with his line of questioning, he suddenly wasn't all that happy about the route he had chosen. Still, he didn't back down. He had a point to make. Among other things.

She dropped her gaze to the floor, crossing her arms uncomfortably over her midsection now. "Um, actually, no. I haven't accepted any of them."

"Why not?" he asked.

"It, uh . . . it was never convenient."

He paused a telling moment before asking, "In twenty years, it's never been convenient for you to go out with a man you found interesting, and who was interested in you?"

"No."

"Then I guess you *haven't* ever kissed a man, have you?"

She glanced up at him, long enough for him to see that her blush had deepened, then back down at the floor. "I, uh . . . no," she finally said. "Just that once. Just . . . Brian."

Just Brian, Julian thought. That was the only experience she'd ever had with a man. "So then you have no idea what it's really like," he said quietly.

"No," she agreed. "I suppose I don't."

"And yet you say you know what you're doing. You say you've gotten over what happened."

"I have," she insisted halfheartedly. "I have gotten over that. I just haven't . . ."

"What?"

She expelled an anxious breath. "I have put what happened with Brian in the past," she assured him again, more adamantly this time. "But I just haven't . . ." She released another one of those troubled sighs, then said, "I just haven't been able to move forward, that's all. In some ways, I kind of got . . . stuck. Life has just sort of . . . happened to me, Julian. I haven't really consciously chosen any of it. Not until this opportunity with Brian presented itself. This is the first time I've ever really decided I was going to do something, and then done it. That's why you have to trust me. That's why you can't interfere."

"All right," he said reluctantly. "I won't interfere. Not with Brian."

She closed her eyes, clearly relieved. "Thank you."

He took another step forward, bringing him close enough to her that their bodies were almost flush against each other. He didn't touch her, though, not right away. He waited for her to become accustomed to his closeness, waited to see if she would take a step backward in retreat. And when she didn't, when she stood firm and tilted her head back to look at him curiously, he lifted a hand to her hair, and slowly, gently, twined an errant strand around his finger that had escaped the knot atop her head. Her eyes widened at the innocent touch, her pupils expanding to nearly eclipse the blue of her irises. But she didn't move away, didn't discourage him, didn't say a word.

"I can't quite help interfering, though," he told her softly, "with this."

And then he dipped his head forward, very, very slowly, pausing when his mouth hovered only millimeters above hers. He wouldn't kiss her if she didn't want him to, he promised himself. It was her call. And he was reasonably certain that he'd survive if she decided to push him away.

But she didn't push him away.

She did lift both hands toward his chest, palms flat, but hesitated before touching him, as if she was uncertain about what she wanted to do. So Julian waited. He was a patient man. He could wait all night, if that was what it took. Hell, he could wait forever, if the prize at the end of eternity was Simone Van Dormer.

As Julian hovered over her, neither kissing her nor moving away, Simone felt panic rise from the pit of her belly, souring the back of her throat. He was so big, she thought. Even though she knew better these days how to take care of herself, he could, if he really wanted to, overpower her. And she'd had no preparation for what he clearly wanted to do. Oh, she'd seen the way he had looked at her this week, had heard the suggestiveness in some of his comments. And she wasn't so naive that she didn't understand when a man wanted to jack things up to the next level.

In the past, she'd always been very good at discouraging such interest in men the moment it appeared.

With Julian, though, she hadn't discouraged it. She told herself that was because she hadn't thought he would act on his interest. He was so cool, so composed, a man who seemed to control his passions the same way he adjusted the temperature of his tap water. She just hadn't thought she needed to discourage him—he seemed so successful at discouraging himself.

Now, however, she wondered if she hadn't discouraged him because . . . well . . . because she was interested in him, too. No, he wasn't the first man she'd found attractive over the years. She'd told him the truth when she said there'd been one or two who'd caught her fancy. But they'd never caught enough of it for her to breach that invisible wall she'd erected around herself twenty years ago. She'd never been interested in them enough to step outside her fortress and make herself vulnerable to them. With Julian, though, for some reason, she did want to break through that self-imposed barrier. She wanted out. She wanted to liberate herself. She wanted, for the first time in two decades, to see what it was really like on the outside.

So, without thinking any more about it, reacting on instinct alone, Simone pressed her hands against his chest and tilted her head back a bit. She pushed herself up on tiptoe, and in the breath of a second, her mouth connected with his. And the moment her lips grazed his, she was nearly overcome by the softness, the warmth, the tenderness of his touch. She hadn't thought such a large, solid man would feel so sweet, so pleasant. She had feared she would feel overwhelmed by having him so close. But Simone didn't feel overwhelmed. She didn't feel fear. What she felt was . . .

Oh, my.

The quiver of sensation that wound indolently through her was simply too delicious for words. Slowly, she moved her hands upward, over his chest, toward his shoulders. As she went, she located the pulsing of his heart, and she realized it was racing with the same erratic, uncertain pounding as her own. The recognition of that gave her courage, made her feel bolder, and she curled the fingers of one hand around his warm nape. She threaded the others through his dark hair, cupping the crown of his head, pulling him down to herself so that she might taste him more deeply. And when she did, Julian followed her down willingly, looping his own arms loosely around her waist.

He didn't press her, didn't take the lead, never tried to seize control. He let her set the pace, let her call the shots, let her take possession of him. And as Simone kissed him more completely, as she opened her mouth to him and tentatively pushed her tongue inside his, she realized she wanted very much to take possession. And once she had him, she thought vaguely, she didn't think she would ever want to let him go.

"Kiss me," she said softly against his mouth, surprising herself. And Julian, too, judging by his expression. "Please, Julian," she added even more softly. "Kiss me back. Show me . . . show me how it can be."

It was all the invitation he needed. Even so, when he took the initiative, it was with a gentleness and solicitude she hadn't expected. Although Simone had never really been afraid of men after the episode with Brian, she hadn't ever been entirely comfortable around them, either. She'd never fully trusted them. With Julian, though, she realized she did trust him.

She was comfortable around him. Because she knew he would never hurt her. She knew that because he, too, had been hurt in his youth.

At her soft petition, he tightened one arm around her waist and pulled her to himself, then cupped a hand gently over her cheek. For a long moment, he gazed down into her eyes, then he dipped his head to hers and, very gently, covered her mouth with his. Simone closed her eyes so that she might better appreciate the responses keening through her, the heat, the wanting, the need, the desire. So much . . . There was just so much, she thought. And all of it was so new, so wondrous, so elemental, so . . . so nice.

So this was what it was like, she thought. This was how it was supposed to be between a man and a woman. The easy and equal exchange of surrender and capture, of thrust and parry, of give and take. She'd only known half of it before. The capture, the thrusting, the taking. Having the whole picture now was quite . . . enlightening.

Julian kissed her more deeply then, exploring her mouth this time with his tongue. Sharp heat exploded in her belly and her chest at such an intimate penetration, rocketing to her extremities, to her very soul. Her response to him was so visceral, so innate, that she wanted to become one with him right then. But she knew it was too soon. It was one thing to kiss a man and quite another to join her body with his. There would be time for that ultimate coupling later, she told herself. For now, she just wanted to feel, to explore, to learn more about how it could be between a man and a woman.

Reluctantly, she tugged her mouth free of his and pushed herself slightly away. She looked at his face and saw a man tormented in much the way she was herself. His cheeks were ruddy with his passion, his mouth was swollen with the intensity of their kiss. His hair had been tousled by her fingers, and his breathing was ragged and hot. Simone swallowed hard and tried to quiet her own rough respiration. She told herself they should stop, that this experiment, though successful, had gone far enough—for now.

Instead, she said quietly, "Show me more, Julian. Please. Show me more."

His smoky eyes grew even darker at her declaration, but he said nothing in response. He only gazed at her intently for several taut moments, his hands on her back moving lightly up and down, up and down, up . . . and . . . down. Then, suddenly, he pulled her body against his again and skimmed a hand lower. Past the small of her back, past her waist, over her fanny, to the lower curve of her derriere. He bunched a small handful of her dress in his fingers and rubbed the soft fabric languidly back and forth over her heated flesh. Slowly, methodically, he dragged the skimpy material up and down, left and right, each circular motion drifting the fabric over her sensitive skin, moving the garment higher, until Simone felt the cool kiss of air on her naked behind. She thought it the most erotic sensation she'd ever experienced. Until she felt the warmth of Julian's palm cupping gently over her bare bottom.

Her heart kicked hard against her breastbone at the contact, and she opened her mouth to tell him to stop, that they'd gone far enough, that even though she was the one who'd made the request, she was starting to feel frightened now, and *please, Julian, please don't do that, not yet, not until I'm ready, which I thought I was, but I changed my mind and now I don't want to, so please stop.*

But before she could get the words out, Julian himself spun away from her, walking uncomfortably to the other side of the room. As he went, he expelled a long, lusty groan from deep inside himself, as if he'd just been struck. Her dress fell back down to cover her, but Simone still felt naked somehow. Where before she might have panicked at feeling such a thing, though, with Julian, such emotional nakedness wasn't quite so alarming. Because he'd bared himself to her, too, in a way. And the moment he'd turned away from her, every bit of her fear had fled.

"Julian?" she said softly. "Is everything . . . okay?"

For a moment, he said nothing, only kept his back turned to her, his shoulders rising and falling as he tried to level off his breathing. Little by little, though, he calmed himself down. Then he raked both hands deliberately through his hair and inhaled one final, fortifying breath. Still facing the wall, he told her, very gently, "I want to make love to you so badly, Simone. But not until you're ready for it." He pivoted back around to face her, his dark eyes still turbulent, his cheeks still flushed, his breathing still a little uneven. And he added, "And not until I'm ready for it, too."

She gaped softly at him, confused by his declaration. Then, gradually, she began to understand. Neither one of them was ready for the explosive responses they aroused in each other. She had shaken him as profoundly as he had shaken her. They both had much to learn—about themselves and about each other—before they could take that next monumental step. She smiled as the heat he had sparked to life inside her banked a bit and began to smolder. That fire would never go out completely, she knew. But for now, she could contain it. She could manage it. She could learn more about it. And then, when she was ready, when Julian was ready, the two of them together could spontaneously combust.

"I want to wait for the right time, too," she told him. "But, um, how long, uh . . . When do you think that will be?"

He grinned at her. "We'll know when the time comes," he said. "And the time will come, Simone. Don't doubt that. But right now . . . it's just too soon. For both of us. We need to give ourselves time. Time to do it right."

She nodded her understanding. Julian was right. They needed time. Time to get to know each other. Time to become comfortable together. Time, perhaps, she thought further, to even fall in love.

And time for something else, too, she knew. Time for her to put the past well and truly in the past, where it needed to remain forever. Time to see to it that Brian Richie paid for what he had done, and to make sure he never did anything like that again.

Tomorrow, she thought, she would take care of that last item on the list. Tomorrow, she would sneak out without Julian's knowledge somehow, and she would go to meet with Brian, before the reception. She would do what she had to do. And then, finally, she would be free to get on with her life.

When Julian awoke on Friday, he knew immediately that something was wrong. The hotel suite was too quiet, too dark, too lonely. Although he'd always awoken a couple of hours before Simone, he'd awoken with the knowledge that she was there, too, sleeping peacefully in her bed upstairs. This morning, however, he felt her absence as keenly as he felt his own presence. She'd slipped out without his knowledge, something he would have sworn she wouldn't possibly be able to do. He was a light sleeper by nature, and when it came to Simone Van Dormer, he'd developed a strange kind of sixth sense over the past week. Hell, it was his job to know where a person was when he was assigned to protect her. Simone, however, had managed to outmaneuver him.

Damn. She was good.

She was also gone. And Julian knew—he just *knew*—where she was. She was on her way to meet Brian Richie. To even the score. However she meant to do it.

Julian didn't bother to shower or shave or eat. He simply grabbed the same clothing he'd worn the night before and tugged the garments on as quickly as he could. The keys for the rental car weren't where he'd left them the night before, which came as no surprise at all. In spite of that, he hurried up the stairs to check Simone's bedroom, in a last-ditch effort to see if maybe he was wrong about her leaving.

But he wasn't wrong. She wasn't there.

Shamelessly, he searched the room and sorted through her possessions, hoping he might turn up some clue as to her whereabouts. And although he did find a few interesting tidbits among her belongings— not the least of which was a well-read copy of William Blake's *Songs of Innocence and of Experience*—there was nothing to indicate where she might have gone.

Julian was on his way out of the room when he saw the purse Simone had been carrying the night before, lying on the chair that was tucked beneath the desk. It didn't look big enough to hold more than one or two of the basic feminine necessities, but he snatched it up anyway and opened it. Much to his surprise, though, it didn't hold *any* basic feminine necessities. Not unless one considered a full clip for a .25 caliber automatic weapon basic, feminine, or necessary.

Oh. My. God, Julian thought. To put it mildly.

Because where there was a clip, there must be a gun—even though that gun wasn't, technically, with that clip at the moment. That only meant that the gun was somewhere else. And where there was a gun, he feared, there was Simone Van Dormer. And where there was Simone Van Dormer, there was Brian Richie. And where there was Brian Richie, there was trouble.

Oh, God, Julian thought again. Surely she wouldn't. Surely she wasn't planning anything like that. Surely there was a very good reason for why Simone Van Dormer had come back to Cincinnati packing heat—a reason *other* than that she planned to fill Brian Richie full of lead. If only Julian knew where she was, he could ask her about that very thing. Unfortunately, he had no idea where she might be. Although she'd been absent from Cincinnati for some time now, she was still a native. She almost certainly remembered her way around. She could be anywhere.

But, hey, a complete lack of knowledge had never stopped Julian Varga before, no way. He was an investigator, after all. He could find anyone. Even Simone Van Dormer. Probably.

He just hoped that, when he did, she wasn't standing over a body, holding a gun whose clip was empty.

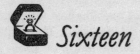 *Sixteen*

"Hey, Cincinnati! Thank God it's Friday, huh? We have something special for you this fine Friday afternoon. We're going to bring you an eighties flashback weekend, starting today. Enjoy. A personal favorite of mine is up next. Indulge me. It's Josie Cotton, with 'He Could Be the One.'"

Eve grinned at the appropriateness of the musical selection, then leaned forward and nudged the volume a little higher. Wyatt had more than made good on his promise to arrive in Cincinnati by dinnertime on Friday. In fact, they crossed the Ohio River and rolled into downtown just before four in the afternoon.

The entire Cincinnati skyline had changed, she marveled upon their approach, feeling a mix of melancholy and satisfaction at seeing it. Buildings rose up against the bright blue sky now that hadn't been there twenty years before, and the old ones she remembered seemed different somehow. There was even a new baseball stadium on the riverfront. *What next?* she wondered with an idle shake of her head.

When they pulled to a stop in front of the Stanhope Hotel, Eve saw that it, too, had experienced its own share of changes. At some point over the last twenty years, a massive renovation had occurred. The last time she'd stood here in front of the place, on prom night, the stately old hotel had been charming, to be sure, though in a somewhat neglected state. It had been tired-looking and poorly lit, the carpeting faded, the woodwork dull. Now, though, it shone like a bright jewel. Green awnings spanned the front entrance and first-story windows, their beveled glass sparkling like diamonds in the late afternoon sun. Scarlet-clad bellmen with bright brass buttons scurried about the cobbled walkway, and beyond the front doors, big marble urns boasted huge bouquets of flowers in every color imaginable. Even from outside, she could see that a richly patterned, emerald-and-ruby carpet spanned the lobby from mahogany paneled wall to mahogany paneled wall, and an elegant marble fountain babbled at its center.

"The Stanhope looks great, doesn't it?" Wyatt said when he noted where her attention lay. "It was bought by a big chain about five years ago, and they completely renovated the place."

She considered the old place again and sighed. "Yeah, but I kind of miss the way it was before."

He said nothing in response to that for a moment, then told her, "Things change, Eve. There's nothing we can do to stop it. We just might as well try to make the best of it. Especially if things change for the better."

"Yeah, but who's to say what's better?" she asked.

He smiled at her. "We are."

And before she could comment on that, he opened the back hatch on the SUV and began to unload their bags. He looked gorgeous and yummy, his faded jeans molding his hips and thighs, his dark green polo hugging his broad shoulders and lean torso. She still had trouble believing how sweetly and perfectly they had made love the night before. Twenty-four hours ago, she'd been feeling lost and lonely and uncertain about herself and about the future. But suddenly, today, the entire world was different.

Wyatt was right, she thought. Things did change for the better sometimes, if you let them. Naturally, there were still some things between the two of them that they needed to address before she could really focus on the future. But that was just the point—after last night, she was thinking about the future. And she'd stopped worrying about the past. Better still, she was enjoying the present, because it was no longer the empty, lonely place it had been for too long.

She loved Wyatt, she realized, not altogether surprised by the discovery. She had loved him twenty years ago, and she loved him today. But her love now was different from the love she had felt for him in the past. It was more profound, more passionate, more precarious. It was an adult love, and therefore more frightening. Because where teenaged love was by no means stable or permanent, this one, she knew, would last forever. And she had to trust that Wyatt's love for her was the same. That was a lot of trust to give to one person. And Eve wasn't yet sure whether or not she could do it.

As quickly as Wyatt placed their luggage on the ground, a bellman appeared to load the bags onto a dolly. After explaining that they were meeting up with guests who had already arrived, they headed off for the desk. Eve, however, needed to make a quick side trip, because in their anxiousness to get to Cincinnati as soon as they could, they hadn't stopped at all for their final two hours on the road.

"I need to use the ladies' room," she whispered to Wyatt as they took their place at the end of a short line at the reservations desk.

He threw her a much put-upon look. "Can't it wait? This shouldn't take more than a few minutes."

She shook her head. "Sorry. I'll be right back. By then you'll have us all checked in, and we can head on up to find Simone and Julian."

"But I don't want to let you out of my sight," he said with a smile. He leaned forward to brush his mouth lightly over her neck. "You could be in danger, after all," he reminded her in a low voice meant for her ears alone. "Mainly because you look good enough to . . . eat."

Heat flared through her entire body at the way he uttered that final word, and she was thankful for the breezy, loose-fitting flowered jumper that she wore. Hopefully nobody but her would notice the physical repercussions his words had on her fevered body.

"Oh, God," Wyatt groaned softly beside her, "I love how your nipples get hard when I talk dirty to you."

Okay, so hopefully nobody but her and Wyatt would notice, she hastily amended.

"I'll be right back," she said, before she embarrassed herself right there in the lobby of the Stanhope Hotel.

"Hurry," he told her.

As she scurried off to find the ladies' room, Eve

found herself hoping that Simone and Julian, as much as she wanted to see them, had decided to go out for a little while this afternoon. That way she and Wyatt could steal a little more time alone together. Although what they'd discovered in St. Louis was still new enough to be thoroughly exciting and arousing, she didn't think there would ever come a time when things *weren't* thoroughly exciting and arousing between them. Wyatt was just that kind of guy. And, Eve admitted with a smile, she was just that kind of girl.

After tending to her business in the ladies' room, she paused in the adjacent lounge to evaluate her appearance, wincing at the image that gazed back at her from the mirror. She dragged a brush through her hair, applied a light coat of lipstick, then gathered up her purse and headed out of the lounge to return to Wyatt. She halted abruptly in the hallway before making it to the lobby, though, because she saw a familiar figure leaning against the wall, between her and her final destination.

Before Eve had a chance to react, the man pushed himself away from the wall and was quickly joined by two others.

"Eve," he said in a chillingly smooth voice, "long time, no see."

And before she had a chance to say a word in response, the trio of men lunged toward her.

Twenty minutes after Eve's departure, Wyatt stood leaning against the concierge desk, impatiently awaiting her return and totally annoying the concierge. Okay, he knew women took a long time in the rest room, but this was ridiculous. Eve had promised to be right back. And he'd made an erotic suggestion she'd clearly been enthusiastic about. No way should she be taking twenty minutes. He glanced down at his watch. Twenty-*two* minutes, he corrected himself. Okay, enough was enough. He was about to go storming off for the ladies' room when a slim, gray-haired woman approached the concierge desk carrying what looked very much like Eve's purse.

"Excuse me," she said to the man behind the counter. "I found this handbag on the floor near the ladies' room. I'm sure someone must be looking for it."

Wyatt studied the handbag closely. Yep. It was definitely Eve's. He knew that, because he was the one who'd given her the Powerpuff Girls key chain—Buttercup, natch—that dangled from one end of the strap. It was one of the prizes he'd won for her at the amusement park in Amarillo.

"I know the owner of that bag," he told the concierge as the woman handed it to him.

The concierge appeared in no way convinced.

"I do," Wyatt insisted. "Check the driver's license in the wallet. It will belong to Eve Van Dormer of Santa Barbara, California. Or maybe Eve Walsh of Los Angeles," he amended reluctantly. "I'm not sure if she got her name and address changed back on her license after her divorce."

In spite of the concierge's clear dubiety, the man did as Wyatt instructed and checked the wallet. His eyebrows arched in surprise when he looked at the driver's license.

"Eve Van Dormer," he said. "Santa Barbara, California."

Wyatt couldn't quite keep the snottiness out of his voice as he retorted, "Toldja." And he couldn't quite stop the warm feeling that washed over him when he realized how completely and quickly she had divested herself of her ex-husband.

Then he realized the significance of Eve's purse being here without Eve being attached to it, and something in his belly went rancid. He turned to the woman who'd brought it over. "Where did you find this?" he asked, snatching it back from the concierge. "Show me exactly."

The woman led him across the lobby and down a hallway, past a bank of telephones and two water fountains, to where it ended with an emergency exit flanked by a men's rest room on one side and a women's rest room on the other.

"I found the handbag here," she said, halting scarcely a foot away from the emergency exit. "It had fallen open, and a few of the things inside had spilled out. I can't imagine someone dropping it without realizing."

Yeah, neither could Wyatt. And that bothered him a lot. What bothered him even more was that the emergency exit door was slightly ajar. He pushed it open and passed through, and found himself on a sidewalk bordering a parking lot that appeared to be infrequently used, judging by the lack of cars parked there. He looked left, and he looked right, but he saw no sign of Eve.

"Thanks," he said over his shoulder to the woman, having nearly forgotten she was there.

She nodded and strode back down the hall, and Wyatt took a few more steps into the parking lot. He was about to turn away when something small near the street exit caught his eye. He jogged over, that sick feeling in the pit of his stomach roiling now. That sick feeling turned to terror, however, when he bent down to pick up Eve's sandal.

Oh, God, he thought wildly. *Oh, God*. Some matriarch-fricking bodyguard he had turned out to be.

And then that thought was superseded by another: Luther. Eve's father. Could this be one of his setups? Wyatt wondered. Even though the old man had promised he wouldn't interfere again? Even though it made no sense for the guy to have his daughter kidnapped in Cincinnati? Not that it made sense for him to have his daughter kidnapped anywhere else, either, but still . . . Luther Van Dormer wasn't exactly *Make Room for Daddy* material.

Could Luther be behind this? Wyatt wondered again. And if he wasn't, he thought further, growing sicker with each passing second, then who was?

"Of course I called the police, and small world that it is, the detective I spoke to turned out to be somebody I graduated with. And then what the hell was I supposed to tell them?"

Wyatt paced from one end of Julian and Simone's suite to the other—overlooking, for now, the fact that it was *Julian and Simone's* suite—and tried not to feel like a trapped rat as he recounted the day's events to his partner. " 'Yes, Detective, I'm sure she was taken against her will. No, I'm positive she wasn't trying to ditch me. Well, yes, as a matter of fact, there *was* a rumor that I tried to molest her on prom night, but that was a total lie. In fact, we'd just discovered and declared our undying love for each other. Yes, I'm sure she felt the same way I do. Yes, trust me. No, I'm not stalking her. Yes, she does share my feelings. Really. Honest. She does.' "

He stopped pacing and turned to his friend. "Hell, I'm lucky they didn't arrest me. Somehow, Julian, I get the impression that they're not going to go out of their way on this one. Not until Eve's been gone for a good, long time. Or else not until her body turns up floating facedown in the Ohio River."

In addition to the police, Wyatt had also called Luther—in fact, he'd done that first—only to hear Eve's father tell him that, number one, he most definitely had *not* arranged a phony kidnapping for Eve once she arrived in Cincinnati, and, number two, he would catch the next flight out of Santa Barbara and be there as soon as he could.

Now Julian was looking decidedly disturbed by all that Wyatt had told him, which only went to show how very serious the matter was. Even in the most dire circumstances, Julian never let anybody see him sweat. Now, though, he looked ready to tear the sofa in two with his bare hands. *God, what happened to him this week?* Wyatt wondered. Julian looked like he'd slept in his clothes, he hadn't bothered to shave, his eyes were shadowed, and his expression was bleak. Wyatt had known the effect that the Van Dormer women could have on a person, but he'd been so sure that Simone and Julian would be much too cool to ever succumb to . . .

Well, to each other, evidently.

"Simone's been missing since this morning," Julian said. "I thought I knew where she went—or, at least, *why* she went—and I thought she went there under her own speed. But now I'm not so sure. Maybe someone took her, too."

Wyatt nodded. "Maybe we were all a bit hasty in deciding that Luther Van Dormer was just being paranoid about his daughters coming back to town," he said. "Because you know, Julian, it's not paranoia when people really are out to get you."

"Let's not jump to conclusions," Julian said. "We don't know for sure that Simone and Eve were taken against their will."

"I know Eve was," Wyatt said.

Julian didn't contradict him. What he did say was, "I think Simone is carrying."

"What?" Wyatt exclaimed.

"I found a full clip in one of her purses, but no gun to go with it. I figure that must be because she's got the weapon on her, wherever she is."

"Why the hell would Simone be packing?" Wyatt asked.

But Julian only shook his head silently in response. Even so, Wyatt could tell that he knew something Wyatt didn't know himself but wasn't going to share it. For the first time in their four-year friendship and partnership, Julian was keeping something from him. And Wyatt couldn't help thinking it was on account of a woman. Which was the last thing he'd ever thought Julian would keep secrets about.

"So what do we do now?" Julian asked.

"I don't know," Wyatt replied, that sick feeling boiling up in his midsection again. "They could be miles from here by now, apart or together, who knows?"

"We should call the FBI," Julian said. "There's a good chance they—or at least, Eve—may have been taken across state lines. Hell, the next state is right there," he added, pointing out the window, across the Ohio River toward Kentucky.

Wyatt inhaled a slow, deep breath, willing his heart to stop pounding so hard against his breastbone. He nodded his agreement with Julian and was about to go look for the phone book when the scrape of a key card in the door jerked both his and Julian's attention in that direction. When Simone Van Dormer entered the room, they each lurched forward, startling her so badly that she instinctively took a step back.

"Where the hell have you been?" Julian demanded with all the outrage of . . . of . . .

In spite of everything, Wyatt smiled. Because his friend was showing every sign of being totally smitten by the other Van Dormer sister. Then again, seeing as how Simone was wearing a frothy little dress the same pale blue as her eyes, with a wide, scooped neck and none too long hemline—and, good God, she didn't appear to have on a stitch of underwear beneath it—Wyatt couldn't quite blame the guy for being smitten.

"I've been out," she said crisply, her cheeks coloring, her eyes going dark. "Jeez, you're worse than my father."

Wyatt shook his head in disbelief. Wow. Julian and Simone. He never would have guessed the two of them would hook up, but now that he saw them together, he realized how appropriate the pairing was. Looked like he and Eve weren't the only ones who'd undertaken a long journey this week.

"Oh, yeah?" Julian charged. "Well it turns out that maybe your father wasn't so wrong to be worried about you and your sister after all."

Simone narrowed her eyes first at Julian, then at Wyatt. Then her eyes widened when she realized who he was. "Wyatt?" she said. "When did you get here? Where's Evie?"

"Gone," Wyatt said succinctly.

"Gone?" Simone echoed. "What are you talking about? Where is she?"

"We think someone took her, Simone," Julian said, his voice gentling some. "I was worried . . . I mean, *we* were worried that they might have taken you, too."

"No, we *know* someone took Eve," Wyatt countered. "Her purse was found near the women's rest room off the lobby downstairs, and I found one of her shoes out in the parking lot. Someone took her against her will. And we're afraid she's been taken out of town, out of state. Julian and I were just about to call the FBI when you came in."

Simone's mouth had dropped open as Wyatt spoke, but she closed it now and eyed first him, and then Julian, with much consideration. "Don't worry about calling the FBI," she said.

"Why not?" Wyatt demanded. "I think we need them on this."

Simone expelled a resigned sigh. "Because they're already here, that's why," she told him.

Wyatt only gazed at her in confusion for a moment, but it took Julian no time to figure it out.

"You work for the FBI?" he asked.

Simone nodded. "And if someone took Evie against her will, then I'm fairly certain I know who it was."

Wyatt studied her curiously. "Who?" he asked.

Simone met his gaze levelly. "Brian Richie."

"Lemma get this straight," Wyatt said a little while later, after Simone had made a couple of phone calls . . . and he and Julian had poured themselves a couple of stiff drinks. "You're a *fed*?"

"I'm not a field agent," Simone corrected him. "Not anymore. I've been out of the field for a couple of years. Now, I'm an instructor at a federal training facility just outside Santa Barbara. My specialty is domestic militia groups—I teach other field agents about them. But I'm also a firearms expert."

Wyatt gaped at her in disbelief for a minute, then turned his attention to Julian and found that his friend was . . . well, gaping at her in disbelief, too.

"And Brian heads up a militia group?" Wyatt asked.

Simone shook her head. "No, he has nothing to do with anything like that. It wasn't my expertise in that area that brought me into this investigation. It was my familiarity with the Richie family. What I didn't know when I was a kid, though, was that Brian's father, William, had his fingers in all sorts of illegal pies, as did his father's father, Stephen, before that. The entire Richie family has been on the wrong side of the law since before Prohibition, but no one was ever able to make anything stick. Not until recently."

Wyatt shook his head, too, harder than Simone had, as if that might somehow clear it of his utter and profound confusion. "I'm still totally lost here."

"Brian took over the family business, so to speak, after his father's death," Simone said, "but he's not nearly as intelligent as his father or grandfather were. Nor," she added meaningfully, "does he have the head for business that his wife did."

"His *wife*?" Julian echoed. "What the hell does his wife have to do with anything? She's dead."

Simone nodded. "She is now, but she wasn't three years ago when she took over *her* father's business."

Wyatt narrowed his eyes, afraid to ask what he wanted to ask. "And what was Brian's wife's name?"

Simone met his gaze levelly. "Alice Portman. Being

the liberated woman—and mob matriarch—that she was, she kept her name after they married."

Wyatt nodded knowingly now. "And Alice Portman is—"

"Dennis Portman's daughter," Simone finished for him.

"And Dennis Portman was the source of the original threat made against you and your sister twenty years ago," Wyatt said, recalling what Luther had told him and Julian that night at The Keep . . . God, had it only been a week ago? He felt like he'd lived a lifetime since then.

"So when Dennis Portman died," Julian concluded, "Alice took over his business affairs . . ."

"His illegal business affairs," Simone interjected. "He was Brian's father's partner and his family was just as dirty as the Richies were. Alice and Brian's marriage was pretty much arranged when they were kids. Kind of like two sovereign nations combining their power with an arranged marriage. Only here it was two crime families combining their power. And Alice, until she died, was the head of it all. Brian only took over after her death. But, as I said, he's not as smart as she was. He's made some mistakes and been very sloppy since he took control. The FBI has been collecting information on him all along, and eight months ago, we got a break when Brian did something especially stupid. And I'm not at liberty to discuss the details," she added when Wyatt opened his mouth to ask for them.

"So how'd you get involved in all this?" he asked instead.

"The investigation into Brian's and Alice's affairs

eventually included all the people the Richies and Portmans had ever done business with, which included my father. That's how I found out about it. And when I did, I volunteered to make myself available in whatever capacity they needed me, because of my history with Brian. As I said, I've been out of the field for a while, but I still know the ropes. Now that it's come time to reel Brian in, I'm the person they decided to use for bait."

"Why didn't you tell me about all this, Simone?" Julian asked. "I could have helped you."

She hesitated for a moment, as if she was weighing just how much she should reveal. Finally she said, "Number one, I didn't need any help. I know exactly what I'm doing. This is my job. Number two, I can take care of myself. I've been trained at self-defense, and I'm an expert marksman. And number three . . ." She shrugged apologetically. "I didn't want you to get hurt, Julian. I couldn't have stood it if something had happened to you."

This, Wyatt noticed, clearly moved Julian. If the man hadn't already been halfway over the moon for the woman, her admission would have had him doing laps around the cow.

"Even though I knew Brian was dangerous," Simone continued, "I honestly didn't think he'd come after me or Evie. I really thought Alice's gripe with the Van Dormers was *Alice's* gripe with the Van Dormers. Not Brian's. Plus," she added, gritting her teeth a bit, Wyatt noted curiously, "Brian's relationship with the Van Dormers was of a more . . . personal nature. And it was with me, not the rest of the family."

The comment confused Wyatt, but judging by the

look on his partner's face at the moment, he didn't think it would be a good idea to press the issue right now.

"Still," Simone added, "I didn't think Evie would be in any danger. Especially with Wyatt around."

Oh, sure, throw that up in my face, Wyatt thought.

"And I really did think that this operation would go off without a hitch," Simone continued. "Especially when Julian told me you and Evie were driving in and wouldn't be here until the weekend. That gave me plenty of time. All I was supposed to do while I was here was wear a wire and lure Brian alone somewhere and get him to—"

"You were wearing a wire last night?" Julian interrupted.

She nodded. "Yes."

"Under *that* dress?"

"Yes."

"And you're wearing one now?" he demanded further.

"Yes."

"Under *that* dress?"

"Yes."

"Where the hell did you put it?"

She smiled. "Modern technology is an amazing thing."

"Man, I'll say."

"Anyway, I was supposed to get Brian alone," she continued, "and try to get him to incriminate himself, or, at the very least, say something that might offer us additional information we didn't already have. I mean, we have a lot, but one solid, incontrovertible piece of information would tie it all up nicely with a big, satin bow. And then, once Brian incriminated himself, my colleagues were going to do the rest.

"But I never had the opportunity to do my job last night," she added, turning her attention pointedly to Julian.

"Uh . . . sorry about that," he said sheepishly. "See, if you'd told me what was going on . . ."

"What? You would have left me alone with him?" she asked dubiously.

"Well, no," he told her. "But I might have hung back a little."

"Yeah, right," she said. "That's why I went out alone this morning, hoping to find him," she continued. "Unfortunately, I never caught up with him. Obviously, because he had other things to do today. Like snatch my sister. He's probably planning to come after me, too, but his game with me is evidently a bit more elaborate. He's going to toy with me first."

She began to think hard about something, and Wyatt and Julian remained silent while she did. Then, finally, she said, "I can still meet with Brian tonight, the way he and I originally planned, and try to finish up what I started. But that doesn't help Evie now. If I could just figure out where he took her. If we just knew of someplace he used for things like—" Her eyes suddenly went wide, as if something of monumental importance had just occurred to her. "Oh, God," she said softly. "I think I know where he might have her."

"Where?" Wyatt demanded.

But instead of answering his question, Simone glanced down at her watch. "The class of eighty-one's reception will be starting in a little over an hour. Brian doesn't realize we're on to him. Or does he?" she pondered aloud further. "Wyatt, did he see you and Evie together this afternoon? Would he have made any kind of connection between the two of you and get suspicious?"

"I have no idea," Wyatt answered honestly. "For what it's worth, *I* never saw *him*. But that's no guarantee of anything."

Simone chewed her lip thoughtfully for a moment. "We'll just have to risk that he didn't," she finally said. "He and I agreed last night to meet down in the lobby at seven and go in to the reception together. I'm thinking he's just stupid enough—and just arrogant enough—to go ahead and meet me as planned. Hey, he'll probably get off on it, knowing he kidnapped my sister this afternoon and is squiring me around tonight." She blew out an unsteady breath. "I just hope he hasn't done anything to hurt Evie."

Wyatt really, really, really wished Simone hadn't put voice to her fear. Because until that moment, he'd been marginally successful at keeping his own fears for Eve at bay. But once Simone said aloud what had been lurking at the back of his mind for the last hour, all those fears came rushing to the fore. And Wyatt began to feel sick all over again.

Then Simone seemed to think of something else, because she turned to him with a speculative little gleam in her eyes. "If Brian *doesn't* know you're involved with Evie," she said, "you could be at the reception tonight, too, as nothing more than a returning member of the class of eighty-one. And Brian wouldn't be suspicious."

"Yeah?" Wyatt asked. "So?"

"So if memory serves," she said, "you have a twenty-year-old bone to pick with Brian, too. Isn't he the one who spread rumors about how you assaulted Evie on prom night?"

Wyatt nodded stiffly. "Yeah."

Simone grinned. "Then I think I have a plan. And, better yet, I think it just might work. Wyatt, you stay here at the hotel with me—I'll need you at the reception. Julian, you can go with my colleagues to get Evie."

"You're sure you know where she is?"

Simone nodded. "Ninety-nine percent sure. Let me make a few more phone calls. But here's what we're going to do."

Wyatt listened closely as she outlined her plan, but he felt a little numb about everything he'd discovered. Boy, you leave town for one lousy week, he thought, and when you come back, nothing is the same as it was when you left. He'd found and fallen in love with Eve Van Dormer all over again, only to have her stolen right out from under his nose. His best friend and partner, whom Wyatt had never seen show more than a passing interest in a woman, had fallen head over heels in love, too. Simone Van Dormer was a fed. And Brian Richie, all-American boy next door and rescuer of stranded, rejected women was actually a scumbag criminal who would stoop to kidnapping and terrorizing the very woman he had rescued all those years ago.

Man, he thought as Simone's plan took shape. High school reunions sure could bring out the worst in a person.

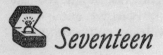 *Seventeen*

Simone inhaled a deep, shaky breath and expelled it as slowly as she could, and she somehow refrained from pacing anxiously across the hotel lobby. She stood near the fountain, where she and Brian had decided to meet, dressed in a tiny little black strapless cocktail dress she just knew would grab his attention. She'd accessorized it with drop earrings and a choker of jet beads, smoky sheer stockings, black heels, and her favorite listening device. And she tried not to clutch her little black beaded evening bag too tightly, because she had a couple more essential accessories in there—not the least of which was her sidearm. And although the safety was on, she didn't want to risk blowing her cover too early by blowing off one of her toes. Besides, limping around would just spoil the line of her dress.

She only hoped Brian was, in fact, stupid enough

and arrogant enough to show up tonight. Then again, she wasn't especially worried about that. She was fairly confident that he would show up. Because she was more than confident that he was stupid and arrogant.

And speaking of stupid and arrogant, there he was, right on time, she noticed, striding through the main entry of the Stanhope Hotel. He looked dapper and handsome and charming in his dark suit and ruby necktie, and he made Simone's flesh crawl. She forced a gentle smile and took a few steps forward, meeting him halfway across the lobby.

She was an excellent judge of people—or, at least, had been since prom night—and her instincts were impeccable. She studied Brian closely as she approached him, and she detected not the merest hint that he suspected she was here for anything other than his irresistible allure. Gag. Evidently, he hadn't seen Evie with Wyatt earlier that day. Or, if he had, he hadn't sensed anything suspicious about them being together. For now, she thought, everything was going according to plan.

"You look absolutely bewitching," he said as he took both of her hands in his.

She forced a faint blush and dropped her gaze to the ground. "Oh, Brian," *you stupid, arrogant pig*, "you do say the nicest things. Thank you."

He threw a surreptitious glance over her shoulder, as if he was looking for someone. "You don't have your bodyguard with you tonight?" he asked.

Heat flared in Simone's belly, but she managed a puzzled smile. "My bodyguard?" she asked. "What do you mean?"

"Percy," Brian fairly spat. "Your cousin. I figured

he'd be intruding onto our good time again. Ruining everything."

"Oooh, Percy," Simone echoed, relief washing over her. "No, he had to go back home. His mother called him."

Brian oozed out an oily little smile. "Excellent," he purred. "Then I'll have you all to myself tonight."

Simone tucked her arm through his, sighed contentedly, and tried not to throw up. "I think we're going to have a wonderful time tonight," she said. "I can't wait to see some of our former classmates. I bet we're going to be surprised by what a lot of them have become."

"Yes, well," Brian said as they strode toward the elevators that would take them to the ballroom on the second floor. "I've encountered several of our former classmates over the years, Simone. And very few of them are leading lives that are anything but ordinary."

He regaled her with stories of some of those ordinary lives as they ascended to the second floor and strode toward the ballroom. And although Brian clearly had nothing but contempt for the ordinary, Simone found herself envying most of those lives that he described. There had been a time in her life when she'd fantasized about such an ordinary existence for herself—a career in a field she enjoyed, marriage, family, and a house in the suburbs. But that fantasy had never materialized, thanks to the road she'd begun traveling—or, perhaps, had retreated down—after what had happened to her at the prom. She'd known after that night that she would never feel ordinary again. That she would never have a life she totally enjoyed. So she'd done what she could to exist as happily as could be expected.

And in a way, she had been happy. At least, happy

enough. She'd always liked her work, and she had friends and a loving family. She'd been reasonably happy, if not completely so. Still, she'd never quite been able to shake the feeling that there was something missing from her life, something big. She would have sworn that that something was *not* a man. Now, however, after discovering Julian, she realized that that was exactly what had been missing. Not a man, so much, but . . . affection. Affection she could give to another human being. Affection that another human being could give to her.

She glanced over at Brian and pretended to hang on his every word. Now if she could only survive the evening, she thought as she ignored him, then maybe, just maybe, she would discover what it was like to find the total happiness she had never thought she would know.

"Ah, here we are," Brian said as he came to a stop before the ballroom entrance. " 'Welcome, Woodhaven High School class of eighty-one,' " he read from the banner that hung over the door. "Let's see who we can find, shall we?"

They greeted the table hosts at the door—Mike Lindley, Simone was surprised to see, whom she recalled as being a complete thug, and a man he introduced as his partner, Stephen. Though the way he said *partner* suggested that the relationship between the two men was much more than just a professional one. Well, the way he said *partner*, and also the way he put his arm around the other man's waist and pulled him close. Suddenly, several things about the angry adolescent Mike had begun to make sense. Simone smiled as she greeted both men, then moved to fasten her name tag to her dress.

"Allow me," Brian said before she had the chance.

And before she could stop him, he plucked the plastic badge from her grasp and affixed it to her dress for her. To do so, he thrust his fingers down the front of her bodice, pressing the backs of his knuckles shamelessly against her breast. It was all Simone could do not to double a fist and whale him one upside his head, to send him flying backward.

Later, she promised herself. Later, she would give Brian exactly what he deserved.

"Thank you," she said a bit breathlessly when he completed the action.

"My pleasure," he assured her in that oozing, oily voice of his, having obviously interpreted her breathlessness as the result of passion, not loathing. "Let's not stay too long at the reception, all right?" he added. "Being at the Stanhope with you tonight is rousing . . ."

He met her gaze levelly, his blue eyes utterly void of anything even remotely resembling a soul. How could she have ever found him attractive? she wondered. How could she have ever believed that he might be the one for her?

"Being here with you is rousing all kinds of memories, Simone," he continued. "Memories I'd like very much to relive. I can't wait to show you the boathouse. It's always been a special place for me." His smile grew even oilier than before. "And I think you'll be surprised by what you find there tonight."

That's what you think, Simone thought. *And you're going to be even more surprised, you contemptible little worm. By what you* don't *find.*

She made herself smile and said playfully, "We have plenty of time for that, Brian. First there really are some people I want to see."

He feigned impatience as he said, "If you insist."

Then again, she thought, maybe his impatience wasn't feigned at all. Brian Richie, she knew, had big, big plans tonight. Only what he didn't know was that she had big, big plans tonight, too. And her big, big plans were going to send his big, big plans right into a big, big toilet.

"Oh, I insist," she told him, feigning charmed delight to counter his feigned . . . whatever.

For the next two hours, Simone kept a close eye on Brian, her wristwatch, and the main entrance to the ballroom as they circled through the crowd. Then, shortly after nine, she glanced toward the ballroom entrance to see one of her colleagues from the Bureau standing at the ready, his single nod her signal that all was well. And she expelled a slow, silent sigh of relief when she realized her sister was safe and sound. Now all Simone had to do was get Brian alone and make him an offer he couldn't refuse. Or else shoot him. She wasn't really particular.

But he saved her the trouble of having to conjure a pretense just then by abandoning all pretense himself. "I think this evening has dragged on long enough," he said suddenly, after he'd separated himself and Simone from a small group of old classmates. "I'm getting bored. I want us to be alone." He smiled a vicious little smile. "You'll come with me now, Simone," he said with complete certainty. "You'll come with me, because I have Eve."

"But Evie's not here yet," Simone countered, pretending to misunderstand. "She's driving from Santa Barbara and won't arrive until tomorrow."

"Wrong," Brian corrected her. "Funnily enough, I came to the hotel for *you* earlier today—"

"For me?" she interrupted, laughing. "What a coincidence, Brian. Because I was out looking for *you*."

"Well, I doubt you had the same intentions for me that I had for you," he told her.

"Oh? And what were your intentions for me, Brian?"

"Actually," he said with another one of his evil little grins, "I had intended to kidnap and torture you, and then send you home to your father in little pieces."

Oh, my, Simone thought. That was going to sound good on tape. She forced her eyes wide in what she hoped looked like stark, raving terror and tried not to giggle triumphantly.

"But, instead," Brian went on, "lo and behold, fate dropped your sister right into my lap. I saw her walking across the hotel lobby, and when she turned down a hallway, I, and my companions, followed her."

"Goodness, Brian," Simone said. "Don't tell me you kidnapped and tortured Evie, then cut her up into little pieces. That's going to put a damper on the reunion, don't you think?"

This time Brian was the one to widen his eyes. And his mouth, too, because he only gaped like a dead fish at her response. Simone was just about to express her gratitude to him for being so specific about his threats—on tape, too, no less, how very thoughtful of him—when their conversation was interrupted. Right on cue.

"Hey! Hey, Brian Richie! I have a bone to pick with you, you lying little sonofabitch!"

Brian and Simone glanced up as one to find Wyatt crossing the ballroom toward them, holding a half-empty glass of Scotch in one hand. His necktie was askew, one side of his collar was bent upward, his hair was appropriately mussed, and he wove back and forth as if he had tied on a mean drunk. Before Brian realized what was coming, Wyatt grabbed the lapel of his jacket and jerked him hard forward, toward the largest group of their classmates who had gathered nearby. Caught off guard, Brian stumbled along behind Wyatt, righting himself just before he would have fallen, something Simone realized belatedly that she would rather liked to have seen.

"Hey, everybody!" Wyatt shouted, more drunkenly—and more loudly—this time, rousing the attention of, oh . . . just about everybody in the ballroom. "C'mere! Come over here! Look who I found! It's that lying little sonofabitch, Brian Richie!"

Simone had followed the men to where they stood now, and she noted that Brian had gone a little pale. She also noticed that he was gazing at her curiously, as if he couldn't understand why she wasn't using this opportunity to oh, say . . . run for her life.

"Wyatt Culver," he said disdainfully when Wyatt reeled to a halt beside him. His attention ricocheted from Simone to Wyatt, then back to Simone. Ultimately, though, it was Wyatt who finally commanded it. "If you have a bone to pick with me, Culver," Brian added coolly, masking his confusion well, "it's one of your own making."

Wyatt opened his mouth to respond, then glanced past Brian at Simone. "Do I know you?" he asked her, slurring the words together and narrowing his eyes as if he were trying to remember.

"Simone Van Dormer," she said cheerfully.

"Ooooooohhhh," Wyatt replied drunkenly. "No. I don't remember you. But I do remember your sister."

He turned to look at Brian again. "Which brings me back to you, you sonofabitch." He stepped right in front of Brian, then thrust his free hand forward, against the other man's chest, pushing him backward, closer to the crowd.

Brian stumbled again but recovered well, then jerked his head upward, meeting Wyatt's gaze levelly. "Maybe we should take this outside," he said.

"Oh, no," Wyatt told him, shaking his head as if *very* intoxicated now. "No, no, no, no, no, no, no, no, no, no . . ." His voice trailed off as his eyes seemed to glaze over a bit. "Where was I?" he asked no one in particular. "Oh, yeah. Oh, no, you don't. You sonofabitch. We'll keep it *riiiiight* here." He swept a hand toward the crowd milling behind them, a very large group of people now, who seemed to be moving closer. "I think the *whoooole* class of eighty-one deserves to know what a lying little sonofabitch you are," he added. "Tell 'em."

Brian arched his eyebrows idly. "Tell them what?"

"Tell 'em how you lied about what happened between me and Eve Van Dormer on prom night. Tell 'em how I never hurt her and how you made it all up, because . . . because . . ." He hiccuped in a much inebriated fashion. "Because you're a lying little sonofabitch, you lying little sonofabitch. That's why. Go on, tell 'em."

"I never lied about that," Brian said. "I saw you walking away from the car, Culver, and I found Eve inside, in a state. It was obvious what had happened. And I, for one, can think of nothing more contemptible than a man forcing himself on an unwilling woman."

Oh, Simone *really* had to bite her tongue at that one. And she had to use every last scrap of self-control she possessed to keep from pulling her gun on him and riddling him with enough bullets to qualify him for Swiss cheese status.

Wyatt, on the other hand, evidently had no such qualms. Not that he pulled a gun on Brian—more's the pity—but he did toss his half-empty drink in Brian's face. And when he did, the crowd that had gathered around them gasped as one, then went deadly silent.

"I never forced myself on her," Wyatt said, straightening, all traces of drunkenness suddenly vanishing. "And if she were here right now, she'd tell you that herself."

With surprising calm, Brian withdrew a handkerchief from his breast pocket and wiped his face dry. He then stuffed it back into his pocket and narrowed his eyes at Wyatt. "You—"

"It's true," a voice from behind Simone interrupted him.

Brian and Simone both spun around at the sound of it, Simone smiling in relief, Brian gaping in disbelief. Because Eve stood at the very front of the crowd, with Julian standing on one side of her and three federal agents standing on the other. She looked healthy and safe and happy, and she was dressed in a spectacular little blue dress that Simone had to admit did wonders to bring out her features.

"Wyatt never hurt me that night," Eve said, loudly enough for everyone to hear. "Brian Richie is a big, fat liar. Among other things." She offered Wyatt a dazzling smile and crossed to where he stood. Then she lovingly adjusted his necktie and collar and hair, and brushed an affectionate kiss across his lips. "Wyatt was a perfect gentleman that night," she added. She then turned her attention to Brian. "You, on the other hand, Brian, are no gentleman at all. Which is what I told the police and these nice FBI agents just a few minutes ago when I formally pressed kidnapping charges against you. You're just lucky no one got hurt when they came to get me at your boathouse. Your colleagues, as it turns out, are as gutless and free of honor as you are. They ran off. Or rather," she amended with a smile, "they tried to run off. I think they're currently chatting with the police and the feds, telling them all sorts of interesting things about you."

Now the crowd that had gone silent suddenly came alive with murmurs, gasps, and whispers. Brian, too, came alive, ready to turn and bolt from the room. Simone, however, anticipated his attempted escape— go figure—and hurled herself against him, shoving him to the ground. In one swift, graceful motion, she straddled him, reached into her purse for a pair of handcuffs, and snapped them onto his wrists.

"Brian Richie," she said, "you arrogant, stupid, loathsome pig, you're under arrest. For too many things for me to list here now. But let's start with kidnapping my sister, shall we? And threatening to cut us both up into little pieces. And all those nasty dealings you've had with nasty people you shouldn't be having dealings with. I'll let my colleagues outline the details of everything else."

Signaled by her statement, two men and a woman wearing plain dark suits arrived beside the prone body of Brian Richie and jerked him to standing. Simone stood, too, straightened her little black dress, and happily handed her capture over into their care. She wanted to check with Evie to be sure she was okay, but one look at the way her sister and Wyatt were eyeing each other made Simone think she should wait a bit.

As her colleagues escorted Brian away, outlining his right to remain silent, yadda yadda yadda, she moved to stand beside Julian and watched calmly the retreating back of the man who no longer posed any threat to her, either literally or figuratively. He was going to be put away, in a very icky place, for a very long time. And he was going to be out of her memories forever.

"Was that a gun I just saw in your purse?" Julian asked as she took her place by his side.

"Mm-hm," she told him. "My favorite automatic."

"Have you been carrying that all week?"

"Yep."

"I'd like to know where you had it."

"I bet you would."

He smiled. "I love you," he said.

She smiled back. "I know." When she looked up at him, it was to find him gazing at her expectantly, and her smile broadened. "I love you, too," she said. "I can't wait to start showing you how much."

"And *I* can't wait," he said softly, bending down to nuzzle the side of her neck, "to find out where you hid that wire."

Eve looped her arm through Wyatt's as she watched the authorities escort Blond Brian Richie to the door. Boy, she thought, this was really going to wreak havoc with Simone's plans to marry the guy. Then Eve gazed over at her sister and Mr. Julian Varga, saw the way the two of them were gazing at each other as if they had some really big plans, and realized that maybe, just maybe, she had been making assumptions about her sister—and a lot of other people—for a long time that weren't exactly, oh . . . accurate.

"Wanna dance?"

She turned her attention back to Wyatt and smiled. "There's, um, there's no music playing," she pointed out.

"Yeah, well, considering how the feds—who weren't even invited to this shindig, I might point out—"

"Neither were you, from what I hear," she interrupted.

But Wyatt ignored the comment. "Considering how the feds just took the class president out in handcuffs," he continued, "music, at this point, wouldn't exactly be in good taste. And also," he added, "considering that we went to high school at the height of the disco era, having no music is probably not such a bad thing. Talk about not exactly good taste . . ."

"That's right, I forgot," Eve said, remembering. "You were the one who led the movement to have our prom theme changed from Kool and the Gang's 'Celebration' to Pink Floyd's 'The Wall.' "

"Hey, 'The Wall' would have been a totally appropriate theme," he assured her.

She laughed. "Looking back, I'm not inclined to disagree."

As if cued by their discussion, the music did start up again then, the hired DJ having evidently decided that music might improve the sudden downturn in the mood of the crowd. But it wasn't "The Wall" that began playing, or even "Celebration," for that matter. Still, the song was something slow and mellow and strangely familiar.

"Do my ears deceive me?" Wyatt asked, tilting his head to better hear the tune. "Is that Barry Manilow I hear?"

"I believe it is," Eve said with a slow nod.

He stepped back a pace and opened his arms wide in an unmistakable invitation. "Come on, baby," he told her. "They're playin' our song."

Eve chuckled as she went to him, curling her hands against his chest and snuggling close as he folded his arms over her back. His warmth and his scent surrounded her, and she sighed silently her contentment at being so close to him again. There had been a few points during the day when she had feared she might not ever see him again. Now, though, she was absolutely certain they would never be apart.

"You're sure you're okay?" he asked softly, as if he'd sensed the avenue of her thoughts. "I don't think I've ever been more afraid in my life than I was this afternoon when I realized you were gone. And when I found out who was responsible, I wanted to kill the sonofabitch. With my bare hands."

She nodded against his shoulder. "I was surprised, too, when the people from the FBI explained everything. But I'm okay, Wyatt. I was scared, but that's all. Nobody hurt me. Brian locked me in the bedroom and left a couple of his goons outside. When the federal agents showed up, the two henchmen about wet themselves trying to surrender. Julian got in a couple of good licks on my behalf before they did—he must have been some kind of hell-raiser in his day."

"Julian?" Wyatt asked incredulously, pulling back far enough to gaze down into Eve's face. He didn't seem to believe her. "*My* Julian?" he echoed. "A hell-raiser?"

Eve nodded enthusiastically. "If his right hook is any indication, yes."

Wyatt gaped for a moment. "Boy, that kid's been holding out on me. Had I but known, he and I could have been having a good time together. Gee, you think you know a guy . . ."

"Anyway," Eve continued, "as I understand it, the bad guys are cooperating fully with the good guys now. All in all, I'd say the world is revolving just the way it's supposed to be."

Wyatt pulled her close again, tucking her head beneath his chin. "You got that right, sweetheart," he murmured. "You definitely got that right."

They danced in silence for some time, letting their hands slowly, surreptitiously explore each other, reacquainting themselves with fondly remembered places. At one point, Eve opened her eyes to see her sister and Mr. Varga—though she supposed she should get used to thinking of him as *Julian* now, she thought with a smile—as they danced past, Simone looking happier and more at peace than Eve had ever seen her look. Julian, too, appeared to be in a place of utter bliss, so Eve closed her eyes again and melted into Wyatt. Everything, she thought, was exactly as it should be.

"I just realized something," Wyatt said suddenly.

"What's that?" she asked without opening her eyes. The rhythmic to and fro of their bodies was seductive, narcotic, and she had no desire whatsoever to disturb her own place of utter bliss.

"We never danced at our prom," he told her.

She smiled. "No, we didn't, did we?"

"So that's two things we missed out on that night."

"But we're dancing now," she pointed out.

"So we are," he said.

"And, if you want," she added, "we could go out to the parking garage later and look around for a 1978 Chevy Nova. I think that's what Stuart was driving that night."

"Chevy Novas are for kids," Wyatt told her. "Grown-ups are allowed much greater freedom."

Freedom, she thought. That was exactly what lay at the bottom of it all. That was why she was feeling so good right now. She was free of the past. Free of her less than pleasant memories. And now she was free to stop trying to recapture the girl she once was, and free to become the woman she'd always had the potential to be. That, Eve decided, was where she would find her happiness. There, and somewhere else, *with* someone else, too.

She pulled her head back to look at Wyatt, and he gazed down at her with undisguised affection. No, more than affection, she thought. What he felt for her was clear.

"I love you," she said.

He bent to brush his lips lightly over hers. "I love you, too," he replied as he pulled back again.

"We'll never be able to go back, will we, Wyatt?"

"No," he said. "We never will. But you know what, Eve?"

"What?"

"We can go forward. And something tells me that's a much better place to be."

At 3:00 A.M., Eve and Wyatt and Simone and Julian sat in the main salon of their suite, finishing up the last of the hors d'oeuvres and munchies and wine that room service had sent up just after midnight. They'd finished giving their statements to the authorities, had all explained to the absent parties how everything had come about, and now all they wanted to do was relax. Well, relax and then get on with the rest of their lives.

The men had removed their shoes, their ties, their jackets, and the women had gone one further and changed into their sleepwear—a white cotton gown for Simone, ruby red silk pajamas for Eve. Eve couldn't speak for the others, but she was nearly hoarse with all the talking they had done. Never in a million years would she have guessed that Blond Brian Richie was just a punk and a creep and a thug. And never in a million years would she have guessed that her sister Simone would step in at the last minute and save the day.

"I still can't believe you remembered that stuff about Brian Richie's boathouse," she said to her sister now. "But thank God you did."

Simone's expression was a little bleak as she replied, "I've never forgotten anything about prom night, Evie. And when Brian mentioned the boathouse again at the restaurant the other day . . ." She shrugged, but there wasn't an ounce of carelessness in the gesture. Eve could see that her sister was still shaken by all that had happened—both this week and twenty years ago. "I guess it just stuck in my head," she said. "I equated that boathouse with Brian's ugly deeds. I'm just glad he didn't hurt you."

"I wish he hadn't hurt you," Eve said softly. "And I wish you'd told me what happened on prom night."

"It's over," Simone said. "It's in the past." She glanced over at Julian. "It's time to move forward now."

"And here I always just thought you were working as an office manager or something at that FBI facility," Eve added with a slow shake of her head. "I mean, you never specified, and it never occurred to me that you were an agent." She smiled. "Serves me right for making assumptions about the good, obedient, invisible twin."

"Daddy didn't know what I did there, either," Simone said with a shrug. "And, hey, I was sharing a house with him."

"And speaking of your father," Julian interrupted, "anybody know where he is?"

"He got as far as Atlanta," Simone said, "but he missed his connecting flight, so he's kind of stranded. He knows Evie's okay, though. And he told me not to worry." She smiled. "He says he has a plan."

"Oh, great," Eve said. "We probably won't see him until the end of summer."

"Anyway, you couldn't have known about my job, Evie," Simone continued, "because, like you said, I never told you, and besides you were—" She halted abruptly, though, before finishing whatever she had been about to say.

Probably, Eve thought, it was because Simone didn't want to bring up the subject of her ex-husband. "Because I'd pretty much estranged myself from you and Daddy while I was married to Edwin and barely ever saw you," she finished for her sister. "It's okay, Simone. We can talk about it. And then," she said, "we can forget about it. As you said, it's in the past. That chapter of my life is over." Eve, too, turned her attention to Wyatt, who sat beside her, his fingers twined with hers. "I want to start thinking about the future, too. I'm just not real sure where that future will be taking place," she added.

"You're really not going back to California?" Simone asked.

Eve shook her head. "California's not my home. It's never felt like home. It's not where I belong."

"So then where do you belong?" Wyatt asked.

She smiled. "With you," she said simply. "Wherever that winds up being."

He smiled back. "I'm glad to hear you say that, because, you know, I've been thinking."

"Uh-oh," Julian interjected. "That can't be good."

Wyatt picked up a sofa pillow and threw it at his friend. "Now I *know* what I want to do is a good idea," he said.

"And just what is it you want to do?" Eve asked.

He gazed at her in thoughtful silence for a moment, as if he wasn't sure whether or not he should say what he had on his mind. Finally, though, with a very secretive little grin, he told her, "I want to leave Cincinnati and go somewhere else."

She narrowed her eyes at him curiously, but a warm, wistful, sensation wandered through her whole body when she saw the look on his face. "Like where?" she asked.

"I don't know," he said. "But this last week on the road with you . . ." He shrugged. "It was a lot of fun, Eve. And I can't help thinking that maybe the two of us could have a lot more fun for a while, just . . . driving around. Having adventures. Getting to know each other. Living life. *Enjoying* life. I seem to recall a couple of ambitions from our senior yearbook that involved world travel and writing the Great American Novel," he reminded her further.

"And we're going to be able to pay for this . . . how?" she asked with a smile.

His grin broadened. "That'll be part of the adventure."

"Gee, I don't know, Wyatt . . ." she began. Though, in spite of her objection, she found herself warming to the idea.

"Hey, you charmed a lot of people there at Bonita's Pie Kitchen that night," he reminded her. "And I can bus tables like nobody's business. I bet we'd always be able to find work when we needed it."

"Plus," she said brightly, "my father is filthy, stinking rich, and I have a nice, fat trust fund."

"Well, yes," Wyatt agreed with a grin, "there is that."

"But what about me?" Julian asked. "What am I supposed to do for a partner, if you abandon the business to go gallivanting across the country?"

As one, Wyatt and Eve turned to gaze expectantly at Simone.

"What?" her sister asked. But she, too, was smiling.

"When we were kids," Eve said, "you always said you wanted to be in business for yourself."

"Yeah, but I was thinking more along the lines of a Kool-Aid stand," Simone said. "There's not much overhead with that."

"And just a little while ago," Eve continued, ignoring her sister's protest, "you were telling us about how you just sort of fell into your work at the FBI, because they were on campus recruiting, and you fit their 'lone wolf' profile so well. How you never really planned to stay with it your whole life."

"Yeah, so?"

"So," Eve said pointedly, "you don't seem like such a 'lone wolf' anymore. And even if you did leave the field voluntarily, you looked like you were having way too good a time tonight, taking out the bad guy. *I* think you'd like to be in the field again—or the equivalent thereof. *I* think," she added meaningfully, "that you and Mr. Varga here would probably do very well in business together."

"Business," Julian said with a smile, stretching his arm across the back of the sofa, dropping his hand over Simone's shoulder. "Yeah, I think we could be good together there, too," he agreed. "What do you say, Simone? Wanna start a partnership together?"

She gazed at him with much speculation—most of it very appreciative, Eve could tell—and then suddenly stood. "Maybe we should go upstairs and . . . talk more about it," Simone said. "If you think you're *ready*, I mean."

Julian nodded. "Well, certainly we could . . . talk about it," he said. "If you think *you're* ready."

"Only one way to find out," she told him.

Julian stood, too, very eagerly, Eve noticed, linking his fingers with Simone's as he followed her up the stairs to the second level of the suite. Where the bedroom was, Eve recalled belatedly. Which left her and Wyatt down here with the sleeper sofa, she thought. Oh, well. They could be creative, she told herself. They didn't *have* to use the sofa. The bar, for instance, showed great promise.

She turned her gaze toward the stairs Simone and Julian had just ascended. Hmm . . . Those stairs showed promise, too. "Boy, who would have guessed Simone and Julian would hit it off so well?" she said. "But they really do seem like they belong together."

When Wyatt didn't respond right away, Eve turned to look at him, only to find that he was watching her with as much appreciative speculation as her sister had shown for Julian just a few moments ago. "Hey," he said softly, "after what happened twenty years ago, who would have thought that you and I would hit it off so well? Who would have thought you and I belonged together?"

"You think we belong together?" she asked.

He arched his eyebrows in surprise. "Don't you?"

This time Eve was the one to gaze back at him with appreciation. "Actually, Wyatt," she said, "even twenty years ago, even being as confused and befuddled by you as I was, I pretty much thought that you could be the one for me."

"The one what?" he asked with a smile.

She snuggled closer to him, lifting a hand to the third button of his shirt, where he'd halted his attentions when he'd made himself comfortable earlier. "The one to be my soul mate," she said as she slipped the button free of its mooring. "The one to be my other half," she added as she freed the next button, too. "The one to be my Zen partner, the one to be the cream in my coffee, the one to make me totally complete," she enumerated as she liberated the remaining buttons. She spread his shirt open wide and buried her hand in the dark hair scattered across his chest. "I was just too young back then to realize what you were," she told him. "What you would become to me. I was too young to understand what was going on."

He nodded, lifting a hand to twine his fingers through her dark hair, then tucked her head into the curve where his shoulder met his neck. "I think we both had some growing to do before we understood the importance, the significance, of what we had," he said. "In some ways, we were lucky to meet early in life. But we were just too young to know that."

She sighed as she snuggled closer to him. "So do you think it would have lasted if we had made love on prom night?" she asked, resurrecting the subject they had never decided in St. Louis. "Or do you think we would have messed it up and ruined everything?"

Wyatt shook his head. "It doesn't matter what happened twenty years ago, Eve," he said. "All that matters is what happens from here on out."

And then he bent his head to hers and covered her mouth with his. He kissed her deeply, druggingly, possessively. And more than anything, in that moment, Eve knew he *was* the one.

An amazing contemporary romance debut
By an author you'll never forget

Something About Cecily

An irresistible love story by

KAREN KENDALL

He's tall, dark and handsome . . . and determined not
to succumb to the charms of sexy, scatterbrained
Cecily. But when Chas Buchanan agrees to hire her
as a temporary secretary, Cecily brings chaos to his
office . . . and spice to his love life. But can opposites
really attract, or just drive each other crazy?

Coming in May
An Avon Contemporary Romance

"Sexy and sassy—a writer to watch!"
Susan Andersen, author of *ALL SHOOK UP*

ACA 0401

Discover Contemporary Romances at Their Sizzling Hot Best from Avon Books